SAN DIEGO PUBLIC LIBRARY
3 1336 02676 5306

D0049322

The Translator

Books by Ward Just

FICTION

A Soldier of the Revolution (1970)
The Congressman Who Loved Flaubert (1973)
Stringer (1974)
Nicholson at Large (1975)
A Family Trust (1978)
Honor, Power, Riches, Fame, and
the Love of Women (1979)
In the City of Fear (1982)
The American Blues (1984)
The American Ambassador (1987)
Jack Gance (1989)
Twenty-one: Selected Stories (1990)
The Translator (1991)

NONFICTION

To What End (1968)
Military Men (1970)

THE Translator

Ward Just

A RICHARD TODD BOOK

Houghton Mifflin Company / Boston / 1991

Library of Congress Cataloging-in-Publication Data

Just, Ward S.
The translator / Ward Just.
p. cm.
"A Richard Todd book."
ISBN 0-395-57168-5
I. Title.
PS3560.U75T7 1991 91-12789
813'.54—dc20 CIP

Printed in the United States of America

BP 10 9 8 7 6 5 4 3 2 1

Book design by Lisa Diercks

To Sarah

Going West

THIS IS one of the German legends.

After frightful adventures in Pomerania an itinerant dwarf arrived in the once-prosperous hamlet of A——, on the northern flatland between the Elbe River and the Baltic arm known as the Kieler Bucht, monotonous terrain north and east of the present city of Hamburg. The dwarf quickly gained the respect of the people, who were angry and dispirited. They were threatened by one of the neighboring villages. They were short of weapons and short of food. The harvest had gone badly, drought followed by flood. The population was disoriented by the constant north wind, which had brought a painful plague. They believed an evil spirit was among them, and that there had been a displacement of the center of gravity. They listened when the dwarf told them that he had magical powers. God had granted these powers to him as an indemnity. Be of good cheer! Together we will overcome misfortune.

The dwarf told the people of A—— that they were in the position of the wounded man who feels pain in his foot after his leg has been amputated. The amputation occurred long in the past, beyond the reach of memory, and it was good that they had not forgotten. They had been insulted. Their destiny was to be under attack always, and their mistake was to assume that forbearance was a virtue. They must meet attack with attack. They would be victorious. Even if casualties were taken, the issue would at last be forced and the people regain their lost pride and their rightful place in the scheme of things. Avenged, the phantom pain would disappear. The dwarf would lead them as he had led other beleaguered communities. That was his destiny, indemnified as he was by God. But the people had to have faith in him. Your hearts are made of iron! the dwarf boomed. The townspeople, frustrated and near despair, agreed to go to war. Even war was better than waiting patiently to be overwhelmed.

Presently they ventured to the very heart of the enemy camp. It was poorly defended, and indeed the neighboring village was less populous than they had imagined. Yet the fighting was fierce and at the end of the day nearly everyone on both sides was dead. Those who had survived retreated to the hamlet of A—— and were applauded as saviors. The northern flatland was tranquil at last, and the people, having gained their rightful place, were glad, except for the many widows and children of the fallen. Still, they were proud, and as if in approval of their deeds, the north wind ceased to blow; the plague vanished.

Here the storyteller pauses, perhaps scratching his ankle.

The itinerant dwarf commanded superbly, but it is not known if he survived. Presumably he did; he had survived everything else. He was last seen at the head of a column. With his sword held high, he was almost the height of a normal man. But he did not return to the hamlet, and the townspeople, having counted the dead and the few coins left in the treasury, began to have second thoughts. The cost of tranquillity had been high. The surviving soldiers continued to praise the dwarf as a great prophet and general, others to curse him as a provocateur. The community divided, suspicious and fearful, sullen and hostile, its deepest anxieties submerged and unspoken. There were quarrels concerning Rightful Place. In their hearts the people of A—— began to doubt themselves and vowed never again to follow one who claimed divine inspiration. Yet the fault was not the dwarf's alone. In such an affair pride was the logical pretext, but heartbreak the natural consequence. In any case, the dwarf had vanished and they were well rid of him, whoever he was, wherever he was, dead or wandering Pomerania or Masuria, that ancient region of Northern Europe where each city and village has two denominations, its German original and its Polish alias.

* * *

In the legend the name of the hamlet is not given. But the people of Ilsensee, situated on the monotonous flatland north of the Elbe and south of the Kieler Bucht, believed it was their town, and their ancestors who had trusted the itinerant dwarf. There were many stories the old people told, of mysterious visitors and inexplicable events. Ilsensee after all was very old, continuously inhabited since the Dark Ages, mentioned casually in the ninth-century annals of the Frankish Empire as a depressed market town with an unfortunate history, though the nature of the misfortune was not specified. Charlemagne was said to have paid a visit in 810. There were numerous tales of the chivalry and piety of the Teutonic Knights, who administered the region for two centuries. Goethe wrote about the church and its cloister. The people of Ilsensee insisted, on no evidence whatever, that it was the dwarf's legend that inspired Nietzsche's incendiary dictum "One should die proudly when it is no longer possible to live proudly."

Of course no one cares about that today. Ilsensee looks to the future, not to the past, as farther east Danzig is Gdansk and Stettin is Szczezin. In Ilsensee there is no one to keep the dwarf's legend living. There are not so many old people now, and those few are understandably not superstitious. Interviewers are brusquely turned away. The last time a reporter from one of the Hamburg papers arrived in town to write about the legend, she could find no one who would speak to her and had to go away without filing the usual Dwarf Update. They've forgotten, the reporter told her editors. Herr Dwarf is only a tourist's souvenir.

What would you expect? Ilsensee is now a modern suburb in vogue with young stockbrokers and bankers from prosperous Hamburg. There is even an industrial zone north of town with a computer company and a textbook-publishing concern. There are two seafood restaurants and a Mexican take-out and a sports center and a Cinema 1-2-3. The pretty hotel beside the lake is popular with tourists visiting Schleswig-Holstein. Before the war the wooden church attracted visitors from everywhere in Europe. They came to admire the superb tympanum, carved in 1110, and the gnarled oak dwarf at the base of the raised altar, the dwarf so grim and bad-tempered that the tourists were moved to shudder and smile. The dwarf's forehead was concave and luminously silky from the touch of the fingers of thousands of parishioners who believed it a talisman. But Ilsensee had always been unlucky. The church was destroyed during the bombing raids of July 1943. Most of the town was destroyed in an afternoon, owing to a navigational error. The target was the people of Hamburg.

The van Damm house, down a narrow macadam road near the lake, was spared. Major van Damm was in Berlin, and his wife and young son were at home, crouched in the basement, terrified. It seemed impossible that they could live through the explosions. The boy thought they would surely be killed, and never understood why he and his mother were spared while so many were not. In the basement his mother prayed, and insisted that he pray with her. While they prayed the bombs fell and their neighbors died. The boy could not believe that God was selfish in that way, to pardon them and condemn others simply because his mother asked Him to, unless God was an impetuous tyrant, like all authorities. However, his mother believed. She believed in God and the German legends, the Teutonic Knights and the courageous dwarf and certain ancient folk customs, such as the sewing of comforters made from the feathers of fifty geese. All afternoon she prayed and told stories of defiance and survival, her voice high with fright but never breaking, not even when the bombs fell as close as fifty meters and shrapnel banged against the house. In the morning they found a dud bomb in the rose garden next to the front porch, causing her to smile grimly and give thanks to God.

Almost two years later, Montgomery's troops swept through Schleswig-Holstein on their way east, camping finally at Lüneburg Heath to accept the surrender of the German command. By then, Major van Damm was dead, and his wife, Inge, and son, Siggy, were starving, living hour to hour in the pockmarked half-timbered house by the lake, on the margins of the ruined hamlet.

They were always hungry. Germany was finished, the men were all dead or in retreat, but miraculously the war went on and on. God's will, according to Inge van Damm. Nothing could stop it or end it. Every few days they saw stragglers, pathetic half-dead men who would arrive at the front door searching for food. Sometimes they were rough, ransacking the kitchen and threatening Inge. They were wild men with strange famished faces and sunken eyes. When they found anything to eat, they took it; but there was rarely anything to find, and Inge was clever in concealing what there was.

In this disorder her duty was to herself and her son. The stragglers were soldiers separated from their units, often wounded or sick or deranged, desperate for food, terrified that they would be found and executed. Inge explained to them that there was no food anywhere. She spoke slowly and patiently, and firmly, as if to children. Sometimes the stragglers believed her and went away. More often they burst into the kitchen to search for themselves. She never moved from her usual place during these depredations; and incredibly, she was never harmed. Her faith never wavered. She and her son were under God's protection.

Time seemed not to advance, each day very like the last, until the boy looked out his bedroom window one spring morning and saw a British soldier urinating in the driveway. The boy knew he was an officer from the insignia on his helmet. Three comrades were sitting in their jeep, smoking, lounging the way soldiers do. All four were unkempt. They looked like healthy savages. The urinating soldier was facing the house, making no attempt to conceal himself. Siggy could hear them talking, and suddenly he knew that he and his mother would be killed, shot dead. He accepted this with resignation. They had been through so much for so long and he knew that his father was dead. Germany was a nation of dead. He had never expected that he and his mother would survive the war, so little fuel, so little to eat, always threadbare, always afraid. The sky was constantly full of warplanes now, none of them of the mighty Luftwaffe. The stories from Hamburg were frightful. The Fatherland was destroyed. They would be killed because no one was allowed to surrender. The British did not take prisoners; everyone knew that.

The officer had finished and was closing his trousers, looking up the driveway to the house. He turned to say something to his comrades, who alighted wearily from the jeep, complaining. They seemed to be in no hurry, as if there was nothing on earth that could stop them from doing what they planned to do. It was the way soldiers everywhere behaved. The boy could hear his mother moving about downstairs in the kitchen. He ducked away from the window, knowing that he must go to warn her. No woman was safe when enemy soldiers were in the vicinity.

The boy was in his room with a headache. He had them frequently, of such ferocity that tears would jump to his eyes and his ears roar, as if the bombing had begun again. The pain commenced in the back of his skull and worked its way forward, filling his head until it scratched the back of his eyeballs. Nothing helped, and he never complained. He knew in a subconscious way that he would have headaches all his life; that they would be as much a part of his days as hunger and fear; and that the headaches would arrive without notice and withdraw gradually, inch by inch. The headache was the reason he had put the American novel aside. He was reading at the rate of a page a day, so much of it beyond him even with the English grammar and the German-English dictionary at his side and his mother to help out, though she did not approve of his reading a book in English. He had found it in the library downstairs and his father had said it was all right, good enough for what it was. The boy was fascinated by Americans, and his father knew that so he let him read the book, which was the book about "a month's action" in Africa. He did not understand most of it because he did not understand English grammar and syntax. German words were composites, the sentences as heavy and implacable as a freight train. The English sentence was an express. He did understand that the passage had rhythm because it reminded him of the Bach his parents listened to on the radio. He tried to put the words into German; but the feeling behind the words was American, and that would not translate. He knew that one day he would be able to do it, but he couldn't do it now.

He had put the book aside and begun to look at his photograph album, trying to take his mind off the pain in his head. There was one photograph in particular. His father had taken it in 1941 and had it enlarged. They had gone to Hamburg for his birthday, a grown-up lunch and then the surprise, an American film, the adventures of a private detective. It was a black-and-white film and the setting was California. The private detective wore a gray fedora hat and a trenchcoat and talked out of the side of his mouth while tugging on his earlobe. There were subtitles in German, but the boy paid no attention to them. He loved the sound of English, so crisp and inflected, so natural, like swing music. The actors' speech suited the California ambiance. The private detective belonged to no organization. He worked alone. He was attractive to women, seeming to treat them no differently from the way he treated men, employing the same side-of-the-mouth manner with both. Sometimes he took off his fedora when he met a woman. The private detective had no connections to anything, neither family nor government, yet he was never afraid. You could not imagine his parents, who they were or what they looked like; perhaps he was an orphan. At any event he was free and unattached; apparently that was what was meant by the word "private." At the end of the film he had captured the gangsters and the woman but didn't seem to care about either. The boy remembered one line all his life: Twenty-five dollars a day plus expenses. The expenses were taxicabs and liquor, and an occasional telephone call. And he gambled, though never recklessly; when he gambled, he won. He seemed to have all he needed. He had a small anonymous apartment and he had his office. He was more at home in the office than he was in the apartment, which was furnished like a hotel room. But the main thing was that he wasn't tied to anything. None of them were. The woman wasn't. The gangsters weren't. Of course the police were arrogant; but they did not seem to be disciplined. The gangsters were tied to money and that led to their downfall. The private detective didn't care about money any more than he cared about women, though he kissed the woman halfway through the film and seemed to enjoy it. He seemed to enjoy everything that he did without making too much of it or boasting. The private detective led a dangerous life in California but was never daunted.

The boy couldn't stop talking about the film, the look of California, its naturalness, its tension, the palm trees, and the cars on the street, particularly the cream-colored convertible. He asked his father to explain the parts of the film that he didn't understand. Had his father ever been to California when he visited the United States? No, California was western and his father went to southern states. But America was wonderful, wasn't it? Not necessarily, his father said in a tone of voice that suggested the subject was closed. He remembered two sentences in English and spoke them aloud, deepening his voice to imitate the private detective.

Twenty-five dollars a day plus expenses.

You'll shut up and like it.

His father looked at him and laughed. That's excellent. Your accent is really very good, Siggy. Isn't it good, Inge?

I suppose it is, his mother said.

No, it's exceptional. Truly, Inge. One afternoon at a cheap American film and he's speaking like an actor.

Yes, she said. A cheap American film.

Even so, his father said.

How much is twenty-five dollars, Papa?

Not very much, his father said. Enough.

Remove your hat, Siggy, his mother said. It is time for dinner.

On their way home his father had pulled the car off the road, where a Gypsy caravan had set up a carnival and flea market. There were animals, the usual muzzled bear and leashed monkey, and stalls where the Gypsies were selling odds and ends, used toys, household articles, and clothing. Tucked in the corner of a shelf was a battered gray fedora hat. It was identical with the hat the private detective wore. He begged his father to buy it, and to his amazement his father did, laughing, saying something to the Gypsy. When they got home, the boy posed for a photograph, standing on the stairs, leaning on the bannister, wearing the hat. He pulled the brim down over one eye and adopted a sober expression, one that indicated that the wearer could not be surprised or fooled by anything. This was the expression of a reliable man who could bear anything that came his way. His father had the photograph enlarged, and now it was his greatest possession, propped on his bureau next to the family album. It was thrilling, seeing himself enlarged. The hat had been lost but at least he had the photograph. If he should somehow survive the war he would become a private detective, would learn English and talk out of the side of his mouth, never becoming excited or betraying his real thoughts or feelings, but always alert, always operating on his own, enjoying everything without making too much of it or boasting, wanting enough only to meet his own needs in order to maintain his cherished independence. He would live in an apartment and wear a trenchcoat. A cream-colored convertible was too much to expect, except in a dream. But he would not be afraid, he hoped.

Later that night he heard them talking about him. They were discussing his future, what he would become in the new Germany. He would be a soldier, of course; he had the stamina but more important the temperament and the intelligence. When he was of age — Klaus van Damm spoke as if the moment were at hand rather than many years off — he would take his place in the Wehrmacht. The Reich would then be secure. But the Wehrmacht would have a significant role to play in the organization of Germany and of Europe. France was benign to the south. The British were fighting well but could not fight forever. The Communists were something else, Russia so vast and untamed. Bonaparte discovered that. But Bonaparte did not have panzers.

He must not leave Ilsensee, his mother said.

But Inge. He must leave home.

No, she said.

A soldier leaves home, Klaus van Damm said.

Then he will not be a soldier, she said.

The English infantrymen were walking up the driveway now, carrying their carbines. They walked slowly, in single file, looking left and right. Siggy called to his mother but she was already on the stairs. She told him to stay in his room, on no account to come downstairs. Be quiet, she said. Make not one sound. I will talk to these soldiers as I have talked to the others, our own.

He hurriedly took the photograph from the album and stuffed it through the long crack in the molding above his bed. He worked it carefully between the molding and the plaster until it could not be seen. They would soon be dead or in prison but the photograph would remain. He thought it was evidence of his existence, a thing belonging to him alone, separate from the war. And it would always remain in his memory, himself at six in a fedora, leaning on a bannister, looking at his father with a no-nonsense expression. The photograph and what it represented was no one else's business. It was not the enemy's business and he would not disclose its whereabouts even if tortured. That was what the English did, and they were efficient at it. They were merciless. There were many stories of tortured civilians, even children.

He heard low voices in the kitchen. They were speaking English. He waited for sounds of violence but heard nothing. The conversation seemed to go on for some time, though it was probably no more than a few minutes. He was standing in the shadows near the window. He heard the front door slam and watched the soldiers walk away down the driveway, their carbines slung now. The officer stopped to light a cigarette, suddenly looking up, seeing him in the upstairs window. He froze. The officer moved to unsling his carbine, then didn't. He exhaled a long stream of smoke, ending in a perfect smoke ring. The smoke ring hung a moment before it collapsed, but by then the officer was already walking away down the driveway, whistling, jerking a thumb in the direction of the upstairs window; one of the soldiers turned around and, seeing him watching them, laughed.

He ran downstairs, where his mother was washing potatoes, two of them, for the evening meal.

He said, "Are you all right?"

She said, "Of course. They were very correct."

When he asked her what the English wanted, she said they wanted to know the direction to Ilsensee. They were lost. So she gave them directions as they had asked.

"And they weren't English. They were Americans."

He didn't believe her. What would Americans want in little Ilsensee?

"They wanted to see our church," she said. "They had heard of it, the tympanum and the dwarf. It was the dwarf they wanted to see, to touch its forehead. They had read about that also, our quaint medieval custom. I told them it was not possible because they had destroyed it with their bombs in 1943."

"That was the English, Mama. They were English bombers."

"They are all the same to me," she said.

His mother always amazed him. She had not looked up from the cutting board where she was carefully peeling the potatoes, setting aside the skins. She must have known that the Americans would have no interest in two poor potatoes. He noticed a pack of Chesterfield cigarettes on the counter, a sight as foreign as meat on the table. He rubbed his eyes, smiling suddenly because his headache had begun its slow retreat.

"And what did the Americans do then, Mama?"

She said, "Nothing. They thanked me and went away. The officer spoke German, but I replied to all his questions in English. They left me this." She picked up the pack of cigarettes and turned to drop it in the garbage pail, hesitating at the last moment, then replacing it on the counter. She could barter the cigarettes for food.

He remembered the perfect smoke ring. It was the sort of dapper farewell an American from California might make, a gesture suited to a cream-colored convertible or a cocktail lounge. *Americans,* he thought. If Americans were in Ilsensee, they were everywhere and the war was over. He rushed to the door and ran down the driveway to the macadam road. There were cigarette butts in the road, and a stain where the soldier had urinated. A way up the road the jeep had stopped, the Americans motionless, their arms raised. They were circled by soldiers of the Wehrmacht, if you could describe the wasted men in the road as soldiers. They did not wear helmets or badges of rank, and their weapons were American or English. He took a step toward them, believing he could in some way mediate. The soldiers of the Wehrmacht could not know that the war was over and there was no need to continue fighting. He called, but they were too far away to hear him, and his voice was thin. And then the guns began to fire.

The Americans were hit, and tumbled from the jeep, trying to get away. It was no use. They were hit again and again, falling crumpled and silent, or out of control, screaming. The noise was terrible. The dapper American officer sat in the road holding his stomach until one of the German soldiers stepped behind him, aimed carefully, and shot him in the head. Siggy began to cry. One of the dead Americans was hanging over the side of the jeep. A German pulled him into the road and began to go through his pockets, ripping the cloth in his frenzy to discover what they contained. He took the American's wallet and his wristwatch. The boy was crying uncontrollably now, calling to the soldiers, a kind of high-pitched wail such as a woman might make. The soldiers were rummaging through the knapsacks, searching for food. The knapsacks flew out of the jeep, landing on the macadam road. The Germans were yelling at each other, blizzards of words that the boy could not understand. One of the Americans sat up, screaming something, and a German soldier shot him, the gun jerking up and down, the bullets flitting everywhere. The scream ended suddenly but its echo remained, along with the sound of the shots and the voices of the Germans, cursing now. None of them noticed the boy, who had tried to move toward them but found that his legs would not work. Finally, willing himself, he began to run and reached the Germans as they climbed into the jeep. One of them stared at him with — it could have been hatred or pity. The soldier's face was distorted and inhuman. He raised his hand, but the jeep was already moving, spinning wheels, scattering gravel. The Americans lay in their own blood. They did not move, and then Siggy felt a hand on his shoulder and turned to press his face into his mother's stomach, the fume of potatoes.

"Oh, Mama," he said and struggled to say what he believed, that his heart was broken.

"You must forget about this," she said.

Klaus van Damm, no longer a major, died in a Berlin prison early in 1945. Illness, malnutrition, execution, no one knew. The death certificate arrived one day in the mail, no cause given; it was what Inge van Damm wanted to know. She stood in the kitchen with her back to the sink and read the document, top to bottom. Then she broke down, weeping in a fury of despair. Siggy was horrified; it was the first time he had seen his mother cry, and it was shocking. She wheeled and hurled the paper into the sink, turning the tap full force, drenching the paper until it began to disintegrate. When Siggy tried to retrieve it, she pushed him roughly away.

Lies, she said. All lies.

One day we will know the truth about Klaus.

But they never did. Klaus van Damm was briefly cited in several histories of the Third Reich as one of the more capable staff officers at Berlin headquarters, a meticulous technician of the old school, disciplined and aloof. He was known to admire certain aspects of American military theory. In the 1930s he had made a number of trips to the United States, studying the great sieges of the Civil War, Vicksburg, Chancellorsville, Antietam, Shiloh. He had walked the ground with his maps, his compass, his binoculars, and his sketch pad and pen; everyone was very helpful. He was a professor from Heidelberg studying the cradle of modern war — was it not Hegel who said that governments never learned anything from history? He even found a survivor from Shiloh, but the old man's memory was gone and he was unable to give a clear account of the progression of the battle, though he had been an officer and in a position to know. My feet hurt, the old man said. I had a cold. I slept in mud. I missed my wife. It was helter-skelter. Klaus van Damm did not put much value on the Southerner's remarks, the ramblings of an old man. He did not assign value to chance or chaos, the atmosphere of the battlefield, but that was because he was staff and not line. Staff suited his orderly and unimaginative temperament.

No one ever discovered why he was arrested. Klaus van Damm was not an intriguer, and he had no known political views. He was an army officer whose specialty was the enemy order of battle, and perhaps his offense was that he told the truth. He was unprotected. He had few friends on the general staff and even fewer in the defense ministry, and none at all among Adolf Hitler's entourage. None of his acquaintances was in a position to help, and none did. Of course he was not a Nazi. Too proud, his wife said.

The van Damm house is owned now by an accountant, an executive with the computer company in Ilsensee's industrial park. There are other houses round and about, many of them with small swimming pools. Audis and Mercedeses crowd the driveways; no one remembers the van Damms. Siggy's photograph is still immured in the small bedroom at the top of the stairs. He was never able to retrieve it, and after that frightful afternoon had no heart to do so. His bedroom is occupied now by an au pair from Sweden, and occasionally by the accountant when his wife is out of town.

Siggy — no one calls him that anymore — returned in the fall of 1975 with his American wife. They were touring Schleswig-Holstein in a rental car. It was their honeymoon, begun at a hotel in Sylt in the Frisian Islands. But Sylt had not been a success, so they had returned to the mainland and driven to Ilsensee, staying at the pretty hotel by the lake. He had not been back in years. He thought his American wife would like to see where he had lived as a boy, during the war years and later, but everything was a disappointment. Ilsensee had been rebuilt, with curving streets, lamps that arched like striking cobras, and low-slung stucco buildings in the modern style, part Bauhaus, part warehouse. Of course it was an improvement over the results of July 1943. But nothing was familiar. He recognized no one, not even the hotel staff. The hotel had been a billet for American officers after the war, and he worked there as a waiter, earning money and learning American English. He spent all his free time at the hotel, eavesdropping on conversations. In the evenings he fetched beer for four majors who played poker at the table near the bar; when he asked them to correct his pronunciation and grammar, they did. All the American officers were fond of him, so grave and polite, so willing, so intelligent. They gave him food to take to his mother. They gave him books and magazines. And when one of them made a mistake one night and called him Sydney, he did not object; he took their name as he had taken their language, their food, their books, and their magazines. They knew that his father had been an officer in the Wehrmacht but did not seem to mind.

Of course the hotel was now owned by a Swiss concern. The management was Swiss, except for the maître d' from Hannover. The souvenir shop in the lobby sold little wooden dwarfs, with concave foreheads and imps' ears. Adorable, his wife said. Sydney thoughtlessly recounted the legend, each detail, and at the end of it she turned away without buying a dwarf.

Angela was pregnant and out of sorts.

Dinner was expensive, and he tried to lighten their moods with a bottle of *Sekt,* German champagne. But it was not a success any more than Sylt or the dwarf had been.

"It isn't Taittinger, is it?"

"It isn't supposed to be Taittinger."

They were on opposite sides of a great divide. She had wanted to go to fragrant Tuscany, to the hill towns and to Florence. She wanted to sit in the warm sun. She wanted to visit the Botticelli room in the Uffizi, stroll on the Ponte Vecchio, dine grandly at Harry's Bar, and make a bella figura at love afterward. Instead she had gotten Sylt, surly, charmless, northern, and cold. Now they sat at a table for two in a zone of silence, dreading the bedtime chores.

"Shall we take a walk?"

"Why not," she said. "Let me get my coat. I'll take my scarf, too. Do you think I'll need my mittens?"

"I don't think you'll need your mittens."

"It's pretty cold. It might snow."

They strolled around the lake, ghostly with evening mist rising in waves, steam from a simmering pot. The night was very still. He pointed out the various absent landmarks, where the church had stood, where the playground had been, where he had gone to school, the corner where the infirmary had been, the beer garden where he and his mother and father would go for Sunday lunch and listen to the German band. He explained about the famous tympanum, the carved door of the church. Odd that one of the meanings of tympany was arrogance or pride. Probably there was a connection somewhere, a pretentious façade concealing a poverty of spirit. Something like that. He would have to look it up when they got back to Paris, tomorrow or the next day from the look of things.

And suddenly they were there, looking up the driveway at the half-timbered house. They were standing where the American had stood urinating. That spring afternoon came back to him in a flood, and he turned away to collect himself. It was more than thirty years ago and he had never described his broken heart to anyone, and did not want to explain himself now to Angela. When at last he looked again he saw that the house was larger than he remembered it, and then he noticed the glassed-in porch, an addition since his time. The house looked tidy and well cared for. The rose garden was still there, but the shrapnel scars had disappeared, filled in and painted over. There were bony saplings tethered to the lawn and hedges along the driveway. He remembered the dud bomb and his mother's grim smile, an acknowledgment of God's grace. What an extraordinary woman she was, how passionate to defend what was hers, how fearless. He looked at the hedges, dead in November, trying to connect now with then. He was silent a long moment, fighting the fragments of things, the day his father went away, the day the English bombers came, the photograph, the Americans, his mother's tears, and the disintegrating paper. Then he was fighting the memory of the American soldiers falling, the shouts and the explosions, the appalling frenzy of it, and his inability to intervene.

Forget about this, she had said.

But they had only wanted to look at the church, and the others had only wanted something to eat.

He shuddered and Angela said coolly, "What's wrong?"

"This was a mistake," he said thickly.

"No kidding," she said.

He did not reply, only stood looking at the yellow light in his old bedroom.

"I knew it would be," she said. "That's something I've known all along."

"Good for you," he said. "Excellent. How did you ever get to be so clever, a little American girl? Angela wins again. Aren't you proud of yourself?"

"God, van Damm," she said. Her voice was loud in the night stillness. "God, I'm tired of you and your German mood."

He watched her walk away briskly in the direction of the hotel, listening to her heels click on the macadam. He watched her until she reached the place where the Americans were killed, and then he turned back to face the house. There was a tricycle on the front porch and a small red Audi in the driveway. The ground floor was dark and now the light in his old room went out, and the house became a silhouette. Apparently they went to bed early in suburban Ilsensee. He wondered about the photograph, whether it had survived all this time, or whether it had decayed like a corpse in the grave, or the Americans killed that afternoon. His mother had washed the blood from her hands; and had bartered the Chesterfields later for six eggs, a beef's tongue, and a tin of sugar, an excellent bargain.

That afternoon she told him to go back home. Her voice was like a whip, and he backed away, down the road. When he saw what she intended to do he stopped and called for her not to, please, that she mustn't. She heard him but paid no attention. She went through the knapsacks methodically, one by one, to see if anything had been left by the German soldiers; any food or cigarettes or money, anything of value. She moved the limbs of the dead and went through their breast pockets, knowing that was where soldiers kept cigarettes and chocolate bars. She lifted the American officer and let him fall, his helmet clattering on the macadam. But there was nothing at all to take, so she returned, her face hard as stone, and led the way back to the house where she cleaned her hands of blood and finished preparing the potatoes for their evening meal, as if nothing at all had happened.

The light in his old bedroom went on again briefly, and then off. If anyone found the photograph, what would they make of it? A six-year-old boy with a man's fedora around his ears. He had picked at the molding until his mother told him to stop, he was defacing the wood. His efforts were clumsy and halfhearted because he associated the photograph with the careless Americans, particularly the American officer, who had blown a perfect smoke ring and then jerked a thumb in his direction. After the Americans had been killed, he did not want to think about the photograph, or anything.

The cold deepened. The stars were brilliant overhead, the houses dark. His breath plumed in the hard air, and he remembered it was cold that other season so long ago. He looked east where the sky was black with cloud. He said a brief prayer because east was where his mother was, living in the village where she was born. Inge van Damm's family had lived there for many generations, and there were cousins nearby. Once the family had been prosperous and respected. He did not know much of her life in the East, except for bare-bones accounts furnished by an American friend. They seldom corresponded, and in any case the mails were unreliable; and what they had to say to each other could not be written in a letter. She seemed to be content in her ancestral village, east almost to the Polish border. The terrain was very like the flatland near Ilsensee and the life not much different from the life before the war. Ilsensee had been a pretty village then, old-fashioned and slow-moving, removed from the affairs of the nation.

She wrote him that they were good to old people in the East. She had a cottage with a garden. She had plenty to eat. At the clinic, medical care was supplied without charge. One of her distant cousins was a nurse, so she had everything she needed. She was permitted to attend the small chaste church, rebuilt since the war. However, she did not trust the pastor, a sickly cleric from Swinemunde whose interpretations of Luther were reactionary. A Russian battalion was bivouacked nearby, but they kept to themselves; they were just boys far from home. Modern life was a nuisance, but at least in the East there was not the criminal materialism that corrupted the Federal Republic. The Federal Republic was only North America without inflation. It was a pig of a state, worse even than the fascists. I am happy enough to be alive, she wrote, and signed the letter, *As ever, your mother, Inge van Damm.*

She had gone east after her son went west, having waited a decent interval, realizing finally that there was nothing to keep her in Ilsensee, with her husband dead and her son living in France, an infrequent visitor. She believed he had run away and had denounced him then, accusing him of dishonoring her and her gallant husband and the Fatherland itself. That, as with so much else in the world, was the work of the Americans, rootless cosmopolitans whose culture was worse than any narcotic; the Americans believed in amnesia. No one ever left Ilsensee, or any city or hamlet of the Fatherland, with a glad heart. To live in another country? Was this why we survived the war? She was beside herself. You believe you will make your own history, live in harmony, find a Rightful Place. You believe you will be able to leave us behind. But you cannot, because we will always be at your elbow, whispering in your ear, visiting your dreams, tugging at your sleeve. We of the previous generation will always be present, so whatever you do and wherever you go, we will be part of it. You will search for a joyful life, but you will not find it. You will not find it abroad among our enemies. We will weigh on your mind always.

Sydney heard a rustle behind him, something small fleeing into the dead reeds beside the lake, and then a splash.

So that was that.

Time to move along, to return to his American wife, who was tired of his German mood, tired of Schleswig-Holstein, tired of the northern flatland, tired of the November chill, of the war dead and the legends of charismatic dwarfs, of *Sekt* and sausages and so much else, who wanted only sunny Tuscany and a cheerful, obedient husband. It was time to return to the hotel and make a bella figura, agree that his German mood was discouraging, and apologize sincerely; but Ilsensee cast its own spell, as Sylt had, and he had been a fool to forget that and to think that Angela could understand. She was American.

He turned abruptly and began to walk away when he heard a cry, a breathless meow like a child. But there was no one about and the house was dark. Only the spirits of the past remained, along with the thick sour odor of the lake; that, too, so familiar. He tried to remember the expression on his mother's face the day she denounced him. He remembered the words, their weight and timbre, but not the mouth that spoke them nor the look in her eyes. What a dreadful scene it had been; and he had given her no comfort. Bad enough to remember the words.

Sydney was walking swiftly now. The lights of the hotel were in the distance, dimly seen through the mist rising on the lake. She said, was this why we survived the war? Yes. Yes, it was. We survived the war in order to become Europeans again. We survived the war in order to move on. Damn the war, damn the fascists;

damn the old people with amnesia one minute and total recall the next, a flash of light in the unimaginable darkness. He tried to conjure up the expression on his six-year-old face, the grave expression that his father had caught with the Leica. He could not remember the name of the American film or any of its actors. He recalled the cream-colored convertible as a Buick, and of course he recalled the two terse lines of dialogue. Over the years he had inspected gray fedoras, trying to match the one his father had bought from the Gypsies, but none of them was quite right, and naturally he was never able to duplicate the expression in the photograph. He thought of these things as a sort of phantom pain. It is so difficult to see ourselves as we were when young because we are always on the inside looking out; and on the inside there are no mirrors. Not that he had any great desire to do so. Compulsion was not always desire. He did not believe that the boy was necessarily the shadow of the man, so he did not yearn for his six-year-old self, yet he strained for an understanding that was always just out of reach.

He wondered if she was at peace in the cottage in her ancestral village, with her vegetable garden and the reactionary pastor in the rebuilt church. No doubt she could gossip with the distant relatives, perhaps reminisce about German life before the war. But where in that was consolation? The hotel was in front of him now, its lights bright as beacons. His American wife was waiting. Sydney turned, raising his arms to the stars, heaving a great sigh. All of it was lost, the legends, the tympanum, the old people, his father, even the Gypsies, who began to disappear not long after, in late 1941, early 1942, one of those frightful years.

2

For the rest of his life, often late at night in the minutes before sleep, Sydney van Damm remembered his arrival at the Gare du Nord aboard the day train from Hamburg. It was a golden evening in the autumn of 1956, an anonymous year except for the restless Hungarians, who were at the end of their rope. He was twenty-one years old, a robust German provincial who knew less of Europe than a casual medieval traveler. He knew nothing firsthand of Paris, though he had read selectively in the books that celebrated its materialistic and cynical yet liberal and welcoming character. He knew that Paris was flexible and temperamental, and could become anything that you wanted it to be. The French were in a continual state of flux; the meaning of so remote an event as the French Revolution was still a matter of debate, even Robespierre's Terror. In France nothing was ever settled finally and for good. Sydney believed that as soon as he knew what he wanted to be, he would know what he wanted Paris to be, and that Paris would obey.

And of course he knew little of Germany beyond dour Ilsensee and the university quarter of Hamburg, so as the train hurtled south he stared with fascination and dread at the countryside, thickening with each mile as it became a strangled foundry, Krupp's and Thyssen's furious factories and blast furnaces at Dortmund, Bochum, Essen, and Duisburg. This was the foundation of the nineteenth-century German Empire; at Bochum they even had a museum of mining, one and a half miles of galleries as lovingly constructed as any wing of the Louvre. The cities had only been names, and now they acquired faces, but it was difficult telling them apart. Probably they were no different than Pittsburgh or Nottingham. The Ruhr lay under a pall of soot, though here and there you could see a patch of bottle-green pastureland, metallic in the sun. Soon those would be covered by new factories and assembly lines, roads and parking lots and office buildings and apartment houses. Five kilometers north of Cologne he saw the spires of the immense cathedral, the one that by God's grace had escaped war damage. And then the train slipped across the Rhine to pause at the station before continuing into anonymous Belgium and, an hour later, into pastoral France.

There was a moment's difficulty with his passport, the official working the pages back and forth, staring at the picture, at him, at the picture again, asking a question in rapid argot, and Sydney answering, Yes, I have employment at the German-American Foundation. It is indicated on the second page. I am a translator, he added, using a bit of complicated French slang that caused the official to look again at the passport, at his picture and at his name, before handing it back with an anonymous grunt and a puzzled shake of the head. It was well known that Germans spoke French badly, using an obscene accent that grated on the ears. Probably this *schleu* had grown up somewhere near Strasbourg, though the document listed his birthplace as Hamburg.

The train was still moving when he swung down from the second-class coach. He felt a moment of vertigo, the sense that he was the only fixed point in a world that was spinning wildly. Travelers moved around him as he stood alone, his heavy suitcase at his feet. Sydney remembered touching his wallet, and being reassured by its bulk; and then he raised his eyes to the roof of the vast iron terminal, watching the engine's steam vanish in the last rays of the dying sun. He was grinning, and at the same time he was apprehensive. He lit a Gauloise and pitched his unread German newspaper into a trash can, squaring his shoulders as he put out his hand to greet the young American hurrying toward him. Sydney knew that he was an American because the Foundation said they would send one, to show him around and help get him settled. But he was surprised that the American was so young and so well tailored and self-assured in the racket and density and utter spinning confusion of the glorious Gare du Nord.

"Welcome to Paris," the young man said. "I'm Lem Poole, but my friends call me Junko."

And at that moment in his recollection Sydney would smile and shake his head, perhaps turning in his bed, making himself comfortable, knowing that it would be a few minutes before sleep came.

They walked across the street to the Alsatian restaurant, where they drank one beer and then another, getting acquainted. At first they spoke French and then switched to English after Junko remarked, Jesus, Sydney, your French is god damned *good.* Junko Poole's French was not god damned good, and Sydney had the feeling he was being examined; and that he had passed. They ordered more beer and plates of choucroute — on Uncle Sugar, the affable Junko Poole said, and Sydney nodded without knowing who or what Uncle Sugar was — and more beer to go with the choucroute, and at eleven that night piled into Junko's Volkswagen and drove to the Latin Quarter, where Sydney had a room in a sour little hotel. The room was his until he could find a place of his own. Junko Poole had a list of addresses.

They became friends, at work and after hours. Junko found Sydney a tiny flat in the Jewish quarter of the Marais, and helped him furnish it. He explained about the street markets and identified the obscure cafés where the portions were large and the bill laughably small. He introduced Sydney to the expatriate American community, struggling artists and journalists and willing debutantes from the North Shore of this or that who came for junior year and stayed on. Junko maintained that it was necessary to create your own community in Paris, since the French one was closed, with restrictive covenants as severe as any yahoo golf club in the American suburbs. Fortunately, in Paris you didn't need the French. You needed them less than an army needed generals. You were better off without them, although from time to time you found a good one, meaning a young one, under thirty years old. That was the dividing line. And they don't like us any better than we like them. They don't like it that we're here, where the living is easy.

Junko seemed to know everyone in the expatriate American community, either in person or on sight. He knew musicians and foreign service officers and Americans who lived on the margins, avoiding work and taxes. Sitting in a café, he would nudge Sydney and gesture at a burly man in a trilby and say, That's James Jones, the very famous American writer. He's a denizen. Jimmy and Irwin Shaw have a killer poker game that I intend to join one of these days. And, rising to leave, would pass by Jones's table and touch his arm and say, Hi, Jim, and the famous writer would nod and say, How's it going, and return to his newspaper; it happened all the time.

Sydney's work at the German-American Foundation was undemanding, only tedious. The Foundation sought to improve cultural ties between the two great nations and to that end published a newsletter and furnished unspecified support to a literary magazine that featured political essays and the occasional short story or poem by east European writers, mainly Germans. The essays were smuggled to Paris in diplomatic pouches or brought back by Junko Poole on his mysterious trips to Prague and East Berlin. Junko was in charge of the unspecified support and often gave Sydney a short story or poem to translate, for which Sydney was paid handsomely, off the books. My slush fund, Junko explained. And he always got a credit: *Translated from the German by Sydney van Damm.* The work was noticed, too, by publishers and others. Once or twice Sydney performed the duties of a *nègre,* the in-house ghostwriter of manuscripts that were otherwise unpublishable. But he did not care to be a ghost, and his boss did not insist. Sydney's usual chore was to work on the newsletters, where the articles had to do with economic conditions in the German Democratic Republic; always bad and getting worse, owing to the criminal Marxist straitjacket.

The Foundation office was a third-floor walk-up located over a bookshop near the Jardin des Plantes, the botanical gardens and zoo a short walk from the Gare d'Austerlitz. On fine days Sydney would take his manuscripts to a bench in the herb garden and work in the sun. There were many old people who came with their dogs to sit quietly on the wooden benches, and young mothers wheeling baby carriages. Nurse's aides from the Hospice de la Salpêtrière came to eat their frugal lunches in the garden. They were flirtatious and unexpectedly sexy in their pale blue uniforms. Gina and Monique and Danielle were a relief from the unruly Americans Junko collected, and before long Sydney found himself in a world the other side of the expatriates', a working-class milieu of making-ends-meet, surly fathers and tyrannical mothers in crowded apartments in districts like Père Lachaise and Daubigny. The girls were clever and goodhearted but uneducated and unrebellious. They wanted to get married and have children, but since Sydney was a foreigner doing intellectual work that paid badly he was not a candidate; they liked him but the odds were too long. They believed he would never settle down. Gina insisted that one day he would go home to Germany and not return; everyone went home sooner or later, this was natural. You will find a German girl, Sydney, and then you will become a little bourgeois, just like us, except you will need to earn more and also become less grave. You work too hard, Sydney, for too little. You allow people to take advantage of you.

The girls did not dare present him to their suspicious parents, so he made do with long sensual afternoons and evenings in the narrow bed in his apartment in the Marais, followed by the merry trek home to Père Lachaise or Daubigny, a lingering kiss on the mouth, a whispered confidence, and a playful squeeze before the fading clatter of heels on the steps upstairs. Monique and Danielle were married within the year, and then Gina announced that she, too, had found a boy, a shy, religious boy of good family, a technician at the hospital; and he wanted to be married soon. Sydney said, truthfully, that he was happy for her and that he would miss her; he would miss them all, but Gina especially. No one would ever take advantage of Gina; she went her own way wholeheartedly. She saw a future for herself beyond a malodorous walk-up in Père Lachaise, her parents in one bedroom and she and her sisters in the other. She dressed with style, a kind of lilt; sexy to my fingertips, she called it. To be a bourgeoise is not to be unfeeling. In some ways she reminded Sydney of himself, determined to outrun a bitter childhood. It was only a feature of their childhoods that Gina ran in one direction and Sydney in another. He wondered about the shy, religious boy — Gina was neither — but concluded that she knew what she was doing. That is, she knew what she wanted.

If only you were different, Sydney.

He laughed, knowing they were not suited for anything permanent, and regretting it.

If you were French, she said. If you had more ambition.

I'm ambitious, he said.

Not in the right way, she countered.

She went out of his life, as the others had. Monique had introduced him to Danielle, and Danielle had introduced him to Gina. From now on, Gina said, you're on your own. He was an afternoon man, a hand-me-down. The girls came to the Jardin des Plantes at lunchtime, flirted, went to bed, and went away. This had continued for many months, a harmless and agreeable routine for a single-minded young man with no wish to settle down and start a family, not now and perhaps not ever. He was still exploring, discovering who he was, and what Paris was, and how they fit.

Sydney was surprised a month later when Gina arrived at his apartment. She sat on the bed and told him she was pregnant.

After a moment's silence he asked her what she wanted to do.

"Get rid of it," she said, looking at him with a hard face.

"How many months —" Sydney began.

She brushed the question aside. "Jean-Pierre and I will be married the month after next. He is not an idiot. He can count."

Sydney looked at her, so slender and small with her gamine's haircut; it was the mode that year, and it made Gina look even younger than she was, until he looked at the thin line of her mouth, which seemed to conceal clenched teeth. He was not prepared for her stubborn realism, the cold self-interest of the French businesswoman, the shopowner or concierge or keeper of the caisse. Her manner said, This is your responsibility. Don't get sentimental. This isn't a sentimental affair.

Sydney said, "What do you want me to do?"

She said, "Find a doctor."

"I don't know one," he said.

"I didn't ask if you knew one. I asked you to find one."

A good one, she added. Not some pig butcher. She said she would come by the next day. And then she left.

Sydney had only one worldly friend, Junko Poole. It was Junko who could locate an apartment, or a car for the weekend, or an after-hours casino, or an unlisted telephone number. The Lord will provide, he said, a reference to Morris Lord, the director of the German-American Foundation. Sydney dreaded going to Junko, expecting his customary sarcasm and knowing that all favors were repaid, in one coin or another. But Junko listened without comment, except to agree at the end that Gina was in a fix and it was up to them to help her out. As it happens, he said, I know a man. Tell Gina to make no plans for the next few days.

They went to a small private clinic in the Sixteenth Arrondissement not far from the Étoile. Junko insisted on accompanying them, and to Sydney's relief he was tactful and considerate. He brought with him a pretty silk nightgown, since Gina would spend the night. You're a very pretty girl, he said, and a pretty girl should have a pretty nightgown. She smiled and thanked him, admitting for the first time that she was frightened. Junko did not tell her not to be frightened, only nodded in understanding. When she was called into the operating room she turned without a word and followed the doctor inside. She was wearing a simple coral-colored shift and flats. Sydney and Junko remained in the corridor, smoking cigarettes.

Sydney put his hand on Junko's shoulder, thanking him. He said, I'm indebted to you. Gina is. You've been a real friend and I won't forget it, at which Junko smiled and said that friends stuck together and one of these days it would be Sydney's turn. She seems like a nice girl, and it was too bad that it had to happen, but that sometimes it did and when it did it was good to know — people who could help.

Then the nurse came to the door, opening it and standing aside to say something to the doctor. Sydney saw Gina in the stirrups, the coral-colored shift hiked up around her thighs, her face pale in the harsh white light of the overhead lamp. He thought, some of this pain should be mine. What he had was a hand-me-down pain, willed rather than felt. He felt no pain, only pity. He wanted to turn away but did not. He forced himself to look at Gina, and then the door swung shut.

It was over in thirty minutes. The doctor vanished after a few whispered words with Junko Poole. The nurse wheeled Gina back to her room. She was groggy with anaesthetic. The room was dark. Sydney bent down to kiss her but she turned her head. When Junko squeezed her hand, she squeezed back, though she did not look at him.

When Sydney returned the next morning, she was gone.

Yes, the nurse said. Everything went well. Why wouldn't it? She is a healthy girl and she will have many more children. As no doubt will you, monsieur.

The nurse handed Sydney a soft parcel, the nightgown.

She said to give this to your friend, with thanks.

Each year brought something new and unexpected. The city had never been so vibrant with possibility, indisputably the capital of Europe, the only balance or counterweight to the coarse American colossus. A Gauloise in his mouth, his hair uncombed, his sweater shabby even by the standards of Montparnasse, Sydney became a late-night fixture in the cafés. There was always a new film to discuss, or Sartre's view of civil disobedience, or Breton's view of Sartre. Was it true that the philosopher could have lived as readily under Hitler as under Stalin? In the Latin Quarter there was always a rattle of language, Italian, Slavic, Arabic, Vietnamese. German was rarely heard. Sydney compared the Paris of the fifties to the Berlin of the twenties, a fertile time, loose and voluptuous, self-conscious yet brimming with energy and ideas. Hard to know whether the city was moving forward or backward, toward one ideal or in retreat to another. Governments came and went; but that seemed not to be the point. There was so much to learn about

Paris and about oneself and one's craft, and the turbulent times themselves in which, miraculously, Germany did not figure. Germany's exiguity allowed Sydney to move about anonymously, unidentified, unencumbered by the weight of the war or of nationality; or so he believed. It was true that the French were difficult to know, more difficult even than the Germans. In any case, he was no longer a regular at the Jardin des Plantes. And in the meantime, there were Junko Poole's unruly and forgetful Americans.

Three years after arriving at the Gare du Nord, Sydney quit the Foundation. Junko advised him to do it without delay and do it with *politesse*. It isn't a place where you want to stay too long, old Sydney. You're in their files and there isn't anything you can do about that and, who knows, perhaps it'll come in handy sometime; maybe you'll need them; and you can hope that they won't need you. Everyone and his brother knows what we've been doing here except those who are too stupid or greedy or idle or blind, and one of these days there'll be a nasty article in one of their smarmy little Marxist propaganda sheets, and it'd be just as well if you weren't around to catch the flak, German tool of crypto-fascist CIA warmongers. You're trying to make your own independence, and in those circumstances it's wise not to leave footprints, *comprenez?* You can leave now and say you dint know nuttin from nowhere. Take my advice and bow out, Syd.

Sydney had decided to quit even before Junko's warning, and his reasons had nothing to do with the American intelligence service. Life was too comfortable, and too much of it given over to talk. Gina disappeared, another liaison went sour, and the Jardin des Plantes seemed too convenient, even haunted. He began to think that he was suited to the single life. Like the American detective in the fedora hat, he had enough for his own needs. He kept irregular hours; it would be difficult for another person to fit into them. And as Gina had said, he was not ambitious in the right way, meaning the usual way. He knew that he needed to take a fresh step into the unknown. His reputation as a translator, German to English, French to German, was solid and growing. He had his first book contract — the novelist Josef Kaus had asked for him, having read his translations in the Foundation magazine — and the promise of piecework from Junko. Sydney was polite about it and Morris Lord understood. He gave Sydney two months' salary and a fine reference (and you'd better be careful where you use it, hear?) and said they were sorry to see him go, he did the work of two people, and it was always accurate and timely and often brilliant work. Your temperament is exactly right for us, you're resolute, discreet, stable, and modest. You don't dick around, van Damm. Which is more than I can say for your buddy, that cocksucker Poole, LeMessurier Sebastian Poole, phonus-balonus babyfaced duplicitous prick. My dear friend at Langley named him Junko. And I'll bet you can guess why. I'd stay away from Brother Poole, if I were you. He's trouble. That's friendly advice; do with it what you want. You're a smart lad. Lucky for us that we got the word from your professor at Hamburg and acted on it, which we don't always. He said that you were the best student he'd ever had. He said you were a prodigy, and that you'd flourish in Paris. You've a great future and we won't forget you, Herr van Damm. And don't you forget us. *Au revoir. Auf Wiedersehen.* Godspeed. Come see us when you're in the neighborhood. And you can bet that we'll stay in touch, *Kamerad.*

Junko Poole bought Sydney a farewell dinner at Lipp, the downstairs dining room melancholy in the early evening. It's on Uncle Sugar, he said, and of course this time Sydney knew who and what Uncle Sugar was. Junko listened while Sydney told him what Morris Lord had said; and then he murmured that it didn't matter, the director was about to be handed a hatful of shit himself and would soon return to Washington, where he belonged. Junko watched Sydney's slow smile, the one that always had a touch of sorrow to it. You couldn't help liking him even as you wondered who he was really, what animated him, and where he was headed in his life. The poor bastard. He would never be conspicuous. He lacked the capacity to re-invent himself, though that was difficult in Europe and often unsavory as well. What in America was praiseworthy was in Europe — suspicious. Still, it left a man at a disadvantage.

They ordered oysters, cassoulet, and beer, despondent in the funereal atmosphere. Lipp was subdued because Albert Camus had died the day before, and the breath went out of Paris. Even his enemies were saddened. People didn't believe it until they saw the photographs of the Facel-Vega wrapped around the plane tree; and the New Year had scarcely begun.

Junko picked at an oyster and said, "What did your people think of him?"

Sydney shrugged. "Mixed. I suppose Germans would admire his sense of duty."

Junko waited. Lipp was unnerving, so quiet.

"Of course he was obsessed by suicide and that would not appeal to us. Germans are not interested in suicide. Too personal," Sydney said with a smile. "Unless it is an affair of honor or of love."

"Romance," Junko said.

"It would be something sentimental," Sydney said.

"Camus thought it was the only serious question."

"He was wrong," Sydney said.

"Yes," Junko said. "The question is not how to die but how to live."

"I think that's what he meant," Sydney said.

"Well then," Junko said. But Sydney was concentrating on his oyster, carefully detaching the muscle, squirting lemon, taking it in whole, chewing, swallowing, sighing, taking a long draft of beer, sighing again. He was very good in the war, Sydney said suddenly. The Germans and the French have different memories of it, shame on one side and disgrace on the other. And which is worse? Apparently shame, for Germany was silent as a tomb, shut in on itself, obsequious in its dealings with the outside world, while France was as noisy and assertive as a jazz band. Vichy was forgotten. Collaboration was unmentionable. When Sydney raised his glass, Junko saw that his hand was trembling. If he did not know better, he would have said that Sydney was grieving.

"With Camus gone," Sydney said, "the French will lose their way. They have lost their conscience. He was the only one they had. And when conscience goes, art dies."

"Art has nothing to do with conscience," Junko said.

"Art is conscience," Sydney replied.

Junko Poole leaned forward, the better to unnerve Sydney. He said, "What the hell do you care?"

"Albert Camus was a great soul," Sydney said.

"He was a better than average Frog, that's all."

"But not a fighter in your Cold War? Of course he was over thirty."

"He fought some. He was better than most of them. Better than that bastard Sartre. Put him in the United States and he'd be Adlai's minister of culture. Or probably the UN, since we don't have ministries of culture in the Land of Lincoln. He'd cut quite a figure on the East Side in his trenchcoat and his Bogart fedora, arguing with the Reds. Freedom died today, or was it yesterday."

"Look at that," Sydney said. In the corner of the room near the entrance a young woman was drying her eyes and drinking wine, all at once.

"So what," Junko said.

"They're going to miss him," Sydney said.

"For a while," Junko said. "Then there'll be the five-year revision and the ten- and fifteen- and twenty-year revisions of the revisions. In fifteen years he'll be a bum and in twenty a hero and in thirty forgotten, mostly, and so forth and so on and I suppose finally he'll be an icon like Flaubert. Or not quite like Flaubert, because he was born in Algeria instead of Rouen. He was a colonial, after all. Not quite one of them, you understand."

Sydney said, "Yes and no."

Junko was watching the woman near the entrance. She was dressed simply in a sweater and skirt, gold bangles on her wrists. She looked like one of Bergman's women, her fingers touching the stem of the glass, her head tilted to one side in an attitude of melancholy languor. You could write a movie around her, Junko thought. Make her naked in the second reel. She was evidently waiting for someone, because she looked at the door every time it opened.

"Remember what that Frenchman said. France will enter the modern world when the last Resistant kills the last Collabo."

Junko turned away from the woman to look at Sydney. "Don't expect any mea culpas from them, Syd. It's not their style. I don't notice the Germans doing any, either, and they've got more to account for. Maybe they're doing them silently, so that no one can hear."

"Not yet," Sydney said.

"Not ever," Junko said. "But they don't have to worry about it because Uncle Sugar is here to keep them safe and sound, from the Reds or inflation or instability or insurrection, you name it. They don't have to think about anything. It's better that they don't."

Sydney laughed. "Uncle Sugar? Forever and ever?"

"Long enough," Junko said.

"You won't get tired?"

"Sure," Junko said. "But that's another story."

In the corner near the entrance a middle-aged man had joined the woman, and now they were holding hands across the table, the woman talking, explaining something, the man shaking his head. She dabbed at her eyes with a tissue. Whatever she was saying, he was rejecting. The waiter arrived with two fresh glasses and filled them with Champagne. You're sexy when you cry, Junko thought; and when she looked at him sharply, Junko smiled.

"This city's dying," Sydney said suddenly.

"So what are you doing here?"

"I like dying cities," Sydney said.

Part 1

One

SYDNEY VAN DAMM met Angela Dilion at Junko Poole's apartment in Montparnasse on the last day of April 1975. Sydney had not wanted to come; Junko's parties were always cumbersome, noisy, and crowded with aggressive American visitors who were ill at ease in Europe and galled by Germans. They were either solicitous or curt. Many of them had never met a German and were frankly curious, and not subtle about their curiosity. At Junko's Lincoln's Birthday bash two months before, an American had rolled up her shirtsleeves — Isn't it warm in here, do you mind if I make myself comfortable? — so that Sydney could not miss the row of blue numbers burned into her arm.

I think we've met before, haven't we, Herr van Damm?

Since Americans always asked what you did and where you came from, Sydney's nationality was impossible for him to avoid. When they asked about the new Porsche or the new Fassbinder or the latest spy scandal, what they really wanted to know was Sydney's analysis of the Third Reich. Could it happen again? Every German was an expert on the fascists. The Americans looked at him closely, trying to calculate his age, a date of birth being the focus of personality no less than a stutter or a club foot. Nineteen twenty-five was the generally agreed-upon year, the moral equivalent of a smoking gun. There were evenings at Junko Poole's when he felt like an astronaut at a press conference. So you've been to the moon! Tell us about the moon! Were there any signs of life? When the woman exposed her arm he was mortified. She was a little older than he was. Her skin was fair and the numbers stood out. They were as conspicuous as a diamond bracelet and for a moment he gaped; but of course that was the first time he had seen numbers on a human being's skin, and the American woman seemed to understand that and understand also that they were engaged in a complex transaction. When he replied that no, he did not think they had met, she smiled and did not answer, turning away to say something to her husband; and a few moments later they left. Sydney wanted to leave but didn't; in fact, was the last one out the door, drunk and depressed, thinking about the American woman who had asked him if she could make herself comfortable. There were certain acts that could never be undone, only pondered. It was not any easier drunk than sober, and Junko Poole's Lincoln's Birthday bash was not the place to go about it.

But now Junko insisted. We're all in lousy moods, Syd. We're distressed. We need you here. There won't be any strangers around to ask questions, except one, and you'll like her. We need your light German touch to cheer us up, the effervescence for which your people are so justly famous. And then he went on to describe Angela Dilion, his new American discovery, a class act, very pretty, very willing, a sharp tongue, a little money on the side, smart as a snake, no layabout, lonely like you. Angie's a real American girl, Junko said with a wink. It's time you met one.

They were not attracted to each other at once. Angela thought him a dour academic, and he thought her a self-centered bourgeoise, and neither was entirely wrong. Listening to him, she was convinced he was an American, perhaps a scholar who fed at one of the foundation troughs. That would account for his scrupulous diction, and Junko loved scholars. Looking at him, she was as certain of the reverse — a European intellectual who had spent most of his life in America, Berkeley or Morningside Heights. It was like meeting a European film star — Yves Montand or Curt Jurgens — and hearing the voice of Marlon Brando. No question, though, that Angela was Yankee through and through. She had a rangy walk, a pug nose, and a sharp voice. She held her head high and talked straight at you, too bluntly for Sydney's taste. He could not tell how much she held in reserve, probably not much. He listened hard to her accent, which was unfamiliar. He had never met anyone from the state of Maine, though hers was not strictly speaking a Down East accent but the Dilion Trill, whose scale began somewhere near Bangor and ended in the Home Counties.

Junko said later that he knew they would get on, at least for an evening, Sydney's introversion complementing Angela's openness. That woman lets it all hang out, he said. Angela wanted to know Europe, and Sydney was as close to the modern European as anyone she was likely to meet, a survivor of the war who meant to survive the peace as well. Junko wondered if Sydney was a bit too intellectual, too dense and preoccupied for Angela, then dismissed the thought. Angela Dilion had the ability to see around corners, even Sydney van Damm's corners; and Syd was amusing once you loosened him up. What he could do for her was less certain. She was finely made and light on her feet, ambitious, with a quick reaction time, not the first words that leaped to mind when you saw Sydney, his square head and broad shoulders, his concise build, his deliberate movements, his oceanic patience. You looked at him and thought immediately of a workingman, one of the skilled trades, bricklayer or army sergeant. He was a man who looked as if he had advanced through the ranks.

Junko brought them together early in the evening, preparing them separately, spinning little mysterious biographies, which they did not believe and which he didn't expect them to believe. So they were cautious with each other, knowing Junko was often mischievous. Junko tried to help them along, but the introduction didn't take and they both wandered off after a few moments of forced conversation. Sydney was more taciturn than usual and his appearance worked against him. He had not shaved and his clothes were rough. Angela was always eager to meet a new face but Sydney's was not promising. She was happy to be at Junko's, though. She did not want to be alone on this night, when the Americans were being thrown out of Vietnam at last, and about time. There were drawn faces and tears at Junko's that night, but Angela was dry-eyed. While she talked to Sydney her eyes strayed to the television set in the corner, where the first appalling pictures appeared, people falling out of helicopters, helicopters falling out of the sky, men shouting and waving weapons, scrambling to save themselves. Many of the men were hysterical. There were wounded civilians in the street, women and children and old men beside a burned-out bus. A soldier struck one of the old men in the face with his rifle butt and then tumbled himself, apparently shot dead. Saigon was disintegrating, bombed to the Stone Age, stinking of cowardice and corruption.

She watched a furious sequence of discontinuous images. Now they seemed to be evacuating the American embassy, refugees pressing against the gate, more helicopters on the roof. This was the last ghastly aria — and all of it acquired from a television set in the corner of an anonymous apartment in Montparnasse while she talked quietly to one Sydney van Damm, a man she had never seen before and would probably never see again. He could have no idea what this meant to her. The war was finished.

She said, "Have you known Junko long?"

"Many years. How did you meet Junko?"

"Around. That's where everyone meets Junko, 'around.' And you?"

"I do some work for him."

"He said you were a linguist of the Romance languages."

"Romance languages? Junko said that?"

"That's what Junko said," Angela said, turning again to watch the television screen. Junko Poole and two American women were blocking her view, but she could hear the sound, excited French punctuated by gunfire. She said to Sydney, "I suppose you didn't have anything to do with the war because of your age." He seemed to stiffen and when he answered that he did not fight in the war, she said, "But they were giving college deferments, so you wouldn't've been affected anyway. You wouldn't've gone no matter what. Lucky you."

He said, "I beg your pardon?"

"You would've been deferred even if you were young enough to go because you're what my father quaintly calls 'a university man.' That's a compliment, by the way." She was watching a small part of the screen that had become visible, talking to Sydney out of the side of her mouth. "But you might have been good at it. You look tough enough. Why are you staring at me like that?"

"I am not an American."

"You sound like one."

"Do you want to see my passport?"

"You're not English," she said doubtfully. "Canadian?"

"I'm German."

"You look German, come to think of it."

"Is that a compliment?"

"Sure," she said. "I suppose so. Why not? Let's watch what's happening here, on the other side of the world. You'll be interested in it." She took him by the hand — a heavy, calloused hand, she noticed, dry in spite of the warm room — and led him to the window next to the poster of Cézanne's naked oranges, where they had a clear view of the television screen, archive footage of Eisenhower and JFK and Johnson and Nixon with crosscuts of antiwar marches and rallies. She recognized some of the campuses and government buildings, and half-expected to see her girlish self carrying a banner with a slogan of the period, US OUT. When the face of a snarling teenage girl filled the screen, Angela sighed and shook her head.

"That could have been me, that one right there."

"Were you in college then?"

"For a few years," she said. "I was miserable. I dropped out, and then I came here to live."

"Because of the war?"

"Yes," she said.

"Amazing, that ordinary people could stop a war. No one ever did it before, at least without a revolution."

She snorted. "Don't give us too much credit. We didn't stop it. We slowed it down a little. We harassed them. We ruined Johnson. That's all we did. It was something, but it wasn't enough."

"In Europe it seemed incredible."

"I suppose it did," she said. "But we were in a place we had no business being. We were far from home."

"And you came to Europe because of the war."

"Because my brother was killed in the war."

Ah, Sydney said. It was a groan. He touched her hand. "I'm very sorry. I had no idea. You were close?"

Yes, she said. Yes, they were close, so close that the night he was killed she dreamed he was hurt. The dream was vivid and when she woke she remembered each particular; and stayed in bed all day long, frightened, pleading illness, waiting for the telephone call. When it didn't come, she wept with relief. How stupid; she had never been superstitious. They were not a superstitious family. That was Tuesday. On Friday afternoon two young officers arrived at the front door of the house at Old Harbor. Her father listened to what they had to say and collapsed, simply fell down. The officers were still there when she got home from school. They were unnerved, it was their first death detail. One of the officers stuttered as he gave her the news, reading it from a piece of paper. When he was finished, she told him to leave, to get out and not return, and then she was sorry she had been rude; they were scarcely older than she was, two young soldiers from the army base near Bangor. It was November 1968, a few days before the election. She fixed her father a drink and they sat in silence, thinking about Shake. It seemed to her now that the silence lasted two years. She had thought about the war every day, seeing it through Shake's eyes, from the letters he wrote. They were amusing letters, written with manic energy. It was looney tunes in Nam, you had to be there to trust it. Shake was assigned to a supply battalion in a rear area, far, far from harm's way, no prob. They had hot meals and movies at night and there were tiny whores, featherweights. In his letters he described the mechanics of the drug trade, organized and thriving as any great industrial concern. They had fifty-seven different varieties of grass. They even had opium and pipes to smoke it in. She reread the letters from time to time, trying to understand Shake's war. It was nothing like the war she saw on the evening news; and that night, when she tried to talk about it with her father, he only stared into his drink and shook his head. Now that the war was ending, she tried to find some satisfaction and could not. She wanted to believe that something would be salvaged, but could not believe that either. The beginning, middle, and end; all of it was squalid.

She said to Sydney, "He was only a teenager. He was a dropout too, from high school. I tried to talk him out of it, we all did. And I followed his sterling example, because of the bad vibrations."

They were silent a moment, listening to gunfire and the excited shouts of the French commentators.

She said, "Did you have any brothers killed in your war?"

"My father died," Sydney said. "I have no brothers."

"I'm sorry," she said. "Your father was in the army?"

"A staff officer," Sydney said.

"You must have been very young."

"I was ten when the war ended."

"I was ten when our war started, if you believe that our war started in 1957. Many do." She smiled at the coincidence, a bleak little irony. She was determined not to cry in front of this German stranger. "That makes us different generations, doesn't it?" Then, softly, "Look at *that. Look* at them," she said contemptuously, leaning forward for a better view. American sailors were pushing a damaged helicopter off the landing deck of an aircraft carrier. The helicopter staggered, rising, then plunged into the sea, where it wallowed like a drunken insect. The camera lingered for a moment, and then the screen went dark, brightening again with fresh scenes of panic in the capital.

Someone handed them glasses of wine, and they stepped back from the television set. Junko Poole and the two American women were standing motionless in front of it, their faces stricken as if they were in a mortuary and the television set was a corpse, a departed loved one.

She said, "Shall we leave them to their grief?"

Sydney smiled and turned his back on Saigon.

She said, "Do you mind talking about your war?"

Sydney raised his shoulders and let them fall.

"What did you think about on the last day of your war?"

"I thought about food," he said. "And I thought about freedom."

"Freedom?"

"In a war you are never free. And we were always hungry."

"Tell me this, Sydney. Were you humiliated?"

He looked at her strangely. The Second World War was not an electronic war. You did not tune into it. You lived it every hour of every day. You had no power over it, and it controlled your life completely and mercilessly. He said, "No. I was hungry. And I was afraid also. We did not know what would happen next. Anything could. The Red Army was not far away and we knew that they were worse even than the English. And our own army was a rabble, disorganized and starving as we were. We were relieved when the war was over, and we were frightened. Humiliation played no part. Humiliation is a luxury indulged in by the well fed or the cowardly."

"But you were defeated."

"We deserved to be."

"I'm sorry," she said. "You know all about this business. Defeat was good for your country; perhaps it will be good for mine. Was it good? I suppose it was. God, I hate them for it, though. I loved my brother so. I loved him to death. I won't forgive them, tonight or ever. Now I'm crying, and I promised I wouldn't. I haven't cried for months. Let's talk about something else. It's over now anyway. See the picture? They've taken the flag down. They've struck the colors. Is it true that you're a translator, Sydney? What do you translate? Whatever it is, I'll bet you're good at it. You were pretty good just now. Let's make a bargain, Sydney. Let's try not to be well fed or cowardly."

Later that night, when the party had gotten loud and disheveled — everyone had forgotten about Saigon or pretended to and was gossiping and philandering in the usual ways — Junko Poole noticed Sydney and Angela in a corner, head to head. The roar of conversation rose around them, but they paid no attention to it. They were both sweating in the spring heat, and Angela had taken off her shoes. They were sitting on the windowsill, where they could see the huge framed poster, Cézanne's naked oranges. The window was open and the street sounds close by. Sydney was talking and Angela was listening and nodding sympathetically. He was describing his life to her. He called it marginal. He lived on the edges of Parisian life, alone and without the consolation of citizenship. He had no family, except his mother who lived in the East. They were out of touch. He translated German novels into English or French, mostly English. He preferred reading German, writing English, and speaking French. He worked at his translations every day, slow and lonely work that paid badly. When he got too far behind or wanted an expensive meal or a weekend in the country, he called Junko Poole and accepted piecework, which was undemanding and paid extremely well. Every few months he took a weekend in the country, alone or with a friend, and hiked and fished. Often he went to Normandy, the invasion beaches near St. Aubin. They were wonderful beaches, wide and unpopulated. They were beaches with a history.

And you? he said.

I keep the wolf from the door, Angela said. Except when I let him in.

Junko said you were private, Sydney said.

Junko's a liar, as is well known.

And a philosopher.

Not that either, she said.

That wolf, he began.

She said, Look, Sydney. I don't *do* anything. I don't write poetry or novels or make films or design publicity or underwear. People don't understand that. They don't like it. Women think I'm letting down the side. They think I'm lazy or a dilettante. But I don't believe you are what you do. I believe you do what you are, and what I'm doing is living my life. I like art. I go to galleries and museums with my friends and try to discover what's happened to the artists in this country, because most of what I see isn't art. I could say I'm writing a novel, but I'm not. I could say I'm getting my head together, but my head's fine. Unspeakable, isn't it? Probably this is the wrong century for me but it's the only one I've got. I'm a marginal character, Sydney. I'm sort of like you. I'm far from home and I like it.

Junko said you were ambitious, Sydney said.

What Junko doesn't know would fill the Louvre, she said.

Their faces were almost touching. And then Sydney laughed and kissed her on the mouth, suddenly, as if he were uncertain of her reaction. This was an impulsive act, very out of character. He was aware of Cézanne's naked oranges, the sounds of Montparnasse below, and Angela's closed eyes. They broke and looked at each other, and then she kissed him back.

Junko Poole watched all this from the kitchen doorway. He was holding a bottle of Champagne, thinking that a sardonic toast to the lost war was in order. But he did nothing. Junko was a man of the world and knew a *coup de foudre* when he saw one.

Ten days later Angela moved into Sydney's tiny apartment in the Marais. She preferred it to her own studio near the Invalides, though her studio was smartly furnished and had an elevator and Sydney's was five flights up and barely furnished at all: a bed, a table, two chairs, an armoire, and several hundred books, most of them in German. She believed Sydney's apartment the more atmospheric of the two, and his life more composed. She had been living in Paris for five years, the first three at the Sorbonne, the last two at liberty. She thought of herself as a witness, a sort of UN observer, sent to monitor the skirmish lines of a worn-out war of attrition. This involved café life, long nights in St.-Germain-des-Prés discussing the meaning of the 1968 uprising with the journalist whose hand was under your skirt and his baby blue eyes on your tits but whose conversation was dazzling if marred slightly by a tendency to lecture, his discourse having the feel and flavor of the classroom, unsurprising since the classroom was his true venue. How they loved to talk! Thrilling in its way, four or five of them at one of the front-row tables at the Flore drinking pastis and debating the merits of urban sabotage, and then at three in the morning the good-looking French boy who had been to prep school in Virginia and whose stepmother was a movie star suggesting that they go to Cannes at once, just for a few days, lie in the sun and slip naked into the Med and *float.* Money slapped on the table and away they'd go, taking the waiter with them, the waiter's white apron sailing into the interior of the café as he renounced the workaday world; alas, he did not know how to drive after all. The few days became a riotous week, the sun burning all day long. And this was the wolf-life she kept from the door, and sometimes admitted.

And Sydney? Sydney was living in Paris the way an adult was meant to live, sparely and without affectation or money, and he had lived that way for years. Café life in St.-Germain-des-Prés was part of another life long ago. Cannes might as well have been Chicago. When he went to the beach, he went to Normandy. He had not strolled the Champs-Élysées in years and knew nothing of the races at Longchamps or the little jazz club in rue St. Benoît or the disco at Place de la Bastille. He had never eaten in a three-star restaurant nor taken a boat around the islands at night.

Language weighed him down. Language was the cause of his terrible headaches. He told her that his head came apart because there was too much language in it, competing idioms. But it seemed to him that his headaches were less frequent now; no less severe but less frequent, and she was the cause. She buoyed his spirits with her tales of the wolf-life, not so different from his own life fifteen years before.

Make you feel young again, do I, van Damm?

Your life is more stylish than mine, he said.

Tell me about it, she said.

Long afternoons in the Jardin des Plantes, unimaginably lonely. I was often ill and required round-the-clock nursing care.

Am I supposed to believe that?

He said, Believe that and you'll believe anything.

Still, it's not Cannes.

No, he said. Your Cannes was fun?

Yes, she said. It was. I liked it, going on the spur of the moment late at night when no one was around. Did I mention the golden-haired French boy who owned a château in Touraine and a pied-à-terre in Nice? And he had a title. He was a young baron.

Third-rate title, Sydney said. Bonaparte *fils* gave them out like gumdrops.

The château was as big as the Ritz, she said.

He said, Would I like it, Cannes?

She laughed and laughed. Maybe, she said. Maybe you would. I don't think it's your kind of place, though. It's Mediterranean, Syd. It's pastel. It's soft, except of course the people, who are hard as rocks.

And Maine? Would I like Maine?

Definitely, she said. It's northern, cold, and monotonous, short days and long nights and killing summer frosts. The only trouble with Maine is that my father lives there.

Yes? Sydney said, cocking his head.

My father and I do not get along, she said.

Angela watched him in the evenings working at the small wooden desk by the window that looked out on a synagogue. He liked watching the religious come and go and often on the Sabbath he heard them singing, melancholy airs filled with the heartbreak of Central Europe. That was how he heard it, though perhaps the religious heard it differently, since they were the ones who were doing the interpreting. In any lamentation, the song belonged to the singer.

Sydney seemed always to be reading books by German writers she never heard of, strange sensual stories, often cruel and sexually perverse, vibrant with struggle. She knew nothing of German literature beyond Rilke and Mann and the unreadable Goethe. German literature was not part of an American university curriculum and not an advertised specialty of the Sorbonne, either. It was as if German politics had discredited German literature. The novels seemed to happen in a barren and tormented region of the mind, and when she told him that, and how difficult it was for her, he said no, not barren. *German.* Broch, Lenz, Musil, Roth. And Austrian, he said with a smile.

She read his German writers in translation and found them unforgiving, pilots' jargon for inarticulate and therefore dangerous aircraft. In their disdain of the forms of everyday life the stories resembled Sydney's cramped Marais apartment, which became more adverse to live in as the weeks passed. She thought of it as a cell, indisputably his alone, and she found it monotonous, like Maine. Perhaps some decoration, she suggested; no ornamentation, nothing elaborate, merely something cheerful. Remember your sainted Goethe. More light!

She set about cleaning the windows and the threadbare carpet. She brought a cactus plant and a ficus tree from her own place, and some of her own books and framed photographs. The first item she purchased was the poster of Cézanne's naked oranges, which she hung over the narrow bed. The second item was a bigger bed.

She was thrilled, somewhat to her surprise. She thought that at last, after so many boys, she had found a man.

Two

THEY WERE MARRIED in the fall. Carroll Dilion came for the wedding, though Angela urged him not to bother, there was no point to it, the trip was arduous et cetera and unnecessary et cetera, and the ceremony only a formality. We're having it because Sydney wants one. We've been married in heart and soul for six months and I'm pregnant, she said. But her father insisted, she was all he had left (as he put it), and he wanted to meet his new son-in-law, father of his first grandchild. The one who finally caught you, he said. I want to shake his hand. He instructed Angela to book him into the Ritz, where he had stayed with her mother on their honeymoon after the war and had a fine time.

Angela was resigned. To Sydney she complained that her father had never been there when she wanted him and now insisted on being there when she didn't want him. Is that perverse, or what? He thinks his money entitles him to do whatever he wants, Dilion's alleged millions. He's a nuisance, she said.

Angie, Sydney said. If he wants to come, let him come. It's a sentimental thing. He's entitled to see his only daughter married. Don't be so harsh. You should have heard him on the phone, he was so pleased.

Yes, I'm harsh, she said. Sorry about that. I have reason to be. And don't be fooled by his act, which he's perfected really well over the years. He takes it on the road, too, for out-of-town tryouts. He's loaded with charm and it's disarming. Naturally that's his point, to disarm the enemy so that he can get his way. That's what he does in life, get his way. Carroll Dilion lives for himself, period.

As opposed to the rest of us?

Yes, as opposed to the rest of us. Don't argue with me, van Damm. Not about Carroll. I'm an expert on Carroll Dilion. I've had a lifetime's experience with him beginning when I was a little girl and my mother died and later when I was in college and my brother died. Probably I expected too much. No doubt I did. And I don't anymore. Now this: this is a happy occasion so naturally he's up for it. Nothing's required of him. Carroll's great at ceremonies like this one, when everyone's smiling and happy. But let me tell you something. When you need a strong shoulder, forget about Carroll. He's so selfish, so in need, he soaks up all the sympathy and there's never any left over for anyone else.

They went to the Mairie in the morning for the civil service, then had a light lunch and strolled in the Luxembourg Gardens, waiting there until it was time to go to the church. They sat in the sun, watching old men play boules. The garden was fading in autumn, leaves littering the gravel paths, only a few hardy flowers remaining in beds here and there. Angela was uneasy, chattering aimlessly, the surprising amiability of the formalities at the Mairie, the twinkle in the eye of the magistrate, his firm handshake at the end; when she offered him her cheek, he kissed it.

Carroll was not listening, sitting slumped in his chair, staring blankly at his hands. Angela knew he was thinking about Shake, because his demoralized bearing reminded her of the autumn day in 1968 when he sat in his heavy chair in his study at Old Harbor, drinking Scotch after Scotch, saying nothing that was intelligible. The room, with its heavy wood and brass fittings, its spyglass and mariner's compass, was reminiscent of a yacht's saloon. She had never felt comfortable in it; from its windows you could see a sliver of blue ocean. When she sat next to him, taking his hand, it was like taking the hand of an indifferent stranger. When she leaned her head against his shoulder, he flinched, then relaxed enough to put his slender fingers around her arm, sighing, murmuring something. He began to speak, but it was not to her but to the room itself, his sanctuary. What he said were expletives, garbled phrases, some code to which only he had the key. Her heart was breaking and after a moment she ceased to listen.

And when the calls began to come — how did the news spread so fast? — she took them, accepting the condolences, regretting that, no, her father could not come to the telephone but she would let him know that you called, thank you so very much. She wrote the names on the pad next to the telephone. Food and flowers arrived and she accepted those, too, standing in the front door saying how much she appreciated the thoughtfulness, but her father was too — distraught. She was behaving the way she thought her mother would have wanted her to behave.

She made only two telephone calls herself, one to her current boyfriend, who was out somewhere, and the other to Carroll's lawyer, Tommy Borowy, who was in court in Bangor.

Yes, there is a message. Tell Mr. Borowy that Shake Dilion was killed in South Vietnam.

She remained in the study, sitting in a chair in the far corner of the room. After a while, she did not bother to answer the telephone. She stared out the window at the sliver of ocean glittering in the moonlight. Later that night, the bottle of Scotch almost gone, Carroll rose and commenced to inspect his books. He looked lost and apologetic, a man who had blundered into the wrong house. He stepped slowly to the wall of books, leaning forward, on familiar ground now, running his fingernails along the spine of a leatherbound set, Herman Melville. And below Melville, Twain and Hawthorne. He moved right to Anthony Powell, Aldous Huxley, and Evelyn Waugh, slowly clicking his fingernails along the grainy spines of the books, staring at them, his lips moving silently. He shook his head then, as if these Englishmen had nothing to offer him at this time. He stopped at Conrad, his fingers stroking the leather, his feet set wide apart, a worried seaman on the foredeck gazing at a troubled horizon. He seemed to be in conversation with Joseph Conrad, a confidential matter, something man to man. Carroll knew Conrad's work well. He used to read aloud from *Lord Jim* and *The Secret Sharer,* explaining that the Pole wrote often of the very end of experience and what was found there. Every man had to test himself, and if he was courageous and lucky he found maturity. This was all the reward you could ask for, or were entitled to: growing up. It was always more a matter of courage than of luck, though naturally you had to put yourself in the way of things. Luck was barometric pressure, that day's weather. From her chair in the shadows near the window, Angela could see Homer's little watercolor, a fisherman alone in a boat, the wind rising, the fisherman's face lifted to the heavy sea, gambling.

The watercolor had been her mother's. Someday it would be hers.

She remembered Carroll tapping his foot, taking a long swallow of his drink, and turning, looking at her, puzzled, as if wondering what she was doing there. He hesitated, then drained his glass, turning to the window, tears jumping to his eyes. It was very late. They listened to the wind a moment, gusts that rattled the windows, and then he began to speak of his son, her brother, such a wonderful boy, so confident, so headstrong, a boy heedless of consequence. "He grew up like Huck Finn. He thought he could do anything, just anything at all. He was a boy without moorings, but we put our hopes on him, didn't we?" He refilled his drink, ice and then Scotch. "Now he's gone, too." For a moment, she did not know whom he meant. But of course it was his wife.

"You must look after yourself now," he said.

Then Tommy Borowy, huge in a camel-hair coat and muffler, was through the door and into the room, his chest heaving as if he had run miles and miles. Carroll let out a strangled cry and they fell into each other's arms, the lawyer rocking her father to and fro in a bear hug. The lawyer's vitality filled the room. Her father was invisible now behind Tommy's broad back. She could only see the fringe of white hair and his feet, incongruous in red leather slippers.

She heard her father say, "It's finished for me."

And Tommy: "Christ, Carroll. Oh, Christ."

Tommy had not seen her and her father had forgotten about her, so she rose and stepped quietly to the door and opened it and slipped through it, looking after herself, as she had been told she must do. She sat in her bedroom with the lights out. She believed that if she tried hard enough she could reach the spirit of her mother. Her mother would have words of consolation, something hopeful and decent. The night she died she had given Shake a hug and a huge smile and then turned and said she would be with them always. What a wonderful daughter you are, Angie. Then, I'm going to leave some of me with you. And she winked in her old way, the way Angie winked today, the wink that startled her mother's friends. So she went to the mirror and winked and that seemed to bring her mother a little closer. She listened with all her might but heard nothing, until a light tap on her door. Carroll, of course. But she pretended to be asleep and at last he went away.

She looked away from Carroll to Sydney, who was watching the boules players. There was a dispute of some kind between an old man and a young one and at last, with a gesture of disgust, the young one gave way.

"Almost time," Sydney said.

"I love you, Sydney."

Sydney blushed, as he always did when she spoke privately in public.

"You're sexy, too, van Damm. Do you know how sexy you are? For an older gentleman. For a man with some gray in his hair."

Carroll said, "Isn't it time to go?"

Angie said, "Van Damm? You're not ever going to let me down?"

"Never," Sydney said.

"Because I've been let down a lot and I don't like it."

"Not by me," Sydney said.

"By men in general."

"What happens if I do? I'd better be prepared."

"I'll hate you," she said.

"Let's go," Carroll said.

"I'm joking, Angie."

"Hate you to death," she said.

The boules players were arguing again, their voices rising. They had attracted a crowd. The young man was shouting and waving his arms.

"What are they arguing about?" Carroll asked.

Angie laughed. "The young one got screwed over once too often. And now he's telling them that they can take their game and stick it."

Sydney turned and looked at her queerly.

"He's telling them that he doesn't need them, that he has another game. Another game in a better part of town, he's saying. And that's the game he's going to."

"Time to go," Sydney said. "It's time to get married." He rose, taking Angela by the hand. She winked at him. Full of surprises was his bride-to-be. They weren't arguing about boules at all, but about the football game that night, who was favored and who wasn't, and which bar to go to in order to watch it on television.

They were married in a small Protestant church in Montparnasse. There were no attendants, not even Junko Poole, who had introduced them. Angela wanted a private wedding because she did not believe in official vows. She had no confidence in the church and even less in the state, or perhaps it was the other way around. She explained to Sydney that she was superstitious. Wedding parties made her nervous. Ideally there would be just the two of them and whatever officials were required, a concept he agreed with theoretically. He was honoring the wish of his mother and didn't care whether there were witnesses or not so long as a Lutheran minister spoke the proper words.

It was something she would want, Sydney said. I'm sure of it.

She should be here, Sydney.

They wouldn't give her a visa.

Did she apply?

I doubt it, Sydney said. What would be the use? I'm not sure she got my letter.

Still, Angie said.

It's better this way, Sydney replied.

So there was only Carroll standing at Angela's side. He remarked that the church in Montparnasse reminded him of the Little Church Around the Corner in New York, where he was married just after the war. It was not the façade nor the interior, God knows; perhaps it was the light falling through narrow windows into the choir. Isn't it kind of gloomy? he asked. His wedding was a full-dress affair, eight ushers and eight bridesmaids, with a reception at the Barclay that lasted until midnight and then some. The church was filled with flowers and everyone agreed that the wedding party was especially glamorous, the ushers in their thirties or older, the bridesmaids all younger. Many of the men had gray hair and children almost as old as the bride. Carroll was thirty-six, Camilla only twenty-one. There was a downpour that afternoon, but no one minded. The war was behind them and how proud you were to be an American, free, white, and twenty-one, as they said then; the future spread before them without limit. They had a wonderful wedding and reception and a riotous time in Paris, and then drove south to Cannes, where someone had lent them a villa. Souvenirs of the war were everywhere but they paid no attention to them, ancient history. At Camilla's insistence they tried to find the place where his jeep had overturned during an airstrike; it was somewhere north of Orléans, but he didn't look very hard and they never found the place. Focke-Wulf 190s, he said. They attacked low and flat. But what the hell, it was a long time ago, ancient history.

Of course in those days you came and went by boat, a leisurely passage, black tie at dinner and dancing later.

Romantic, Carroll said. The ne plus ultra.

But the real difference was the way we felt about ourselves and our country, he said. We'd won a world war! I wonder what happened to the confidence we had.

She said, You mean confidence game.

The service was swift. It seemed only a few minutes, and they were on the street again. Carroll seemed dazed and afterward complained that he didn't understand a word of what was said, and his French used to be quite passable. It had been one of his majors at Williams, and of course Camilla spoke it like a native. She had once spent a year abroad; her parents had taken her to Burgundy when she was just a girl. They lived in Nuits St. Georges. That was when your grandfather decided to learn the wine trade, Angie. It didn't work out for him, like most of his schemes. Everyone could see that war was coming, so they left Nuits St. Georges and never went back.

They walked slowly from the church to the Café Flore on Boulevard St. Germain, where Carroll and Camilla went on their honeymoon and later. Camus sat right over there, Carroll said. He was with a beautiful woman the afternoon we saw him. She had dark hair cut very short and was wearing enormous sunglasses. He was in a trenchcoat, which he didn't take off. She was a dish. She looked like Garbo but it wasn't Garbo; she was French through and through.

Carroll ordered Champagne and toasted his daughter and new son-in-law, the German-American alliance, ha-ha. Long life, happiness, prosperity. And here's to my grandchild! Grandson, please, he said, an oblique reference to Shake.

Sydney and I are hoping for a girl, Angela said.

It was dark when they finished the Champagne and left the café to stroll down the boulevard. The evening promenade had yet to begin. The apartments on the upper floors of the great stone buildings of St. Germain were rosy with light. In one of them they could see a maid arranging flowers. In another a man and woman were in evening dress, standing at the window admiring each other. Sturdy wrought-iron balconies in front of each window gave the apartments a palatial look, stone tiaras calling attention to plump, satisfied faces.

They walked across the bridge to Place de la Concorde, standing a moment to admire its proportions and the majestic sweep up the Champs-Élysées to the Arc de Triomphe. Then they struck off down rue de Rivoli to rue de Castiglione, leading to Place Vendôme. Carroll stopped several times, peering up the straight line of rue de Rivoli to its vanishing point. The apartments facing the Tuileries put him in mind of a mountain face made of stone and glass. It was perfection, so composed and harmonious that it was like something found in nature. He stood quietly in the bustle of rue de Rivoli, contemplating the geometry, and then turned to Angie.

Your mother and I were here many times. Standing on this very spot admiring the view. She loved Paris and always wore a red beret. It made her look like a coed, so adorable. We were here in 'forty-six and again in 'fifty and 'fifty-five, before she got sick. In 'fifty and 'fifty-five we stayed at the Meurice, just up the street. It had been Nazi headquarters during the Occupation. In 'forty-six things were still tough for the French. There were shortages and a new government about every ten minutes, and for a while it looked as if the Reds might take over. The dollar went a long way, though. We stayed at the Ritz for peanuts. Did your parents ever get to Paris, Sydney?

They were here once, I think. In 'thirty-five or 'thirty-six, before the war. It was their anniversary and they went to Paris to celebrate it.

Everyone loves Paris, Carroll said.

Let's go, Angela said. I'm hungry. Thirsty, too.

But Carroll did not move. He said, What did your father do in the war, Sydney?

He was a staff officer, a major. He died in Berlin in 'forty-five.

In the air raids?

They killed him, Sydney said.

Was he involved in the plot, then?

No, he was just a staff officer.

Carroll nodded, sighing.

I want to go now, Angela said.

They dined at the Ritz. Conversation was general, Angie and Sydney making most of it. Sydney described their new apartment in Montmartre, a Bauhaus building on a sickle-shaped street that swept up the butte to the Place du Tertre. The neighborhood was straight-ahead Figaro country, bourgeois to the core; everyone kept a dog and a Renault and read *Le Figaro*. They would take possession of the apartment after a honeymoon in the Frisians. Carroll thought to ask where the Frisians were and Angela laughed. They were off the beaten path, all right, islands in the North Sea off the coast of Germany. They were sand dunes in the North Sea. It was well after the tourist season and no one would be around.

The Frisians are deserted now, Sydney said. Like Maine in the winter.

But not so cold, Angie said.

Carroll smiled. It doesn't sound like you, somehow, Angela.

She wanted to go to Tuscany, Sydney said.

The worst way, she said. But van Damm talked me into the Frisians. They are very German, according to Sydney.

Carroll said quickly, What does that mean? What does it mean to be 'very German'?

Only Germans go there, Sydney said. There are jokes about the thick-witted Frieslanders. They don't like strangers, but Angie will win them over.

Is it pleasant, then?

Very pleasant, Sydney said. And fashionable.
These German islands —
Brahms in the morning and the Brothers Grimm in the afternoon, Sydney said dryly.
Carroll said to Angela, You always hated cold weather.
Not when I'm with van Damm, she said.
You always hated the winter in Maine, Carroll said.
She said, That was Maine. No one likes Maine in the winter.
He smiled disarmingly. Why, I do, he said. It's a fine place to live when you're alone.
You're lucky to live there then, she said.
It sounds as if you two have got things figured out, he said.
Angie said, We do.
Carroll said, It's amazing. You honeymoon on these islands and then you come back to live in Paris on your sickle-shaped street where people read *Le Figaro* and keep cats. Or is it dogs? Sydney translates and you do whatever it is that you do. What *do* you do, Angie? Anyhow, it's a long way from Old Harbor. But who wants to be shut up in Old Harbor? You know what we say up there, Sydney. There are two seasons, winter and August. But I've lived there for years and I'll die there. Paris is a long way from your homeland, too. I hope it works out for you. I truly do.
We appreciate your coming, Sydney said.
In six months I'll be a mother, Angie said. I'll do that.
We're glad you came, Sydney said.
Carroll turned to Sydney then, reaching to pour the last of the wine into his glass. He said, I have money. But I expect you know that. I have no family except for Angela, so one day you both will be rich. Of course it's never wise to count on an inheritance, the times being what they are. I expect we'll go through a bad patch now because they've lost their minds in Washington. But if things don't get too much worse there should be a nice nest egg for you, and as you know Angela has an annuity from her mother. It's given her independence, which is what her mother had in mind. Probably the reason that Angela doesn't work is that I never have. I never needed to. And now I'm too old to start. But if you ever need anything, I wish you'd let me know. Will you do that?
We don't need anything, Sydney said.
In case, Carroll said.

Yes, Sydney said.

I wish Angela and I were closer. Do you think we could be, Angela?

She hesitated a moment before she answered. Yes, we could be.

I'd like that, he said.

I would, too, she said.

I wish I were different, Carroll said.

Angie said quickly, No, you don't.

He laughed shortly. Perhaps not.

She said, Have a good winter, Dad.

Yes, he said. You, too.

Good-bye, Sydney said.

Take care of her, Carroll said.

I will, Sydney said.

Not that she needs it. She's always taken care of herself, haven't you, Angela? Carroll pushed his chair back, rising with both hands flat on the table, looking around the dining room at the waiters standing at attention. He said, I'm tired. It's been a long day. I must go to bed. My flight's early. I've still got the jet lag and here I am, turning around and going back home. It's strange to me, being in Paris. It's been such a long time. And I'm sorry about my mood in the Luxembourg Gardens. I was remembering Camilla and Shake and that made me sad. I couldn't help it. I didn't want to spoil things on your day. Last thing I wanted, believe me. I wish you every happiness, now and in the future.

Sydney rose and they shook hands.

Carroll smiled thinly, leaning down to kiss his daughter on the cheek. Tears filled his eyes. She smelled his familiar shaving cream and felt the scratch of his evening stubble. He retreated slowly, smiling back at them from the glass doors of the entrance. Angela looked at him, thinking that if she did not know him she would take him for someone's rich American uncle, paying for a spree at the Ritz. Carroll Dilion gave a last wave and disappeared into the corridor, leaving Angela and Sydney alone at last. One door closed and another opened and they realized that they were free to lead their own life together, and that they had no idea what life would hold, where it would lead, and how it would flourish or if it would flourish. But of course it would. Sydney raised his glass, the wine sparkling in the crystal.

To us, he said.
To us, she agreed.
I like him, you know.
I know. Men always do.
Do you think —
Yes, she said. He is what he is. You can't make him into anything else. I've been so angry with him for so long; and he with me, though he'd never admit it. But I'm going to forget about that now. I don't need him anyway. I've got you. We can be nice to him together. All right?
They clinked glasses and sat a moment in companionable silence. She inspected him in his wedding suit, a white rose in his lapel. She had never seen a bridegroom with a white rose in his lapel, but Sydney insisted so she bought him the rose and a white handkerchief to go in the breast pocket. For herself, she had bought an off-white suit at Chanel, a short skirt and a round-necked jacket. She wore her mother's short gold chain around her neck, gold bracelets, and a little gold pin on the jacket. It was make-believe, Miss Golden Girl of 1975. She shook her head, beginning to smile and then to laugh.
You look almost presentable, she said.
What do you mean, almost? He feigned high indignation.
She said, You darling. You're not the sort of man who wears worsted suits with side vents and a white shirt with a silk tie and a white rose in your lapel. The suit fits you but you don't fit it.
I thought I looked dapper.
Van Damm? You look like a workingman.
I am a workingman.
I, on the other hand, am in perfect character.
You are the toast of Paris, he said.
Here's to you, Sydney. I hope it wasn't too awful.
It wasn't, he said. I was nervous, though. Our Lutheran was dour. The magistrate was better. He was a man who liked his work.
Marrying people, she said.
Making them legal.
I don't want to go just yet, she said suddenly.
Shall we order another bottle?
Why not? she said.
Not on his tick, Sydney said.

Any way you like, she said.

Sydney turned, found the waiter's eye, and pointed at the empty bottle in the silver bucket. Angela watched him do it, liking the way he turned and gestured, as if he had ordered bottles of Champagne in the dining room of the Ritz every day of his life.

She leaned slowly across the table and kissed him. This was what she wanted to remember, she and Sydney alone at a round table in the middle of the Ritz dining room, newly married, one bottle of Champagne gone and another on its way, she spectacular in her Chanel suit, Sydney handsome in his worsted with its silk tie and white rose, his mouth breaking into a grin. He said something and she laughed. They would have a beautiful honeymoon and return to their new apartment; and in six months they would have a child. Her bracelets glittered in the candlelight. The waiter arrived, presenting the bottle for Sydney's inspection. She felt she was on the edge of a great discovery, an adventurer discovering an ocean lying flat and enormous as far as the eye could see, the surface concealing the riot of life beneath. The waiter popped the cork and refilled their glasses, paused a moment, and went away. A vast benign hush surrounded them as they toasted each other again and again.

Three

IN THE GRAMMAR of their life the honeymoon was an embarrassing solecism, a misplaced modifier or dangling participle remembered forever with a raised eyebrow and a comical shudder. Remember the second day in Sylt? The day you said it reminded you of March in Maine or was it Maine in March, only worse? And that was a carnival compared with Ilsensee and the German mood. They looked on the honeymoon as a writer looks on apprentice work, ambitious and earnest but distraught. They had affection for it, as anyone does for early error, and they would never, ever denounce it; but they did not want to repeat it either. They were trying hard in Sylt and Ilsensee, but they did not know the rules. At the time it looked as if the beginning of their marriage would be the end of it. There was one false step after another.

Sylt was a sand dune fifteen miles long and a half a mile wide and a millennium deep, a few miles from the mainland but utterly separate, a feature of the sea. The sun did not shine and there was wind all day long. The hotel was a Frisian masterpiece, furtive eyelid windows and a thatched roof, hundred-year-old shadows inside and dirty green hedges outside, the quintessence of glum. The staff — if you could call the manager, two chambermaids, a cook, and a waitress a "staff" — did not know what to make of Angela, an American so far from home. They had never seen one before, except the manager, who confided to Sydney that he had retreated all the way across France and into Germany in 1944, pursued by

Americans. He had wounded two of them near Aachen. It was the worst year of his life, if you didn't count 1945. If it were not for the American air force Germany would have won the war, would you not agree, Herr van Damm? The landing at Normandy succeeded by chance only, the Luftwaffe criminally withheld from the battle. If it were not for the landing, and for the air force, Germany would have won and there would be peace today. Germany would have crushed the pig Russians and eradicated Bolshevism.

Angela listened to Sydney's translation and then asked him, "Is that true?"

"No," Sydney said.

"Why don't you tell him that, then?"

"Because he doesn't want to hear it. And if he did hear it, he wouldn't believe it."

"I think you ought to set him straight, Syd."

"Think so?"

"He's a fool, Sydney."

"It was a long time ago," Sydney said.

"No kidding," Angela said.

She was used to the French, so merry and conversational, so absorbed with the style of things, food and wine, and decoration, the symmetry of it, the ambiance. France was sexy; Germany was numb. At Sylt the chambermaid was sullen and did not respond to instructions, or even Angie's confident *Guten Morgen*. She looked at the tangled sheets and sneered, tearing them off the bed as if they were contaminated, fouled by lovemaking. Angie wondered if perhaps the Germans made love on the floor or standing up in a corner or in the chairs or on tables.

These island Germans were dense and monosyllabic, and that seemed to suit van Damm's new mood, preoccupied and reflective. He was ardent; it wasn't that. They were both ardent, exploring their raw sexuality beyond the physical claims of their bodies, slipping into the ethereal realms of soul (his word) and heart (hers). She showed only the slightest evidence of the baby growing inside her, a roundness and hardness that excited her husband and her, too. The fact of the baby freed them both. There were no taboos. From the big bed with the heavy comforter they could watch the North Sea pitch and heave, the sea making love as they were. Its depths were theirs also. He put his hand on her belly and smiled a smile of the purest delight. We have it now, he said, and we won't ever lose it.

But when it came time to leave the connubial bed and take a light-headed walk before breakfast or after dinner, he fell silent, concerned now with his own private thoughts, which he did not share. When he tried to explain, he was inarticulate. She thought of it as his German mood and wondered if he was spooked by his homeland. She was often spooked by hers; why couldn't he be by his? At first she was tolerant, vaguely amused, comparing him to a great scientist who was lost and incompetent outside the laboratory of the connubial bed, obsessed as he was with new abstract theories of raw sexuality, soul and heart.

The second night of their honeymoon she watched him stride up the beach, hands plunged into his coat pockets, hair flying, his broad back and heavy bent head reminiscent of the physique of an American football player. She watched him a moment — this romantic German, she thought, my husband — and then sprinted to catch up, linking her arm through his, excited at touching him. He gave off a wonderful smell. They stopped to look at the sea, so gray, gray the color of death, and unquiet at dusk. It was an ugly sea, the sea of Norse legends.

She said, "It would be hard to live here."

"For us," he said. "Not for them."

"It's lonely," she said.

"It is that," he agreed.

"Your Frieslanders," she said. "They are not a jolly people."

He turned to her and said with great seriousness, "Don't be too hard on them. They're good people, simple people, but they're isolated here. They haven't had any advantages. They've been left behind and they resent it. They don't know how to leave home, so they stay here and watch tourists come and go. They're used to the big blond types from Hamburg, and they're suspicious. They're suspicious of us. We're foreign to them, even me. They distrust outsiders."

He had lapsed into German: *Ausländer.*

She said, "Even you?"

"They don't know what I'm doing with an American. They don't believe we're married. What do you call that?"

"Dirty weekend," she said.

"And after all, it's the off season."

And then she thought, But whose honeymoon is it? He seemed to be saying that it was her duty to please the Frieslanders instead of the other way around. Then, having thought it, she said it out loud.

He looked at her with his flat gray eyes, and she remembered the look from the first time they met and she had not liked him. She was conscious of the noisy wind and the racing waves, gray as far as the horizon, clouds low overhead, and the buxom dunes behind him, grass here and there and no houses at all, no sign of human habitation. It was as it must have been in Saxon times. She thought, How at ease he is here, how much a part of the land and the water, and the weather. Somewhere a foghorn growled. The wind bit into her cheeks, and she turned, looking behind her; in the distance the lights of the hotel glowed dully. She realized suddenly that she did not want to return to the hotel, with its heavy furniture and faded wallpaper and animals' horns over the mantel, a puny fire sputtering in the grate, and chipped porcelain at their places each night. At night they were the only people in the dining room, forced to keep their voices low and their laughter muted because the atmosphere was so ponderous; it was heavier than they were. She could not wait to leave the table to resume their lovemaking upstairs, but how much better if they could love each other any place they chose, even at dinner. The connubial bed was not supposed to be a refuge, nor her honeymoon a dirty weekend. They were not refugees. She and Sydney were not casual lovers. She wanted to leave Sylt to the Frieslanders, leave them to their own isolation and prejudice. Peasants were the same in every country, no exceptions.

"It's our honeymoon, Syd."

"That's right," he said.

"Reminds me of the state of Maine in March."

"I remember it from many years ago," he said.

"Here?" she said.

"We were here when I was very young, my father, my mother, and me. We drove over for the day and then spent the night in a lodging, bed-and-breakfast. It was in the summer. I couldn't've been more than four, five years old. It was sunny and warm.

People were sunbathing nude along this beach. There was a cult of nudity then, a health-fad thing to begin with and then others took it up. They were everywhere on the beach. They offended my mother, so we left early."

"Well," she said, laughing.

"They had an argument about it but my mother won."

Angela said, "Even better."

"I remember seeing the hotel from the beach. How sturdy and happy it seemed. I remember a bandstand close to town where they played German music in the evenings, everyone was there listening. Brahms." He was silent a moment, evidently recollecting his German music, and then said bitterly, "It's only a few more days, if you can stand it. Then we can go home. And next year we can go to Tuscany."

He had spoken with such vehemence, had said "Tuscany" as if it were a curse. She was dismayed. It was such a simple thing that he refused to understand. In a few short sentences they had reached impasse. And she had only spoken her mind, as she had always done, as she would always do. That was her way, and if he found it intolerable . . .

"Next year?" she said. "But this is now. This is our honeymoon right now. I don't care about next year. Who knows what will happen next year? This place is haunted. It's — tortured. This is not a place for people who love each other as we do and will always. Isn't there any place in Germany besides this sand dune? Is this the only hotel in the Federal Republic? Is this the only place we're allowed to be? What's the matter with you?"

She spoke crisply, her head high. She stood on a little sandy rise, looking down at him, watching his eyes, waiting for an answer. He stood as motionless as an animal caught in the headlights of a car, blinded by the sudden glare. Violence drew near, in the wind and the restless sea, and the lonely dunes rolling away to the gray horizon, and the great brooding sky above. What a sinister beach it was, and now she tried to imagine it teeming with young nude Germans, ripe in the summer sun. Her breath caught, her chest aching. She wanted him to speak but she was frightened and suddenly at a loss. She was tired and cold. Her feet hurt. She was unstrung. She wanted him to put his arms around her, but dread was in her heart.

Yes, he said at last.

She looked at him. What did that mean? Yes what?

"Yes there are other places," he said.

"Then let's go to one of them," Angie said.

It was dusk now, the wind rising. They walked back to the hotel in silence, Sydney deep inside himself thinking that he was forty years old and suddenly a husband, and that he was unprepared. He was unprepared for Germany also; whatever he expected, this was not it. He was unable to explain himself and his acute unease. He was a German who had lived among French for twenty years, the *Vaterland* sovereign but invisible, *la patrie* in front of his eyes but immaterial. Now he was back and alarmed to discover that he knew intimately every hill and tree, the touch of the wind, and the unspoken thoughts of the population, and how precarious things were. And he was unable to tell her. It was like trying to describe the workings of his own brain, in the profoundest sense impossible. The truth was, he knew nothing but translation, the moving of a thing from one condition to another; it was the same thing but changed utterly. He was happiest when listening, as he was doing now, to the rising wind and the roll of the waves and his own words, inadequate even to himself. He was listening to the words as if they were being spoken by a doppelgänger; but of course that was the German way. His days were devoted to rendering the words of others. He rarely thought about making himself intelligent or even clear. That wasn't the point. No one cared what he thought. Why should they? He didn't. He was as imprecise with himself as he was exact with his manuscripts, Josef Kaus for example. When he was translating Kaus's novels he cared about Kaus and in a certain sense became Kaus. Still, it wasn't him; it was Kaus. So when he began to tell her about the summer day at Sylt before the war, it was an effort to put the words together correctly, and an effort to explain about the Frieslanders. He had not thought about the island or its people in years, and had not known that he cared. He defended them because they were compatriots, and because she could not know the state of Germany during the war and after. She was an American and innocent of the feast of vultures, the rapacity, the misery, and the residue. She listened to him and thought he was favoring them over her, as if it were a popularity contest. How could she make such a mistake except willfully? He was only doing his job as interpreter. For twenty years he had worked at it, living blamelessly with his memories, his manuscripts, and his knowledge of three languages; and the one he knew best he rarely spoke, because he was rarely in the company of Germans. But these were his assets, his life, and his duty. He did not understand how she could fail to see that, she who saw so much. The Germans were a unique people who were often misunderstood. Too often it was said that they were a complicated people with a difficult past, but that was true. They lived in an operatic world of myth and legend, of giants and dwarfs and sorcerers, none more so than those who had been left behind. It was the nature of Germans to be divided against themselves; and those who are divided against are divided within, and probably that was true of him, too.

He had seldom spoken of these things to anyone, and never to a woman. He had never allowed a woman into his inner life, not because he regarded it as too precious or intimate to be shared but because it was undeveloped, like film in a camera. Women came and went, Italian, French, Scandinavian women. Never a German woman, and never an American until Angela, introduced by Junko Poole as an American masterpiece, the class of the field. And Junko was not wrong. None of the women counted in the way that Angela counted; and she hated Germany. You could not despise Germany and love a German. He understood suddenly that he had not immigrated to France because he loved France, but in order to leave behind Germany. He was not the first. But it was well known that Germans did not make good expatriates.

He reached out and took her hand. "I'm sorry about this."

"Look," she said, pointing.

Well out to sea a freighter struggled against the rising wind and the incoming tide.

"Is that us, Syd?"

"No, it isn't," he said.

"It sort of looks like us, low in the water and night falling."

"It isn't," he said again.

They made up that night with a happy bella figura that lasted, as she put it, into extra innings. Then she was up and out of bed, pulling a sweater over her bare skin, pouring glasses of schnapps for them both, talking nonstop as she returned to lie beside him while she did leg exercises. When he asked her why she had more energy after sex than before it, she said that sometimes she did and sometimes she didn't, it depended on the quality of the experience. Tonight she did.

"And because we're leaving this dump," she whispered, laughing to show that she didn't mean it exactly as she said it.

"Not that bad," he said.

"Pretty bad, Syd. But it's almost over, so let's forget about it and plan tomorrow. Tomorrow's another day, just as Scarlett said it was."

"Who's Scarlett?"

"Never mind," she said. "An American legend, just like your Siegfried." She cranked her legs furiously, riding her imaginary bicycle, and then let them fall. She looked at him sideways and said it was good for the baby.

He sipped the schnapps, rolling it around on his tongue, then letting it scorch his throat. He was developing a picture in his mind and wanted to describe it to her, even though he suspected she was weary of the subject. He reminded her that he had not seen his homeland in years and in some respect had put it to one side in his memory. As if one could successfully mislay Germany! But he had wanted her to see it and to refresh his own memory as well. Or no: not to refresh his memory but to see what the Federal Republic had made of itself. This was a mistake. He confessed his mulishness and apologized for suggesting Sylt, a Shangri-la only a German could love. He thought it would be charming, deserted in the off season, forgetting how particular Sylt was. The inhabitants had always had a reputation for stubbornness and irascibility. He thought that he and Angie would have Sylt to themselves, their private island; and they surely did, except that there were shadows everywhere and the great silence of their lodging seemed to cast the longest shadow of all. He had his vague but persistent memory of German music and the sturdy hotel and sunny beach, wide as an autobahn. He had imagined them making love on the beach — as they did, once, bundled like Eskimoes. Remember, our first afternoon? It stopped raining and the sun came out and we went behind the dune?

"How could I ever forget?" she said. Sand in every orifice

and the pencil in his coat pocket scratching her left breast.

He smiled in the darkness and took another swallow of the schnapps. They were under the goose-down comforter. He was talking to the ceiling, and outside it was raining again, bright flashes of lightning in the far distance and the growl of thunder. He admitted he liked remote places and remembered Sylt as vivacious, and when it wasn't he thought they could transform it by their presence, the way Cézanne transformed oranges. They could subdue it by an act of will.

"Dumb of me," he said. "I wanted us both to like it, and I didn't want to be defeated by it."

"The schnapps is good," she said.

"I was damned if we would be but I guess we have been."

She said, "I think it's stronger than we are, Syd."

"It's been around a lot longer." Then: "It's like being manhandled. It's a kind of mugging." He laughed. "A hand from the grave, a skeleton's cold fingers around your throat."

She shuddered, moving closer to him. It was just an island, after all. A *place,* not quite like any other but still a place. You could find it on any map.

He said, "Does it really remind you of Maine?"

"No," she said. "It doesn't remind me of anything."

He said, "Poor Sylt."

"It scares me. It's spooky. You scared me."

"I didn't mean to," he said. "I wouldn't scare you for anything."

"Today on the beach," she said.

"I was in a mood," he said.

"You were not yourself." He moved beside her and she put her hand on his thigh, feeling the lumpy muscle under the skin. She remembered the last time she was in Maine, arguing with her father over life's small change; perhaps this was like that for Sydney. She said, "All of us are different people when we go home. We're one way where we live and another way when we're home, and it's not that we're children again. It's not that at all. It's that we can't believe we're adults, and all the time there's this racket of memory telling us how we ought to behave and what we ought to believe in and we're appalled that we're hearing it all over again and it throws us off." She felt him moving under her fingers. "Right, Syd?"

"Close," he said.
"We're going to laugh about Sylt someday."
"I will if you will."
"It's just a darned *island*," she said.
"So where shall we go?" he said.
"You say," she said.
"No, you say," he said and then he said, "Denmark."
"No," she said firmly. "We stay in Germany."
He shook his head doubtfully, staring into her eyes. "Maybe we've had enough of Germany and Germany of us. Maybe we ought to give Germany a rest. Denmark's only a few kilometers north."
"No Denmark," she said. "I want to see more of your Germany. I just don't want to see more of Sylt."
He was silent a moment, turning to look out the window. The storm was moving out to sea. The wind had abated and there were only brief bright flashes in the distance. He said, "It'll be good weather tomorrow." Then, softly, "We can go to Ilsensee, where I grew up. It's not far, a morning's drive." He embraced her in the darkness, pulling her toward him. He said something she could not hear, and then put his head under the comforter and kissed her belly, where the baby was.
She sighed, closing her eyes.
"Feeling good?" he said.
"Feeling fine," she said.
"Are you thinking of names?" he said.
She said, "Brunhilde."
He laughed at that, kissing her on the chin.
He said, "It's not like Sylt."
"What's it like, Syd?"
"There's a hotel beside the lake."
"And what else?"
"The house I was born in."
"And you'd like to go there," she said.
"I'd like to go there with you, Angie."
"You promise to be a bella figura?"
"Absolutely," he said. "It's a promise."
She was suddenly very tired. She was distressed that he wanted to revisit his childhood, a place so miserable that he refused to dis-

cuss it; at least he would not discuss the worst of it. Compared to Sydney, she had had a happy childhood, though she had never thought of her childhood as happy, anything but. Perhaps that was what divided them.

"And then we'll go south," he said. "The Sauerland or the Rhine Valley."

"You'll remember whose honeymoon it is?"

"Yours," he said.

"Yours, too," she replied. She was moving away now; he relaxed his embrace. She smiled to herself, thinking that you never went partway. In for a penny, et cetera, so they might as well go to miserable Ilsensee. At least it wasn't an island. It wasn't Sylt.

"Sydney?" Her voice was thick.

"Bella," he said. "We can call her Bella Figura Dilion van Damm."

"I think I felt the baby move," she said happily.

Four

IN HER DREAM she was with Sydney in a hotel at the shore. Things were unfamiliar, the cramped room, its plain furniture, a wooden crucifix above the bed. They were in near-darkness. She heard the sea below, the muffled crash of the waves and the hiss of the drawback. Sydney stopped talking and she began to cry. She tried to explain what had happened but was unable to form a sentence. She was feverish, poised between tears and laughter. She wanted to make love but her legs hurt.

She was dreaming deeply. Round about dawn she went to the window and stood there alone, her forehead against the glass. She was confused. The black water turned purple and then deep blue but the stars were still bright. The sun was hidden over the watery horizon. She did not know if it was dawn or dusk because she did not know whether she was on the coast of France or of Maine. She believed this was Normandy, but she could not be sure. It was all the same ocean. Things seemed to her uncertain and she knew she must be cautious. She was fearful of what lay beneath the surface of the sea.

A way down the beach a man was surf-casting. Gulls floated above his head, riding wind currents. His dog, a comical dachshund, waddled back and forth, barking at the gulls. How particular it was, how lonely, how beautiful in the ambiguous glow, the sun not visible but poised over the horizon, either rising or setting. Back of the surf-caster, in the notch between two grassy dunes, was the ruin of a revetment, a souvenir of the last war, either of the German occupation or the American defense, depending on the continent. The tide was turning now, the waves curling in the light breeze. She thought that the waves looked like the damp dark curls of a woman's bob. The tide brought with it dozens of blood-red oranges which rolled here and there in the sand.

Was that Sydney lying full length on the bed? His eyes were closed but she knew he was pretending, allowing her a moment to herself. She turned back to the window, the fisherman on the edges of her vision, illuminated by a pale blue light. He set his feet, threw, and reeled in slowly, the lure dancing on the surface of the water. He looked solid as granite, an old man, older even than Carroll, but very fit. He had the build of a wrestler. She smiled, collecting herself, watching him, observing his rhythm as he set his feet and flung the lure into the soft surf. Its hooks were sharp as needles, yet he had not caught anything. But probably that wasn't the point. Probably the point was to be present at the shore at dusk, with his gear, the gulls, and his comical dog, and no one else about except for the thousands of ghosts that always gathered around this particular beach.

This was certainly Normandy, the invasion beaches. She felt herself gravitating home to Paris.

Things were suddenly clarified. They were at Courseulles-sur-Mer. Sydney had described the deployments, the Canadians and the British here, the Americans farther west, beyond Arromanches. The German defenses were thin because Berlin had been deceived, believing the invasion scheduled at a point farther north, the Pas de Calais. She had not listened to him carefully, vaguely bored because many of the words and phrases were unfamiliar, and the day was so sunny and warm, unseasonable. There were people here and there on the beach sunbathing. The fisherman returned suddenly to her vision as he reached down to swipe at the dog, who was snapping at his heels, and then to angrily cast once again. The dog had a human face, and catching fish was the point after all.

A great weariness overtook her. As she gazed beyond the fisherman to the open sea she imagined a mighty fleet on the horizon. It was the incoherent moment before the bombardment, prelude to the furious invasion, and occupation by a hostile force.

* * *

Sydney was sitting by her bed, his expression as mournful as a hound's. She smiled gamely, he looked so comical, as comical as the dachshund in her dream, which feathered away now, receding until it vanished; she would never remember it in her lifetime.

She said, "Hi, Syd."

He kissed her, holding her lightly and loosely, as if she were fragile and might break.

"It isn't any fun," she said.

"No," he said, his mouth moving into something resembling a smile.

"It's hard work and it hurts."

He said softly, "I know."

"No, you don't, Syd. You don't know a damned thing about it." She looked at the ceiling, surprised at its height, surprised to find a clear glass bottle suspended above her; a tube ran from the bottle to her forearm. "He tore me up pretty badly, didn't he?"

Sydney put his ear next to her mouth and she repeated what she had said.

"He's big," Sydney said.

She said, "How big?"

"Eight pounds," Sydney said.

"I told you we should have had a girl," she said.

"Next time."

"Not right away," she said.

He said, "What did you say? I didn't hear."

She said, "I'll sleep now."

"Go to sleep, Angie."

"I'm sleeping," she said.

When she opened her eyes a few hours later he was still there, in the chair by the window. He had a book opened in his lap but he wasn't reading. He was staring into the dark street, smoking a cigarette. He was blowing smoke rings, the smoke hitting the window glass and collapsing.

She said, "I hurt, Syd."

"Can you stand it?"

"What do you mean, can I stand it?"

"You've had a lot of morphine."

She said, "Shit."

He said, "The doctor will be back in a few minutes." He rose and reached for her hand, holding it tightly.

"He did a good job, didn't he?"

"He did a fine job. You did, too."

She said, "You lamb."

"Rest awhile, Angie."

The doctor came and talked pleasantly at her. She did not understand everything he said, except that she was fine but needed rest. When he went into the corridor, Sydney went with him. It seemed to her Sydney was gone for hours, though she knew it was only a few minutes. When the doctor came back he gave her two pink pills and water to wash them down with. She looked at him closely, remembering him from the operating room. He was a good-looking young Frenchman with brown curly hair and a masculine pout, and a voice to go with the pout. She wanted to ask him something important but forgot what it was. She was so out of it. Well, she remembered what it was now.

Sydney was standing with his back to her, looking out the window.

"Syd? When can we see him."

His shoulders moved fractionally when he sighed, turning, his hands in his pockets. He looked at her from the shadows, knowing that he would have to lead her into the deep water a step at a time and not knowing for the life of him how he was going to do it, wishing he could speak in German, wishing, really, that he did not have to speak at all. He had to do it without breaking down. He dreaded the question that was sure to follow.

"We'll call him Max, as we agreed."

He smiled in spite of himself, nodding, still in the shadows so she could not see his face.

"Are they going to bring him up soon?"

"Not for a while," he said.

"Stand by the bed where I can see you, Syd."

"He's in the operating room, Angie."

She held her breath when he sat down on the bed, taking her hand, looking directly at her now.

"They're operating, Angie."

"He's alive, then."

"Yes." He moved closer to her, watching her eyes fill with tears. Sydney said, "He has such a sweet face."

She lifted her chin, smiling suddenly.

He waited a moment, then continued. "It had to be done at once, Angie. That was what they told me. They explained the procedure. They had to have permission and I gave it. The operation had to be done right away or not at all, so I told them to go ahead and do it now."

"There was a choice?"

"Yes, Angie."

"It is a dangerous operation?"

"Very dangerous, Angie."

She nodded, trying to take it all in as you would collect the cards when they were dealt, taking them into your hand and looking at them, each one, before putting them into suits. She did not understand about the choice and the urgency. And there was one big question that she had not asked and could not pull from her memory. It was stuck there, the obvious question. She felt a fool. Then she remembered.

"Where are they operating? I mean, is it his heart?"

He was holding her now, rocking slowly back and forth.

"He is not normal, Angie."

She closed her eyes, exhaling.

"They knew that immediately," he said.

"And the operation?"

"He will die without it."

"And if the operation is a success?"

"He will live," Sydney said.

"He will be all right, then?"

"No, Angie."

Her mouth was beside his ear. She said, "Is he in pain?"

"No," he said. It was Sydney's one lie, and harmless. No one knew whether the little boy was in pain or not. Probably he was, though he did not cry. He had uttered something at the moment of his birth, enough to force air into his lungs. But the doctors then were worried about the mother and did not turn their full attention to the child for a moment or two.

She said softly, "How did it happen?"

He did not know what she meant and did not answer.

"Whose fault," she said.

"No one's fault," he said.

"Oh," she said. She was limp now in his arms. "You said he had a sweet face."

"Yes, very."

"Maybe," she began.

He did not reply to that. They sat quietly in the near-darkness listening to hospital sounds, a telephone somewhere, the muffled tread of a trolley. He did not know if he had done the right thing. He had had only a few moments to decide and the doctors were no help. They were doctors, not moral philosophers. Neither were they the child's father. Here you are, Monsieur van Damm. Here are the choices. There are two of them. You can do this or you can do that, and with this the child dies right away and with that he lives for a while, perhaps five years, perhaps longer. He will never lead a normal life. He may speak, he may not. He may be violent, he may not. He will never be able to look after himself. Love will make him more comfortable, perhaps. But love will not cure him because what he was born with, or more precisely born without, is not curable. So make up your mind, Monsieur van Damm. You have five minutes. Of course Sydney's mind would not work. It would not weigh and sift; it could not foretell the future. And in the end he chose life.

"The Russians," he began, then stopped. He had been thinking about it for twenty-four hours, what the Russians said about such a child. But now was not the time. He had not taken her all the way in.

"Our Max," she began.

"Yes," he said.

"You were right, Sydney. *You were right.*"

"I think so," he said.

She said, "How terrible for you."

He shook his head.

"Yes," she said.

"I wanted you to be there so we could decide together, but you were out."

"Out like a light," she said.

They heard the bleat of an ambulance in the street, and then she kissed his ear, nibbling it. They were silent a moment and he thought he was as tired as he had ever been in his life, tired all the way through his body.

She said, "What about the Russians? Have the Russians landed?"

He smiled at her. "No."

"What about them, then?"

"The Russians believe that such a child is touched by God," he said.

When he left to go home to shower, shave, and eat something and perhaps have a stiff drink or two or three, she waited until she could no longer hear his footsteps and then broke down. She buried her face in her pillow. Her body went hot and for a moment she could not breathe. She saw bright lights behind her closed eyelids. She tried to speak but no sound came; and there was no one to hear her if she did speak. She thought she would faint. In that way she got through the night.

She wanted to see her baby, but they would not let her. The baby was in the recovery room and they would not know for a while whether the operation was successful. Numerous tests were required, and they would take time. When a human being is that young, the brain . . . The doctor shrugged and did not finish the sentence. Perhaps it would be a week, perhaps longer. She could look at him through the glass of the nursery. She must believe he was receiving the best possible care, as good as anything in America. But of course she never doubted that. They were doing everything that was humanly possible, and the nurses were kind. It was only that she wanted to hold him, as any mother did with her child.

Angela became withdrawn, overcome by fatigue. Her bones ached and she was unable to concentrate on anything for more than a few minutes. Really, it was melancholia, the fear of the known and the fear of the unknown, and the fear that she would be unable to cope. Life was suddenly a mystery, formless, charged, changed utterly. She felt years older, making forced conversation with friends who arrived with flowers and the morning newspaper. Junko Poole arrived with flowers and two bottles of Château Lafite Rothschild. One glass of wine made her tipsy and she was afraid she would break down again, but Junko told joke after joke, some bad, some worse. Even Sydney was laughing, and for a moment she remembered their old life. Junko and the other friends were shy about the baby. They did not want to ask awkward or probing questions, or push her beyond her limits, whatever her limits were. No one knew. She didn't, but believed she was always in sight of the boundary. One shove and she was over the edge. The friends were naturally apprehensive about the answers. So the visits were strained, sometimes to the breaking point. Her eyes would fill with tears, she would shake her head, and the friends would go away.

When at last they allowed her into the little room off the nursery, she approached the basket slowly, then surged forward as if pushed. His head was heavily bandaged but she could see his button nose and his mouth and the fringe of dark hair, Sydney's legacy. He lay very still on his stomach. She bent over to get a closer look. He looked adorable. Angela touched his shoulder lightly and resisted when the nurse wanted to take her away. She said to the nurse, Just a moment more. She moved closer. Sydney was right, he had a sweet face. Her breasts were hurting and she wanted to feed the baby, but the doctors would not permit that. She noticed the IV concealed behind a screen. She felt a flood of tenderness, and then was being led back to her room in the maternity ward, where she immediately called Sydney at home. She was reassured, hearing his voice. He was working and things were fine at home; he had half a dozen cards and letters for her. She realized she had not asked about his work, and when she did and he replied that he was having trouble with Josef Kaus's new novel, a particularly dense passage, she asked him to read it to her and then was able to suggest a word, "bluff." The passage had to do with a card game. He was delighted with her word. They laughed together a moment and it was like old times, when there had been only the two of them. Sydney was always coming to her for Americanisms. She loved hearing his dry laugh, complaining that Herr Kaus was eloquent in German but that the German, antique as it was, resisted translation. German resisted translation generally. Still, he had had a fair day, two pages with possibly a third before dinner.

He asked her if she wanted anything from home.

Yes, she said. She did. "I want my copy of *Little Women.*"

He said, "Come off it, Angie."
She laughed. "No, it's what I want."
"It's a children's book," he said.
"No," she said firmly. "It is not a children's book."
She hung up without telling him that she had visited Max, and that it broke her heart, seeing him bandaged like a fallen soldier, bandages on his head and an IV in his arm, motionless in the hospital basket. He was so tiny, so defenseless, it was cruel and inhuman. And she did not know what she could do to aid him, or what anyone could do. He was alone in the world.
That evening she and Sydney made a visit together, and Sydney felt a moment of vertigo. He suddenly seized her arm, teetering, out of breath. The baby was awake, eyes open, staring at them — and in his eyes they believed they saw something resembling recognition.
In five days Angie was discharged. She loved being home, in her own bed among her own things, listening to Sydney rattle around in his office, responding to his requests for Americanisms. She went to the Faubourg St. Honoré to look at clothes, anticipating the time when she would be thin again. On rue de Lille she bought a mirror in a golden frame and on rue Jacob she bought a glass coffee table, and when she was finished met Sydney for lunch at La Coupole, two dozen oysters and a bottle of Sancerre. They picked up their old routine, listening to the evening news, then walking to the neighborhood restaurant for dinner. The first night the patron presented them with the cocktail maison. Welcome home, we've missed you. We've been thinking of you. He did not ask how things were. Everyone in the quarter knew that Angie and Sydney had had a difficult time, and that their child was not normal.
Every day Angie visited Max in the hospital, although some days she was not allowed to see him. He was subject to seizures and high fever. He was struggling, they said, but he had a strong will. Often she would stay awhile, talking to the nurses, whom she had come to know quite well. Every few days she saw the curly-haired doctor; but he was not in charge of Max and seemed ill at ease talking about him. She came to realize that a hospital was a community, like a newsroom or the theater, and there were insiders and outsiders. She was grateful to be welcomed.
Angie and Sydney spent hours with doctors, therapists, and a

young psychiatrist recommended by Junko Poole. Stupid of them, boneheaded, but they did not understand that the psychiatrist was for them, not for Max. But this gave them a moment of amusement because they did not believe in psychotherapy. The psychiatrist began by talking about anger and guilt, the twin pillars of modern times. They must grapple with both and defeat both; the struggle would be titanic, because anger and guilt were tenacious fighters, skilled in guerrilla war. He thought it would be wise to schedule three appointments a week, one each for Angie and Sydney, one together. They had to understand that there was much to work out between them. In this way the various resentments could be identified and, if they were audacious and honest, expunged. In order to purge anger and guilt it was important to understand them root and branch, and a psychiatrist was indispensable. A psychiatrist was vital no less than rain on parched earth.

Or a pig to a truffle, Angie said.

She wanted to talk about fate, how the Christians understood it, how the Jews did, how the Muslims, Confucians, and Hindus defined it and accounted for it. Perhaps it was necessary only to contemplate it, as religious contemplated the face of Buddha. But the psychiatrist knew nothing about fate and cared less, expressing his indifference in exquisite, formal French. She loved listening to him. His voice was as melodious as an oboe and it was with regret that she sighed, no, she and her husband were not divided nor were they burdened by feelings of anger and guilt, except that some guilt was part of every adult's scheme of things, no less than indigestion or a hangover. There were questions of melancholy and responsibility, but those questions were ethical and they would have to figure them out for themselves.

When they were outside on the street Sydney turned to her and shook his head.

She said, "Didn't he have a beautiful voice?"

"I don't think you should have compared him to a pig and a truffle," Sydney said.

"He's a big boy, Syd," she said.

They read widely. They bought books and medical journals and went to see parents and other experts with experience in — the disabled, the retarded, the handicapped, the backward, the simple-minded, the Mongoloid, arrested, damaged children.

Enough, Sydney said at last.

Angie looked at him, stricken.

That's *enough,* he said.

The baby came home in August, accompanied by a nurse. In six months they were able to do without the nurse, except for those days when they wanted to go out, to lunch or dinner or to a movie.

They sent Max away when he was ten. He had become too unpredictable, his sudden bursts of energy frightening in their intensity. The apartment was too small to contain the three of them, and finally Sydney suggested that they do the sensible thing. That was the word he used, "sensible." He also used the word "humane." He couldn't work properly, his balcony office being neither private nor secluded, and Angie — Angie sat with Max by the hour, reading to him, or knitting while Max watched, fascinated for a moment, then insisting that they go to his room and lay out the farm, tugging on her arm and pointing. Angie had bought a miniature farm, a house and a barn and silo and a farmer and his wife and children and animals, cows, pigs, ducks, and a collie dog. He seemed to enjoy the miniature farm more than any other thing that he did; and sometimes he would sit with the animals for as long as an hour, as long as Angie was there by his side. Often he came to her late at night, tugging on her arm and pointing, and Angie, half-asleep, would rise and go with him to lay out the farm and watch him while he moved the animals about.

Sydney had looked into hospitals. There was one on the downside of the butte, on a quiet street below rue Caulaincourt, not far from their apartment on avenue Songe. They could visit him regularly and he would be well cared for by the nuns and the state would bear most of the expense.

We have to do this, Angie.

I won't, she said.

We have ourselves to consider, also.

He's *ours,* she said. And I won't let him down.

He'll still be ours, he said.

Not if he's there. If he's there he's not ours. Max doesn't need a hospital. Max needs a farm in the country. If we lived in the country, the boy would be at peace. I know it.

Come look at it with me, Sydney said.

I'll look but I won't touch, she said.

She explained what she meant. Something was given to you and you had to bear it because it was yours and therefore you were obligated. In our case it's this child. But it could be a memory or a belief. It could be almost anything. Max was unable to care for himself and lived in a world inaccessible to them or to anyone else. He was behind locked doors. She and Sydney were all he had and God knows he had little enough and there was no way to know how much they meant to him because he did not react in normal ways. He was not a normal child. He had a fire in his brain, or perhaps it was only smoke, but whatever it was it did not allow him to love or laugh or cry *or exist* in a comprehensible way, except of course — You are being unfair, Angie, Sydney interrupted, grinning in spite of himself because she was being wicked and knew she was — when he kisses you good night or throws his arms around me and laughs and laughs or sits with that dear expression looking at Cézanne's oranges. Right, Syd? And the measure of things is the devotion we have not to the strongest but to the weakest. Otherwise it's just fascism. Agreed, Syd?

"So forget about your fucking hospital, Sydney. It's not going to happen."

He was furious. "Are you suggesting that I want to send him to Dachau?"

She shrugged. "Might as well."

He glared at her a full minute and then spoke to her in German. He said things he never would dare say in English. They were things he didn't mean. But he said them, in part because he knew she could not understand them. When he finished he was in tears, which frightened her because she had never seen him in tears. Tears streamed from his eyes as he glared at her, silent now.

"I'm sorry, Syd."

"Don't ever say that again," he said.

"I'll go see your hospital," she said.

"All right," he said. "I'm sorry too."

"What did you say to me?"

"You don't want to know," he said.

The next week Max had the worst of his episodes. He was restrained and then sedated. Sydney took Angela to the hospital below rue Caulaincourt, where they had an interview with the director and were given a tour. The rooms were small but clean and the staff seemed cheerful and capable. There was a small courtyard in the back of the hospital with a garden and a wee fountain. They would be allowed to visit any time during the day and could take Max home for a few hours now and again if he was well enough. Yes, Angie said at last. All right, Syd. I agree. But not forever. There are other places in France, in the country, and when we can afford to send him there, we will. I hate to think of him here forever. I'd like to think of him in the country with farm animals and an orchard and a big field to play in, as long as he can't be home with us.

Max was taken to the hospital in an ambulance, though an ambulance was not needed, strictly speaking. It was one of his good days. He spent the morning watching Sydney work at the typewriter, fashioning sentences. He seemed to approve of the typewriter's rhythm, and sat with Sydney's posture, slumped shoulders, crossed legs, bent head. But when it was time to go, he went without complaint. Angie explained to him that he would be living in another place for a while but that they would see each other every day, as always. She promised him that he would be comfortable and loved there as he was at home. Under her arm she carried a duplicate of the poster of Cézanne's oranges and a toy typewriter to remind him of home, and of course the miniature farm with its buildings and animals. The farm fit into Sydney's leather portmanteau.

They walked slowly down the stairs and into the courtyard, Max between them, Sydney carrying the portmanteau and the other suitcase. In the ambulance Max stared incuriously out the window and seemed not to hear the siren. They went with him to his room, unpacked his things, then stood tentatively by the door. One of the nuns and an attendant were there to assist them. Angie taped the poster to the wall and put the typewriter on the bureau. It was only a cloth pillow made to look like a typewriter. When Angie unpacked the farm, the nun looked at her with alarm and said such toys were dangerous and should be kept out of sight. They represented temptation.

The nun said something to Max but his concentration was fierce and he did not move. Angie turned away, leaning against Sydney. The corridor seemed to stretch forever into darkness. She remembered the night he was born and the night she first saw him in the nursery. She remembered Sydney's vertigo. There were those nights and ten years of days and nights when she thought she would die of love for this boy, remembering always Sydney's Russian proverb. Max never spoke an intelligible word.

Part 2

One

THE APARTMENT BUILDING on avenue Songe presented a Weimar face to the world. Back of the porte-cochère were three narrow courtyards, red tile underfoot, three tiers of irresponsible balconies above. The style was Bauhaus with a nod to the pharaohs. From a certain point in the far courtyard you could see a spire of Sacré-Coeur, the spire vaguely phallic. The courtyards were at angles to each other, the iron grillwork over the windows fashioned in a diamond pattern that seemed to change shape as you looked at it, à la Maurits Escher. A gaudy belt of blue ceramic ran along the courtyard wall. Eight-foot-high ferns in green glazed pots flourished despite the lack of sunlight. Sunlight rarely touched the tile, and street noise did not intrude because avenue Songe was strictly residential.

The place was solid as a fortress, which was what everyone called it, had called it for years — Fortress America. Edward Hopper was said to have lived in apartment number 24, though there was no verification of this and it might have been wishful thinking; in sunlight the whitewashed upper courtyard walls were truly Hopper in their pitiless glare. Harry and Caresse Crosby once danced nude by moonlight on the second-floor balcony, stairway B. After the war, Eisenhower supposedly played bridge in number 18, driving in from his suburban headquarters to join — and here the accounts differed, but the evenings were said to be rowdy. In the late 1950s, an American actress had a liaison with a French cabinet minister in number 12. Some confusion here: it may have been the actress and the cabinet minister in number 18 and Eisenhower in number 12. What was indisputable was that in 1943 and 1944 a unit of the Maquis operated out of the basement caves under stairway C. Everyone in the building knew they were there because their commandant loved American swing and played Glenn Miller and Benny Goodman by the hour on a wind-up Victrola.

The building had the look and ambiance of a very large, well-kept Mediterranean villa occupied by a single extended family. The apartments were designed for artists, with eighteen-foot-high ceilings, windows almost as high, and wide doorways. The artists had long since given way to commercial photographers, so that many of the windows now had heavy curtains, usually drawn. It was common to see leggy models with ditty bags swinging through the porte-cochère into the courtyard and then hurrying up stairways to the photographers' studios. One of the photographers was a specialist in hands, another in necks, and a third in the shape of the products themselves, cosmetics. The cosmetics photographer placed vials of perfume or deodorant in a box lined with black velvet and shot as carefully as a hired assassin, or an Impressionist composing a still life.

Three stewardesses rented number 8, living there between flights. A soprano lived in number 23, practicing her scales each afternoon at three; permission to do so was written into her lease, though that did not prevent Milda, Consuela, and Ingrid from complaining to the management. An actor lived in number 16 and an English businessman in number 20, but they were seldom seen. Prices rose, not high enough to attract the newly rich, not low enough for Bohemians. There were always Americans in residence, apartments sublet or sold, friend to friend. No apartment ever remained on the market for long, so rich was the history of Fortress America, and so beguiling the shape of things within.

For fifteen years Sydney and Angela had lived in number 24, Edward Hopper's alleged studio, a duplex one flight up, stairway C. "Duplex" made it sound grander than it was, a small kitchen and the living room on the ground floor and on the upper floor the big bedroom, a bathroom, Sydney's balcony office, and a small bedroom unoccupied since Max left four years before. The apartment was crowded, shelves of books floor to ceiling, books stacked on the floor, books on the coffee table and under it. There were photographs of Max, Max alone, with his mother, with his father, on avenue Songe patting a dog. Here and there on the walls were spaces for etchings, Sydney's Germans and Angela's French, Kirchner's Berlin streetwalkers leering at Dufy's Montparnasse flower sellers. There were two very well-worn couches and three less well-worn chairs and a round table that could seat seven for dinner, eight if you were careful of your elbows. The living room resembled an ancient civilization whose stages of development were mysterious except to the natives. The most organized affair in the room was the bibelot table with its carefully arranged ivory ornaments, seashells, glass animals, Fabergé eggs, scrimshaw, and nest of brilliantly colored Russian dolls. The bibelots rested on a pretty red and gold cloth that fell in folds to the floor, concealing the tiny television set under the table. In the evenings, exhausted from work, Sydney would often spend a few minutes rearranging the ornaments, pushing the dolls back and the eggs forward, placing the scrimshaw among the seashells.

Their civilization was small and crowded, like a village in an isolated valley somewhere in superstitious Central Europe, things close at hand, sentimental things, things that were there because they had always been there. They had a talismanic value, more to Sydney than to Angela. She often had an urge to throw everything out and start over, except that Sydney liked the apartment as it was, loved it really, as she could see when he fussed with the bibelots like a gardener tending rosebushes.

When she was pregnant with Max she was frightened they would have to move. Sickle-shaped avenue Songe was lovable and the neighborhood was familiar and everyone said the air was good, up on the butte. But Weimar was unsuited to family life. She and Sydney spent afternoons prowling Montparnasse looking for a place with two bedrooms and windows that weren't drafty, close to the Métro; second or third floor would do, on a tree-lined street where there were other children, perhaps one of the short streets above the Luxembourg Gardens. Montmartre was so far from the center of things. Sydney offered to get an office somewhere else, but she didn't like that idea and of course he didn't either.

I want the three of us at home, she said. We can be more of a family, near the Luxembourg Gardens. I can take the baby there every day in a spiffy new carriage and we can all go together on the weekends. You and I can have lunch at home as we've always done. So they looked and looked but found nothing suitable, and then Max was born and the heart went out of her.

In her confusion she thought of returning to the United States. American doctors were very good with children like Max. Sydney could find work with one of the American publishing firms. She wondered if France had been a mistake after all, so self-conscious and closed in on itself, so sensual and narcissistic. But then she thought of the kindness of her neighbors and friends — Junko Poole called her every day and after she returned from the hospital took her to Lasserre for a lunch that left her dizzy with fatigue but laughing as she had not laughed in many months and at the end of it promised, in his conspiratorial whisper, Anything, Angie, anything at all that you want please call me because you and Syd are like family and whatever needs doing, I'll do and do gladly — and decided, No, Paris was home. Stagnant, rapturous Paris. And where would they go in the United States? She had no connections outside the state of Maine, where her father was no less conspicuous than Bonaparte in the Invalides. New York was out of the question and the West Coast unimaginable. And no doctor anywhere on earth could help Max.

So they stayed on in Montmartre. She established a routine, Max most mornings, a museum or art gallery most afternoons. There was always a new exhibit or a lecture. Sometimes she took notes but most often sat and listened, like any casual tourist. In the evenings she and Sydney would share their days, Etruscan pots or Flemish portraits on her side, German novelists and American slang on his. She could easily imagine herself a sly courtesan living in Perugia or a plump goodwife counting coins in Antwerp. Well, she said to herself, I am an appreciator. I am not a critic nor a cultural show-off. I do it because I enjoy it, and that's reason enough. My bargain with life, she called it; and every year they took a trip, to Normandy or the south of Spain or Tuscany, and once to Mauritius.

On Tuesdays and Thursdays she lunched with friends, the lunches long and hilarious, thick with gossip. Most of the women worked in offices but business talk was avoided, too boring. On

Thursday afternoons she often accompanied her friend Simone to the grammar school to collect Simone's twin boys, the period known as *l'heure de maman* — mother's hour, the mothers (and a few self-conscious fathers) all gathered on the sidewalk behind the Panthéon, the children bursting through the school doors, raising their faces to be kissed on both cheeks, their excited voices describing the day's events, studies and scandals. Angie had gone to *l'heure de maman* with Simone for years, since Max was an infant. At first she forced herself to do it, as a way back to ordinary life: normal women with normal children. Then she found herself looking forward to mother's hour with Simone and Simone's twins, who were adorable but devilish, brimming with good health and voluble as birds. Life went on, she told herself, and it would be nice to know where it went on *to.* One of the things it went on to was the moment on the crowded sidewalk when the boys lifted their faces to be kissed by tante Angela, who also had a son, though it was understood that he was an *enfant attardé;* they always asked after Max, and Angela always replied that he was fine. She liked listening to the boys, their high voices trilling sentences in children's argot, Simone attentive as a mother should be; until their energy overwhelmed her and she rolled her eyes, *boys.*

The years slipped by. There was the winter that Sydney had pneumonia and the summer that Angela broke out with eczema. The year after that, Muslim terrorists bombed a department store. In a single ten-day period in November 1988, Sydney won a prize for translation and Angie won the lottery, three thousand francs that paid for curtains in the living room and a tiny bronze Buddha for Sydney's office. The apartment filled up, more books, more ornaments. Angela was unnerved, wondering if she was destined to live her whole life in the place they called the Fortress. The dollar rose or the dollar fell and they seemed to get no further ahead — though "ahead" meant one thing one year and another thing the next. The annuity from her mother helped, but Carroll was having unspecified money trouble, obliged now to "dip into capital," by which he meant disposing of various "holdings." His infrequent letters were filled with complaint and foreboding, causing Sydney to smile. Capitalist intrigue, he said. The family finances were Angela's province, and he had full confidence et cetera in her abilities et cetera and knew that if there was a problem she would find a solution to it and in the meantime he was translating as fast as he could, and by the way what was slang for insolvent? Busted, she said. Broke, flat, on the rocks. We are healthy, Sydney replied. And our papers are in order.

She continued to contemplate the future. One year she wanted a small car, the next a farmhouse in the country. She began to think of these things as the necessary components of a well-lived Western life, and then wondered if she was just a spoiled brat after all, coveting a dwindling inheritance that was years away in any case. Still, it was not a crime to want a house in the country.

They were always hard up, perhaps not in Sydney's terms, but in hers. When American visitors came for drinks or dinner — they were usually prep school or college roommates with whom Angie corresponded — the visitors would exclaim about the apartment's charm, how cozy and quaint it was, how *tout Parisien*, how *intime*, how tasteful and cheerful and, well, *Bohemian*. Did you ever see such an interesting arrangement of rooms? Did you ever see so many books? Books in English, books in French and German, art books, guidebooks, reference books, poetry and prose, dictionaries and atlases. How do you find time to read them all? They did not say that from the flamboyant courtyard they had expected something else altogether, something sexy, memorable, and smart; but Angie could hear it in their voices. You didn't have to be clairvoyant to hear the perky condescension. How cunning! And you've lived here for fifteen *years*, Ange, you and Sydney? You rascals! That's amazing. That's Europe for you, here today and here tomorrow. Bottom line, *Magnifique!*

The truth was, American visitors were not comfortable in it. The apartment reminded them of students' quarters, with the worn chairs and frayed carpet over the creaky parquet floor, the posters and the exposed wine rack and the modest Philips stereo and the damned books everywhere. The bibelot table was adult, true; and the mirror had an Empire quality, though, God, you can hardly see your face in it. Their adorable daughter in college at Wherever had a larger suite, a damn sight more comfortable, with a view of the quad.

And in the cab later they began to laugh. How can Angie stand it? She wasn't brought up like that, the Dilions had money; Dilion's millions, they used to call it. The old man never worked a day in his life. I feel sorry for her. There's no room to turn around in that place, no space to breathe. They must fall all over themselves, or fall over the books. What do you suppose keeps them there? Europe is dead, everyone knows that. Well, she made her choice. And it doesn't look as if it's worked out.

If this is the way you have to live in Paris, the American visitors said, give me Cleveland.

It makes you thankful for what you have.

I like Angie and he seems all right. But *God.*

Did you see the kitchen?

That kitchen was obsolete during the reign of the Sun King.

Well, probably they like it.

Angie doesn't like it. That, I can assure you.

Then — Angie improvising freely now and not, as it happened, wide of the mark — they would come to the choice that she had made, the one that hadn't worked out. She was the only one of our crowd to leave home, go abroad for the sheer hell of it, and stay. How we envied her, flying off to Europe, learning French in more ways than one. Remember how romantic we thought it was and principled, too. Political. Up yours, Richard Nixon! And we were envious of her German, who was handsome in a coarse sort of way, and of course there'd been scads of affairs before him. We wondered if he'd been a Nazi or if his father had or what. We thought she had the world by the tail, and maybe for a while she did. She said she did.

But it's been kind of off again, on again, that marriage.

The problem is, you don't know where they belong.

I don't know where he belongs. She belongs in the U.S.A.

She's very bright, Angie is. No one's ever accused Angie of dumb. But I think things have been rough for them. And she had that poor boy right away and what can you say about that except there but for the grace of God. It was a terrible shock for her and maybe she's never recovered. You have to wonder if someone's sending you a message.

It's a mistake, you know, living outside your . . . boundaries. Marrying into another culture. But Angie's always been headstrong. She's always had her own view of things, and if you didn't like it you could go shit in your shoes. But this time our Angie got more than she bargained for. And that's the trouble with rebellion, darling. Sometimes your little revolution succeeds and you get what you want, or anyway what you deserve, and you have to live with it and defend it, having expended so much energy to get it.

About like that, Angie thought.

Fortress America had its singular charm, including frequent power failures owing to wiring that dated from the Great War. For that reason Sydney used manual typewriters, one French and the other polyglot for English and German. The typewriters had different diacritical marks and of course the French typewriter had its singular keyboard. It was like playing similar musical instruments, each requiring its own fingering. The typewriters sat side by side on a long table next to the knee-high railing that separated the floor from the window. He could lean over the railing and look down into the living room. The high windows gave out onto the courtyard. If he lifted his eyes, he could see over the roof to the branches of the maples that shaded avenue Songe. Directly opposite, above the porte-cochère, at eye level, was a photographer's studio. He was the neck man. Once when the power failed Sydney looked up from the typewriter to see the photographer angrily part his heavy curtains and yell something. He was furious, the camera useless in his hand. Behind him the model was lighting a cigarette. She was nude, a jeweled necklace at her throat. She looked infinitely weary, her knees apart and her shoulders slouched, her thumb hooked on the necklace. She stared blankly across the courtyard to Sydney's apartment but did not notice him. The photographer shook his fist and turned back to her, shooting now in natural light. She smiled tentatively, winding the necklace around her throat like a noose. When the lights came on she was suddenly blinded and threw her arm in front of her face, the smoke now curling through her hair. The photographer was shooting wildly. Sydney looked away and when he turned back the curtains were drawn again.

The north light was always wan, no matter the season. Sydney liked the balcony office for its modesty and charm and loved his solitary work, Angie always handy for consultations. He translated in longhand, then transferred the work to typescript at the end of the day. He was slow, four pages a day being exceptional. Three pages a day was his speed with any of Josef Kaus's novels, which were written in a dense, antique German, without color or light. His prose had an inner rhythm, though it was far from verse. It had the rhythm of the foundry, muscular rather than supple.

Josef Kaus enjoyed a modest vogue in America. He insisted on Sydney van Damm as his translator, and indeed this was written into his contract. They had never met, even though Kaus lived in Montmartre, a few blocks from avenue Songe. Sydney knew little about him and had never seen a photograph. Josef Kaus was sixty-five. He had studied at Heidelberg and at Berlin. He was married. He had no children. All this, according to the publisher's terse biography. Sydney suspected that Kaus liked to gamble, because there was always a scene at a card table or a racetrack and this was unusual because Germans were not, as a rule, passionate gamblers. Kaus had apparently lived in France for many years, though France did not figure in any of his books. Kaus was formidably learned, perhaps too learned for a novelist. He had the mind of a philosopher. Sydney thought it better that they remain strangers. What if they disliked each other on sight or were politically at odds? Better to be well met through the text, the whole text, and nothing but the text. Sydney had translated six of Josef Kaus's novels and was at work now on the seventh.

The look of Sydney's office had not changed in years. On the bone-white walls were a Dix graphic and a poster from the Maison de Balzac on rue Raynouard, the great writer staring off at a slant, his shirt undone and his eyes bright with mischief, as if he had just finished a novel, perhaps *Pleasures and Miseries of Courtesans* — Are you working now, Cher Maître? Yes, I'm writing a novel, I'll be finished in a minute — though it might have been sex. As the master himself said, "One night of love, one less novel." His hair was disheveled. His knuckles were dirty. His right hand was over his heart as if he were making a pledge. In the glare of the photographer's phosphorus his flesh looked pasty and soft, the skin of an indoor man. Balzac's work was in every respect the reverse of Josef Kaus's. Kaus honored him, though. In a rare whimsical passage he described the nineteenth-century French novelists as an army, the great clanking infantry of Zola, Stendahl's heavy artillery, Flaubert's sharpshooters, Maupassant's gallant cavalry, all of it commanded by the field marshal himself, the Viscount Hugo. "But they all marched to the music of Honoré de Balzac."

Next to Balzac was a photograph of Sydney's father in uniform, and a framed document in German. On the long table next to the railing were the well-worn dictionaries and grammars, the typewriters, and two ashtrays, one of them usually full. Number 2 pencils were scattered here and there, along with big gum erasers and liquid correction fluid for typescript. On the desk facing the wall, the desk where he worked in longhand, was the little Buddha and a photograph of Angie clowning on the beach at Arromanches, the ruins of invasion fleet Mulberry behind her. Unpaid bills were piled on one corner of the desk, unanswered correspondence on another. Above the desk was a gilt-edged mirror from the Empire period — it was the companion to the one that hung in the living room — and when the translator looked up from his work he saw his own face, with its broad forehead, compact jaw, and deep-set eyes, a severe face without dance. It had become more severe with age, the lines carved, the complexion dark. He had been thought handsome as a young man and Angie thought he was still, "if only you'd take care of yourself a little, Van, get some exercise and give Kaus a rest and take a vacation once in a while with me, and if you could cut down on the tobacco a little, that would be good, too, and one less glass of beer at dinner wouldn't hurt and might help."

Looking up from his work, imprisoned in the novelist's iron sentences, van Damm did not recognize himself in the mirror. He resembled a mechanic looking up from under the hood of a car, or Balzac on a bad day. The mirror threw back an Expressionist portrait, straight lines at odds with one another, suggesting moral struggle, or perhaps a migraine headache. At such times, staring myopically into the glass, he wondered if he had an identity beyond the text, Kaus's furious alienated machinery. And of course he did not, during the daylight hours when he was working at his desk in the balcony office, a creature of Kaus, the number 2 pencils, the big gum erasers, and the typewriter at the end of the day.

There was always music in the courtyard, drifting from the open windows on warm days, mostly taped music but sometimes improvised, bongo drums, guitars, pianos, violins; and of course the soprano at three. Lately there were voices also, the excited news readers of radio and television. It had been years since anyone had attended the news in any attitude other than tired irony, civic exhaustion at more of the same. Now, suddenly, there was news that was news, arresting, momentous, and unpredictable. It was the year things began to break down, old Europe moving backward at astonishing speed, reforming itself as it had been before the Great War. Czechoslovakia, Romania, Bulgaria were suddenly part of Europe again. It was hard to say exactly where they had been for the intervening decades; out of mind certainly, except for the press reports detailing the various tyrannies, and the exiled novelists and playwrights who fulminated from Paris or Toronto. Suddenly on television there was the king of Romania, interviewed at Zürich, his old-world eyes betraying nothing as he looked down his nose at the camera. The interview betrayed nothing either. Only his soft chin suggested a weakness, perhaps for Cognac, perhaps only the tedious evenings among exiles at Monte Carlo or Estoril.

"He can't want to go back to Bucharest," Angie said.

"Yes," Sydney said after a moment, listening to the king's languid French. "I think he does, bless his heart."

They listened in the morning and again at noon and in the early evening, before the televised news at night. Each day brought fresh revelations, and the effect was of an orchestra — or five orchestras, or ten — with no conductor and no score, and at the moment when you thought that the house lights would go up and the authorities clear the stage, the musicians would commence a new melody. All this was happening just out of eyesight, in Berlin and Leipzig, Warsaw, Budapest, Prague, Sofia, Bucharest, and Moscow, the syncopation unmistakable, a scintillating ragtime. For twenty years the news had been elsewhere, Indochina, the Americas, southern Africa, the Middle East, hopeless wars and appalling famines. Now it was just beyond the Elbe, fascinating and exhilarating at first, then troubling. It was difficult in these times to see good news as only that. In these times it was the function of good news to conceal bad. Sydney thought it was like watching the ball bounce on a roulette wheel, not knowing whether the wheel was honest or fixed and, if fixed, who had done the fixing. And if it was honest it still favored the house.

Germans commenced to dominate the news as they had not done since the war. Sydney was accustomed to thinking of his country as a neutral quantity, a non-nation. It had no foreign policy, nor any international aims other than a desire to remain sober, responsible, and out of sight. Not that the past was out of sight, to the dismay of younger Germans and the fury of older ones. There was no statute of limitations on the Third Reich. From time to time a Nazi was unearthed in Paraguay or Bolivia. Such was the pull of the past, and so moonstruck and credulous the believers, that forgers sold their clumsy Hitler diary to an American newsmagazine. The scoop of the century! The exclusive that remained exclusive. People averted their eyes from the successor regime, the Federal Republic. A dwarf of the civilized world, it was assigned a freak's role in the carnival scheme of things. The business of postwar Germany was business and it behaved like any obtuse privately held family concern, furtive but anxious to be seen as a good citizen. As old Prussia was an army with a state rather than a state with an army, so the Federal Republic was an economy with a state — no wonder that the iron law of the German Economic Miracle was *no inflation* — and went about its business shyly, the least charismatic of nations, misshapen, a huge head and a short powerful body, its hand on its wallet, a burgher's wary smile concealing clenched teeth, its voice seldom heard. Ven vill da vorld vorget? Germany frightened people, it had been docile for so long, its situation unnatural. As a nation it resembled Chicago, central to its region, a furious engine that advanced on its own inner logic, closed in on itself, with resentments enough to fill all the couches of Vienna — yet beneath the surface there was faith, patience, and an implacable sense of destiny. The intellectuals, Sydney among them, wondered: Was the profit motive sufficient for the nation of Goethe? If you gave Young Werther a BMW, would his sorrows vanish? Would he feel good about himself at last? And that was only the Federal Republic. On the other side of the Wall were thirteen million more consumers, Germans also, whose appetite for capitalism's supermarket was ravenous, almost cannibal —

What's he saying, Syd?

He's talking about the seduction of capitalism, the discipline of German workers, their cannibal appetites, their ambition.

Angie said, I wish some of that had rubbed off on you, Syd. So you'd step up the production.

Quiet, he said. I'm listening to the news.

And we could buy a new *rug*.

Naturally there were dissident voices. The Romanians and the Bulgarians tried to hold the line. Give Stalinism a chance! In Poland no one wanted to govern — and no one did. It had been so long since anyone had worked a full day — we pretend to work, and you pretend to pay us — that the economy had vanished. There was no economy in the ordinary sense of something directed or managed. One emergency followed another; the Berlin Wall breached, reformist regimes established in Prague and Bucharest, the Soviet Union abruptly bankrupt so that the president decided that he had to destroy his system in order to save it, and dismantle his empire in order to save *that,* and proposed that the Deutsche bank underwrite the experiment. If Moscow was on its knees, could Bonn fail to respond?

Europeans at first were thrilled by the idea of Europe whole again, Europe as it was idealized in the last decades of the nineteenth century, a whole continent, stable and prosperous, purposeful, ideologically relaxed, incredibly tranquil — great powers, small powers, nobles, peasants, Christians, Jews, Muslims even. It could be a new age of empire, the former satellite states a Third World of white people! A fantastic market of familiar faces eager to participate in the New Europe, all of it financed by the Germans as treasurer for the European Community. If only the Germans would broaden their horizons and turn away from their own dour vision of history, which was decadent Europe supervised by the German *Übermenschen.* The last days of 1989 had the look of the end of a century. And of course the beginning of another.

Sydney and Angela attended the evening news, astonished. At eight o'clock on TF 1 or Antenne 2 or La 5, the Brandenburg Gate and Wenceslas Square became as familiar as the Eiffel Tower or Place de la Bastille. Now and then a correspondent would report from the Ellipse in Washington. In America the turbulence was good news, the antichrist mortally wounded at last, history itself at an end; either that or a monstrous deception, a Red sleight-of-hand designed to lull and bewitch the credulous Western democracies. And as the winter wore on it became fashionable to speak of Eastern, now Central, Europe as entering a prerevolutionary phase, such as 1787 in France, a condition of extreme peril. That was why NATO was more important than ever and American occupation forces a check on the German vision of history. NATO was a vaccine. You did not discontinue cholera inoculations because cholera had vanished; it could re-emerge at any time.

Angie listened to the American news with foreboding. Bush was present much less often than Reagan had been, the French fascinated by the old hoofer, his lopsided grin and fancy footwork, a casting triumph reminiscent of Charlie Chaplin in *The Great Dictator. Très amusant!* The old man's disdain of facts seemed to suggest an idiot savant's definition of deconstruction. Then Kohl replaced Bush and days went by without news from America, except the breathless reports of civic outrage. She had been away for so long she did not recognize the locations, could not distinguish between the Pentagon and the State Department, or Times Square and any other inner-city combat zone. She remembered when she first came to Europe, she had watched the fall of the American empire with glee. She thought of herself as the satisfied vacationer in Florida, lying on the warm sand and checking the papers daily to see how bad the weather was in Chicago or Boston, laughing when there were reports of below-zero weather, sleet, snow, freezing rain, power failures, and school closings. She remembered the savage joy she felt at the fall of Saigon, the rightful end to an unjust war, the bully beaten, the dead not dishonored but avenged. Defeat ensued when a country did not mind its own business.

Angie was a little less happy with Desert One and not happy at all with the *Challenger* explosion. Unemployment, disease, uneducated and uneducable children, violence of every sort, disequilibrium and despair everywhere. What she felt now was — pity. As they watched the news she was defensive and then sarcastic when Sydney made his snide remarks about baffled, self-indulgent America, land of nightmares and vigilantes.

It makes you sick, Sydney said.

Yes, she said. Yes, I guess it does.

The *guns,* he said.

The constitutional right that seems to override all others, she said.

I used to love America, Sydney said.

And now you don't?

There doesn't seem much to love, he said.

Feel let down, do you? Poor Sydney.

She found to her surprise that the euphoria she felt at the liberation of Central Europe was almost exactly balanced by her depression at the disintegration of the United States, and wondered if she were witnessing a zero-sum game, Europe rising at the expense of America. America had prospered at the expense of Europe, and now was it the other way around? On the margins of the rivalry between America and Europe were the obscure struggles of Lebanese, of Indians and Pakistanis, of Liberians, Ethiopians, Sudanese, Tamil separatists, Colombian warlords, ANC guerrillas, and the monstrous suppression of Palestinians in the occupied territories of Israel. These were bloody. Every night on television, late in the broadcast, were reports from famished nations. A teenage girl cradling a Kalashnikov seemed to Angie the emblem of the times; and she hated it. Europe was not safe. No place was safe.

Fear of the unknown began to replace fear of the known. All through the spring, summer, and fall of 1989 the residents of Fortress America, as elsewhere in Europe, watched events unfold in the East, one dizzying climax after another, applauding the Soviet leader's audacity and puzzled by Washington's irresolution, now silent, now defensive, now sentimental, all too plainly powerless, fallible, and out of it. Washington let Germany go without a murmur, so perhaps — perhaps the Americans required another banker, now that the Japanese were losing heart.

That was the news on New Year's Eve, 1989.

Sydney and Angela were having a glass of Champagne, waiting until it was time to leave for Junko Poole's to welcome the new decade. She was reading the newspaper and Sydney was watching Eyebrows, the anchor dapper in black tie and red boutonnière. Sydney was listening carefully. On screen was a videotape of the interrogation of the Ceausescus. The president was contemptuous. While he talked he made a chopping motion with his right hand, and when he stopped he glanced up as if expecting applause. There had always been applause before. Sydney watched him carefully, wondering if he knew what was coming. Probably not. The dictator assumed that he was still a dictator and could wish the trial away with a chop of his right hand. He and his wife sat at a plain table, location undisclosed. It was assumed to be somewhere in Transylvania.

Ceausescu was shaking his head. Not a denial of the charges but a refusal to dignify them with an answer. His wife sat beside him and looked at her hands. She had a peasant's shrewd face and large hands. Suddenly she looked at her husband, and Sydney said aloud, She knows. He doesn't know but she does and she's trying to tell him but he won't listen to her, because he still thinks he's a dictator and she knows he isn't. Of course neither of them knew the videotape would be shown worldwide. People from Bangladesh to Monaco would watch it, this Romanian drama. Other tyrants would watch it, seeking clues.

Angela rattled her paper and said, What's happening?

Suddenly the tape stopped and the screen was filled with the animated face of Eyebrows. He talked excitedly and then he paused, to let the next picture speak for itself. It was the dictator lying at the base of a wall, his tie askew, blood on his shirt. He still wore his dark overcoat. The camera moved in close to capture the wound in his temple, and his half-lidded eyes in the colorless face. Snow clung to his chin. Then a fuzzy picture filled the screen, this one made from long range. It showed the wall and the body and a window above. Eyebrows shot his cuffs and pointed at the window, observing that it was likely that the dictator was killed elsewhere, or perhaps allowed to commit suicide, since no one would arrange an execution by firing squad in front of a *window* —

Angie rattled her paper again, looking up. But the image was gone now. Eyebrows was explaining that those who owned the camera were careful to permit no photographs of themselves, the interrogators. You heard their voices but what you saw were the Ceausescus at the table. No doubt the interrogators were frightened of whatever or whoever might still be loose in Transylvania. Madame Ceausescu's fate was not known; but it was unlikely she was still alive.

Very unlikely, Sydney thought, but then again who knew? Perhaps the trial and executions were contrived, some video deception like lip-synch or docudrama or re-creation. It all seemed straightforward enough, the dictator lying in the snow, a wound in his temple, blood on his shirt. But no Christian had questioned the divinity of the Roman Catholic Church until Martin Luther wrote his theses, and that had followed fifteen centuries of unrelieved turpitude and misrule. The reformation of Central Europe seemed to be taking place from television's pulpit. You had to communicate it on television; otherwise no one would believe it. Disinformation was a sacrament like any other. So don't be surprised if the dictator rises from the dead, Sydney thought.

Angie said, "Are they dead?"

"Looks like it. Hard to tell."

"I didn't see it," she said. "I'm glad I didn't. What do you think?"

"It was on television," Sydney said.

"I know that. What do you think about it?"

Sydney took a sip of Champagne. "Live by the sword, et cetera."

"An eye for an eye, is that it, Van?"

"If it is, they've got a way to go. They're not finished. They'll have to kill them over and over again, thousands of times, and each time they'll have to do it on television."

"That has possibilities," she said. "Every day there'll be a program, midmorning for the housewives worldwide. *The Ceausescus Die.* It would go on forever and ever, like *The Cosby Show* or *Wheel of Fortune*."

Sydney grunted, thinking that on the last program they could drive a stake through the dictator's heart and watch his soul vanish. On the television screen a teenager in her underwear was embracing a kitchen appliance. She was a shapely teenager and Sydney watched her a moment before turning off the set.

Angie said, "It's time to go to Junko's."

Sydney stepped to the window and stood looking into the courtyard, silent now in early evening. It was chilly, with a thin drizzle. The apartments across the way were dark, as they were most evenings. He tapped his Champagne glass on the windowpane, thinking that the courtyard resembled a deserted ballroom. He said, "Let's stop by the hospital, wish Max a Happy New Year."

She said, "That's a nice idea, Sydney. But he'll be asleep."

"Let's do it anyway," Sydney said, draining his Champagne.

Two

RISING SLOWLY in the iron elevator, Angie felt like a jeweler in his cage, claustrophobic and cramped but secure. Over the soft click of the elevator gears she heard the sound of the party on the fifth floor, already able to identify laughs and voices. She did not feel like a party and was trying now to work herself into a festive mood for the new decade. She looked at her watch, knowing they were late but knowing also that Junko would understand. Sister had been difficult and did not want to admit them to Max's room until Sydney explained carefully that it was a ritual with them, always seeing Max on New Year's Eve. They had done it every year Max had been in the hospital and there had never been any trouble and wouldn't be any trouble now because they only intended to peek in and say hello if he was awake and blow him a kiss if he wasn't.

Angie threw on a little false smile trying to force herself into a state of conviviality, something suitable for the brave new decade. What she really wanted was to be invisible. Her blue mood had deepened when she began to read about the latest maneuver in the Central Park jogger nightmare, and then peeked out from behind her newspaper to see Nicolae Ceausescu and his wife interrogated, Madame Ceausescu plainly terrified, the tyrant filled with bravado. He hadn't the imagination to grasp the consequences but she did and it showed everywhere in her face, her eyes and her nervous mouth; and then her long-fingered hand was on her husband's sleeve, pulling, and Ceausescu was oblivious. Perhaps there was a Romanian version of wilding and this was it, political wilding, a TV trial and an execution, legal maneuvers a kind of commercial jingle. Ceausescu's reign had been a form of wilding — and if you struck at the king you had to strike him dead, preferably on television, television a necessity. She had made a crack about a long-running serial, they had finished their Champagne, and Sydney had capped the bottle for a nightcap later. She put the paper aside, the New York jogger forgotten. And when they looked in on Max she had almost broken down because somehow the Cézanne poster had fallen off the wall and lay on the floor, torn and crumpled like any discarded bit of refuse. She was heartbroken. Sister explained that Max had been anarchic that afternoon. Do not worry, Madame van Damm. It is not dangerous to him. We will dispose of it in the morning.

Weeks ago she had said to Sydney, I have the blues. A shadow has fallen over my spirit and will not go away. She thought about her brother Shake in ways that she had not done in years, and there was no reason for that, he had been dead a very long time; she had come to terms with his death in 1975 when the war ended. Sydney had looked at her in surprise and said that he thought about his father all the time, as if there was nothing unusual or morbid about it. She thought about the past all the time now because she could not get a purchase on the future; and that was not like her. She began to worry about her father, alone and irascible in Maine. His letters were pathetic and his handwriting so feeble he had taken to dictating into a machine and giving the tapes to his lawyer, who had an underworked secretary. So the letters arrived on stationery that read Thomas Borowy, P.L.C., attorney at law, and below that the date and Darling Angela. The secretary's spelling and punctuation were worse even than her father's, and Angie wondered what the woman thought when she typed the inventory of complaints, weather, illness, taxes, the modern world, and the obituary report. She had no idea Carroll had so many friends. He was veiled in his references to his diminishing income, no doubt because of the secretary. But each letter contained hints — securities sold, bonds cashed. Times are hard here, Angela. It's a depression, and don't let anyone tell you any different. He was especially passionate on the iniquities of the capital gains tax, so unfair to wealthy individuals who had bought securities many years ago when prices were low. Same story, he said. Tax and spend, tax and spend. And who bears the burden? Old people, those least able to carry it. When are you coming to see me? She had not been home in two years and thought now that it was time.

The elevator came to a sudden stop and Sydney opened the glass doors, holding them for her. She did not move, listening to the sounds of the party inside Junko Poole's apartment. Sydney had a strange expression on his face, as he almost always did before an evening with Junko Poole. He said to her once that he had no idea why they were friends; they did not enjoy the same people or believe in the same things, and their temperaments were at odds. They were opposites, he supposed that was it; and they had known each other for many years. For himself, he was beguiled by Junko's life, its scale and ambiance and purpose. Sydney claimed it was like being intimate with a professional athlete or actor, without, of course, the publicity. There was a spectacular quality to the way Junko lived, always in motion, always disciplined, always preparing the next star turn. He was a devil, all right, some people might even call him a phonus-balonus baby-faced duplicitous prick. But where Junko was, entertainment was also. And he was loyal to a fault.

She lifted her chin, hearing a babble of party voices, thinking suddenly of her father's house at Old Harbor, how dark and silent it had been when she saw it last, how discouraged and inert. Her mother's spirit had vanished along with Shake's, and there were only the familiar shapes of the rooms and furnishings, books and pictures and photographs, ghosts, dead memories, life stopped dead. Nothing was as she wanted it to be, and she was not consoled.

Sydney said impatiently, Come on.

Angela's false smile was slipping, so she put it back on and followed Sydney to the door, which flew open at his knock. It was the devil himself, tempting in white tie and tails.

Junko Poole had watched them through the peephole in the door, his custom with late arrivals. He heard the elevator and went to the door and put his eye to the glass, hoping to catch a guest at an unguarded moment. Their expressions gave him clues to the night ahead, whether it would be festive or fractious; of course the second did not cancel the first. Bitter argument was often amusing, character revealing as it was. Angie was smiling. Hard to tell what Sydney was feeling or thinking but his expression did not promise much. Probably he was not a New Decade man, believing that 1990 was the last year of the old rather than the first year of the new. Typical of Sydney to go against the world's grain. If he were a member of the United States Supreme Court, he would be a strict constructionist and the pansies and hippy-dippys would picket his house, not that he would give a fuck. Syd, Syd, Junko thought. When are you going to learn?

He watched Sydney straighten his tie, grimacing. Sydney in black tie was reminiscent of the Max Beckmann self-portrait, the picture the artist called composition in black and white. Better he should have titled it composition in Kraut or composition in German naturalness. Sydney had the artist's iron jaw and fierce unhappy eyes, a Leipzig face that seemed to combine anxiety and remorse. Of course it was a face that was attractive to women, and invited confidence from men as well. It appeared to be a face that reflected the dense character of the man and alas it was not a face that promised quick reaction, not a face that knew how to look for opportunity, not a face for the celebration of the naughty decade now at hand, the one that offered such hope. The world was breaking apart and a man had to be willing to pick up the pieces and not to worry about dirty hands. A man had to seize opportunity by the throat and squeeze until it screamed for mercy, turning its pockets inside out, letting the coins fall free. You had to believe you were entitled to it, and had the will to make it stick. You had only to be natural, knowing that you were doing what others would do if they had the wits, nerve, and vision.

Junko opened his arms, welcoming them.

Angela stepped forward, Sydney touched his tie.

Aren't New Year's Eves a pain in the ass? Junko sighed.

It's a new decade, Angela said.

Last year of the old, Sydney murmured, touching his tie.

Junko laughed. Sydney was at ease in a tux the way a lunatic could be said to be at ease in a straitjacket, the uniform of the day, all the inmates had them. Yet Sydney was smiling now, putting out his hand, saying something sarcastic about the white tie and tails. And what he did not know was that the soup-and-fish was a hand-me-down, father to son to grandson. Its wide lapels and subtle frogging were fashionable now as they had been in 1912, when Harry Poole made his first crossing of the Atlantic and met the French divorcée who would bring him such grief, their marriage a titanic Franco-American struggle that lasted half a century until they died within a week of each other, snarling to the end. The great prize was their delicate son Philip, named for Pétain, the hero of Verdun, and appropriately enough because the boy was a battleground no less ravaged than Fort Douaumont or the homicidal hill known as Morte Homme. Before Philip disappeared into a lurid Montparnasse twilight he married an American woman, a coldhearted gold digger, according to Harry, who produced a son and immediately returned to the United States, settling in Chicago, where she had "connections." When Junko was ten his mother informed him that the father he had never met was dead, circumstances obscure; perhaps he had been hit by a taxi, she said. Harry was handling the arrangements and there would be no funeral. So when Junko dressed himself in the white tie and tails — all the Poole men were the same size, a 38 long, broad-shouldered and narrow waisted — he looked into the mirror and saw a raffish family history, handsome boulevardiers and their cunning women, a great ocean liner in mid-Atlantic, his grandfather waltzing with the high-spirited French woman; the Artists and Writers Ball in Paris, his father two-stepping with avid Minnie LeMessurier, a self-created heiress apparent; himself at twenty with some wisecracking midwestern debutante at a suburban golf club, waltzing again, tails flying, the girl excited because he was so handsome, so *assured*, so mature in formal evening dress. No one could talk as sweetly, or as amusingly, as Lemmy Poole. And from the sidelines, within range of dashing Lemmy's eagle eyesight, the girl's parents would look at each other, raising their eyebrows. Murder Maud, I hope the son is not the shadow of the father. That degenerate. Or grandfather, the man would add, that con man, one step ahead of the sheriff his entire sorry life. What a family! And Junko, winking at himself in the mirror as he liked to wink at debutantes, giving a final twist to his white tie and a hitch to his trousers, would laugh out loud. He did love times past, filed but not forgotten.

Sydney rolled his eyes and Angie lifted her face to be kissed, putting her arms around Junko's neck. Her body was soft, having lost the wiry tension that had made her so provocative years before. Champagne was on her breath; perhaps she was tight after all. Was that some gray in her hair? Hard to tell in the dim light of the corridor, not that it mattered. Angie Dilion was still the class of the field — *a real American girl, Syd, it's time you met one*. Another good deed that went unrewarded, as he had reminded Angela more than once after she had been swept away by her European. Her German knight. *Man*, she made that clear. And what did she mean by that? You know, she said. But Junko had shaken his head; no, he didn't know. In *his* family . . . but Junko did not finish the sentence. He said, In bed, what? Do the Germans know something about bed that we don't? Never mind, she said coyly. It's like jazz music. If you have to ask what it is, you'll never know.

"We're late," Sydney said. "Sorry."

"We went to see Max," Angie said.

"No cabs, so we took the Métro," Sydney said.

Junko suppressed a smile; only Sydney van Damm would take the Métro on New Year's Eve. He opened the door and stepped aside, allowing Angie to precede him. Then he touched Sydney's arm.

"Someone here, want you to meet."

"All right."

"You'll like him."

"Why will I like him?"

"He's a German, Syd. Just like you."

Everyone was drinking Taittinger waiting for the New Year. At the precise moment, 00:00, the lights of the Eiffel Tower would be extinguished and they would witness the show from the big double windows of Junko's living room. Angie and Charles Delahaye were bent over the ebony backgammon board near the fireplace, the Steinmillers kibitzing though distracted by the noisy laughter from the other guests — Sydney, Henry Green, Gretta Delahaye, Françoise Fontaine, and the German, Erich, all standing in a circle listening to Junko tell an involved story about NATO position papers and Henry Green's great coup of a decade ago.

"Henry's too shy to tell you about it, so I will," Junko said.

"All lies," Henry Green said mildly.

"The gospel," Junko said. "They still talk about it in Brussels. At Brussels headquarters, it's legend."

"It's because there isn't anything else to talk about in Brussels," Henry Green said.

"Position papers," Junko said. "NATO's life blood. Anyone want to guess how many position papers NATO's had in the past forty years? Covering every contingency under the eye of God? Two thousand? Two hundred thousand? Who knows, and it doesn't matter except it's plenty. Every paper since the founding of the alliance has contained two words. Most important two words in the alliance, a position paper without them is like the Apostle's Creed without the Holy Ghost. Henry managed to get a paper through the bureaucracy without the two words. This was in about 1982, when it mattered. It mattered like hell. But they were inattentive in Brussels. They didn't notice. Henry promised to do it and we made a bet. I didn't think he could. I didn't think he had the nerve to try and I didn't think he could do it if he did try. He was putting his career on the line. Brussels is a stinker of a bureaucracy. It's a beehive full of sticky honey. Know what the two words are?"

"No," Françoise Fontaine said.

"Soviet threat," Junko said.

Françoise and the others began to laugh except the German, Erich, who leaned forward, perplexed.

Junko added, "Usually preceded by three words, *to counter the*."

"Hats off to Henry," Françoise said.

"One paper out of thousands and Henry wrote it and slipped it by them. The paper was so bellicose that no one noticed that the threat went unidentified." Junko rocked on his heels and guffawed. "Want to know something else?"

"I think I can guess," Sydney said.

"Soviets picked up on it right away, thought it signaled a new policy, a fresh détente. They thought we'd repealed the Evil Empire. They made inquiries, toot sweet. The assholes in Brussels denied there was such a paper, said there'd been a malfunction in the word processors. Machinery run amok. Disregard. Then they traced the sabotage to poor Henry and there was some concern on the Potomac that Henry might not be what he seemed to be, if you're following me here." Junko beamed, flicking an imaginary ash from the lapel of his black coat. He glanced around him, as if to verify that no hostile party was in earshot. Then he murmured, "There was a thought that Henry might be a sinister force. Want to tell what happened next, Henry?" Henry Green smiled and inclined his head toward Junko, now in full throat. "They didn't fire him right away but they might as well've. They sent him down the hall, made him liaison to the fucking Swiss. Terrible fate."

"I had to resign," Henry Green said.

"And that's when he came to work for me," Junko said.

"For a year," Henry Green said.

"Yes, for a year."

"That's when you were in oil," Françoise Fontaine said.

"I was in oil at that time," Junko said. "Oil and this and that. Whatnot. A volatile business, oil. Subject to rapid mood swings and unforeseen circumstances, like that," he said, pointing to Angela and Charles Delahaye at the backgammon board, the rattle of dice and the click of counters.

Sydney turned, nudged by Erich. The German had been standing to one side, distracted, evidently baffled by Junko's rapid English. He had been staring at the raw silk wall covering, a static scene of provincial France, wigged men and voluptuous women in a moment of repose. Horses and peasants stood nearby, ready to be of use. The German was staring at the spectacle with loathing. The tiny Matisse above the fireplace had caught his attention also and without taking his eyes from it he asked Sydney to translate, please, the story that had made everyone laugh so.

Sydney obliged, but it was not as funny a story in German as it had been in English.

"And it was a joke?" Erich said. "How can this be?"

Sydney explained about the thousands of NATO position papers, the Brussels honeycomb, and the monotony of the Soviet Threat. Of course this was a few years ago, when you knew your enemy.

The German sighed, gulping his Champagne and refilling the glass from the bottle on the sideboard. He moved heavily, with what seemed like infinite weariness. His eyes darted here and there, from the raw silk wall covering to the Matisse to the Meissen stallion on the mantel and the tubs of caviar and slices of foie gras on the low glass table near Angela and Charles Delahaye. Erich said, "We did not think NATO a joke. NATO was a threat. NATO still is, no matter what they say." He slid closer to Sydney and whispered, "Who is this Henry Green?"

"A friend of Junko's."

"Junko?"

"Junko Poole, your host."

"You mean Sebastian."

It took Sydney a moment to recall Junko's middle name. Yes, he said. Sebastian.

"And this Henry Green. What sort of man is he?"

"A man with a sense of humor," Sydney said.

"But they fired him."

"They don't have a sense of humor," Sydney said. Then, looking closely at Erich, at his wiry widow's peak, his pallor and his bloodshot eyes, his box-shaped suit and worn woolen tie, Sydney thought: DDR goon. Sydney said, "Henry Green and Junko were in the oil business together."

"Sebastian was in the oil business?"

"For a while," Sydney said.

"I did not know that," Erich said.

"Junko specializes in import-export. This and that. International whatnot." There was no precise German word for "whatnot," so Sydney substituted a slang commercial expression. "But of course you know that already."

The German moved his hands, neither yes nor no.

"You are from the East?"

"Yes, of course," Erich said. "The German Democratic Republic," he said proudly.

Stasi, Sydney thought. He said, "You work in the embassy here? In Paris?"

"I live in Stralsund. It is north, on the Baltic."

"I know where it is," Sydney said.

"It is only a small city."

"My mother was born in a village near Stralsund."

"You have the Saxony accent."

"I was born near Hamburg."

"This is the true Germany," Erich said. "We are the soul of Germany. We are a hard-working people. But we have many enemies."

Sydney nodded but did not reply. Behind him, Junko was telling another story and Françoise Fontaine was laughing. Henry Green had replaced Charles Delahaye at the backgammon board and from Angela's posture Sydney knew that she was losing. The

Steinmillers were standing at the window admiring the view of the Eiffel Tower.

"There are those who do not wish us well."

"When unification comes," Sydney began.

"I hope it will not come," Erich said. "It will destroy everything."

"The Wall is already breached."

"They are idiots," Erich said. "They will rape us. They will destroy everything that we have worked for. We have broken our backs for them. Of course we are different sides of the same face, our doppelgänger Deutschland." Erich helped himself to more Champagne and filled Sydney's glass also, his hand trembling slightly so that some wine spilled on his fingers. The German seemed not to notice, his eyes half-closed now. "Sebastian and I are friends. He is a loyal friend. Have you not found that to be true, Herr van Damm?"

"Very loyal," Sydney said.

"It is a rare quality," Erich said. "He has told me about you. You are the translator. He hoped that we might meet."

Erich was staring again at the Matisse, squinting at it, so Sydney said, "It's one of Junko's favorites. He's loyal to it. He's had it for years."

"Who is the artist?"

"Henri Matisse."

"A simple drawing," Erich said. "Two, three strokes only. Very French."

Junko was concluding his story now, something to do with the price of weapons and the price of oil. When the price of oil rose, the price of weapons also rose, though the reverse was not always true.

"It is hard for me to appreciate the French," Erich said.

"They are not a simple people," Sydney said.

"Sebastian thinks they are."

"He would," Sydney said.

"Sebastian said that you have known each other for many years."

"Once upon a time we worked for the same firm, Junko and I. It's out of business now."

Erich laughed. "Oh, I think not. I think it's very much in business."

"But we don't work for it anymore."

Erich raised his eyebrows and let them fall.

"So you've gotten acquainted!" Junko cried, moving between them, reaching for the Champagne bottle and filling their glasses. Erich's was empty again, and so now was the bottle. "Erich is a new friend, Syd. I wanted to get him together with you, a countryman. How long ago was it that we met, Erich?"

"Not so long ago," the German said morosely.

Junko laughed. "It was the day the fucking Wall came down. Never forget it." He turned to Sydney. "Erich and I are going into business together."

"Moving to Stralsund, Junko?"

"Stralsund? No, not Stralsund. Why the devil would I want to go to Stralsund? Stralsund's a little pissant town near the Baltic. What the hell do I care about Stralsund, except as a port of embarkation. That's all it's good for. It's an exit." Junko Poole craned his neck this way and that, surveying his guests. The noise level had fallen now that there were no more stories. "Erich works for the interior ministry in Dresden."

"You mean he's Stasi," Sydney said.

"No, Sydney, he's not Stasi."

"Not Stasi," Erich said quietly.

"You're like those yahoos you're always complaining about who think every German they see is a Nazi. Christ, Syd. Grow up."

"So he's not Stasi. So what?"

"Erich's going to go private, Syd, because of all the changes and so forth and so on. There won't be any place for an east bureaucrat when unification comes. They're out on their ass and that's a mistake because these are the gents who know where the bodies are buried. So Erich and I will be working together and that's why I wanted you two to meet, Syd, because I'd like to talk you back into the fold, for just a little while." Junko Poole turned to the German. "Sydney's a damned good translator. Best I ever saw, as a matter of fact. Discreet, reliable."

"Yes," Erich said unconvincingly.

"We have to have someone who's bilingual absolutely in German and English, and French won't hurt, either."

Erich sighed, nervously twisting his fingers, blinking rapidly. His glass was empty and now something like panic crossed his features until he saw a full bottle in a silver cooler on the coffee table. He excused himself and walked off, refilling his glass and remaining to watch Angie and Henry Green at the backgammon board. Angie was animated now, apparently winning.

"Where did you find him, Junko?"

"Don't be hard on Erich, he's demoralized. He loves his DDR. He's devoted his life to it. It's his oldest friend and he forgives it its trespasses. If you press him he'll tell you the great myth narrated by Aristophanes. According to Aristophanes human beings were originally twice as large as they are now, with two sets of everything, brains, genitals, hearts, faces. Four arms, four legs, two noses. These original human beings were not so different from us, proud, arrogant, and aggressive. And so they offended Zeus — who cut them in half, and tied the skin in a knot visible now as the navel. With me so far, Syd? Each human being was destined to wander the earth in search of its lost half. The human creature was never to know contentment unless, miraculously, it found its — brother. Or sister. The human condition: unsatisfied longing. Of course Erich uses the German, *Heimweh*. Erich's eloquent on the subject. He believes it is the story of Germany."

Erich was standing behind Angie, who was rattling her dice cup and saying something to Henry Green. They were at the endgame and suddenly she turned the doubling cube, laughing as she did it; and Henry Green doubled back. Erich frowned, as if he had witnessed a breach of etiquette. He was conspicuous in his box-cut suit and heavy shoes, and exhausted face.

"He's a sweetheart," Junko said.

Sydney shook his head. "Horseshit."

Junko said softly, "Sometimes I forget that you're not a Yankee, Syd. You think like one, talk like one, even look like one, up to a point. You know, Syd, it's your *hair*. Your hair grows in a funny way, just like Erich's. It's un-American, straight where it should be curly and curly where it should be straight. It's your distinguishing feature, like Kissinger's Bismarck accent even though he's been tenured in the U.S.A. for forty years."

"Call it *Pferdedung*, then."

"I thought you'd have more sympathy for a countryman caught behind the lines. It's not his fault."

"It's Angie," he said. He watched her across the room. She

tucked her tongue between her teeth, rattled the dice cup, and threw. "Live with an American, you adopt their habits. Their habits are always more efficient and practical, their way of looking at things, the way they react. At first, from a distance, you think that Americans are simple, that they behave the way they do because they can't bring themselves to think about consequences or the dark side of things. But that isn't true, they're just more independent than we are and things have been sunny side up for so long that they can't imagine them any other way. But they're learning, at least *you* are, *mon vieux*. But probably you've always known. We're just different sides of the same face, as your friend Erich might say."

Junko grunted and took a step forward, laboriously, as if he were a tank moving into enemy territory. "Been wanting to talk to you a while now. I've been spending some time in the East, talking to the commissars. I like them, and they like me. My commissars are pretty much normal businessmen at heart except they haven't got the know-how. It bothers them. They're at a disadvantage and they know it, and it eats at them. They have the grab, though, and that's the main thing. They have the *will*. You don't do business over there in the usual ways, and in fact 'business' isn't the word I'd use."

"What word would you use, Junko?"

He thought a moment. "Heist. Problem is, they're not accustomed to contracts and lawyers and the *t*'s that have to be crossed and the *i*'s that have to be dotted and so forth and so on that you have to do to ensure that you're not getting screwed. It isn't that they don't want to screw you, they do. It's that they don't know how to do it the way we do it and of all the god damned maxims they've taken from the American way of life the one they practice, as opposed to preach, is from Chicago and it's the toughest to get around. 'Never write when you can speak, never speak when you can mumble, never mumble when you can nod.' And, Christ, Syd. Half those countries don't have direct dial and that means no fax, no nothing. But if you have Erich, you don't need fax. So what the shit. We'll do things their way."

"What are you selling, Junko?"

"Not selling, Syd. *Buying*."

"And what's the commodity?"

"That's why I need a translator because there's one piece of paper after another and while there's some know-how the commissars don't have, they do know how to screw you. So I have to have someone there who's on my side, looking after my interests, reading the pieces of paper and listening to the conversations, the talking, the mumbling, and the nodding from a single point of view: Junko Poole's."

"And what does Erich get out of it?"

"Security, Syd. Erich wants security."

"He gets security?"

"I think that's what he gets. That's what he wants, so why not give it to him?"

"I'm booked up, Junko."

"It's a little like the Florida land boom out there in the East. And the thing to remember is that before the bubble burst a hell of a lot of people got rich. And the secret, and it's always the same secret, is to get in early and get out early and keep your greed under control, though I have to say that the definition of greed's more spacious each and every day. And that's why I need you on this deal." Junko took a dainty sip of Champagne. "Thing about you is, you're a cat. Everyone thinks cats're dumb and dogs're smart. Know why? The dog comes when you call it and does a trick or two, stands on its legs and goes arf-arf. But that's not intelligence. That's obedience. Cat, meanwhile, goes its own way. Cat says, Fuck you, hombre. So who's smart and who's dumb? Syd, this is the best intelligence operation I have ever run. It is exquisite. I have not put a foot wrong and I do not intend to. Now what in the hell do I have to offer you to give me a big meow?"

Sydney began to laugh.

"You know, Syd. You make things hard on yourself." He pointed to the backgammon table, where Henry Green had taken out his checkbook and was writing in it. "I'm offering real money. I'm making it and I'll share it."

"You and Erich," Sydney said.

"Erich's a gloomy Gus, no question. Maybe Erich bears watching. But we're going to teach them a lesson. I'm like a professor to them. I'm giving them a seminar in the modern world, and like all professors I don't come cheap. I believe that the commissars ought to stick to their five-year plans, and the playwrights to writing plays and the poets to reading in the coffee houses. But if they want to play in a market economy, let them play. I'm their man. There're rules they can learn, just like we did. It only took us a couple of hundred years. Probably they can learn it in less, they're not dumb. But they're going to need instruction, capitalist know-how, hands-on. An off-the-shelf stand-alone independently funded market capability. To coin a phrase, Syd. And I'm offering you entry on the ground fucking floor."

While Junko talked, Sydney was looking at Angela. Henry Green handed her a check, which she folded carelessly and dropped in her purse. Her expression was almost studious, and then she glanced up and winked at him. She was idly moving the dice cup back and forth, a conductor with her baton. Henry Green was disbelieving. Sydney thought of Nicolae Ceausescu at the plain table somewhere in Transylvania. Henry Green seemed to occupy the wan share of a room filled with blind energy, Junko's braying bombast, Angela moving her dice cup and looking covetously at the Matisse above the fireplace, the Steinmillers hilarious now at the big window overlooking the Champ de Mars, the Delahayes and Françoise Fontaine helping themselves to caviar and foie gras. These locations were like regions of a country, you could travel to them. You could enter Hilarity or Disconsolation as easily as Bavaria or Schleswig-Holstein. And then he saw Erich slumped in the easy chair near the bookcase, apparently asleep.

Junko was again in full throat. "I hope you've been following the momentous events, Syd. Aren't they thrilling? Does your German heart go pitapat? It's a great day for Democracy. I've been following events in my own small way, keeping in mind always the wise words of Vaclav Havel. That Czech turd. Havel's *système philosophe*, as they say, is always to be horizon bound. Eye on the horizon and so forth and so on and there you find God or the true soul or some fucking thing. So Erich and I think about the horizon, too. When the Wall comes tumbling down for good and the two Germanies are together in the same bed, Hansel and Gretel doing the horizontal mambo in Central Europe, what does this mean for the honest businessman who wants to make a dollar in the free market system? It means you have to have a man on the inside, who's giving you a piece of paper and a transcript maybe, an intercept of this and that, so you know where you are every minute of every day. So when it's one bed, it's Hansel and Gretel and Junko, too, and all of us are mambo-ing together. And we just strip that little fucker clean." He looked away, laughing. He said, "What's up with Angie? She looks bored."

"I think she just won at backgammon."

"Good for her," Junko said. "Henry Green's good. He's a shark."

"I think she knows that, Junko."

"She has that look. I thought she was bored."

"Angie never gloats," Sydney said.

"What the hell's the use of winning if you can't gloat?" Junko put his hand on Sydney's shoulder. They were both looking at Angela in her zone of silence, staring now into the middle distance. Henry Green had wandered off. "Think about what I said, will you, Sydney?"

"Sure," Sydney said.

"You'd never regret it," Junko said.

"I'll think about what you said and I'll think more about what you didn't say, the so forth and so on and the whatnot and the this and the that."

Junko laughed and looked at his watch. He clapped his hands loudly, turning to the big window with its view of the Champ de Mars and the Eiffel Tower, brilliantly lit like a great iron candle. He raised his arms as if sighting a rifle and said softly, Bang! And the Eiffel Tower went dark. It was 00:00.

"Happy New Year, Syd. It's the beginning of the last decade of our century."

Later that night, drowsy with wine and lovemaking, Angie lay in her bed thinking about her life. Through the open window came sounds of a party, laughter and someone playing a sitar, a less sedate affair than Junko's where she had won two thousand francs at backgammon and at supper later she had found herself next to the mysterious German who spoke almost no English, or French either. He was so drunk that he wobbled when he walked, so his language skills were moot in any case, and he seemed not to notice when his toast to the two faces of Germany — incomprehensible until Sydney translated — was joined only by Junko. She thought the German opaque, his drunken face a locked door. She could not imagine what he had to do with Junko, although many of

Junko's associates were . . . odd. This one was sinister, he frightened her. Then Charlie Delahaye began to play cabaret songs on the piano and the German slipped away, out the door and into the early morning with only a stiff wave of his hand by way of farewell. No one was sorry to see him go. No one said, Be careful. No one offered to call a cab. It was understood that Erich was a man who could take care of himself.

Wide awake now, she listened to the slide of the sitar. At such reflective moments she was more than ever aware of her discontent. She felt herself neither here nor there, poised always between the land that she had left and the one she had adopted. It was hard knowing where reality was, because it was hard knowing where she belonged truly. And now she was overwhelmed with memories of Shake and guilt — she supposed it was guilt, though it may only be anger, perhaps curiosity — about her morose father. The lament of the expatriate, she had heard it a hundred times. Yet France was home; it was inconceivable that she could live anywhere else, certainly not in Sydney's country, or hers either. At times she thought they were marginal people, noncitizens, neutrals far from home. They belonged to nothing except each other, and Max belonged to them. A sinister German proposing somber toasts, Junko Poole telling worn-out stories about mischief at the North Atlantic Treaty Organization, two thousand francs won at backgammon, the Eiffel Tower dark, an ordinary New Year's Eve in the Seventh Arrondissement. In a month the evening would be forgotten.

In the cab she had asked Sydney what he saw for them in the 1990s, and he did not know what to reply. He liked his life as it was, and saw no need for change. He had his work and she had her life and on the whole they were doing all right, weren't they? She said that what she saw was a house in the country, perhaps Normandy, where she and Sydney and Max could live together away from the capital city. I feel hemmed in, she said. The high cost of living, the society that you could neither enter nor ignore. It reminded her of Maine, so closed-in and particular. She wondered if she was nostalgic for Old Harbor. Maine was down and out, according to Carroll. The whole country was down and out, yet lately she was drawn to it. Perhaps it was only the idea of it, its hard soil, its fog and cold ocean, its salty wind. Normandy could be their first step west, so she told him that what she saw in the 1990s was a house in the country, a sort of farm where she and Max could be out of doors.

You and I and Max, she said. A nation of three.

But Sydney was preoccupied and did not answer directly, muttering something about Junko Poole and his German friend, then saying loudly that he intended to go to work first thing in the morning, begin the New Year on a positive note. That's what the decade has in store, he said.

You'll think about Normandy? she said.

Of course, he said.

You wouldn't hate it?

I suppose not, he said.

You grew up near the water, she said.

Yes, he said. But so what?

What do you suppose it would cost?

No idea, he said.

Less than the Fortress, she said.

Renting, yes.

I don't want to rent again, she said. I want to buy. I want our place, not to live in someone else's place.

She remembered the little Homer on the wall of the study at Old Harbor. It had been her mother's, and now it was hers. It was a little watercolor, a mariner in trouble, scanning the horizon, clouds boiling in the distance. She loved art with a kind of indiscriminate ardor, the way men loved sports. There were a couple of fine Homers in the Musée d'Orsay. If you had one, it would be a tragedy to sell it. It would be a tragedy for the Musée d'Orsay to sell its Homers or Whistler's Mother or the Louvre to sell its Vermeers or its one great Goya. A thing that you loved was part of yourself, so it would be like selling your left thumb or your kneecaps. The living room at the house at Old Harbor was no different from the various rooms of the Musée d'Orsay or the Louvre. If you went there and the pictures were not where you expected them to be, then what was the point; you were heartbroken. Still, there was life itself. Art was life but it was not life itself. She did not know what her Homer would fetch, but it was a fine picture and ought to fetch something, perhaps enough for a little farm by the sea in Normandy.

The sitar's notes faded and there was silence in the courtyard.

She sat up and nudged her sleeping husband. "Sydney? Why are we so far from home?" And having put the question in that way, she knew the answer at once. The lost wars, she thought. Shake's war and Klaus van Damm's war had brought them to Paris, ever at the center of Europe. Now it was time to work their way back to the margins.

Three

ANGELA was still asleep when Sydney slipped out of bed, eager to work despite the bite of a hangover. He decided to leave shaving and bathing until midday and went downstairs to the kitchen to prepare coffee. He stood watching the pot come to boil, working to put Junko Poole and his German out of his mind. Then he remembered the conversation in the cab and what Angie had whispered to him in bed, and his irritation. They *were* home. Where did she think home was? But Americans were always restless; it came with the pursuit of happiness. So he had said nothing, pretending to be asleep.

With his coffee Sydney stood staring into the courtyard, gray and silent, slowly filling with early morning light. A crumpled paper hat reposed in one of the green glazed pots. He watched one of the models shuffle into the silence, pause, and shiver in the chill. She gave off a melancholy air, her hair unkempt, her ditty bag slung carelessly over her shoulder. Suddenly she smiled brilliantly, a thoughtful saleswoman demonstrating her merchandise. She held the smile a moment, then lit a cigarette and continued across the courtyard to the porte-cochère. He wondered where she had been; probably stairway A, necks. She had a Nefertiti neck with a chin to match.

With his coffee, and the radio turned to the classical station, Sydney was at his desk before nine, disoriented. He stared at his face in the mirror, tipping his head this way and that, trying to summon old Hoerli, Josef Kaus's dour protagonist. He read the work he had done the day before, then read ahead in the text. He had yet to gain a purchase on Hoerli, to know him as you come to know a part of yourself, an alter ego of your own as well as Josef Kaus's. Hoerli had a life on the page, but also a life in Kaus's mind; and he had a life as his story was translated from German to English. Sydney was concentrating now on Hoerli as Kaus's alter ego, not that this meant very much, an author having more than the usual complement of egos. Herr Kaus seemed to have a new one for each book, as Sydney had one for each translation.

It would help to know a few common facts. When Kaus spoke, was his voice harsh or soft? Did he laugh often? What were his passions? Was he expressive? Kaus called his book *Die Katastrophe*, one of whose English meanings was an event that subverted the natural order of things. It meant also the dénouement of a dramatic piece. The word implied revolution, in the sense of cataclysm; and perhaps other senses as well. It was almost as loaded a word in German as it was in English and French, but the text did not yet support its weight. The story swung on a narrow compass, the narrative flat and without ornament of any kind. It was as if the author wished to put his reader into a trance, deracinated from excitement or feeling. The narrative called for the most formal English, an English without slang or idiom. Kaus's language was demanding even by Germany's industrial standards.

Hoerli was a sixty-year-old bachelor, an engineer by training, a bookseller by profession, an occasional gambler at cards. Little was disclosed of his background except that he was the only child of a government functionary and his wife, and that his face had been disfigured. He had few friends. He lived in a small town in Germany, the town unnamed but apparently in the East. He lived alone and kept a playful cat, Hansi. The time was unspecified but it seemed to be shortly after the second war. There was rationing and evidence of military activity recently concluded. Hoerli lived a solitary life except for those times when he went to the tavern to gamble, arriving early and staying late, winning as often as he lost, taking no special pleasure in winning, resigned when the cards went against him. The card games were meticulously described, although the players were obscure, the single exception being Hoerli's bête noire, the postman. On the weekends he took long solitary walks into the countryside, beginning at the town square and following Moltkestrasse through the quiet neighborhoods to the bleak industrial zone on the outskirts of town to the flat fields behind. On the weekends the factories were deserted except for watchmen with guard dogs. He did not linger in any case, striding into the sun with the resolve of an infantryman eager to locate the field of battle, the vacant prairie, the featureless terrain characteristic of East Prussia. The novel opened on the Saturday when Hoerli came upon two young lovers in a wheatfield, lying naked in the ripe stalks. Unobserved, he listened to their conversation — a harvest of sexual banalities — and then watched them make love. The lovemaking was tenderly, even erotically, described, but Hoerli felt no stirring of desire himself.

When they were finished, he closed his eyes and rolled back into his own childhood, an ordinary Saturday dinner, his father carving a roast, his mother back and forth from the kitchen bringing plates of food. They did not speak. The meal proceeded in silence as it usually did. In the dining room the young Hoerli heard only the clink of silverware against china, and the gurgle of pilsener as his father filled and refilled his glass. Hoerli remembered the smell of food in his nostrils, its taste as he chewed, the immaculate flowered tablecloth, and the dark and heavy look of the room. A head of a roebuck hung on one wall and an official portrait of Kaiser Wilhelm on the wall opposite, the old Prussian's muttonchops bristling with aggression. The family Hoerli dined in the full glare of electric lights, though there were candles on the table.

Sydney van Damm, entirely concentrated now, put himself into that room, guessing its dimensions and its appointments, trying to see it now as old Hoerli was seeing it in his memory; as Josef Kaus wished it to be seen. Narrow windows gave out onto a lawn. There were ragged hedges in the middle distance, and beyond the hedges a flat field. Horses were in the field. The sky was overcast, dusk imminent, rain expected. Hoerli's mother and father were at opposite ends of the long table, father under the Kaiser, mother under the roebuck, the boy between them. The atmosphere was leaden, in sour contrast to the boy and girl making love in the wheatfield. This was atmosphere that Sydney knew well, and he struggled now with his own brimming memory. Kaus's focus moved from young Hoerli to his father and back again, his mother always on the edges. What was the boy thinking? He was inside himself, concealed, there being no room for personal expression at this table, so weighted with the natural order of things. Young Hoerli would be thinking about his studies, naturally, because immediately following the meal his father would ask him about them, never neglecting to mention the poor report last term. His father had his own reputation to uphold, after all. Perhaps he would ask the boy to quote some lines of Schiller, or describe a theorum of the classical physics by way of testing his seriousness and resolve. The electric glare in the room would be pitiless. The boy would eat with dread, his eyes on his plate, though occasionally they would stray to the figured carpet, where he had dropped a piece of boiled potato.

His father raised his glass, sternly contemplating the amber pilsener. Suddenly his mother turned from the table, her hands on her cheeks, uttering a small cry. His father put his glass down with a thud.

"Are you all right?"

These were the first words of the meal.

His mother said, "No."

His father raised his glass again, and took a slow deep draft, wiping his mouth with the back of his hand when he was finished.

"What's the matter then?"

The boy would have cautiously raised his eyes, following his parents, waiting for his mother's response. What would she say now? It was so entirely unexpected. The room froze suddenly, motionless in the great significance of the moment . . .

But Hoerli did not remember the rest of the meal, or that afternoon or evening, or the next day; he did not remember its consequence. His memory stopped with his mother turning and uttering her small cry, his father putting down his glass of pilsener, the question, and the extraordinary answer. Hoerli was living this in his memory, desperately trying to advance the film, finishing the story, while he was watching the lovers, though they had disappeared when he had closed his eyes to wander among the tombstones of his childhood.

Shockingly they were up and dressed and standing in front of him. They were screaming at him. The girl was buttoning her blouse, her fingers trembling. She looked at Hoerli and said, "You snot. You filthy snot." She moved her hips provocatively and said, "Do you like it? Is this what you like to watch?"

"Get out of here," the boy said, raising his fist. But when Hoerli took a step forward, the boy retreated.

Hoerli said, "You shouldn't be here."

"And why not?" the boy demanded.

"People walk here. People from town. It's a popular place for hiking."

"That doesn't give you the right —" the boy began.

"Yes it does," Hoerli said. "It gives me every right."

"Keep to yourself," the boy said.

"Or what?" Hoerli took another step toward him.

"Or I'll knock you on your ass," the boy said.

"Try it," Hoerli said.

"You're an old man," the boy said. He took the girl's hand. "You're older than hell. The hell with you, old man. Old scarface. Look at his face, Käthe. Christ, he's ugly." They had collected their things and were standing arm in arm, looking at him. The girl wiggled her bottom again, causing Hoerli to turn away in disgust. In the distance he heard a clatter, the creak of leather and horses' hooves. A troop of cavalry appeared from behind a low hill, ghost-like, as if they had risen from a great common grave. They were militia on maneuvers, carbines slung on their shoulders, moving at a trot in single file. They were concentrating on some objective and did not see Hoerli, who stood rigidly at attention. The troopers wore forage caps and high leather gaiters; their saddles were polished to a high shine. They were there, and then they were gone, vanishing behind another low hill, the horses disappearing and then the men. The last trooper turned and looked at Hoerli, who nodded pleasantly. The trooper spurred his horse and moved up and over the hill. Hoerli hurried off, back to town. When he had gone a few steps he heard laughter, loud and derisive, the lovers. But when he wheeled on them, they were gone; he could hear their laughter, yet they were nowhere to be seen. They had vanished like figures from a German fairy tale.

He watched low scud drift in from the Baltic, and it was then that the rest of the story from his childhood, or the next few moments of it, came back to him. The film advanced. His mother rose lightly from the table with a proud gesture reminiscent of the classical ballet, threw down her napkin, and left the room, extinguishing the lights as she went. Hoerli remembered her stepping lightly to the door, skipping almost, then gracefully slipping through it. The door closed with a smart click. He suppressed a desire to giggle; she had not looked at either of them, had been as haughty and oblivious as any performer before a suspicious audience. The room was suddenly dark. His father made as if to rise, but did not. They were sitting in darkness, his father humming a strange tune. It began to rain, fat drops striking the windowpanes at intervals. At last his father got to his feet, leaned over the table, and began to carve second helpings from the roast lamb, still steaming on the silver platter. He was maladroit, and drippings slopped from the platter to the tablecloth. He piled his plate, then turned to his son. But the young Hoerli shook his head. No, thank you, Papa. He was dismayed at the events that had played themselves out in front of his eyes. For a moment, his mother had looked like a young girl. The whistling stopped and his father busied himself with dinner. His father poured more beer and the room was silent once again, except for the clink of the silverware, and the gurgle of beer, and the hiss of the rain.

There was struggle now; the text began to wander. Sydney removed his eyeglasses, rubbed his eyes. He needed to see farther into the narrative; but it was beyond reach. This was a boy who would become an engineer, and then a bookseller. In the present moment they would be sitting in darkness, hearing the rain fall. Sydney concentrated on that, before reading the next passage. He imagined old Hoerli in the wheatfield, the soldiers gone, the lovers disappeared, trying to recapture his fifty-year-old memory.

His father had stopped chewing. His elbows were on the table, his chin resting on his knuckles. He was staring at his son.

"Your examinations are near, are they not?"

"At the end of the month, Papa."

"And you will be prepared?"

The boy nodded vigorously, knowing that he would not be prepared.

"You are fortunate, that particular school. It is the best school in the district. Everyone agrees."

After a little silence young Hoerli said, "The boys laugh at me, Papa."

"So?" His father raised his chin, releasing his fingers to cut a thick slab of lamb, which he forked into his mouth.

The boy did not reply, amazed at himself, his impertinence; he never spoke to his father except to answer a question or return a pleasantry. It was unheard of, yet he had spoken; and his father did not scold him, only chewed contentedly, watching with hooded eyes.

He said, "I hate it there, Papa."

"You have your duty," his father said.

He replied, "Yes, of course."

His father turned his head to look at the portrait of the Kaiser. He lifted his glass. "Duty," he said again.

The boy nodded. The matter was closed.

"And when they laugh. What do you do?"

The boy did not reply, concentrating instead on his plate. He moved his knife fractionally, and returned his hands to his lap.

His father said, "Turn on the lights."

The boy rose and did as he was told. His mother's light scent clung to that corner of the room.

"Now answer my question."

"I do nothing, Papa." Then he thought to add, "It is not allowed," though that was not strictly true. He was afraid at school, as he was afraid now.

"Just so," his father said. "At your school, there is discipline."

Though not for everyone, the boy thought but did not say. "I suppose so, Papa."

"Each of us," his father began, but hesitated, his eyes on the ceiling now; it seemed that he had lost his thought. "Has a duty," he concluded.

This was a statement that did not require an answer. They sat in silence a moment, listening to rain on the windowpanes. The hedges swayed in the wind. It was almost entirely dark outside. The boy absently put his hand to his cheek, feeling its ridges, his fingernail on the deepest, most ragged ridge; he listened to the sound his fingernail made.

"Stop that," his father said. He made a gesture of impatience.

"Yes, Papa."

"It won't do any good."

"No, Papa."

Somewhere in the house a door slammed, and his father looked up. An expression approaching pain crossed his face.

"Your mother," he said.

"Yes?"

"She will go away for a while."

"She will?"

"Always respect your mother. No matter what she has done. No matter what happens."

"Of course, Papa."

"Do you know about women?"

The boy was wary now. His father was leading him somewhere. "I don't understand," he said.

"*About* them," his father said. "About *them*." He leaned across the table, the glass of pilsener in his hand. He tipped the glass back and forth, the beer sliding to the lip and back again.

"I suppose so," the boy said. He had no idea what his father was suggesting.

"Evil," he said loudly.

The boy nodded, listening hard. He heard ominous sounds then, the thud of a dropped suitcase, the front door opening and then closing with a soft click. He dared not move his eyes but he knew very well that if he did he would see her proud head with its thick blond curls above the hedges as she walked away down Moltkestrasse to town. He and his father were now alone in the room.

"They have no discipline," his father said. "They *want*. They are never content. They are careless."

Then his father's husky voice softened, becoming almost tender. He seemed to speak with the weight of the nation, knowing that he and his scarred son would forever be united, allied yet at odds, and alone; and that it did not count, it was the way of things, an iron law of nature. He said, "We seek order. Discipline is greatness. It is not the exceptional or the conspicuous, but the 'strict exactitude' of a life that makes it noble." He turned to look at the formidable Kaiser, and then poured the last of the pilsener into his glass. "Good," the old man said. "Now forget about it and go to your studies. Read. Study hard."

Tears filled the boy's eyes. He folded his napkin and rose, moving to the head of the table, where he kissed his father on the forehead. Young Hoerli's heart went out to him. He loved him with all his heart.

Sydney dropped his pencil and rose, stretching. It was noon. His head was thick, still inside the story of old Hoerli, engineer and bookseller, a lonely middle-aged man from a small town in Germany, standing in a wheatfield and remembering an incident fifty years before. Memory resembled the shape of the brain itself, a succession of roundabouts and curlicues, crosswalks, all of it curling in on itself, worn down like the ancient paths of the earth. Some were cul-de-sacs, some great thoroughfares, detours, byways. Some were so tightly wound that they were like bracelets of elephant hair, impossible to pick apart without severing the strands. Severed, the memory died. The soul withered. Memory was never just one large thing but a multitude of small things. Memory depended on the small details that were wound in, a glass of pilsener or an electric light, or hedges bending in the wind. He looked down at his work, two pages, very good for one morning. Exceptional. Of course it would have to be rewritten; some of Kaus's constructions were devilish, and in English impenetrable. A freight train was a freight train was a freight train. There was palpable struggle under the skin of language and this had to be made visible. It had to be as visible in English as Kaus had made it in German, no more but no less either. It had to be faithful.

Evil, he said loudly.

Perhaps the better word was *depraved*, because the father's next statement indicated wickedness or corruption.

"They have no discipline," his father said. "They want. *They are never content. They are careless."*

His translation seemed to him insipid.

"Listen," his father said. "They are not disciplined. In their desire *they are never content. They are unquiet and promiscuous."*

Better, he thought. Not quite there.

Sydney began to smile, then laughed out loud. How far Josef Kaus was from Angie and her America. They may as well be inhabiting different planets; of course Angie did not care for the work of Josef Kaus, the static prose and his men in twilight. She insisted he was a misogynist. She had no affection for his characters, alienated, deracinated, depressed, down and out, nervously broken down with no recovery in sight. Must he be disfigured, too, Van? Isn't that a bit much?

This was old Europe, not an ambiance that would appeal to a skeptical American woman, even an American woman who had lived in Paris for twenty years. Kaus would be difficult for a European of the younger generation, for whom politics and nationality were only sentimental historical notions, not things of the essential moment like the economy, wages, taxes, and social security. Old Hoerli might have something to say to the stateless, though; the immigrant or the unemployed or the indignant, or simply those left behind.

Looking now at the little pile of pages stacked neatly on his desktop, Sydney was pleased. It was a good morning; there was substance at last, Kaus's world with natural features. It was not anything beyond itself. It was not grandiloquent. No life was saved, nothing died, no one wept. God was neither present nor absent, yet an excruciating reverence was evident. Sydney thought that Kaus's narrative was like a pure note from a horn. There was no knowing what would follow. Anything could follow, a hemidemisemiquaver or a whole note; and the translator was charged with interpreting the score. So he submerged himself in the text, turning a word this way and that; and then waiting and turning it again, trying to discover the bottom of the sentence, the fulcrum on which the lever turned, and the sense of it made. The result was a little less confusion in the world.

But first he had to comprehend the family Hoerli, and to separate Kaus's creation from his own experience, now insistently tugging at his elbow.

The time was three in the afternoon, a brilliantly sunny day at Ilsensee. It was the week before Christmas, the year 1943. Miraculously, there were no planes in the air. His father was nervous, admitted even that he was distracted and worried; he could not say what it was precisely, but his colleagues were avoiding him. The atmosphere in Berlin was always fractious, the professional soldiers on one side and Adolf Hitler's people on the other. He turned to his wife and muttered sotto voce that things were not going well in the East, the Russians fighting like tigers; their field leadership had inexplicably improved.

They had finished lunch and were sitting in the parlor. His father was smoking a cigar and his mother was knitting. Siggy was looking at the album of photographs; yes, and the radio was on, an opera, he seemed to remember that it was Puccini. Then his father moved, cocking his head, listening to the faint growl of engines in the driveway. It was cold and the air was still; the icy surface of the lake glittered in the distance. They all looked out the window. Exhaust fumes filled the air as two long Mercedes sedans approached slowly up the driveway, stopping a little way off. Soldiers alighted, gathering in the sunlight, momentous and indifferent. You imagined you could hear the creak of their leather boots as they stamped their feet. Klaus van Damm was not in uniform, preferring a heavy brown tweed suit for a family lunch. He raised his chin, staring coldly at the intruders in the driveway. He put his cigar in the ashtray, and then he spoke.

Inge, you go into the study and take the boy with you. Go with your mother, Siggy.

His mother crossed herself and then rose, taking him by the hand.

She said, God be with you, Klaus.

And you, his father said. He turned off the radio.

Siggy had been frightened all his young life; in the summer, when the bombers came to destroy Ilsensee, he had been terrified. But he was never so frightened as he had been that Sunday afternoon in Ilsensee, watching his father pause and look out the window, and then at each of them, taking a last puff of his cigar, placing it in the ashtray, and reaching to turn off the radio. When his mother crossed herself it was an act not of faith but of desperate habit; the boy remembered that she had sung particularly loudly that morning, in the church they had improvised from a warehouse on the edge of town. Family times at Ilsensee were always ponderous, though the major and his wife were kind to each other, and there were small jokes. Klaus van Damm was often absent on army business, and since the war was home infrequently. But this was ugly with foreboding, and when his parents looked at each other it was with ardor mixed with surrender. The stillness of the room — he could hear the scratching of the heavy tweed against his father's shirt when he turned his head — seemed the held breath of eternity itself. Klaus van Damm had not said he was expecting anyone; this was an afternoon off. Life outside the house was infinitely clamorous, disordered, misshapen, raw, arbitrary, a feral German authority announced by the arrival of two beige Mercedes sedans. That was the authority his father disappeared into.

They went into the parlor. His mother refused to meet his eyes. She stood looking into the cold fireplace, her hands on the mantel. A troop of white Meissen horses pranced across the wide wooden mantel. He watched the soldiers in the driveway, standing about in feather-black uniforms and sunglasses. Some of them were smoking. One of the soldiers fetched a soft cloth from the interior of one beige Mercedes and began to polish the hood ornament, and the chrome of the grillwork. They were in no hurry, and they seemed to him no older than the senior boys at school, though of course the tailored uniforms with their tight leather holsters conferred an immense virility. They made no move to enter the house, were instead nonchalant as they stood in the driveway, talking and smoking. They might have been an honor guard awaiting a general. The senior officer removed his gloves, looking at the house as if he were a prospective tenant, checking the roof and the windows and the shape of the door, the position of the sun at midafternoon, the paint on the shutters. Then he strode quickly to the front door and rang the bell, two shrill chimes, adding a sharp rap of the knuckles. When his mother heard the chimes she started as if physically struck, falling back from the fireplace, her hands over her ears.

She said, Come here, Siggy.

We will stand by the mantel.

Heavy footsteps advanced into the parlor. There was a moment of conversation, vague behind the heavy door. Then without notice the senior officer was in the study, bowing in the direction of his mother, nodding at him. The officer went to the old desk in the corner of the room and looked at it, opening one drawer after another, behaving as if it were his own property. He did not inspect the papers carefully and indeed he took none of them, and seemed to be rifling the desk to prove that he could, that nothing in the house was beyond his reach and authority. He went to the bookshelves, frowning when he saw the military studies, shelf after shelf of histories, biographies, atlases, scholarly studies, memoirs, and twin photographs, in identical frames, of the American generals Grant and Lee.

Siggy was staring at his father, who did not meet his eyes. Klaus van Damm was standing awkwardly, neither a civilian nor a military posture — and suddenly Siggy saw *him*, not civilian, not soldier, not father, but *him*, Klaus van Damm, frightened to death, bent now under the weight of the moment. The tweed suit offered no protection, he might as well have been naked. Siggy realized, shockingly, that his silent father had no standing, controlled nothing, was powerless, was reduced. Unbelievably, he was like anyone else.

"U. S. Grant was a drunkard," the Nazi said.

"And Lee wasn't," Klaus van Damm said. "Yet Lee lost and Grant won."

"It was a matter of supply and manpower. The North was dominant."

"Yes," Klaus van Damm said. "They were."

"And luck was with them. And the Southern politicians were idiots."

Klaus van Damm smiled.

"These photographs of the Americans . . ."

"I made a study of the American Civil War." He pulled a thin volume from a shelf near the desk. "It was published in 'thirty-nine. General Guderian read it. I have a note from him." He handed the book to the Nazi, who looked at the title page, then opened it in the middle and began to read. He read for a little while, shrugged, and dropped the book on the desk.

He said, "We will go now."

His father replaced the book in the shelf, then reached down and took a manila folder from the bottom drawer of the desk. He turned to look at Siggy, a particularly long, searching look. He hugged him, whispering something into his ear; but Siggy did not hear what it was, and did not think he ought to ask. He kissed Siggy on both cheeks, then turned to his wife, embracing her. She seemed to collapse into him. He kissed her on the lips, and walked unsteadily from the room, his heavy shoes thudding on the floor.

His mother was rigid, standing alone in the middle of the study. The Nazi gave the usual salute and followed, stepping lightly. Siggy heard the front door open, and he watched his father through the window. One of the soldiers held open the rear door of the smaller Mercedes. His father got in first, the soldier following. Then the senior officer appeared, walking slowly. He looked again at the house, and at the brilliant sky, of an angry Prussian blue seldom seen in December. There were no aircraft anywhere. Faintly he heard the cries of people skating on the lake.

At the Nazi's shouted order the soldiers piled into the cars and started their engines; and after a moment, they drove away.

"Where are they taking Father?" Siggy asked.

She did not reply for a moment. Then she said, "It is a catastrophe."

We had such good times, she said much later. It was the day he was leaving for Paris, to begin a new life. She would not stop talking. Stories tumbled from her in an urgent clutter. "Before the war, this house was not so quiet, so heavy. It was before you were born, Siggy. You don't know how jolly we Germans were, how quick, the life we had in us then. Even during the very bad times after 1918 we retained our own life. We had our families, those who had survived, and our games and our music and we knew we would again have our Rightful Place in Europe. So many died, your father's brother, my father, his brother; and not only on our side, but in all the armies . . . Your father and I would go to Berlin for the weekend. We would go horseback riding and to the cabarets in the evening, it was naughty then in Berlin. It was where the Reds were. Klaus was so handsome in his uniform, though of course our army was nothing then. Mutilated men were still on the streets of Berlin many years after the war; the army could do nothing for them. Berlin was the center of the universe for us. There was terrible hardship but we never surrendered. And then things began to get better. The young men were gone, but we made more of them. Your father wanted four sons, but alas after you were born I did not have others. When he saw you, Klaus shouted for joy. You must understand this, the way we all struggled and never surrendered and never *forgot.* We were pressed on all sides. We were despised. They tried to make us pay. They tried to take everything away from us. But we refused. We resisted."

He nodded. A taxi was waiting to take him to the *Bahnhof* in Hamburg, where he would board the train to Paris.

She was explaining to him why he could not leave Germany. It was always a mistake to leave your homeland. It was like leaving your church, renouncing God. It left you no place to love, nothing to cherish, no place that you would give your life defending, for the single reason that it is your place, your home, your heritage. Leave it and you insult it. You abandon everything, your language, your soul. To live forever among foreigners was a terrible fate. You will be cursed and derided. And in any case you can never *leave* it; you could walk away from it, but that was not the same thing. It would exist always in your heart. You can never be more than a tourist in someone else's country. How unhappy the Germans in America were! They changed their names, gave up their language, denounced their own culture. They tried to disappear inside America, and the worst of it is, they succeeded! And now they had nothing. In someone else's country you were a guest. A guest worker, subject to foreign laws, rules, and regulations. And when you become inconvenient, you are the first to go.

"They killed him," Sydney said.

"The National Socialists tried to take away our *spirit.* But they never succeeded."

"They killed him," Sydney said again.

"Fanatics, lunatics," she said. "Thugs."

"They were the government," he said.

"Not for so long," she said bitterly.

"And the Jews," he said. "How many of them?"

She recoiled from him, and when he put out his hand — it was a gesture of consolation or reconciliation rather than apology — she refused it, turning from him, her hands gripping her knees.

He said, "We must recognize these things."

She said quietly, "You can't know how things were."

He said, "I have to go now, Mama."

"I lost my father and I lost my husband, those are two things I recognize. In the summer of 1943 I lost my church to the bombs. I almost lost you." Her eyes were hard, bright as gems. She said loudly, "Your father did not *kill Jews*. I did not *kill Jews*. You did not *kill Jews*."

"No," he said. "But Germans did."

"Is this," she said with difficulty, still seated but raising her eyes to look at him. She pointed to the taxi in the driveway. "Is this about your father? Is this about me? Or is this about *them?*"

"It is time for me to leave, Mama. Only that."

"There will come a time when we are allowed to forget that. The world will forget it, too. With God's grace we shall be restored. It is not as though we were alone in our errors. They want to indict a whole people and that cannot be right. You, a German, will see this someday. Or perhaps you won't. You think you can leave Ilsensee, make a new life for yourself, and leave us with our German history; you think it is mine, and not yours. In that, you are mistaken. The world wants us to live in a permanent state of atonement. But we have suffered, too. I have lost my husband. There are women everywhere in Germany who have lost husbands, sons, brothers. You who have made so much of independence, perhaps you can understand this. You know what Papa said. Papa said you were a great mimic." She had remained seated, her eyes half closed as if she were hypnotized, a figure carved in wood.

"Good-bye, Mama."

"Do you remember when he bought you the hat?"

"We had seen an American film."

"From Gypsies, he bought it. Filthy thing. I threw it out."

"So that's what happened to it. I always wondered."

"You think you understand everything, but you don't. You think it's simple, like an American film, good people and bad people and a simple line between them. A script is written and the actors follow it. This is the idea of a child. I loved him," she said fiercely. "I still do. And I did not kill him. Or Jews either."

"I don't think it's simple."

"You are educated now and you will go to Paris for more education. You will read everything and know nothing. From your distance you cannot know how we were, Klaus and I, nor how Germany was." The distance was so great, to her a lifetime. "You want *Freiheit*, take it."

Freiheit, freedom. But in its most profound German meaning, independence.

"Your taxi is waiting," she said, distraught with a formal old-world fury, and it was useless for him to protest further. Her sincerity was not in doubt. When he bent to kiss her cheek he could see her half-closed eyes, dry as marble; and then he felt her tremble.

Never were they to be intimate. She never asked him about his life in Paris, never visited Paris, rarely wrote. He sent her his early translations, of the short stories and poems in the Foundation magazine, and she replied that her eyes were too poor to read small print. And her English was rusty, as it was so seldom used. When he sent her a short story of Josef Kaus she filed it away with the other manuscripts; she knew that Kaus was popular in America and in Germany with the younger element. For his part, Sydney never mentioned the hat. He thought of her as a figure from German folklore, more at home in the previous century. For the modern Federal Republic she had nothing but contempt. It lived like a weasel under the heel of the Americans, worshiping money. It was blasphemous to describe an economy as Adenauer did, miraculous, *Wirschaftswunder.* Germany was surrounded by enemies, as it had always been; and some of the enemies were within.

Twice a year Sydney traveled from Paris to Ilsensee, at Christmas and at Easter. He accompanied his mother to services at St. Michael's in Hamburg, since she disliked the modern church near the hotel by the lake in Ilsensee. There was modern gospel to go with the modern architecture, and that disgusted her. The pastor played a guitar. Sydney and his mother talked mostly of the days before the war, family details, nothing of consequence. He learned that her family was descended from the Teutonic Knights and had lived in the vicinity of Stralsund for a thousand years.

A thousand years?

At least that many, she said proudly.

He believed she was concealing as much as she was disclosing, as if he were an enemy agent. It was not any terrible secret, a crime or misdemeanor, only the true nature of her life with his father, what it was that they shared, and what they wanted for themselves and for Germany. When they thought of the future, what did they see? She did not trust him with her memories, subject as all memories are to interpretation. They were hers and hers alone, and they would vanish when she did. When he tried to describe his own life, how he lived in Paris, the particular vivacity of the French, she nodded and changed the subject. He described his apartment, his office, and the Jardin des Plantes nearby. He thought she would like Gina, who believed that he worked too hard, but that one day he would return to Germany. Gina was as single-minded and determined as Inge. But he never mentioned Gina, nor their aborted child, nor his own collaboration. Abortion disgusted Inge, implying as it did carelessness and modernity. Abortion disgusted him, too, for its waste and its pain. But his was not the final say. He had done what he had been told to do.

She lived alone, maintaining the house as it had been, altering nothing since the cold December day in 1943 when Klaus van Damm was taken away. And the next thing he knew she had sold the house and moved east, one old lady going against the tide of escapees west. People were dying by gunshot and land mine and Doberman pinscher, by drowning and freezing, by poison and by torture. This was the year before the Wall went up. It was not easy to move west to east but she had a special friend, she said. And she intended to live out her days in the village her parents and grandparents and their parents and grandparents were born in. The Federal Republic was doomed, anyone could see that. Reading this short letter, Sydney was horrified, then moved to smile. There was something heroic about it, a move so perverse and wrongheaded. It was escaping into prison, but his mother solicited neither his advice nor his approval so he gave neither. He had never thought of his mother as political, so concluded that this radical act was beyond politics.

So few letters after that, and for a time Sydney was uncertain whether she was alive. He discovered much later that she was, living relatively comfortably and in robust health. She had a small vegetable garden and regularly attended church. She got around the village on a bicycle. She lived alone, a respected member of the community. She was not a party member. This information came from Junko Poole. Sydney had asked Junko if he could find out anything about her and Junko said, Of course, give me a few weeks, and had come back with a report. Every six months Junko would have something to add, nothing of importance. She led a sheltered life. Widow van Damm kept to herself and was a model citizen of the German Democratic Republic.

Sydney sent her a parcel every Christmas, but never got an acknowledgment. He never told her about Max, and for that he was ashamed.

Sydney had smoked thirty cigarettes and his head was thick. He turned to look into the courtyard, surprised to find it dark. Only a moment ago it was filled with white light, the ceramic tiles brilliant in the afternoon sun. He heard a siren in the street, and somewhere in the courtyard a woman laughed, her laugh reminding him of Angela. He glanced at his wristwatch, nearly six. They had tickets to the symphony and before the symphony would visit Max. He had worked all day long without a break, had not eaten lunch or bathed or shaved. But he had been productive, four pages, and they were good pages. He straightened the manuscript of *Die Katastrophe*, noting the sentence where he had finished, old Hoerli retracing his steps back to town, struggling with his torrent of memory. The previous scene was still vivid in Sydney's mind, the old man's scarred face and the glistening flesh of the lovers. He was very close now to old Hoerli, almost close enough to touch.

Four

LATE THE NEXT AFTERNOON the Fortress was dark save for the conspicuous light in 8, the stewardesses back from wherever they had been, balmy Bahrein, Sydney seemed to remember. He stood in the courtyard and looked through their open door at a thicket of hilarious people assembled in front of a television set. These were the idlewilds, always on hand when the girls returned, a kind of layabout welcoming committee. They were mostly French and English, overage students supported by checks from home. Angie thought them vaguely sinister. One of the boys had made a pass at her once, late at night, and when she laughed and told him she was old enough to be his mother almost, he laughed back and said, Yes, that was the point. He was English, the one they called Maximus to distinguish him from his brother Minimus.

Can I tell you about it?

Can I tell you about Mummy?

Mummy was baaaaaad.

They all had nicknames, Pepe and Daddy-O and Sweet Sam and Do-Do and Dingbat and Dee-Dee and Dog, Jolly Jane and Calamity Jane and the Italian Counts, Long and Short. Milda they called Mildew until she told them to stop it. Occasionally one of the stewardesses, Milda or Consuela or Ingrid, would come up to their apartment to borrow butter or cooking oil and it was always amusing to see them, so lighthearted and careless. They would stay for a glass of wine and report the latest adventures with their boyfriends, naughty sheikhs of whom Sydney and Angela had heard much.

Drama attached to the sheikhs, who often turned up without warning on their flights to Rome or Istanbul, once to Bangkok, even.

Can this be true, Sydney? Be honest now.

The sheikhs informed them that Islam required piety on earth but permitted license everywhere else. That was what they insisted, swore to, Allah's Word according to the Koran. The soul of Allah was suspended between heaven and earth, Allah ecstatic. Allah existed in a condition of ecstasy, owing to His weightless state between heaven and earth. Accordingly, the sheikhs rented a Boeing 747 from the national airline — day rates, but that was unimportant — and conducted orgies aloft, obeying the will of Allah, three sheikhs and six girls and Omar-the-eunuch to serve them Champagne and caviar. Omar was also a masseur and a magician who performed lewd sleight-of-hand.

It's unbelievable, Sydney, the flying seraglio, beautiful carpets and cushions everywhere, the finest crystal and china. They had a CD player with the latest tapes from New York and raunchy movies on videocassettes. The movies were hilarious, made in Amsterdam and Copenhagen. There was a real movie star in one of them, honest, Sydney. The girls were given ensembles from Armani, jewels from Fred, lingerie from Frederick of Hollywood, chocolate bonbons from Lady Godiva, Blancpain wristwatches, and just dozens and dozens of scarves from Hermès. For dinner they ate spring lamb cooked over charcoal in the first-class lounge.

We took off from Rome and flew round and round in circles.

Consuela wanted to see the Alps, so we flew to Switzerland.

And they dumped us in Zürich.

Oh, Syd. You should have been there.

You, too, Angie.

He had never met the sheikhs but wanted to. Milda, the German stewardess, had told him they were handsome men with bodies smooth as butter, very athletic, sensual in their own way. Which way is that? he asked her. She laughed merrily and replied, Not the German way.

Now, in chilly late afternoon he observed them from the shadows of the courtyard, his feet hurting because he had walked from the Englishman's bookstore in Montparnasse, stopping to buy dinner, though he wasn't hungry. He had bought dinner only to have something to do in the early evening, and stood now holding two plastic sacks, ready to move along, but fascinated by Milda, who was sitting in a white cone of light painting her nails, her angular face in profile and somehow out of balance, indisputably German; you could imagine her a handsome woman of forty or sixty. She was wearing an officer's cap set at an angle, the visor low over her eyes. She wore no shoes and her shirt was open to her belt buckle. The music was very loud and the people inside were moving to it in rhythm, except for Milda, concentrating on her nails. She looked up then and blew lightly on the nails of her left hand. Consuela handed her a glass of wine but she shook her head, smiling listlessly. Consuela bent down and said something, nodding at one of the men, who was drunk and moving in an exaggerated shimmy. Milda shook her head. Consuela continued to talk and Milda smiled at last, murmuring a few words. Sydney noticed dark circles under her eyes, too many hours in the flying seraglio, although Consuela looked in peak condition as she stood and stretched; it was extraordinary what they wore, Consuela in what looked to be an old-fashioned man's undershirt, two straps over the shoulders, her airline's logo across her breasts. None of the men paid any attention, their eyes on the television screen. Sydney recognized the counts and Dingbat and Dee-Dee. Maximus, whose mother was baaaaaaad, was collapsed on the floor. The apartment looked warm and cheerful, agreeably chaotic, empty wine bottles here and there, overflowing ashtrays. Sydney smelled dope but saw no evidence. He assumed they were watching a rock video of some kind, the noise beating and tearing at the empty courtyard. Someone yelled angrily from an upstairs balcony but those inside the apartment did not respond, ignoring the angry neighbor or pretending to.

Milda turned suddenly and yawned. She stared into the darkness where Sydney was standing, but he couldn't tell whether she saw him or not. He thought not, the shadows were deep, and her eyes were fixed on the indefinite middle distance. She shook both hands, fingers wide apart, drying the nail polish. Consuela touched her on the shoulder and the others parted so that she could see the television screen. It was not a rock video but a pornographic movie. Two young women were tied to a stake, threatened by something offscreen, no need to ask what. The young women writhed and the shimmying man pointed at them, laughing nervously. They were dressed in T-shirts and garter belts, one fair, the other dark; they were ravishing girls. You could see them any day of the week in the St.-Germain-des-Prés in pairs or with their boyfriends, turning heads and knowing they were turning heads. The boyfriends knew it, too, walking with a kind of strut. These two were exceptional, though. Milda watched for a moment as the girls attempted a complicated maneuver to general applause. Then she rose. She buttoned her shirt and gave a hitch to her jeans and then she stepped to the door, staring into the darkness, her face resigned and melancholy. Behind her the girls were comforting each other. The shimmying man laughed again, a high-pitched giggle, and reached for Consuela, who squirted away, out of his grasp. Milda blew on her nails, one by one, whistling an aimless tune.

She saw Sydney and smiled ironically; it seemed to be a wordless comment on the blue movie, so tasteless, so depressing. Moving her head, she motioned him inside. Come into the raunchy warm, Sydney, and watch the teenage girls love each other. Behind her someone gave a whoop. Milda did a pantomime of the girls at the stake, putting her hands behind her back and stretching her neck. She gave a soundless scream, tossing her head, the officer's cap sliding over her eyes and falling, bouncing into the courtyard, falling finally at Sydney's feet. Milda stepped gingerly out of the doorway and onto the cold tile. The others continued to watch the movie and did not notice her departure. Sydney shifted the plastic sacks to one hand, the husband's burden, a little roast chicken, lettuce, a baguette, two bottles of Badoit, and soap for the dishwasher; he lacked dental floss, plaster for the corns on his feet, and aspirin. He reached down for the hat and put it on his own head, Hauptmann van Damm. Milda looked at him and shook her head. Behind her, on the screen, the girls were embracing. When he handed the hat to her, she nodded thanks.

Sure you won't come in?

They're pretty girls, aren't they?

Our sheikhs let us have it. It's rather sweet, there's no blood.

Sydney? You look forlorn.

She hopped from foot to foot and asked if she could come up with him, only for a moment, to get away from the smoke and the blue movie, the noise; the idlewilds were in full throat. I'm depressed, she said soberly.

She ran ahead of him in her bare feet, and began to talk as soon as they were inside. She sat on the couch and talked at him while he put the groceries away and opened a bottle of wine, pouring glasses for them both. He thought of taking schnapps, then thought better of it.

Well, Sydney, she said. It was a mess, everything ruined. They were going to Bahrein but at the last minute there was a bomb threat that was taken seriously, as opposed to most of them, so their crew was shifted to Munich. The Bahrein flight was delayed indefinitely. It had screwed everything up because she and Consuela had made plans in Bahrein, three days at an oasis; and that was difficult to arrange in Bahrein. *Alone*, for a change. But instead they drew Munich, holy shrine of the bourgeoisie, a second-rate hotel, propositions every minute of every hour of every day, none of them worth considering.

They don't know how to take no for an answer.

They see that you are a stewardess and they get ideas.

Those filthy beer halls.

I hate Germans, she said.

German men, she amended.

The women were all right.

Quite nice, really. Great gossips.

The men, ugh. Sometimes I am ashamed to be German.

Sydney was half-listening. The room was desolate even with her in it. It seemed to him a solitary place, insecure, the barbarians just beyond the door, out of sight; but you could hear them murmuring, and the clatter of their boots. He supposed that was the way it had to be sometimes, when you lived on the margins of someone else's society. As his mother had observed so many years ago, you are a guest worker. Of course you were not alone in your marginality. In Montparnasse he had gone to a bookstore owned by an Englishman to buy a German translation of the Italian Malaparte's novel; and it was out of stock. He had had a discouraging conversation with the Englishman, who believed he would be out of business soon. There was no profit in books. Books were a gentleman's trade and he was not quite a gentleman.

Sydney sipped his wine, trying and failing to concentrate on what Milda was saying. He wondered what had happened to the girls tied to the stake in their T-shirts and garter belts. They were good-looking girls, too, beautifully built.

Everyone thinks it's a glamorous job, but it isn't.

She said, It's drudgery most of the time.

The pay isn't much.

You're a high-class maid, and that's all you are.

You're a chattel, they send you anywhere they want to. You put on your uniform and you stick out your chest and you smile and you go. You can't do a thing about it except smile and say yes. We're like those girls tied to the stake, except they don't allow us to wear T-shirts.

They're very good about the bombs, though. They've gotten very thorough and professional, except for the Italians. They're so disorganized in Rome. There's no security in Italy. In that way the Germans are better than most, probably because they've had so much training.

You wonder sometimes if it's worth it. You go here and there and then someplace else. You stay a few days, buy a few things, and then you go home. Your period's screwed up. You arrive early, you chat up the crew, you crosscheck, demonstrate the ha-ha life-saving gear in the event of an untimely ditch in the Adriatic, serve the drinks, microwave the dinner, serve more drinks, maybe flirt a little, maybe not, and then you tell them to fasten their seat belts, extinguish their smo-king ma-ter-ials, have a nice day, and don't forget their belongings in the overhead bin. But there's no future in it. It's a dead end, unless you think there's a future in naughty sheikhs or a Mercedes salesman with a wife and two children in Schwabing.

That's why I'm depressed, Sydney. I think I want to go to America. In America they know how to have fun.

So can I have another glass of wine? There's so much noise downstairs. When our idlewilds come visiting it's always a mess, they stay all night and don't leave until dawn. It's Consuela's way of unwinding, and who can blame her? But do you mind if I just sit a while?

You look sad, my Sydney. Is everything all right with Angie?

She's with Max, Sydney said. A headache was beginning to gather, a rustle of leaves at the base of his skull. It was almost time for the evening news and he wondered if it would be rude to listen to it. Probably Milda would not be interested in the German news, so provocative. Any self-respecting, self-hating German would turn his or her face from the screen, alarmed at the sight of so many countrymen refusing to take no for an answer. It was a rough seduction, and Germans frightened themselves most of all.

Milda said, Every day she goes.

Most every day, Sydney said.

She loves him very much, Milda said.

Sydney nodded, touching his temples lightly with the fingers of both hands.

Sydney? You are not moving from Fortress America, are you? Because when I spoke with Angie the other day she said you were thinking of Normandy, to live in the country perhaps with Max.

Angie said that?

She seemed very sad.

Sydney said, Things are unsettled.

But you are not moving from the Fortress?

He said, No. We have no money.

She said, Good. I like it that you and Angie are here. We have a nice community on avenue Songe. How long have you been married, Sydney?

Fourteen years and change, he said.

She laughed at the Americanism. It's a long time, fourteen years. And of course the change. When you were married I was a little girl in the Kleinwalsertal. Do you know where that is? It's Austrian territory administered by Germans. It's a box canyon cut off from the rest of Austria. So Germans run it. I grew up there. Then my boyfriend became a ski racer and I went around with him for a while until he found someone else. But I never went back to the Kleinwalsertal, even on a visit, even to see my family. The Kleinwalsertal has no future, so I am thinking about going to America. And if America doesn't work out, I am thinking about going to Italy, where it is warm at least, yet Italian men are no better than Germans.

There was a commotion in the courtyard and then they heard someone call, Milda! Millll-da.

She unwound herself from the deep couch cushions and went

to the door, standing quietly a moment, resting her hand on the doorframe before she pulled the latch and looked out.

She said, I'm here. Don't shout.

The man said, Where?

The balcony above you, she said.

The man cursed good-naturedly and said loudly, Come on down, Milda! We're just getting started. We have a new movie, the latest. Things are starting to happen. What are you doing up there? I can't see you.

Having a drink with Sydney, she said, and closed the door.

Sydney had gone into the kitchen for wine and for something to put into a dish, peanuts or olives. He shook two aspirins from the bottle and swallowed them dry. When he returned, she was standing by the window, looking into the courtyard, tapping the visor of her officer's hat against the glass. She said there had been someone in the shadows on the far side, but he was gone now. She put her hand beside her head and turned, as if there were something she had forgotten; but she shook her head. Apparently it was nothing. There were always strange characters lurking about in the Fortress. Sometimes she thought the courtyard was haunted by the ghosts of former tenants, American generals or astronauts or film stars. And of course the heroes of the Resistance, listening to American swing in the basement caves. She laughed suddenly, a kind of trill reminiscent of Angie. She stood with her back to him, her forehead pressed against the glass; they could hear the commotion in the apartment below. She said that at night she felt them moving around, the ghosts. Sometimes they entered her dreams, when she was especially tired or flustered after a difficult flight. She was weary of flying, its instability. No future there. The trouble was, she could not see a future, any future. She almost did not know what the word meant. She did not understand the tense. But the airline business would not be part of it in any case. She had already visited sixty-one countries and, on those nights when she was insomniac, she counted them, beginning with the African countries and ending with the Asian. The way you counted them, Sydney, you visualized the continent and then filled in the blanks, counting as you went, South Africa, Zimbabwe, Zambia, Zaire, like that, always south to north. Each country had its specific location.

This was soothing, and she was usually asleep by the time she reached North America.

Germans have never been travelers, you know. I'm sick of it.

I'm sick of the sheikhs, too.

I'd like to get married and count on fourteen years and change.

I'm going to talk to Angie, ask her how she did it. And if it was worth it.

He said, Let me know what she says.

Milda turned to him suddenly, grinning lopsidedly, then giggling. God, Sydney, I'm high as a kite. We had our stash for Bahrein, for the sunsets at the oasis. It's too good to waste on Munich, so we brought it back here. But instead of mellow, I'm dissatisfied. I was counting on an oasis in the desert and instead here I am in Paris, high in the Fortress, a long night ahead. I'd like to seduce you, Sydney. Are you seduceable? Most men are.

She sat down on the couch cross-legged, modest, her hands in her lap. She blinked her eyes and whispered, Most men like it. Do you think Angela would mind? I suppose she would. Wives usually do.

Usually, Sydney said. Not always. Parisian wives don't seem to mind.

Consuela and I talked about it. We're practical, you know. We would do nothing to offend Angie. But you look so sad at times. And she does, too. She looks sometimes as if her poor heart is breaking. You could use a little friend, Sydney. It's completely normal, this desire. One has a duty to be happy, not to let life get you down. Otherwise, what's the point?

But I have a headache, Sydney thought but did not say. He pulled his chair close to the couch so that they could talk easily. Milda's eyes were very dark and glittering, an appraiser's eyes over a dreamy half-smile. She was slowly stroking her bare ankles. The room was charged now, not so cold and alien, the lamp casting a soft glow on Cézanne's oranges.

She said, Are you faithful to Angie?

Of course, he said.

And she to you?

Yes, of course.

Always? You have always been faithful?

You have to be faithful to something, Sydney said. I chose Angie.

Don't forget your work, she said.

That, too, Sydney said.

She laughed and laughed, her head thrown back against the cushion. What's left, Sydney? What's left over? There isn't much left over. If you are in a cage you must remove the bars. Consuela and I like to know how people live. We don't have many married friends, so we try to learn a little, here and there. It's not encouraging, Sydney. Aren't you always getting in each other's way? Bumper cars in an amusement park? She gave a little fiendish smile. Consuela and I don't know how married people behave.

You mean misbehave, he said.

I suppose that, too, if that is the way you want to look at things. For the idlewilds it's not so much. We try to get along day to day, best we can. Watch a movie at home, fly over the Alps with a sheikh, visit an oasis for the weekend. Watch the camels make love. It fills the time. It seems to do no harm. The big things are beyond our reach, so we do not bother with them. I am sometimes amused at my country, everyone is afraid of us. We're the family next door with the unruly children and the strange noises at midnight. And we are afraid of ourselves sometimes. It is not real, only something remembered from the war. The old people think about it. Each old person is a walking history of war. They know it so well they do not need to speak of it. The Germans prosper. The Germans unify or don't unify. What does it mean for us really? It has no importance today, except for the old people. We young people are on the outside of things, or perhaps on the edges, with our music and our own trolls and our north wind from Limbo. You know our legends, Sydney. We are a limited people. There is so little we can do to change things. We are worried about environmental things but there is nothing we can do about them except complain and sign petitions, make films, demonstrate, practice light urban sabotage. The authorities do not interfere in our personal decisions, behavior or misbehavior. That is for each person to discover for herself. But we like to give ourselves pleasure.

We are unquiet. They are unconfident.

Sydney? Do you think you will ever forget about the war?

I mean old people.

The eastern front, the western front, the Jews, the Communists, the Gypsies.

If the old people can forget about the war, then there's a chance, isn't there?

It was *your* war, not ours.

Sydney? Would you like a toke? I can go downstairs for it, I think you'd like it —

He said, Do you miss the Kleinwalsertal?

She said, I miss my old boyfriend. He was a very handsome boy, very sexy. All the girls wanted him. But he was not successful on the tour and now no one knows where he is. He was in South America and then he went to Australia. No one has heard from him and now he is no longer ranked. A few years ago he was fifty-first in the world, something like that. He did very well at an event in Zermatt. When he left me he said he had to work on his turns. He was in Australia working on his turns, he said. And I guess he still is.

I mean the place, Sydney said.

When I think of the place, I think of my sexy boyfriend. But the place, too, of course. We lived in a chalet halfway down the valley. It was very beautiful. In the winter we had skiing and in the other seasons the hikers would come. They came from all over Germany in their sports cars. They came from the outside world and they treated us like peasants. They were so rich, we thought they had everything. We girls wanted to marry one of them and live in Hamburg or Stuttgart, in a grand house with a coat of arms and servants. My parents hated them. My grandfather, too, who lived with us. He called them pigs, fat and dumb. My grandfather had been in the war, though he never spoke of it. We children were told never to mention the war or the Third Reich. Then one day some policemen came to the house and took my grandfather away to Bonn. He had been a Nazi, Sydney. There was no statute of limitations on Nazis, so they took him away for the trial, though he was an old man then and harmless. He died after the trial. My mother could not stop crying. So I do not miss the Kleinwalsertal, except the natural beauty of it, and the times with my sexy boyfriend.

Your grandfather, Sydney began.

I don't want to speak of him, she said.

How brief and unsettled they were, Sydney thought. So slender and composed, so casually predatory, they floated above the earth like migratory birds, south one season, north the next. Except they never went home; at least this one hadn't. They were not part of any community, except the common market of Europe. When she went to sleep she counted countries, perhaps dreaming of the sexy boyfriend, or the sheikh whose skin was as smooth as butter. He looked at his watch. His headache was fading, and Angela was due home any moment.

And you, Sydney.

I do not miss Germany, he said.

They say Germany is the future.

No doubt, he said. No doubt it is.

We were talking of the future, she said. And the problem for us is that there is none. None at all, and not in any case in Germany. I mean nothing grand, nothing very different tomorrow than today. Nothing to anticipate. We are on the sidelines. We have been on the sidelines since the war and we are accustomed to it. We are waiting for people to die so that the war can be forgotten. I try to explain this to American friends and they do not understand. They forgot the war long ago. They forgot it as soon as they won it. This feeling is unique to the young people of Europe, who want to believe that they are special, that they are a particular part of Europe, that without them Europe would not be Europe. Even so, many young people have been left behind with nothing or no one to turn to, nothing of the past to admire. It is beyond us to construct a new society, something different and something better and more hopeful, because we are all one body now. We draw from the same wallet. Our sheikhs have bank accounts in every capital in Europe and accountants to keep track of them, Swiss francs and French francs, lire, deutsche marks, escudos, kroner, guilders, rials, dollars. Maybe the experiment in the East will bring us all down. But so what. Do we have so far to fall?

Farther than you think, Sydney thought.

I am glad you and Angie are content together, she said after a moment.

Thanks, he said.

I would like to be content, she said. It would be a rare thing. Consuela and I watch you and Angie together, it seems you are very happy with each other. Anyone can see this. It was wonderful to see, except of course for the sadness that we can see also. And the need to be faithful, that is obvious. Perhaps it is a natural thing for an American woman, and the sadness comes from Max.

Sydney watched her, wondering what nerve her discordant spirit would touch next. Milda's gaze was fastened on a point over his left shoulder. As she spoke she unbuttoned and buttoned and unbuttoned the top buttons of her blouse, methodically, as if she were practicing scales. He could see the rise of her breasts where her fingers touched the skin, and her nipples hard as thimbles under her shirt. Her appraiser's eyes, widening, did not waver. When she said wistfully, "I would like to be content," she sounded as if she wanted a new identity, to be a film star or president's wife or Norse goddess, Freyja or Nanna. I would like to be Catherine Deneuve. I would like to be Mrs. Onassis. I would like shelter from the north wind. He thought, Of ordinary life she would care nothing.

After a while she yawned and announced she would take a little nap. She'd had no sleep the night before, and of course New Year's Eve had been late and turbulent. And there were all those people in her apartment, too many idlewilds, too much dope and pornography and noise and it wasn't what she needed just then. What she needed was contentment. Did he mind if she slept for an hour? Give me an hour and then I'll be ready to go back to my friends. Give me an hour and then I'll be myself again, merry Milda. Sydney watched her a moment, her face immobile and warm, eyelids fluttering. Presently her face softened and she turned toward him, her eyes unfocused as they closed, her mouth parted fractionally.

She said, Sydney. Give me an hour.

He said, I'll be in my office working.

Her eyes popped open. Oh yes, she said. You had a visitor this afternoon. He looked like a clochard and his voice was rough. He was very insistent. He was very unpleasant. I said you were not here because Consuela and I had seen you leave. He was in the courtyard poking around and so I went out and asked him what he wanted. I knew he didn't belong there. He was disappointed you were not in, but he left his card.

She dug into her pocket and brought it out, handing it to him. Herr Kaus, she said.

Not ten minutes later Angela was home, turning the latch, stepping wearily into the kitchen. Hearing her, Sydney came down from his office. She stood in a bright zone of light, hands plunged into her coat pocket. She had a newspaper under her arm. It had turned cold and her face was scarlet. For a moment he thought she was ill, but when he touched her arm she looked directly at him and he saw that she had been crying.

Max, she said. He clung and clung, he clung to her and wouldn't let go. He wanted something but couldn't express himself, and all this time his eyes were squeezed shut as if he could not bear to behold his surroundings. He held his breath and for a moment she thought he would have a tantrum. And when Sister heard the commotion she opened the door and that only made Max worse. It's intolerable, Sydney. He can't stay there any longer, and that's final.

He doesn't like Sister. And he hates that place, he always has.

Oh, *God*, she said. She put her head on his shoulder. She still had her coat on, the newspaper under her arm.

I don't know what there is that we can do but we must do something because he's dying there. It's as if we put him into an open grave and each day we throw in another spadeful of dirt. He would not let me go, Sydney. He just clung and clung until finally Sister gave him something and he let go immediately and laid himself down and went to sleep. Except it wasn't sleep, it was unconsciousness. What sort of people are we to force him into that life in that place?

He's not dying, Angie. He had a bad day.

We're no better than they are, she said, throwing down the paper.

Who, Angie?

Them, she said. *Them*, pointing at the paper. It's all over the front page. That hopeless, hopeless country. They're killing little children. They're raping women in daylight. Women give birth to heroin addicts. No one *cares*. They're watching a country destroy itself and no one *acts*. They behave as if it isn't their country, that it's the Sudan or Ethiopia, someplace they hear about on the evening news. I used to think sometimes we'd go back there when we were old, maybe live there for a year so I could get reacquainted, a kind of sabbatical. But now. It'd be like reacquainting yourself with the Gulag or Dachau.

Angie, he said.

Except sometimes you have to do that, too.

He put his arms around her while she talked, winding down now at last, her head sagging.

Why can't we go to the country? If we lived on a farm in the country Max could be with us. We could take care of him. We can live together as a family. Fifteen years of Fortress America is enough. God, I hate that name.

She turned to face him, putting her fists on his chest.

The only thing I have to show for my life is Max, she said.

He did not know what to say to that.

She began to describe the house and its garden, the garden a mélange of flowers and vegetables. The point was to have something beautiful and practical at the same time. The house would be surrounded by roses, with walls thick enough to keep out the heat in the summer and the cold in the winter. It would be away from things, yet close enough to use a bicycle for marketing. It would need repair work. From one of the windows you would be able to see a sliver of sea, as a reminder of the ocean nearby. And of course there would be an apple orchard. Calvados for you, Syd.

She said, But of course there isn't any money, is there?

He said, No.

Maybe there's a way to get some, she said.

My Kaus, he began.

Your *Kaus*, she said. Your Kaus barely pays the rent.

He said, Keep your voice down.

My little watercolor, she said. I don't know what it'll bring but I know it'll bring something, and maybe enough for a down payment. I'll pray for the rest. Sometimes prayers are answered. I think I'll go home in a week, Sydney. Talk to Carroll and see what can be done. The Homer is *mine*, my mother gave it to me. She told me it was mine the day she died.

All right, he said, not agreeing but indicating merely that he'd heard what she said. Then he put a finger to his lips.

Why should I keep my voice down? It's my house.

Milda's here, he said.

Milda? Why is Milda here?

He said, She was tired and depressed. The idlewilds're back.

I know, Angie said. I heard them. Where is she?

On the couch, he said.

And I should keep my voice down?

I think so, Angie.

She slipped out of his arms and stood upright, staring at him. Are you screwing Milda? Are you screwing *Milda*? Then, looking at the expression on his face, she touched his arm and said she was sorry, she was upset. She knew he would never do that and certainly not with merry Milda. Mildew.

Sorry, Van. Forgive me? And I'm sorry I made that crack about your work.

Well, he said, and began to laugh in spite of himself, her, Max, Milda, hopeless America, and Kaus unfinished in his office. It wasn't because I wasn't asked, he said, thinking she might find that amusing but not surprised when she didn't.

Part 3

One

"YOU'RE SHORTER than I expected."

"And you, younger."

Josef Kaus looked at Sydney coolly. "And how old do you think I am?"

"Sixty-five." Sydney smiled. "Am I light or heavy?"

"I am older than sixty-five. Does my work seem like that of a young man?"

"You are more of the last century than the present one —"

Kaus began to laugh, but there was no merriment.

"— but that's only my opinion, shared by a few others. Some critics, for whatever they are worth."

"Not very much," Kaus said.

"On that we agree."

"It is difficult to derive the author from the work. It is a pointless exercise, an affair for graduate students. The work is one thing, the author is another thing. I had the distinct idea that you were tall and spindly, with bad knees and a beard. I had that idea because in the first novel you translated you blundered and got something wrong. I said a man had a weak chin and you translated it weak knees. The words are not similar. From that, I deduced that you had weak knees; for your own reasons, you had identified with the character. Since the man in question was tall, I deduced also that you were tall. To the height and weak knees I added a beard, I can't recall why."

"It wasn't a mistranslation," Sydney said.

"Of course it was." Kaus had taken offense.

"In English, weak-kneed is a more pregnant characterization than weak-chinned."

"But there was nothing wrong with my character's knees."

"Literally, that is true. But there was quite a lot wrong with your character's character. He was a weak man. In English you can call that weak-kneed, if you don't want to hit the reader over the head with it. You make the reference in passing. If you want to suggest an unpleasant trait of character that will be brought out fully in the course of the book, that is how you do it. Weak-chinned is an axe, weak-kneed is a rapier. It is not that in German, it is that way in English. This character, as I recall a minor character, had a failure of nerve at a critical moment. It had something to do with a woman, his mistress?"

Kaus smiled for the first time.

"He backed away from something he shouldn't have. He was like the matador who does not control his feet when the bull charges. Your character was unequal to the moment. Wasn't that it?"

"Roughly," Kaus said.

"So I'm happy to meet you at last. What caused you to introduce yourself?"

"I've lived here for many years."

"I know that," Sydney said.

"I've seen you many times in the quarter, at the café and the post office, and the Métro platform. You and your wife — I assume she is your wife, you appear companionable together — often in deep conversation. And more than once I had the idea that you were talking about me. Or, to be precise, my work."

"Probably so. And of course I have seen you, too. But I had no idea you were Josef Kaus. How did you know who I was?"

"It wasn't difficult," Kaus said.

"It wasn't?"

"I'm afraid the young woman in your building thought I was sinister when I stopped by yesterday and left my card. You were good to call."

"She said you were insistent."

"Yes, I was."

"No harm was done," Sydney said.

Kaus was silent then, and Sydney turned to look at him, bundled in a greatcoat and a fur hat. He looked as if he belonged in St. Petersburg, perhaps a prosperous merchant or government functionary, or Dostoevsky's creditor. He did not look like a clochard. It was snowing and the flakes caught in his mustache, his Stalin whiskers so thick and wiry they looked like the bristles of a hairbrush. Sydney had telephoned and they had met in the little square down the street from the Fortress. Kaus had told him to put on a suit and tie, that they would go out for the afternoon, have a drink somewhere, and talk and get to know each other. It was time they met and talked, Kaus said. Now they were striding down the hill in the direction of Place Clichy, crossing the iron bridge that spanned the Montmartre cemetery, the graves and family mausoleums thickly packed and topped with snow. Kaus paused and leaned over the iron rail, pointing. Zola, there. Farther to the right, Berlioz. Farther still, Greuze and Heine. To the left, Stendhal. Out of sight, Degas.

"Dumas *fils* is there somewhere," Sydney said.

Kaus nodded solemnly. He said, "Do you know Heine? 'Therefore a secret unrest tortured thee, brilliant and bold.' Matthew Arnold on Heine's grave, there." Kaus stood looking over the forest of graves as the snow continued to fall. "Heine here, Marx in London, Mann in California, Rilke and Nietzsche wanderers all their lives. What the devil was Thomas Mann looking for in California?"

"The devil," Sydney said.

"Even Fontane went to London."

"Goethe stayed home, except for the Italian journey."

"Wagner lived in Paris."

"An easy city," Sydney said. "As we have cause to know."

"It is not an easy city," Kaus said.

"Why are you here then?"

"It was convenient," Kaus said. He turned from the cemetery and began to walk again. "The point is, the great unrest leads Germans out of Germany, but it does not lead other Europeans to Germany. No one goes to Germany."

"The American Thomas Wolfe did."

"Not for long," Kaus said. "He was interested in the fascists for a while, and then he left. Even the moderns, the Czechs, the Romanians, the Poles and the Hungarians, when they escape their homelands they go to New York or Boston or Berkeley or here.

They don't go to Stuttgart or Frankfurt or Heidelberg. They don't even go to Berlin. They go to Toronto, even. You would think Germany would be exciting for them, the pressure of it, the egotism. Its neurosis. But they prefer Berkeley or Toronto. Probably they were tired of pressure, egotism, and neurosis. No doubt of it."

"Chekhov died in Germany."

"Poor Chekhov," Kaus said.

They were waiting now at the light, Place Clichy just ahead.

"Watch out, Josef!"

A sedan turned sharply, skidding on the snow, bumping the curb where they stood. Kaus thumped its roof, then stared belligerently as the sedan slowed and came to a stop. A young man alighted and yelled something. Kaus and Sydney did not move for a moment. The young man was slight, half Kaus's size. Kaus told him to learn to drive. Have your mother teach you, he said. The young man screamed an oath, then got back in his car and shot away up the side street, tires squealing.

"Idiot," Kaus said. But he was smiling.

The light changed and they crossed the street into Place Clichy—Place Cliché, as everyone called it, noisy with behemoth tour buses from Antwerp and Hamburg and Madrid and Milan, all surging into the boulevard leading to riotous Place Pigalle, the lumpenproletariat of Europe (in Junko Poole's antique phrase) eager to verify what they had read and heard about dissolute French voluptuaries, high-born teenagers in garter belts and pink berets who whiled away the longueurs of Paris afternoons dreaming of the opportunity to fellate a manure salesman from Cuenca or a postman from Bremerhaven. The tricks they knew! Their enthusiasm! Oh, Paco! Oh, Fritz! So the adventurers in the tour buses lounged sleepily in the deep seats, affecting a bored air as they inspected the sidewalks for countesses.

"As you see," Kaus said. "It is not an easy city."

There was an organ grinder with a baboon on a leash. Sidewalk vendors hawked books, hookahs, beads, belts, copper ornaments, and contraband wristwatches. Blue-aproned *écaillers* patiently stood guard over their slatted baskets of oysters, mussels, and langoustines, the shellfish flanked by bright yellow pyramids of lemons. Sydney smelled the fish as they walked by, the odor competing with roasting chestnuts and diesel exhaust. Entertained by a mime in greasepaint and a derby on his head, a long line of young people waited for the cinema doors to open, an American war story in Version Française. Sydney nudged Kaus, drawing his attention to the poster: American boys brutalized by the Vietnam War. A snarling teenage Marine held a bayonet at a child's throat.

"It was a hard war for them," Sydney said.

Kaus smiled grimly, and did not reply. The restaurants were still open at midafternoon, and when Sydney suggested they stop for a plate of oysters and a glass of wine, Kaus shook his head. Patience, he said, plowing on, seemingly oblivious of the life around them, though he glanced occasionally over his shoulder as if he suspected that they were being followed. Kaus walked with the rolling gait of an outdoorsman; and when he turned to stare at a boy and girl kissing in a doorway, Sydney was reminded of old Hoerli on his weekend walk in the Prussian countryside. Kaus was silent, lost in his thoughts, his long strides keeping him ahead of Sydney, who wondered again where they were going and why he needed a coat and tie to go there. The sight of the oysters had made him hungry. The snow fell more thickly, fat flakes rearranging the familiar look of things; snow was rare in Paris, and when it occurred the city changed personality, diminishing, closing in on itself, its vistas vanishing, hushed. Sydney smiled happily, thinking of oysters, watching Herr Kaus's broad back as he maneuvered around the pedestrians, the sidewalk vendors, the *écaillers*, and of course the frozen tourists with their maps and guidebooks.

And suddenly they were free of Place Clichy, turning now into Boulevard Batignolles. The tour buses disappeared. Restaurants gave way to plain cafés. The sidewalks were empty of *écaillers* and shellfish. The crowds thinned. Kaus quickened his pace; Sydney could hear his labored breathing. They crossed the railroad bridge and a few moments later turned right; this was an unfamiliar quarter, a tree-lined street of private houses and apartment buildings, uniformly formal and eight stories high, solidly bourgeois. It had the aspect of a comfortable residential neighborhood in a provincial city, perhaps Rouen. A curtain moved and it was easy to imagine Emma Bovary in her sitting room, staring into the snowy street, anticipating her impossible doctor. She was listening to the beat of her own heart, and how faint it seemed, how far away; and when she saw the doctor she would turn her head, looking at her hands in her lap, wondering what it was that had brought her to that point —

Ahead of them a man walked his dog, the dog straining at the leash, baffled by the snow. There was no traffic and no sound except for a Schubert quartet issuing from an open window somewhere high above, the notes mingling with the falling snow and muted by it. Then Josef Kaus was stamping his feet, standing before a heavy door, pushing a button, taking off his hat, standing aside to let Sydney precede him as the door swung open and they were admitted.

The foyer was dark, but someone was there to take their coats and lead the way up the staircase. A heavy carpet muffled their steps, but the house was quiet in any case. Sydney heard a low murmur of men's voices, but then they entered an empty paneled room furnished with leather chairs and couches, the walls heavy with portraits of nineteenth-century gentlemen, all whiskers and glower. A waiter came to take their order. Alas, there were no oysters. They ordered sandwiches, whiskey for Kaus and beer for Sydney.

"This is where I come in the afternoon," Kaus said. He gestured at the portraits and smiled. They were someone's idea of a joke. Number Eighty-nine was not a gentlemen's club, though gentlemen were not specifically excluded. It had no name, known always as Number Eighty-nine, its street address. In former times it was known as the Red Club, but no one called it that anymore and the name had nothing to do with politics. It had to do with gambling. A member had once made thirteen straight winners betting red at roulette. The odds against such a coup were astronomical and there were suspicions, often voiced but never proved, that the wheel was fixed. Probably it had been; some of the members had strange antecedents and useful skills. Some had been deprived of passports and had been obliged to arrange nationalities of convenience. Egypt and Lebanon were popular. Several had been in jail at one time or another, for this offense or that, though they were mostly innocent; at least they were innocent of the offenses they were charged with. Number Eighty-nine was a place where a man could go for a drink or a game and not have to submit to questioning. No member was under fifty. All debts were settled at the table. Occasionally there were women in residence, women of the gamier sort, but cheerful mostly. A majority of the members were foreign-born, but there were a few token French and one or two Americans. It always helped to have French members in case there was an irregularity or a police matter. As for the Americans, it was impossible to have a club without them. They loved clubs and they knew everyone. It was impossible to think of the American members as foreign-born, since they seemed to live everywhere as easily as they lived in America. So there were half a dozen Americans, interesting men for the most part.

"I work in the morning and come here in the afternoon," Kaus said.

The waiter served the sandwiches, and Kaus's whiskey and Sydney's beer.

They began to eat, Kaus with the concentration of a scientist at his microscope. He sipped his whiskey between bites, and he was fastidious about crumbs. In his ponderousness he gave the impression of an idling turbine. Sydney took in the room, its worn leather chairs and couches and low tables piled with books and magazines. It seemed a strange sort of club for Josef Kaus. Sydney wondered about the gamy women. Was there a rule governing them, too, no woman over thirty or under fifteen? Was there a passport check at the door? He had always imagined Kaus living a monastic life, innocent of ex-convicts and Americans.

Kaus looked up after a moment and said. "A friend of yours is a member. LeMessurier Sebastian Poole."

Sydney laughed. "He would be."

"He is a popular member," Kaus said. "They say he is a spy. Is this true?"

"I suppose so," Sydney said. "I think he was at one time."

"It is not such a big thing. Most of the men here have lived the secret life on occasion. It was often necessary for survival. Someone asked you to do something and you did it. Sometimes you did it happily, sometimes not. Mostly not because it interfered with other things, you understand? LeMessurier Poole has been helpful to people here also."

"No doubt," Sydney said.

"And he was talking about you one night. I listened but said nothing. He was praising your work and your personality, your skill, your reliability, your tact."

"Tact?"

"His very word," Kaus said. "This Poole is a puzzle to me. I think he is not a reader."

"Not novels, anyway."

"Just so. He was praising your translations. Since he is not a reader, why would he know of your translations?"

"We've been friends for a long time," Sydney said.

"I thought perhaps you had done spy work for him."

"Would it make any difference if I had?"

Kaus cocked his head, thinking, pushing his plate to one side, turning to look out the window. The great somnolence of the room suggested the twilight of the last century, a club perhaps in Vienna or Prague, where men of leisure gathered in the afternoon to speak of worldly things, money, politics, sex, or art. There would be billiards and cigars and a glass of something, and at least one of the men would have a mustache, as Kaus did; and another would feel a little bit out of place, like Sydney. The room was dark because it was snowing harder than ever, the snow collecting in the window mullions. In the leather chair by the window an elderly man was dozing, his chin on his chest. Sydney had not noticed him before. The dozing man made no sound, was perfectly still, his arms hanging straight down by the side of the chair; he might have been dead. Somewhere in the room a clock ticked.

Kaus said, "One must live as best one can. But one has one's work, the work that is important. It makes a difference not because it is spy work but because it is other work. Other work is not important. It is a distraction." He pulled at his lower lip, then took a sip of whiskey. "Still, there are norms. I never did spy work though I had the opportunity, many times. In Europe after the war it was an industry, informing. It was a métier, like automobiles or chemicals or farming. You would be too young to know this, how things were. I was able to avoid them by being unreliable, and I had no tact. I was afraid of them. The spy people, one never knows about them with accuracy, who they are, what they do, who they do it for, and why."

"The why is plain enough," Sydney said.

"Yes?"

"They do it for money."

"Not always." Kaus smiled. "He comes here, most afternoons.

He is an excellent card player, your Poole. Bold, decisive, and a poor loser."

"Does he lose often?"

Josef Kaus shrugged his shoulders. "About as often as he wins."

"And you?"

"The reverse." He turned again in the direction of the window, and the elderly man dozing in the leather chair. The light was so pale it seemed to have no color at all. Kaus lowered his voice. "You see my friend in the chair, sleeping or pretending to sleep. A great pedagogue, and a raconteur. I have known him for many years, since before the war. We were boys together in Prussia. He is the one with the weak chin, though you cannot see his chin now. Take my word for it." Kaus's friend seemed to stir, but that may have been an illusion. "We take a glass together and talk about Berlin before the war, before the National Socialists, before the Americans. In the old days, Herr G.H. knew everyone, the writers, the painters, and the cinéastes. We had wonderful times together and some not so wonderful times." Kaus sighed and raised his eyebrows. Sydney moved closer to him, listening carefully. Weimar elegies were irresistible. But that seemed to be the end of it, for Kaus said no more.

"My mother had wonderful stories of Berlin before the war."

Kaus nodded.

"She and my father went there frequently. My father was an army officer." Kaus said nothing to that and Sydney asked, "Have you been back lately?"

"I have not been in Berlin in forty years." He said, "This is my world now, this Number Eighty-nine. When I want to go to Berlin I talk to my friend. We talk the old slang, the slang of sixty years ago. He has a phenomenal memory. Sometimes I go back to my apartment and write down what he said. Many of the words don't exist anymore. So I invent the spellings."

Kaus took a sip of whiskey.

"My life is here and at my apartment, so we won't talk about Berlin anymore."

Sydney said, "Then I want to ask you about Hoerli."

"What about Hoerli?"

"I am having difficulty with a passage. It's a passage that seems to me in twilight and I cannot bring it out the way I would like. I am obviously trying to freely translate, to give it your depth of field, using very simple English. But it eludes me. This is the passage when young Hoerli is at table with his parents and his mother leaves suddenly, turning out the light as she goes. She utters a little cry and then leaves the table without explanation. The boy and his father remain but say nothing, until the father attempts an explanation of sorts. Young Hoerli listens attentively but is not convinced."

Kaus said, "Yes."

"Can you explain her distress?"

Kaus thought a moment, staring at his glass. At last he said, "No."

"Can't explain or won't explain."

"It's clear in the text."

"It reminds me of an incident —"

"It is its own incident, and no other."

"Yes, of course."

"It's clear on the page."

"It isn't clear to me," Sydney said.

"Then it won't be clear to the reader."

Sydney listened to the clock tick, and tried again. "Perhaps you mean to leave it mysterious, a postmodern solution. Though this does not sound like you, or me either. Do you mean to present an inexplicable event, an event with no immediate cause, symmetrical only in its enigma? Perhaps it is a cry of anguish or of rage, a sudden need to escape. There are many such moments in a woman's life."

"Not only a woman's," Kaus said. "And rage and anguish are different things. And perhaps it is joy."

Sydney pressed on. "So she would have a need to escape her house, which has come to seem like a prison to her, with a prison's routine. She sits under the head of a dead animal, her husband under the portrait of our megalomaniacal Kaiser —"

"*Not* like a prison. Not like a *prison.* A roulette wheel, Sydney. She is the wheel, the universe itself." He was talking quickly now, in a brusque whisper. "All the numbers are hers. She is spun and the ivory ball is cast, by a person or persons unknown. It spins around the sides of the wheel. The wheel's speed diminishes. The ball loses its centrifugal force and its velocity deteriorates, like a dead star falling out of orbit. Exhausted, it settles on a number. Five, fourteen, twenty-three, thirty-two. And someone wins. And the wheel is spun again and again, the ball spins, falls, and someone wins. Or loses, if no bets have been placed. Frequently the case."

"Her dreadful husband," Sydney said.

"He is not dreadful," Kaus said loudly.

"A cold man," Sydney said. "Cold to his wife, distant with his son. His son is bullied at school, and he cannot utter a single word of sympathy. He cannot listen, even. He will not discuss it. A petty tyrant. Silence seems to be his only virtue and obedience his only reward. Except one day his wife is no longer obedient. She utters a little cry, and leaves the table, packs her bags, and escapes."

"Cold, yes. Distant, certainly." There was a sudden ripple of laughter from the adjoining room, the laughter muffled behind closed doors. Kaus glowered at the door and waited for the laughter to subside, as presently it did. "He desires order," Kaus said quietly. "That is what he wants from his life, it is his own freedom, a heavy meal at midday and a glass of pilsener, his son dutiful at his schoolwork, his wife happy in her house. The outside world is endured, not conquered. In his work he is a bureaucrat, one of an army of bureaucrats, some below, many more above. He believes in government. He is not God, he is an ordinary man. Such a man would not want to look at the heavens and see stars falling from their orbits. This would be a terrible confirmation of all his deepest suspicions. It would be a catastrophe, and so he averts his eyes, feigning complacency. He lives in a stable world of dreams and myths. This is a feature of the German personality. You would not necessarily call him great, or even good, in the Christian sense. He is not charitable. His faith, such as it is, does not arise from hope but from despair. But he is not dreadful, either. And there are more like him than you would think, even now, in these modern times."

"He is afraid," Sydney said.

"That is correct."

"Every day."

"And night," Kaus said with a wintry smile.

"And his wife isn't."

Kaus did not answer and for a moment Sydney thought the conversation was ended, or anyway suspended. Kaus was looking at his whiskey glass, empty now. At last he said, "Perhaps his wife has more imagination. Perhaps her routines have given her this capacity, which she conceals as a matter of course. It is unhealthy. She is frequently in a bad humor because she lives within herself, in her own underworld which she can neither pacify nor explain. There are accumulations of things in a life, small things and large, in bed or at the dinner table or staring out the window at the snow, dusting a mantel or signing an official document. Something causes terror. A human being is blinded in that instant, as stars fall out of orbit. It is a mistake to believe that there is always a visible cause to these events, some injustice or iniquity, an insult of society or of history. There almost never is. There are always certain conditions of politics or economics or weather or illness or genes, but these are only natural conditions and cannot be rectified. Only the benumbed and neurotic Americans believe otherwise, or assume that there is anything to choose between old Hoerli and his wife. Old Hoerli has his 'strict exactitude' because he is afraid. His wife leaves because she can no longer be exact. They are good people, Herr van Damm, and they are deserving of our sympathy."

Sydney was listening carefully. Kaus's voice had fallen to a whisper, and then stopped as if there were no more to be said about the matter.

"And the boy," Sydney said. Yes, tell me about the boy.

"The boy is theirs, never forget that for an instant."

It is not likely that I would do that, Herr Kaus, Sydney thought but did not say. "And the boy loves his father."

"A temporary condition. The novel is about the *boy*, conspicuous through no fault of his own."

"Who became a bad-tempered man. A recluse." But he became a *man*, who walked with his own two feet upon the earth, who spoke in sentences, whose life as a recluse was by rational choice, who *lived*, authentic and substantial. Sydney looked at his hands, which were trembling. He moved to collect himself. He said, "LeMessurier Poole has an aphorism."

"Does he?"

"LeMessurier Poole says that in all of life the odds are six to five against."

"Very clever," Kaus said.

"It isn't original with him."

"Perhaps not," Kaus said. "It sounds like him, though. It sounds like something he'd say, but not believe."

"He believes it, all right," Sydney said. "But it doesn't seem to apply to him. Junko goes from success to success."

"Junko?" Kaus leaned forward, a smile softening his heavy features.

Sydney turned away, dismayed and amused. It was what happened when you forgot who you were talking to, when you were concentrating on what the other man was saying and neglected to watch your own tongue. "His nom de guerre," Sydney said.

"Junko," Kaus said, rolling the word around in his mouth.

"It's what they call him," Sydney said.

"And in his war he has gone from success to success?"

"Effortlessly," Sydney said.

"And does he often steal things?"

Sydney thought a moment. "Not often."

"He should be careful," Kaus said. "You go to prison for it, you know. In many countries it's a capital offense or, worse, life imprisonment." He turned to look at the man in the chair, and when next he spoke his voice was soft, almost a whisper. "I can't imagine anything worse than life imprisonment. It's impossible to write in prison. You'd think it would be easy, all that time on your hands and no distractions, no bills to pay, you can't meet a friend for lunch or stay up all night drinking, but it isn't easy, it's impossible. You lose touch with your normal surroundings and with yourself. You are bound by unfamiliar regulations, and living in intimate circumstances with men you would normally avoid. You learn something from it, of course, but it's not knowledge you can use. It's like learning to tie a shoelace when you have no shoes. Often they don't allow pens or paper, so you try to write in your head and that goes for a while, a day maybe, or a week. Then one morning you wake up and your mind's a blank. You can't remember what you were writing and come to believe it was only a figment of your imagination. This is an irony that does not go unappreciated. But you have been writing your entire life and can't imagine how to live without it, and yet you can't do it, in your mind or on paper, either one. What you know is the routine and certain important dates in the future: when you will be given mail or allowed a visit from your wife. These are always at their whim. Your body lacks the necessary vitamins so you are subject to illness, colds and arthritis, and God forbid you should have bad teeth or hemorrhoids. You are self-absorbed to a degree, irascible and unquiet, and you would think that would result in some new insight. But it doesn't. You are imprisoned for a reason and you try to hold on to that. The reason, whatever it was, is the cause of your confinement. You have been identified as a malcontent or a subversive, an enemy of society; soon you lose track of whatever it was that outraged the authorities so, that caused them to ransack your apartment in the early hours of the morning and take you away in your night clothes, leaving your new wife bereft, hysterical with fear. It must have been important, your offense, otherwise you would not be sitting in a cell in the frightful prison near the border; officially, this prison does not exist but everyone knows its name. The other prisoners treat you with respect; or some of them do. The others avoid you or make sarcastic remarks. So perhaps in your former life you were controversial, meritorious in some way, a patriot, possibly heroic; and you try to cling to that as a form of identity. Your former life is a kind of fiction, a dream. Your lawyers make various subtle appeals and by studying the appeals you remember a little of who you were and what you had done to insult the regime, to force the arrest, the hearing, the trial, and the sentence. Then you cease to have any interest in it, you are unable to concentrate. The past seems lost forever, and good riddance. You ignore the calendar. You become apathetic. You are resigned. Your life consists of the present day only. The curtain falls: you sleep, you work, you eat, finding a kind of security in queueing to receive the bland evening meal. It is March of the year, cold outside, cold within. Your joints ache, your stomach is upset. You are standing in line, a guard approaches and jostles your arm; the tray falls. You stoop to pick it up and the guard says something, and kicks you in the ass. At that moment, that instant, you discover the depths of your fate. You sprawl on the cold floor, the guard laughing, the other prisoners silent. You feel a hundred years old, and wonder if it would be possible to remain forever on the cold floor. A voice within says, Rise! This is your own voice, so long suppressed that you do not recognize it. But you obey that voice, as you have obeyed other voices, obedience now a virtue — and discover that you have a life after all. You are capable of feeling pain, and shame. The snot on your upper lip, the lice in your hair, the ulcer in your stomach, the cavity in your molar; all these are human things. And it has nothing to do with *them.* It has to do with you. You decide at that moment to live inside yourself, where they are not welcome and cannot go. They can occupy your body but they cannot occupy your complete mind; some part of it will always be yours. The pain and shame, that is yours. This is your new insight, arrived at last; it has taken years, and can be expressed in a single sentence. You are you and not them. And if the prison does not exist officially, they do not exist officially either. This is what you have discovered after the kick in the ass, and the discovery leads to a new strategy, one that will in time restore the balance of your mind. You decide at that moment not to speak, except for those few words that are required by regulation. You will cause yourself to fade away. You will pass out of the picture. You will look upon yourself as a planet in its own orbit, beyond the reach of their eyesight. You concede that they are the universe — but merely the universe, of which you are an insignificant part, a speck of dust, an ass to be kicked. Their universe is usually hostile, sometimes benign, always in charge. You must remain in your own orbit. If you remain in your own orbit, you will not come to harm. You must avoid friction. Friction will burn you up, like a comet falling from the heavens. In that way you may survive, will survive if you use the force of your entire being, your imagination and your ability to live within, a kind of social invalid. You live in that way, and there is no other way. You do not win because this is not a game and in the finest sense everyone has lost; but you live, and that is no small thing. Yet it is impossible to write, understand that. Even a diary is an impossible thing."

"Josef," Sydney said. Kaus had begun to tremble.

"It will pass," he said.

"I'm sorry. I had no idea you had been in prison, though as I think about it, I should have guessed."

"It is a part of the day," he said. "Like a siesta."

"A European life," Sydney said.

"Yes," Kaus said. "Let us hope that our Junko is careful as he goes about his business here and there, though as an American Junko may be exempt. The normal rules may not apply to him, owing to his nationality. The Americans have been able to avoid much that is frightful, lucky them. They are an old country, older than they know. Is he a careful man?"

Sydney smiled. "Very."

"He calculates the odds?"

"Always."

"It's a way to pass the time and get through the day, cards or roulette. Roulette has a particular appeal, though it is insidious." Kaus looked around him, then laughed sharply. "Well! All of life is six to five against, and yet he succeeds. So we must have sympathy and understanding for him also, lucky lucky LeMessurier Poole. Good for him. Junko. What a name!"

"He earned it," Sydney said.

"And you work for him."

"Not very much anymore," Sydney said. "It was piecework. It paid the rent, barely."

Kaus nodded doubtfully, rising heavily, brushing the breadcrumbs from his vest. Their visit was evidently concluded, and Sydney rose also, surprised again at the other man's size. "It has been a pleasure talking with you," Kaus said. "All these years we have been affiliated, yet we have known each other only through our work, sentences on paper. German words, English words. It's a strange business that we do. I see you are a serious man, but I always knew that, it was apparent from your translations, your care and selectivity, your refusal to hurry, your tact. I wish you well, Sydney. I am happy we have met at last. I thought it was time, the situation being what it is, Europe redrawing its boundaries. We will all be part of the past very soon. And I hope you do not think that this afternoon I have explained too much."

Sydney smiled and said he didn't.

"You are a good listener."

"It wasn't difficult," Sydney said.

"We can meet again sometime."

"Yes," Sydney said. "Of course." But he doubted it. He doubted he would ever see Josef Kaus again.

"It is an unusual life you have, translating the thoughts of others."

"Unusual is not the word," Sydney said.

"Avoid friction," Kaus said with an incongruous wink. "Avoid Americans."

"My wife is one," Sydney said.

"Yes," Kaus said. "I forgot. Someone told me that. Perhaps it was LeMessurier Poole. Our American friend." He looked at his wristwatch. "And now I must leave you for my own afternoon's activity." There was no need to ask what that was. Kaus did a little pantomime of a wheel turning. They shook hands, Kaus smiling, saying something about the bland lunch, apologizing for the absence of oysters, for his own loquacity and self-centeredness; he was old, that was the excuse. At least the beer was cold and the room warm. In the leather chair by the window the elderly man stirred, moving his arms, then flexing his fingers like a pianist. In the hard winter light his corner of the room had a pre-industrial look, as if Franz Joseph were waiting in the wings. The elderly man seemed unaware of their presence, absorbed as he was with his hands. With his dark suit and long white hair, he resembled the august figures in the somber portraits along the wall. His shape as he stood was as round and symmetrical as a Russian doll.

"One of our players," Kaus said. "We were, in a manner of speaking, colleagues. Inside, many years ago." All this was said in an undertone. Kaus nodded at the elderly man, who had turned to look at them, nodding gravely, adjusting his tie, shooting his cuffs, smoothing his hair with the palms of both hands. He said, "How are you, Josef? Who's your friend?"

"Sydney van Damm," Kaus said. "My translator."

"My sympathies," the elderly man said to Sydney.

"This is G.H.," Kaus said. "A jokester."

"Herr Kaus believes in a child's history of the world," G.H. said.

Sydney laughed dutifully, wondering what the initials stood for. They were probably invented on the spot, a run of the alphabet like E.F. or I.J.

"We shared a cell, once upon a time," G.H. said. "It was a trial." Then, to Kaus: "Is he playing?"

"No," Kaus said.

"Our American friend is banker today. It would be a good time for your translator to watch the struggle, you and the American." He rolled his eyes. "Too bad, perhaps some other time."

"Sydney is acquainted with our American friend."

"Is that so?" The elderly man's foxy eyes narrowed in appraisal, but his expression did not change. "He has had an amazing run of luck, our American friend. It's been very impressive, I've never seen anything like it, he can't seem to lose, he goes from success to success."

"Effortlessly, I imagine," Sydney said. "He's very clever."

"Is that it? I was wondering what it was." The elderly man nodded gravely. "So it's cleverness."

"He has good nerves also," Sydney said.

"And good nerves! What a lucky American he is."

"What's the game today?" Sydney asked. "At which he is the banker."

"Roulette," Kaus replied.

"A child's game," the elderly man said.

"The game of kings," Sydney said.

"No, not the game of kings. Baccarat is the game of kings. Roulette is the game of children. Herr Kaus likes it. And the American likes it. I detest it."

"If he's the banker, it means he does not have to win. He's depending on you to lose. All he does is spin the wheel and drop the ball and wait for you to lose."

"That's correct, Mr. Translator. That's all he has to do."

"Shall we go?" Kaus said.

"On the other hand, banker's taking the gamble. Banker's the one with the investment. It's banker's risk."

The elderly man was silent a moment, his animosity apparent. "Are you translating one of Josef's little books now, Herr van Damm?"

"A novel, yes," Sydney said.

"Difficult, I imagine."

"As with any work of art," Sydney said.

"Is that what you call it?"

"That's what I call it, Herr G.H."

"A work of art has consequence, does it not?"

"Usually," Sydney said.

"Yet, you remember what the queer Englishman said. No poem ever saved a single Jew from the ovens."

"No poem ever put one there, either."

"Wrong again, I'm afraid. A poem sent Mandelstam to the Gulag, on Stalin's personal order."

"I thought we were talking about Germans."

"You did? Whatever gave you that idea, Herr van Damm?"

"'Jew to the ovens.' That's normally a reference to the fascists. It is in my experience, perhaps not in yours."

"That is because your experience is much shorter than mine." He snapped his fingers. "Like that, your experience."

"Gentlemen," Kaus said wearily.

"And what is your profession, Herr G.H.? Your long experience would surely entitle you to one."

"I am a cosmopolitan," the elderly man said. "Can't you tell?"

"I would say government functionary," Sydney said.

"Then you would be wrong."

"If it's not a secret," Sydney said. He moved closer to the elderly man, who had shot a malevolent glance at Kaus. "I'm curious, Mr. G.H. What do the initials stand for?"

"Sydney," Kaus began.

"Your translator has become tiresome," the elderly man said.

"My apologies," Sydney said.

"Not accepted," the elderly man said, gave a curt little bow to Kaus, and stalked from the room.

"Sorry, Josef," Sydney said. "I hope you weren't embarrassed."

Kaus laughed sourly. "It takes more than that."

"Once begun, it's hard to put an end to."

"He has a difficult personality. We all know this. But he has had a difficult time, so we make allowances."

"Even so," Sydney said. "He was insulting."

"He is not himself. Or, rather, he is very much himself. He is what he has become, but he was not always that. As a young man he was always gay, a great companion. He is my oldest friend. He has lost his faith. It does not matter a great deal, what he says about me or about my work. My work is almost over. It is not up to me anymore. You were good to defend it in the way that you did, but. He does not believe in art any more than he believes in man or in God." Kaus gave a sudden toss of his head and for a moment looked years younger, boyish almost, a young man about town anticipating a careless afternoon.

They walked out of the paneled room with its portraits and

noisy clocks into the corridor. The great staircase was empty, the hallway gloomy in half light. The chandelier in the stairwell was dark, in silhouette like a daytime moon. The only light came from the leaded glass windows. Outside it was still snowing. The elderly man was stepping through the double doors leading to the salon, where there were two men seated at the rectangular table, the wheel at one end and the betting grid, the numbers, the colors, the odds and the evens, at the other. A bright overhead light gave the room and its mahogany wheel and green baize field the aspect of an Arcadian stage set, perhaps war room. The two men looked up as Herr G.H. took one of the empty chairs, the one opposite Junko Poole, who was standing behind the wheel idly walking a blue chip on his knuckles. Each man had an ashtray and a glass. A bottle of Champagne rested in a black bucket on a side table. There was a single empty chair, Josef Kaus's. All the men were dressed in dark business suits, as if they were attending a directors' meeting or other commercial affair. They were silent and composed, waiting for play to begin. Junko began to collect the chips into little piles and slide them across the green baize, the players' stakes.

"I will leave you now," Kaus said.

"What do the initials stand for, Josef?"

"Ah, Sydney," Kaus said.

"Bogus, I suppose. Like the rest of him."

Kaus looked up, glaring, tugging on one of his heavy earlobes, turning now to stand with his back to the double doors so that Sydney could not see into the field of play. "There is nothing bogus about Felix. Bogus is the last word you would use. If his life had been the least bogus he would be content, but it wasn't. It isn't now." Kaus drew back, wheezing. His breath came in a whistle. "He was in America for some time. He has a daughter living there, I believe, and a son. His wife has been dead for many years, the usual story. Felix was a mathematician by training, though not by temperament; of course that was before the war. In America he made his living as a professional gambler. He played cards. In America they gave him — I suppose you would call it a nom de guerre. G.H. stands for Golden Hands. He called himself Felix DaMurr and became known as Felix 'Golden Hands' DaMurr, and I gather this was not altogether respectful, or complimentary. There was trouble, and Felix dropped out of sight. There was a dispute of some kind and he was obliged to return to Europe. For a while he lived with me, then he found his own place. That's all. Why are you laughing?"

"Golden Hands?"

"It's expressive. He doesn't care for the name. I forgot for a moment and called him G.H., which I do when we are alone. He had quite a time of it, across the ocean. He never should have gone to America, but at the time he had no choice."

"This 'dispute of some kind —'"

"I believe it was in Chicago."

"Why is it so difficult for me to imagine Herr G.H. in Chicago?"

"I don't know," Kaus said. "But there is nothing about him that is bogus."

"An unfortunate choice of words," Sydney said. "I didn't understand."

"He shouldn't play roulette, though."

"Not his game?"

"It seems not to be. He meant what he said when he called it a child's game. But he's drawn to it. Often, gambling, a man is drawn to the wrong game, the game that least suits him."

Sydney said, "Does Junko know about 'Golden Hands'?"

A pained look crossed Kaus's face, then vanished. He waited a moment, then replied, "Yes, Sydney. I think he does."

"Junko shortens the odds any way he can."

"And Felix knows about Mr. Poole. And so do I."

"Good luck this afternoon," Sydney said.

"It's only a friendly turn of the wheel," Kaus said without conviction. "But thank you."

"I'll remember what you said about Hoerli."

"Good-bye, Sydney."

They shook hands again and Kaus walked away, moving heavily, with the gait of a sick old man. It had happened in an hour. Sydney retreated into the shadows, looking now through the double doors, and Kaus stepped inside. Junko Poole stood at attention behind the wheel, arms folded, prepared now to set his universe in motion. Kaus took his seat, saying something, no doubt an apology for delaying play. Twenty-five feet away, Sydney felt the seduction of the moment, its intrigue at once expectant and irresolute, taut as a heartbeat. He had not played roulette in years, and had once promised himself never to play again. It held an infinite fascination and poignance, its combination of chance and probability at the wheel, and the nerve of the players facing it, the necessity of throwing good money after bad, an iron fatalism that is the temperament of the genuine romantic. And always the bitter possibility that the wheel was fixed, doctored in some way by the house, which owned the wheel and the ivory ball, the chips and the numbers, and the clock itself, *time*. To succeed in such an atmosphere was a kind of miracle.

The players' backs were to him, Herr Kaus's bent head, Felix's motionless egg-shaped body, the other two in obscure attitudes, now abruptly bending over the green baize, placing their chips here and there, brusquely or shyly, depending on the character of the man. Junko watched each player's hands as they slid over the numbers, depositing chips. The inactive wheel in front of him was as conspicuous as a stopped clock. There was a tremendous concentration in the puddle of bright light, and then with a twist of his little finger Junko sent the wheel spinning. Play had begun, and with a second motion, as deft and fluid as a fish dashing for a lure, he sent the ivory ball rolling into orbit.

Sydney stepped out of the shadows. Junko looked directly at him with no recognition; at least his expression did not change as he raised his glass of Champagne and saluted the wheel, the wheel's health, good cheer and prosperity, its neutrality — a toast to God, as it were. The only sound in the room was the rasp of the ball circumnavigating the wheel. In the few seconds before it fell, Felix leaned forward and placed his bet, three blue chips on a single number, then with a gesture of indifference withdrew his fingers at the exact moment the ball fell, bouncing, clicking into its slot, Junko murmuring, *Rien ne va plus*.

"*Les jeux sont faits, monsieurs*," Junko said. "Surf's up."

But there were no winners and Josef Kaus had not bet at all, preferring to observe the turn of the wheel.

Junko collected the dead chips. Without looking up, he said softly, "Join us, Sydney. This is a friendly game. Take a chair."

Felix said something Sydney could not hear.

"His credit is good," Junko said.

"With whom?" Felix demanded.

"With me," Junko said.

Sydney stepped through the doorway, feeling the heat of the game the moment he walked into the room. The third player shook hands, mumbling a name that Sydney did not catch and was not meant to catch. The fourth player only nodded. The room fell silent, waiting for Junko. There was a chandelier overhead and heavy curtains concealing the windows. Bookshelves lined the walls, but the only pieces of furniture were the wheel, the betting table, and four chairs. There was a world all its own and the center of gravity was the wheel. Each man had willingly surrendered himself to the wheel. In the courtly atmosphere it was as if they were attending an absolute monarch, a sovereign of the sort the world had not seen since Charlemagne. The wheel was a way of surrendering your independence, and Sydney despised it even as he was drawn to it. No man was ever less a gambler than when betting the wheel, standing before it with the obedient and tremulous assurance of a besotted religious.

Sydney walked up to the table and stopped.

Junko pushed a little pile of chips across the green baize.

"Some other time," Sydney said, stepping back.

Herr Kaus and Felix DaMurr turned in their chairs, looking at him with astonishment.

Sydney said, "I'm a poor gambler."

Junko Poole raised his eyebrows and let them fall. "Do join us, Sydney. It's only a friendly game."

"Not friendly," Felix DaMurr said. "Not a game." He and Herr Kaus turned back to the table as Junko, sighing, prepared to turn the wheel. The men were entirely focused now, and Sydney, released, left the room.

Two

SYDNEY AGREED to meet Junko at La Moelle, a restaurant in the rue de Lille, five tables upstairs and ten down. The waiters were all old men and the proprietor was very old, a devotee of the opera and of literature. La Moelle was a favorite of writers and musicians, and M. Marneffe a source of quality gossip. He was particularly good on literary prizes, the Prix Goncourt and the Prix Fémina, and reliable also on sexual intrigue backstage at the opera. This knowledge was valuable when he was seating his customers upstairs and down.

The food was good but not remarkable at La Moelle and the wine list excellent and very expensive, except for the Brouilly in carafe. The patrons liked the restaurant for its privacy, and for M. Marneffe, who in his huge girth and ribald conversation seemed a character from Balzac or Zola. He was always at the door to greet his customers; the sight of him inspired appetite. You could remain at table as long as you liked, and in that way La Moelle was a kind of club. M. Marneffe forgave Sydney his German nationality and had his own agreeable suspicions about Junko, who did him obscure favors from time to time. And no conscientious Frenchman could ignore the crimson stripe in the American's lapel. Junko Poole was a chevalier of the Legion of Honor. One way or another he had done the state some service.

The *New York Times* correspondent had discovered La Moelle in the early sixties. He passed it along to the press attaché at OECD and the press attaché to a French banker and the banker to

LeMessurier Sebastian Poole, whom M. Marneffe believed to be the permanent deputy of the CIA station in Paris. And M. Marneffe was not alone in this belief. Junko had been around for years, was beautifully tailored, spoke French with an immaculate North Shore accent, and otherwise conformed to the stereotype of the well-born American spy, well fed, well traveled, well connected, handy with his fists, and rich. He had no visible means of support. Junko was attractively vague about his work, often describing his firm as Downtown. Downtown wants this, Downtown says that. Downtown, damn fools who don't know their ass from third base, but let's do what they want, just this once, and we'll pick up the pieces later. He was thought to deal in various commodities, oil, precious metals, uranium, and wheat, and often in manufactured goods, specialized computing equipment, communications gear, and vessels of Third World registry. He bought, sold, traded, bartered, or consulted with those who did.

He was a loyal friend, a man you went to for difficult favors. Useless for anyone to protest that Junko Poole had nothing to do with the Central Intelligence Agency, and in any case there was no "permanent deputy" of the CIA Paris station. It was a fiction. Junko had had nothing to do with the CIA since his salad days in the German-American Foundation and his losing battle with Morris Lord. It was an ingenious cover and unprovable either way. What was the CIA to do, take out an ad like an outraged spouse disclaiming responsibility for debts?

Like accusing someone of being queer, Junko said.

They had finished dinner and were lingering over Calvados and coffee. M. Marneffe had arrived to pour the Calvados himself, beaming because his little restaurant was full and the customers enjoying themselves. All the upstairs tables were filled, the talk loud and punctuated with raucous laughter. They had not talked business. Junko had just finished telling another Henry Green story, how Henry Green had tried to make off with Françoise Fontaine early on New Year's Day, and how Françoise had told him no, she was staying with Junko. She loved Junko even though Junko didn't love her back. She likes a man with a little gray in his hair and a little green in his wallet and some black in his heart, Junko said, looking up and scowling.

"You ever see Gina, Syd?"

"I haven't seen Gina in thirty years."

"I'll be damned," Junko said.

"Why would you ask me that?"

"Because she's sitting over there, the table near the stairs, the women."

Sydney craned his neck. There was a table of hilarious women. They were having a fête of some kind, all of them laughing and talking at once. There were two young women and four women who were middle-aged, and none of them was Gina. Relieved, Sydney turned back to face Junko, shaking his head, mouthing No.

"The one in the pink," Junko said.

Sydney saw the one he meant, a woman in her early fifties, no longer slender, her hair skillfully tinted, falling to her shoulders. He thought she sat rather primly, as if she needed to make an impression. Gina was never prim. She laughed then, a well-used laugh, a laugh the owner was comfortable with. She raised her glass and saluted one of the younger women, and Sydney saw suddenly how pretty she was. She had a lovely smile and a sweet sad look around the eyes; perhaps not so much sad as naked. In bed it would be a look that would stop your heart even as you wondered about it, its origins and what it signified. The woman had a gold band on her left hand and scarab bracelets on both wrists. Her hands were tiny. She was speaking now to the young woman sitting across the table but he could not hear her voice. He remembered Gina's, a soft almost-baritone that could turn caustic and in a second dissolve into a sullen French pout, lower lip leading the way. It was Gina's Bardot look. This woman was big-breasted, which Gina was not; and the primness definitely belonged to someone else. Sydney saw a resemblance, but that was all he saw. In any case, Gina would never find herself at cosmopolitan La Moelle.

Junko said, "Am I right?"

"Looks like her, a little. But it's not her."

"Little Gina," Junko said. "She had the guts of a burglar."

"She knew what she wanted," Sydney said.

"And what she had to do to get what she wanted."

"She went to live in the suburbs somewhere, out near St. Denis, the Red belt. She wanted a bourgeois life, a husband and children, and she didn't see a German getting it for her. I don't know who she married. She told me what he did, but I've forgotten what it was."

"Your harem at the Jardin des Plantes —"

Sydney began to laugh.

"— made me envious as hell. But it worried that son of a bitch Morris Lord."

"Why?"

"He wasn't sure someone wasn't setting you up. We had some funny stuff going on at the Foundation then."

"Nonsense," Sydney said.

"Morris didn't think so. He had Gina and one of those others checked out. I know because I did the checking." Junko Poole sipped Calvados, enjoying the look on Sydney's face. "Gina lived near Père Lachaise and the other one, Christ, I can't remember where. Of course they came back clean. They were just working girls looking for a little fun. And finding it. Maybe Gina found a little too much fun but it worked out all right, thanks to my doctor buttonhook."

"It surprised me, her determination. She had no second thoughts. She never struggled with it. Her family was Catholic, but she knew exactly what she wanted to do."

"*Had* to do, Syd. *Had.* Gina wasn't into martyrdom. One careless afternoon with you ruins her life? No way. She figured she already had one strike against her, who her parents were and where she came from, and saw no reason to take another. Gina wanted to make things easy on herself. She saw her chance with her young man and took it, and God bless her for it. She was a practical young woman and if that's her over there, it looks as if things worked out all right."

"It isn't her," Sydney said.

"As you like. But I admired her. She was tough. She was scared to death walking in there but there were no tears and no whining and when morning came she was out of there, no tearful goodbyes and no thanks, either, except she gave the nightgown back. That was saying thanks in her own way. I hope the guy she married isn't a turd. Let's have another Calvados."

"Sure," Sydney said.

"How's Angie?"

"Max had another episode. It upset her. She thinks the place for Max is somewhere in the country, where he can be around us. Be in the open air. He loves animals, she says. She thinks we're killing him. That's the word she used. She thinks if he gets to the country, he won't die."

"Maybe she's right," Junko said carefully.

"Maybe she is," Sydney said. "Life isn't always rational. But there's no money for it. Maybe I should have joined your little game of roulette the other night. It looked promising. And there were enough losers around that table to populate Bad Homburg. That's where Dostoevsky lost his shirt. How did you do?"

"I did all right."

"As usual."

"Usually," Junko said.

"I'm not a gambler," Sydney said. "Never was. It isn't that I can't see the romance of it, because I can. I understand the attraction, it's a kind of heat you're drawn to. But I never cared enough about money. It never seemed important. It wasn't anything to die for or to live for either, and I couldn't see risking what I had to get more, which I didn't need. There was always enough for me, not quite enough for Angie. Not nearly enough for Max. So maybe like Gina I was never into martyrdom, and saw my chance with translating and took it. And it's all I ever wanted to do. We've always lived decently, except." Sydney paused, remembering Angie in the kitchen, the newspaper under her arm, her face stricken. He changed gears. "The United States depresses her. Hopeless, she says. It's a hopeless country. She's lived here for twenty years but always thought of the United States as home, the home of last resort. But she doesn't think that anymore. Nothing is safe. The world scares her. Germany scares her and the Arabs scare her and the Israelis are as unstable as any of them, and meanwhile it's going to be a fine vintage year in France, where the trains run on time and the cassoulet is as good as it ever was and people are content, mostly, but she's spooked. We have a word for it in German, *Entzauberung*. Truly, German is the language of anxiety. It means disenchantment and melancholy, a profound sense of the falseness of things. It is the sense of a life that falls short. She wants to go to the country because she sees herself as an old woman living in a two-bedroom apartment in Montmartre. The other night she said that at least I had my books. She has nothing to show for her life except Max."

M. Marneffe was suddenly between them, bending over the table, his huge stomach touching the cloth. He poured while he related an anecdote about two flutists and their Corsican governess and the subsequent disorder. He left a bottle on the table and went away chuckling.

Junko said, "This book you're working on."

"Novel," Sydney said. "Remember, I gave you the last one."

"I remember. I'd hoped he'd changed métiers."

"He hasn't," Sydney said.

"I was surprised to see you the other day with Josef. He usually comes to Number Eighty-nine alone, and it was only recently that I connected him to your Kaus. We don't bring the office to the table, as a rule. Herr Kaus doesn't live in the real world. He comes to the table and likes to think that roulette's one of the mysteries of the universe, like Havel's high horizon. But it isn't. It's just roulette. The only thing you've got to know about roulette is whether the wheel's honest, and that means knowing the guy who's turning the wheel. When Josef loses he's disappointed and when he wins he's mystified. It's a hell of a way to live. Roulette's just a way to enjoy yourself, maybe win a little money, maybe lose some. That's all it is. It isn't life and it isn't art or cosmology. Josef likes to think it's something serious, poor bastard. I don't care for his novels. I have trouble with the German pastoral life. Like, I can't get into it." Junko grinned and took a swallow of Calvados. "Was the last book a success?"

"Not particularly," Sydney said. "And this one I'm working on now won't be a success either, except maybe in Kaus's terms. Or mine. I'm working as hard on it as he did, so I have a loyalty to it. The fact that it isn't a success is a recommendation of a sort, wouldn't you say?"

"No," Junko said. "No, it isn't a recommendation." He hesitated, his eyes narrowing in a frown. His whole body seemed to signal disapproval, to move into a kind of wintry twilight. He stroked his chin, bumping his chair back from the table, crossing his legs as he toyed with the glass of Calvados, tilting it this way and that. "Syd, I think you ought to pay some attention to Angie. She knows more than you think she does. She knows a damn sight more than you know. You've got to start looking to the future. Been watching the dollar lately? Falling like a stone. Been watching the Bourse? Frankfurt? London? Been watching the Dow Jones? Some CEO you never heard of farts, or doesn't fart, and the market rises five points or falls fifty. Everybody's watching your compatriots, but your compatriots are watching themselves. Things're unstable and there's a whole world beyond Central Europe that's just waiting to explode. If you think your Kaus is a meal ticket, forget it. This is old Europe, Syd, and the Balkans are stirring now as they did eighty years ago and I don't know how it's going to shake out. Or the Middle East, either, except did you see where the Algerians elected a fundamentalist Muslim? The *Algerians?* If it can happen in Algiers, it can happen in Marseille. So there'll be plenty of shaking going on and a fart every few days and a man's got to be hedged and have something in the kitty because there're opportunities, also because you don't know how dumb some of these people are, the ones who've taken over in old Europe, who've written free verse to the free market. They're going to get a screwing, Syd, and it's just as well because it's the only way they'll learn. It's on-the-job training, no pain, no gain. Welcome to the modern world, baby. Lie down and enjoy it. Now," he said. "Erich."

"I wondered when you were getting to him. I thought the drumroll would go on forever."

Junko leaned forward, both hands on the table, hands clasped together as if he were in his private office. "You didn't used to give lectures, *mon vieux*. And you didn't used to act, when we talked, like you were picking up a wet turd. You used to give my business the respect it deserved —"

"When I knew what it was," Sydney said.

"— and listened without any sarcastic comments, particularly since you knew I was doing you a favor, the piecework and so on, this and that. And some of it was in a gray area and you're clever enough to know that, and you didn't complain then. You took the work, happy to have it. And from time to time I was able to lend a hand in other ways and I was happy to lend the hand and I don't ever remember its being refused. We go way back, Syd."

"Thirty years and more," Sydney said, hardly believing it as he said it. The Gare du Nord, thirty-four years ago, a golden evening in the autumn.

"Erich was very impressed," Junko said.

"With what?" Sydney asked.

"You, *mon vieux*," Junko said. "Your poise."

"Erich's out of his element."

Junko smiled coldly. "In my apartment, in Paris on New Year's Eve. Erich in his Socialist threads and salesman's footwear, no doubt. Not his element, Henry Green and the Steinmillers and Charles and Gretta, not to mention Françoise. Not to mention the caviar and the Champagne. Not to mention my little Matisse. But that isn't where he's working, the fashionable Seventh Arrondissement. He's working in the East, mid-sized port city you're familiar with because it's near the village your mother was born in and lives in now. That's very much his element. Erich knows the village well, so when I asked him for a report from time to time on Frau van Damm he was happy to oblige. More than happy, since I paid him well."

"I see," Sydney said shortly.

Junko said, "I thought you would. Now. We have German product."

"What kind of product?"

"Let me get to that. Call it Cokes and smokes."

Sydney sighed and shook his head.

"Jesus, Sydney. Call it beers and butts then. Call it anything you like. It isn't dope. They don't have any dope in the East, for Christ's sake. And I wouldn't deal it if they did because I don't like the class of people, fucking hopheads. Goons. They're unstable. No, this product is more substantial than white powder. Perhaps not as profitable, but then nothing is." He stared at Sydney, who was listening, poker-faced. "In a week or so I'll be receiving pieces of paper. Maybe they'll be handwritten, maybe not. I think probably they will be. They'll all be in German, which I cannot read, as you know. And I think there'll be some tapes and of course they'll take a minute because the quality won't be very good. This isn't a Deutsche Grammophon, Syd, or even a CBS Masterwork. And the prose won't be of Prix Goncourt quality. Some of the stuff will be technical but nothing you can't handle. These are the damnedest pieces of paper. I got a sample over the transom so to speak and it looks very promising. Erich translated as best he could, enough for me to get the general drift of things." Junko shot his cuffs and looked over his shoulder for M. Marneffe. "You know something, Syd? You need a new wardrobe."

Sydney looked down at his corduroy coat, the bottom button missing. It was a comfortable coat, he'd had it for years. Carroll Dilion had bought it for him in the United States. He did not think of it as seedy, only well worn. Yet there was the obvious contrast with Junko Poole, prosperous in a sleek double-breasted gray suit, bespoke, from the look of it. A silk foulard hankie spilled from the breast pocket. A gold Rolex glittered on his wrist, and his smile was as composed as the rest of him. Sydney wondered what Junko had said to Erich about Inge, and how Erich had gone about his work. A discreet or not-so-discreet check with the Central Committee and, naturally, the local Stasi thugs, then a leisurely surveillance, Inge in her garden, Inge walking to market, Inge alone in her kitchen. He wondered if Erich had seen Inge lately, and if he had any photographs.

Junko was laughing at something.

Sydney said, "You were saying. Paper. Letters?"

"In a manner of speaking," Junko said.

"And transcripts?"

"Syd," Junko said. "The form of it doesn't matter. It'll come in various forms and'll require your most precise touch. I'll need the devotion you reserve for Herr Kaus, but unlike Kaus I'll pay real money. I'll pay more money than you've ever seen in your life, enough money to make a fat down payment on that house in the country that Angie can't live without and some to put away for the rainy day that's coming sure as God made little green apples so that you can go ahead and translate Josef Kaus for the rest of your natural life and not give a rat's ass if the book is successful or not."

"What have you done, snatched Stasi files?"

"Better," Junko said. "Thing is, we'll have to make a trip east, you and I and Erich, too, to close the deal. That has to be done there. Not here."

"Germany?"

"Where else?" Junko said.

There was a stir at the long table near the stairs, the table of cheerful women who had had a hilarious night. They were pleasant-faced women, now somewhat tousled, who were calculating the tip to the last centime. The woman Junko believed to be Gina was doing the arithmetic. They knew they had to leave something extra, perhaps ten percent of the fifteen percent service. They had eaten well and drunk even better, four empty bottles of grand cru Bordeaux and six empty snifters; they had finished with marc, a gamble if you weren't used to it. Now they rose, looking around them, continuing to chatter. Each woman had contributed a few coins to the service bonus. One of the young women was to be married; the party was in her honor. She suddenly picked up her glass and made a final toast to her friends, the toast spoken so rapidly that Sydney did not get it. It sounded risqué and the other women laughed while the guest of honor smiled happily. They were so jolly and affectionate, it made Sydney smile just looking at them, companionable women filled with amusement, well fed, well watered, and still a way to go before the evening ended. He wondered if they were going on somewhere, the Crazy Horse or Le Sexy, some place they could tease their husbands about; and the husbands would be amused or not amused, according to the temperament of the husband. They moved noisily to the stairs, bumping into each other, their voices rising. Then the basso profundo of M. Marneffe, happy to be of service, a long and strong life to the groom, heh-heh.

Junko raised his glass. "Luck to the betrothed."

The young woman inclined her head, acknowledging Junko, beaming. The other women turned toward their table, curious now about the two types who had been staring at them earlier before commencing an intense conversation of their own. The old patron had been solicitous of them, so they were regulars, good-looking men, one smooth and the other rough, raising their glasses now to salute the bride-to-be, who was laughing, happy to have attracted their attention.

"Very good luck," Sydney said. He was looking at the woman with the sweet smile and the well-used laugh, the woman who might have been his long-ago Gina. She returned his look, her eyes narrowing in amusement. These men were trying to crash their party, as men always did. Still, they were attractive men, well-meaning, not forward or inclined to scandal. They were gentlemen of a sort, and the rough one was familiar.

She gave a little nod of her head and said, "Hello, Sydney."

He said, "Gina."

"Isn't this a surprise!" Junko cried.

But she ignored him. "You're looking very well, Sydney."

"And you, too. Very."

"That was my daughter, Sydney. Isn't she sweet? She's to be married next week. She's marrying an American. Can you imagine it?"

"No," he said, grinning to tell her he could imagine it very well.

"He lives here. He's an American in Paris."

"All the best to her," Sydney said. "He's a lucky American."

"He works for a bank and I suppose one day they'll go to New York to live and raise their family."

"She'll like America," Sydney said.

"Yes," Gina said doubtfully. "I suppose she will."

"My wife is American."

Gina laughed and cocked her head, très bien. "Do you have children?"

"Just one," Sydney said. "A boy."

"He is married?"

"No," Sydney said. "He's only — fourteen."

"What an age!" Gina said.

"Yes," Sydney said, his voice thickening so that he grunted the word. "All the best to you, Gina."

"Good-bye, Sydney," she said and followed her companions down the stairs, all of them talking now as they collected their coats. Sometimes the world was a smaller planet than you thought possible. Sometimes it was as small as a neighborhood, or the dining room of a restaurant.

He heard the door slam downstairs, and then he heard their voices in the street. He looked over at the littered table, where the waiter was counting the coins the women had left behind. He picked them up one by one, looking at them, his face resigned; stiffed again, the usual thing. A table of tipsy women was a tragedy. Sydney rose and spoke to the waiter, reaching into his pants pocket to hand him a hundred-franc note, explaining that the women appreciated the service but at the end had become confused, as women will after an emotional evening, a heavy meal, and a glass of wine. As a friend of the mother of the betrothed, he was making up the difference.

"Well, well," Junko said when Sydney sat down. "A handsome gesture."

"Did you see his face? I thought he was going to cry."

"Bravo, Syd," Junko said.

"You were right," Sydney said after a moment.

"Never forget a face," Junko said.

"I do," Sydney said. "I do all the time."

"Bullshit, Syd. You're not telling me that you actually did not recognize her, that you forgot her face, the way she smiled and the way she moved. Her *look?*"

Sydney said, "People change. They change inside and they change outside so that you can't recognize them. It happens all the time. Their circumstances change, inside and out." He thought this was literally true, things breaking down, things disintegrating and accumulating. The strong became weak and the meek became tyrannical. Gina had changed the way a well-loved book changes when you read it years later.

Junko opened his mouth to say something, then didn't.

"It was good that she remembered," Sydney said.

Junko Poole nodded at that.

"It looked as if she got what she wanted, prospering. La Moelle, of all places. Probably because of the American fiancé, the banker."

"She was a pretty girl, the daughter. And Gina's held up well, perhaps a little too well around the hips. She didn't recognize me, but that's only natural; and understandable, I'd say. But she knew you right away and must be thinking now that it's an omen of some kind, perhaps a lucky omen, perhaps not. They were jolly, weren't they? Isn't it good to see people enjoying themselves? A kir royale to start things up, and a bottle of grand cru and an elderly marc de Bourgogne for the digestion, and some oysters followed by a tasty spring lamb and a cheese board and a little chocolate cake to finish. But it costs money, the little ceremonies of life. That meal couldn't've set those ladies back more than two or three thousand francs, but they'll reminisce later and say it was worth it, every penny. Doesn't it make you envious?" Junko shot his cuffs and swallowed his Calvados, setting the glass down carefully. He thought a moment, staring off into the restaurant's emptiness. "Let's see if we can find a way to help each other, Syd. The product needs a steady sophisticated hand that belongs to a mind that's discreet and reliable and knows that the world didn't begin yesterday and won't end tomorrow. I mean a man who's loyal first last and always. The provenance of my product is a little unusual, not the ordinary product, something else. Something out of the way. A hack won't do. Because it isn't only the translation that I'm interested in but the character and personality of the man who wrote it. Or spoke it. And then there's the meeting, where we close the deal."

"In the East."

Junko nodded.

"With Erich."

"Erich's the key that opens the lock."

"What's behind the door, Junko? After the paper's translated, where does it lead? What are you buying?"

Junko shook his head. "Nix. When you're in, we can discuss that. As long as you're out, forget it."

Junko pulled a fat cigar from a silver case, lit it, and blew a great cloud of smoke across the table. Sydney stared into the gloom of La Moelle, lighting a cigarette to protect himself from the pungent Havana. They were alone in the room now. He stared at the long table where Gina and her daughter had been, the table cold now with fresh linen and flatware, plates and glasses, and two small vases at either end, the vases empty because it was almost closing time. There was nothing at all to indicate that moments before six women had been having a fête for a betrothed. There was nothing at all of their warmth and good humor, as a field in winter discloses nothing of the fragrance of spring, though it can be imagined well enough. *Is he married? No. He's only — fourteen.* And she had replied, *What an age!* And he thought his voice would crack because he wanted to tell her about Max, the kind of boy he was, what he had lived with in his life; what Angie had lived with and he, too. He was theirs. They had cared for him, and cared for him still, though he did not live with them anymore. That was his family and now Angela was coming apart at the despair of it, of growing old in a two-bedroom apartment in Montmartre without her son. Theirs was a small society, Fortress America on anonymous avenue Songe, the apartments roughly equal in size, music always in the courtyard, a guardian in charge like the Great Elector or the king in Prussia. People were allowed a place, though. Even Max had a place in the Weimar scheme of things, as he and Angie had, and merry Milda and the others. Now Angie was saying that Max was the only thing she had to show for her life. Max was her product, as Kaus's translations were his. The remark chilled him to the bone, because he feared that it was true, and that her heart was breaking. Sydney was aware of Junko watching him through the great cloud of cigar smoke, his expression pensive, perhaps resigned. Poor Junko, his vision was Schopenhauer's — life as Will, blind energy in endless spasms of birthmaking, random and eclectic, explosive, heedless, now cold, now hot, without meaning except of course for the Will. Probably it was preferable on the whole to the tortured Wittgenstein, who spent his life in search of a truth that could be stated flatly, without embellishment and without exception, and never found one.

Take it, Junko said. Or leave it.

"I'm in," Sydney said.

Junko heaved himself to his feet and stepped across the room to the tray of *eaux de vie*. He stood looking at the garden of bottles, Armagnac, poire, prune, marc, Cognac, Calvados, framboise, sapin, tipping them backward to inspect the labels, checking the vintner and the year. After a moment's deliberation he plucked one and brought it back to the table and set it down, slowly, as if it weighed ten kilos. Then he called downstairs to M. Marneffe for two fresh snifters and sat drumming his fingers, waiting for the patron to arrive, which presently he did.

"And yourself also, monsieur," Junko said. M. Marneffe fluttered his hands, pouring generous measures, complimenting Junko on his brave selection, the most formidable Armagnac in the house, and his penultimate bottle of that tragic year, 1940. Meaning no disrespect, he said to Sydney. A great bottle, a *superb* bottle. The grapes wept copiously that year. An irony, no?

"Great wars make great ironies," Junko said sonorously.

"Your health," Sydney said to M. Marneffe. "May France remain France."

"To Europe," Junko said. "And to our German friends."

"Prosperity," M. Marneffe said solemnly. Then someone downstairs called him and he excused himself, taking the bottle with him.

Junko swirled the Armagnac around in his mouth, then swallowed, sighing deeply. He blew another cloud of cigar smoke across the table, leaning forward, grinning wildly. "*Willkomen,*" he said.

"So what are we buying?" Sydney asked.

Junko laughed merrily and raised his arms, a familiar gesture now, his life-as-Will gesture. He closed one eye and sighted along the imaginary barrel, squeezing the imaginary trigger at the garden of *eaux de vie*. Bang, he whispered. And then he added, "Weapons, *mon vieux*. Buying them low, selling them high."

Three

THEY SHOOK HANDS on the sidewalk in front of La Moelle, Junko hailed a taxi, and Sydney walked slowly down rue de Lille to Boulevard St. Germain and the Pont de la Concorde. A pearly mist had settled over the center of the city. Behind him was the blurred candle of the Eiffel Tower and to his right the National Assembly and high up the great dome of the Invalides, huge and all-seeing but indistinct in the mist. There were only a few other pedestrians, couples, ghostly in the unwholesome light.

He decided to walk along the river as he and Angie often did late at night after dinner or a party. Home the long way, crossing the river at the Pont Neuf. There was a point on the river where you could see the dome of the Invalides, the Eiffel Tower, the spires of Notre-Dame, the edge of the Louvre, the needle at Place de la Concorde, and the Grand Palais looking like an illuminated aircraft carrier. High in the distance, though it seemed close enough to embrace, was Sacré-Coeur — invisible now, owing to the fog. There was always maritime activity on the river, barges and the tour boats. The houseboats tethered along the Right Bank always looked cozy, no matter how mean the weather, lamps inside giving off a rosy glow like an English pub. All the boats had flowers or plants on their decks and round iron tables with folding chairs, a suburban ambiance fifty yards from the Tuileries.

He and Angie paused often, looking at the apartments along the Left Bank, wondering how much they cost and whether the cost would be worth it. There was such a thing as too much beauty, too many sensations, aesthetic gluttony. Sydney preferred a plainer style. In the old days Angie coveted one particular apartment, a penthouse with an enormous keyhole window and a balcony. The window had a surreal look to it, as if it had been designed by Cocteau or Apollinaire. The tenant always seemed to be standing in the window, looking down at the city, a drink in his hand. Angie invented a history for him, a lonely man who drank too much and rarely went out. The city was at his feet, he was a kind of Nero of the Seine. His father was American, his mother French. He had gone to school in France, to America for college; Yale sounded about right, but Princeton would do. He had a fortune but no family. He was always poised on the threshold of life, now French, now American. He was always fitting the wrong key into the lock. He had bought the apartment in the 1950s, when prices were cheap and apartments plentiful. The exchange rate was favorable. An American dollar could buy anything. He had bought the apartment from his father's mistress, who had driven a hard bargain, but wanted him to have it. *Papa and I had good times here*, she said. He looked so much like his father, though he had inherited his mother's melancholy and disappointment. He had been offered millions and millions of francs for the apartment but refused to sell. Where would he go? He was mesmerized by the view. It held him in thrall. If Corot had had such a view, he would never have painted a single tree. This was what the French-American had instead of a wife and children or a lover. He had his view and every night he'd pour a double Scotch and stand at his window and look at it, across the river to the Place de la Concorde and the Madeleine, upriver to the islands, downriver to the Grand Palais and the Trocadero, and of course due north to bulbous Sacré-Coeur, listening to —

Bach, Sydney said.

No, Angie said firmly. Miles Davis.

Piaf, he amended.

Maybe, she conceded. Maybe Piaf. More likely Sinatra, if it was late enough and he was sappy drunk.

At night the apartment was always lit, a minor Paris monument, and you could believe there was a permanent party somewhere in the interior; there would be waiters and a musician in a black tie at a white piano, and the party would last until dawn.

But what does he do all day long? Sydney asked.

He looks at his books.

Looks at them?

He collects rare books. He's a bibliophile, nineteenth-century Americana. He doesn't read them, he collects them. He wouldn't read them any more than a man who collects arms and armor would dress up in chain mail to take target practice with muskets.

How many books does he have, Angie?

Plenty. More than anyone else on the Quai Anatole France.

Late one afternoon they stood on the bridge to look at the apartment once again. Angie had a detail she wanted to add to the biography. The dying light struck the window in a certain glancing way. She gave a cry, throwing her arms around Sydney. She laughed and laughed. It was not a person in the keyhole window. It was a large plant, vegetation of some kind; and what they thought was a hand holding a highball was a crooked drooping branch.

She looked at him sadly. You have to take the facts as you find them, Van. Maybe he turned into a tree, like Daphne. Maybe someone cast a spell, one of the hundreds of guests who'd enjoyed his hospitality over the years and wanted to pay him back in the only way she knew how. The spell she cast permitted him in late afternoon to turn into a tree to observe the setting sun; and each year the bark thickened and soon he won't feel anything.

Angie's fantasies were not to everyone's taste. But how could you not love a woman with such a mind?

Looking up now, he saw that the apartment was lit as usual; and nothing, or no one, was at the window. He wondered if the tree had died. Perhaps the man had, taken away by some contemporary environmental insult: acid rain, radioactive fallout, ozone depletion, tobacco smoke. Whatever, the window was empty. He would tell her about it tonight. It was the sort of thing she would want to know.

That thought took him to the Musée d'Orsay, its plaza deserted, its galleries dark. The iron rhinoceros in the plaza glared at him. Angie had another theory that late at night the paintings conversed, Manet's sexy Olympia discussing boys with the shy blonde with the naked breasts while the bourgeois family on the balcony looked on in their various ways. Fantin-Latour's disapproving doctors lectured Degas's absinthe drinkers as Caillebotte's three workmen scraped the parquet for Whistler's fastidious, house-proud Mom.

Of course (Angie insisted) you could barely hear the conversations because of the racket of the soldiers in the Museum of the Legion of Honor across the plaza, gunfire, curses, the weeping of the wounded, and the summons of trumpets . . .

He continued up the quais, Anatole France to Voltaire, thinking his exile thoughts of Angie, converting the facts to fit her illusions. She was intoxicating though now, walking up the quai in the fog, she began to disappear, along with Junko Poole and the tree in the window and Musée d'Orsay. The sights of Paris were so powerful that they erased everything else. Paris always gave you the feeling of participating in a great aesthetic adventure, although it could also be seen as a kind of municipal fascism, everything organized to a single idea, and if you objected, they canceled your visa; that would be the postmodern view. You got the sensations Paris wanted you to have, yet it was impossible not to wonder about the forms of life that flourished behind the great dazzling façades beside the river, especially now in the fog, drifting on the surface of the water and rising, clear patches here and there like a glade in a forest, indisputably an exile's vision. The exile is obsessed by what the native takes for granted or is irritated by: the damned fog, I can't see my hand in front of my face.

Sydney lifted his eyes, looking across the river, and noticed a couple watching him. The man had his arms around the woman. They were both smoking, and presently a cigarette arched into the water. The man was heavyset with a great shock of gray hair. The fog wrapped itself around them then, and they vanished. Sydney thought they looked sinister, two of Degas's derelicts, smudged, indistinct figures, the trees of the Tuileries in the background and beyond the trees the faint yellow lights of the apartments of the rue de Rivoli. The two figures had not moved and for a moment he thought they were a trick of the fog or of his own eyesight, like the man-tree in the keyhole window. Perhaps they *were* fugitives from the ground-floor gallery of the Musée d'Orsay, spirited across the river to the bourgeois right bank, upwardly mobile at last.

Sydney was passing the small gallery next to a favorite restaurant, empty at this late hour. He paused to look in the window, through the wavy reflection of the streetlamp behind him and, obscurely, of the distant Louvre, at a drawing displayed on a modest wooden easel. It was one of Vuillard's nudes, a sketch of a woman seated at her kitchen table. Her face was in shadows. She was neither young nor old. The time appeared to be early morning of no particular day in the summer. The woman had no plans. Through the open window behind her were the knuckled rooftops of Paris, roughly sketched but vividly alive. The woman leaned on her elbow, her chin touching the back of her hand in an attitude of infinite languor or ennui. It was not *Entzauberung* because this woman was not German or married to one. Perhaps it was only indifference, rising to welcome an anonymous summer morning. She would be feeling a breeze on her skin and noticing the smells rising from the street, fresh-baked bread and wood smoke, and other smells less appetizing. Her hair was mussed, so she had just climbed from her bed, probably out of sorts, half asleep and fuzzy around the edges. A vast silence seemed to surround her, so surely she was alone in the apartment, thinking her own thoughts, alone with her black cat, watchful in the corner of the room.

Sydney believed he was looking into the woman's soul. Vuillard was the savant of French domestic life. The cereal bowl, a knitting basket, flowers in a vase, the cat in the corner. These were the matters of consequence in a human being's life, the family and work. No artist had ever done it better, and most did not care to do it at all. Sydney touched the window glass with his fingertips, experiencing a moment of vertigo. It came and went in an instant, leaving him light-headed. Minute night insects beat against the glass and he angrily brushed them away. He cupped his hands close to the window, peering through them as through a telescope, eliminating the distracting reflection of the streetlamp and the great bulk of the Louvre behind him.

My God, it was a lovely thing, Vuillard's nude. The setting was simple but her face was complicated, lean lines all leading to her mouth, unfathomable in the shadows of the room. On its plain student's easel, unframed, the sketch was perfectly natural. You could look at it forever. He wondered what kind of story Angie would invent around this woman sitting at a table on a summer morning. Was there a husband? A lover? Were there children somewhere out of sight?

She's an artist's model, Van.

The artist has gone away to Provence to paint wildflowers.
She has a free day.
She'll meet a friend at a café.
They'll gossip over a coffee.
That's most of the morning, right there.

He wondered how much they wanted for it. It would be about three hundred thousand francs, fifty thousand dollars. Perhaps more; the art market was lunatic. Junko would know, and know how to kick ten percent off the price. Whatever the price was, he couldn't afford it. Angie would kill for it, as she would have killed for a Braque graphic they saw in the same window a year before. There had been the Braque and one of Nolde's dark scenes of the harbor at Hamburg. He couldn't afford those, either; and no price was too high. They had quarreled over which one they would buy if they had the money; stupid argument. The Braque was cheerful and the Nolde wasn't cheerful, a dense ink sketch of a long dark quai and boats at anchor behind it. You could feel the soot and hear the boats moving at anchor in the cold. The Braque, on the other hand, was just a Braque, though that was not the way Angie saw it. It was exhilarating, seeing what Nolde could do with pen and ink, no cerise or violet or ghastly reptile green. When he tried to explain that to Angie she said, Yes, all right, but it's still Nolde and the port at Hamburg. It's not Braque and that, darling, is the *point*. They stood like two sovereigns of an impoverished nation, peasants dying in the streets, arguing over the construction of a great monument to their benevolent rule: Your visage or mine?

He backed away from the window when he heard footsteps. There was a break in the fog and the Louvre's reflection returned to the gallery's windows. Just then a young man and woman approached, walking arm in arm. They smiled politely at Sydney as they stopped to look at the Vuillard. The woman said something to the man, who laughed indulgently, glancing at Sydney behind them. He gave Sydney a good look because of the deserted street and the fog. They were Germans. They stood looking at the sketch and Sydney knew they were asking themselves the usual question: How much do you suppose it is? Whatever it was, they could afford it. They were prosperous Germans. The woman was dressed in a Hermès raincoat and a silk scarf, and carried an alligator handbag.

Very nice, the German said in French, turning to Sydney.
Yes, Sydney said.
In Frankfurt, we appreciate the Impressionists.
And in France also, Sydney said.
But the prices, the German said, shaking his head.
Naturally, Sydney said.
Still, they are treasures.
Indeed, Sydney said.
How much —
Sydney said he had no idea. A half million, surely.
The German smiled crookedly, hesitating before he replied. A sketch of that quality will be expensive, of course. Three hundred thousand, I think. Perhaps a quarter of a million. It is overpriced at five.
Francs, Sydney said.
Of course, the man said.
A matter of taste, Sydney said. And value.
And pocketbook, the German said. We prize the Impressionists, especially van Gogh and Cézanne. Renoir is too pretty for our taste. The Impressionists appeal to our sense of . . . serenity, naturalness. Perhaps van Gogh is a little less serene than Cézanne. This is a small picture but very fine. It is very well executed. You are interested in this picture?
I would like to own it, Sydney said.
Yes, the German said. That is natural.
The woman said in German, Perhaps tomorrow.
It is possible, the man replied, also in German.
Before we leave, she said.
The German nodded enthusiastically. Yes, we have time before the train. I do not think the Frenchman is serious, and we could outbid him in any case. He turned to Sydney. We are leaving Paris tomorrow, to Strasbourg for lunch and then on to Frankfurt.
The Strasbourg train leaves before eight, van Damm said.
The man looked at the woman, who shrugged. Then we will fly. It doesn't matter. He said to her in German, I would like to see the picture in the morning. And to Sydney in French, Vuillard is not of the first rank, but this is very fine.
You speak French very well, Sydney said.
The German smiled broadly. Yes, thank you. I work with

French people in my business in Frankfurt. Of course in a very few years we will all be speaking English. When our Europe is unified, English will be the common language. An irony, no?

The woman looked to her left, at the printed card in the window. She said, He opens at ten.

That would not give us much time, the German said. Of course we could have lunch here and take the afternoon train to Frankfurt. Or fly.

Sydney listened to all this impassively. They were looking through the Louvre's rooftops to the picture, moving left and right, interpreting it from all angles. The woman seemed to make up her mind. She put her hand on the man's arm, squeezing. Yes, yes, it would be simple, we could come by in the morning, look at the picture, and discuss terms. And then —

We'll see, the German said.

It will never lose its value, the woman said.

That's true, the man said.

We could take it with us. Or the gallery could send it.

The German cocked his head and muttered something. When he finished he was smiling broadly. Sydney knew what it was. The German was saying that with the value of the deutsche mark, it was not so expensive. It was cheap at three hundred thousand francs. So if you want it so badly, why not?

They take American Express, she said in German.

Sydney looked at his watch.

Or we can give them cash, she said. If we make a stop at the bank —

So you see, the German said, turning again to Sydney. We are all prisoners of our wives.

We men of the world, Sydney thought but did not say. He wondered how old they were. Not over thirty, either one of them. They had the complacent faces of the new Germany; and they were about to buy a Vuillard they didn't know existed until ten minutes ago. Well, he didn't either. The nude appeared out of the fog, an apparition.

We'll take good care of the Vuillard, the German said.

I wish you luck with it, Sydney said.

Perhaps we will see you in the morning?

Not likely, Sydney said, using a Berlin street expression.

You speak German, the woman said.

I am German, Sydney said.

You are from Berlin? the man said. Is it not wonderful, our Berlin restored to us at last —

Near Hamburg, Sydney said. But I have not been back in many years.

It is not so far, the man said.

Sydney said, I live in Paris now.

The German cocked his head, smiling. He said, It has been a pleasure speaking with you. I did not recognize you as a countryman. It does not matter so much which of us buys the Vuillard, then. It is either us or the Japanese.

They shook hands, first the man, then the woman, and with a final nod they moved off down the sidewalk and were lost in the fog, which rolled in thickly now. Sydney heard the woman's animal voice, a kind of purr, and the man's harsh laughter.

He moved close to the window again, to see if the sketch was as he remembered it. In a few minutes anything can change, a soul can vanish, a healthy person can become a sick one. They were a polite couple, with a manner older than their years. Perhaps that was one of the effects of prosperity; and the man knew his prices. The woman wanted it badly, though. He wondered what it was that attracted her to Vuillard's nude, the soul of French domestic life. There were plenty of other nudes in Paris, desirable and not, nudes to suit any taste or pocketbook. There were enough of Picasso's raunchy nudes to fill a *Schloss,* even a suburban Frankfurt *Schloss.* No doubt she saw herself, alone and languid in the balmy Rhineland morning, at loose ends after her handsome husband had left for his office, the bank or the trading company, or wherever it was that he worked, leaving her alone to manage the day. Frankfurt was Goethe's city as well as Rothschild's. Her cultivated, industrious husband, whose French was so good, who knew the value of pictures and was not afraid to say so; it would be a comfort, having Monsieur Vuillard on the wall, an expensive souvenir, its delicate composition would remind her always of their holiday in Paris, walking along the Seine in the fog on their last night, the Vuillard appearing as if summoned, there for the taking. So why not take it? An Impressionist, no less, whose work was in great museums everywhere on the continent and in America. The picture was for sale, so why not buy it? They had as much right as anybody, they worked hard, and the deutsche mark was firm. It was a better investment than shares in Siemans.

He thought it was from the passages and interiors series, 1899. These were direct and executed with great simplicity of line, a celebration of the present moment. At the same time, the future was problematical. What would the woman do when she left the table? Perhaps she would go with a friend to have a coffee, as Angie suggested. And perhaps not. Perhaps she would stay forever in the interior, and any passage was an illusion.

He wished he had the money. He could see it over Angie's desk, next to the Cézanne. They could get rid of the oranges at last, though the oranges had sentimental value. Perhaps the bedroom then, the Vuillard over the bed, an exciting thing to wake up with. But there was no budget for Impressionists, and no ship was on the horizon except for Junko Poole's brigantine with its skull and crossbones, a long voyage, tedious piecework of dubious — dubious! — provenance. The fee would make a down payment on a house, and not enough left over for a Vuillard. And if somehow you were able to buy it, you would have to insure it. A complicated business, acquiring artworks. You needed a collector's mentality, a sense of entitlement.

I must have this.

It belongs to me.

I deserve it.

Sydney tapped the glass with his fingernail, trying to work himself into a reckless mood and failing. He had been reckless enough for one night. Well, it was probably a counterfeit anyway. Paris was filled with them, bogus Impressionists; and not all of them were on canvas. Paris was a city where you could look at a tree and mistake it for a man. The sketch looked muddy around the edges and soft at the center. The woman's smile was bogus. The cat was bogus. The rooftops owed more to Mulhouse than Montmartre. The light was wrong.

Sydney turned quickly and walked away, beginning to grin now, remembering Junko Poole aiming his imaginary rifle. The weapons were in the East and Junko intended to buy them and export them, the single difficulty — "hitch," Junko called it — being that they were not, strictly speaking, for sale. But you have nothing to do with that end, Junko had told him. That's Erich and me. You translate, we deal. It would be an interesting few weeks, if they could stay out of jail. What was it that old Hoerli professed? "Strict exactitude." An organized environment, nothing exceptional or conspicuous. That was greatness, as defined by bourgeois Germans. And it was Angela's definition also, if her description of Shangri-la was any guide.

All right, he said aloud. He was talking to Angie. You want your *Rosenhaus,* I'll get it for you.

The fog thickened. He looked to see where he was and found it was the Quai Malaquais. He had known a girl who lived nearby. She edited by day and partied every night, supported by a lavish allowance from her father. She offered to share, she had more than she needed, and Sydney was always broke, threadbare and often hungry. This was after he had left the Foundation. Come on, Syd, who cares? He moved in with her and they lived happily for a month or two until she decided that Florence was more to her taste. She worked for a publishing house and gave it up one afternoon, saying that she was tired of saying no. The manuscripts flew in the door, and she threw them right back. No, no, no. The authors were not known, they did not have provenance, meaning an established patron. The firm already published too many books. So she gave it up, packed her bags, and left for Florence because she was tired of saying no. The rent was paid for another two months, so Sydney stayed on. It was his only experience with trust-fund living. There was nothing wrong with it, either.

Four

SYDNEY AND ANGELA quarreled at breakfast, and then she hurried off to Les Halles to buy a cheap airline ticket to the United States. He had asked her to wait a few weeks, but she refused. I'm taking the first available flight, she said. I'm not depending on Junko Poole for anything, and you shouldn't either. She was furious that he refused to tell her the details of Junko's venture, beyond the fact that he would be translating and that there would be a brief journey east. He mentioned a sum of money and she had laughed in disbelief. She said, Fine, you can go east and I'll go west. She intended to retrieve her Homer from the study at Old Harbor, fly to New York, sell the picture, and fly back to Paris.

Besides, she said. It's time I saw Carroll.

You shouldn't sell the Homer, he said. It was your mother's. It's a family treasure.

All treasure is sold sooner or later, she said.

This shouldn't be. It's a mistake.

It's mine, van Damm. I'll do with it what I want.

As you wish, he said.

The apartment was quiet now, though somewhere on the edges of his concentration Sydney heard voices. He paid them no notice, all his attention focused on *Die Katastrophe*. He was determined to finish the chapter before putting the book aside and doing Junko Poole's business. It was raining softly and all the windows were closed, his office becalmed with cigarette smoke. Sydney was following old Hoerli back to town. Kaus called it Mimerheim. He was intent on describing the landscape in its most minute detail, the flatness of the horizon, a small lake in the distance, trees and low hedgerows, insects, even single blades of grass brought to life in Hoerli's febrile vision. Dusk was coming on. The old man came to rest beside a low stone wall, a wall from the century before. In the meadow beyond it the cavalry troop was practicing maneuvers, moving at a trot and then a canter, swords drawn. The commander shouted orders in a voice that remained strangely soft, almost feminine. The swords flashed in the gray light as they swooped and plunged, lithe as whips. Hoerli heard the rush of air and the creak of the leather. The men called out in a kind of cadence, devout rather than belligerent. Of course this was only a training exercise, yet it stirred another memory of his father. Hoerli remembered his father on a horse, solemn as a statue. It was the quarter centenary of the founding of Mimerheim, and his father had been selected to read the proclamation, even though everyone knew his wife had left him and gone to live elsewhere. There were snickers in the crowd but it was doubtful that his father heard them, so caught up was he in the reading of the proclamation. A cavalry troop had been present at that occasion also, the troop standing at attention in the rain, water dribbling over their golden helmets with the spike at the crown. His father had practiced until he knew the proclamation by heart. At the end of it the horse had become restless, moving its haunches and breathing heavily, shaking its head. The snickering increased, yet his father kept his place and finished the reading of the proclamation in good order, his gruff voice carrying to the farthest corners of the square, despite the rain and the wind that had come up suddenly. He smiled shyly at the scattered applause, and then a brass band began to play a martial air. It was the national anthem, everyone singing. Hoerli had watched it all from a distance as he was doing now, beside the low wall that divided the meadow. The cavalry troop was back in formation, the horses motionless and the men silent. The commander shouted something in his soft voice and the troop moved off at a disciplined trot, swords sheathed, leaving Hoerli bereft.

Sydney looked up, staring into the courtyard, tapping a pencil on the desktop. Nothing moved in the courtyard except the light rain, puddling now on the tiles. He was in a lover's trance, reading

Kaus's next words, which he had put into Hoerli's mouth, *und ich fiel nieder und träumte* — and I fell down and dreamt — and marveling again at his exacting machinery, its equilibrium and power. He thought it sublime, the soul of German naturalness, the order and strength of the language itself. Beside it, French was light as air, and English — perhaps English was water. He hated to leave it, but it would only be for a little while. And when he returned, the machinery would still be there; he had only to turn the ignition key. Sydney tapped his pencil to the troop's cadence. His mind was wandering; he was imagining himself in the meadow with Hoerli, watching the troop retreat. The scene was surreal, the sky a deep violet and the grass a Prussian blue. The men were blond. The horses were black and their hooves seemed not to touch the earth but hover inches above it. The swords clattered in their scabards as they swayed back and forth.

He started at the sound of loud voices and a violent crash, breaking glass. A second crash, louder than the first, brought him to his feet. A book sailed into the courtyard, followed by a cascade of window glass. He heard another shout and then a third crash, and a man's voice — a torrent of words in a guttural, unintelligible language. In the background a woman murmured. He heard the sound of a fist against bone and a ghastly thud and then silence. A candlestick and a picture frame, a second book and a third flew into the courtyard, slapping and skidding on the tiles. A series of splintering cracks announced the breaking of furniture. The woman began to moan, then to cry hoarsely; it was a cry filled with rage, and Sydney recognized the voice as Milda's. A door slammed then and in a moment Sydney saw a heavily built young man in the courtyard shaking his fists. He was unfamiliar, not an idlewild, perhaps thirty years old, wearing boots and a short black leather jacket with some sort of team insignia on the back. His skull was thick with tight black curls and his sausage thighs strained against the leather. He kicked at the books, sending them skittering across the tiles. All this time he was cursing and shaking his fists. He kicked at the books again and slipped, falling into one of the puddles. This seemed to send him into a fresh frenzy.

Sydney was up now, putting the manuscript to one side, hurrying out of his office, running downstairs, out the front door and onto the balcony, taking the stone steps two at a time, into the courtyard at last, hurrying around the corner of the building. Milda was in the doorway of her apartment, holding her elbow. Her face was covered with blood. Blood leaked from her nose and a cut on her chin. Her bloody shirt was torn. She was screaming at the man in German dialect. He was still sprawled in the water, inspecting his hand, injured by one of the fragments of glass.

Sydney tried to move Milda inside, into the disordered interior of the apartment, but she threw off his hand, refusing to retreat.

Then the young man was up, standing ape-like and advancing. He said something Sydney did not understand, then understood all too well. It was an obscene slur delivered in the difficult dialect. Sydney told him to get out and when he snarled something in return Sydney told him to go fuck himself. He told him once and then again, his voice rising, out of control now. Sydney roughly pushed Milda inside and this time she went, telling Sydney to be careful. This wasn't his affair. Paul was a madman. He was crazy with jealousy, rotten with it. Please go away, Sydney. Never mind, Sydney said. It's finished now.

But it wasn't finished. Paul stepped sideways, and Sydney shuffled forward to meet him, trying to remember where to hold his hands and what to watch for. The last time he had been in a fight was Hamburg, the St. Pauli district, many years ago. That one had something to do with a woman also. Students against sailors and the sailors won and weren't gentle about it. Paul looked soft, though, and unsteady on his feet. The leather concealed a heavy belly, and his petulant face did not signal endurance or determination. Sydney knew that he was giving thirty pounds and probably thirty years but he was suddenly furious at his quiet domain invaded, the noise and destruction, Milda beaten, and of course the obscene slur.

Barbarian, he said aloud.

Milda shouted but Sydney was not prepared for the boot that came from nowhere, although he turned so that it caught him high on the thigh, hurting enough so that he cried out. He stumbled forward to grapple at close quarters. Someone had told him to work in close, when they were unsuccessfully fighting the sailors. Paul's leather had the touch and smell of putty, slimy to the touch. Sydney hit him twice in the stomach, then under the chin with the palm of his right hand. He was surprised that his hands went where he wanted them to go and went with speed, but he had never been angrier. Paul grunted, his red face becoming suddenly pale. His arms dropped to his sides and Sydney hit him again in the stomach. He thought it was like hitting a heavy pillow; impossible to know if he was causing damage. Paul turned to move away and Sydney hit him again in the stomach, as hard as he was able. He heard his own breath now, coming in short gasps. He was light-headed with anger and exertion. When Paul began to whimper, Sydney hit him again, although his arm was tired and he did not hit with force. Then he realized Milda was holding on to him and yelling something. He pushed her away and moved close to Paul, smelling his sweat and something else. Milda was on him again, pinning his arms and telling him to stop it, Paul wasn't fighting, the fight was over. You're going to kill him, Sydney. Sydney lowered his hands and Paul sat down suddenly in the puddle of water, making a comical splash. He was holding his stomach and beginning to vomit.

Leave here, Sydney said.

Paul muttered something and rolled over, continuing to vomit.

Sydney watched the *gardien* slowly advance from the porte-cochère. Someone called from one of the upper apartments. If the fighting did not stop at once, she intended to call the police. This was a respectable building, disgusting behavior not allowed. The window slammed.

Milda went to Paul, putting her arms around his shoulders, helping him to rise. They stood there together, and then she turned to Sydney.

He's drunk, can't you see that?

No, Sydney said. He looked at Paul's face, drained of color, and wanted to hit him again.

You hit him too hard, and now he's sick.

Leave here, Sydney said again.

You'd better go, Milda said to Paul. And you should apologize for the mess you made of things.

Paul shook his head, glaring at Sydney. He ran his hand through his hair, ruffling the tight black curls, almost nonchalant.

But when Sydney took a step toward him he backed away, saying a few curt words to Milda. He was still holding his stomach. He had apparently asked her for something because she shook her head firmly. He shrugged then and stumbled toward the porte-cochère. Milda stood looking after him and then followed him, running, touching his arm, saying something to which he nodded slowly. Then she let him go, and walked back to Sydney.

Sydney was leaning against the door, trying to catch his breath and compose himself. He had gone crazy. His leg hurt where Paul had kicked him, and his hands hurt because he had hit Paul, and a headache was gathering in the suburbs of his skull. He did not look at Milda when she returned. When he lifted his eyes at last he saw she was staring at him, trembling and frightened; perhaps it was only anger. She moved her head rapidly, no, no, cleaning blood from her chin and nose, wiping her hands on her jeans. She bit her lip and seemed about to speak, then didn't, cocking her head in the direction of the open door and smiling a wisp of a sarcastic smile, listening hard. On the stereo Billie Holiday was singing, "Lover Where Can You Be?"

He followed her into the apartment, surveying the wreckage, a bookcase knocked over, a wooden coffee table smashed. Cigarettes were ground into the carpet. One was smoldering and he picked it up and put it out in an ashtray. Pictures were askew on the white walls, papers and books scattered everywhere on the carpet. A man's hat, a dapper Borsalino, rested primly on the end table next to the couch. There was a sweater on the floor and he picked it up and handed it to her. She covered her chest with it, nodding thanks. He stepped to the kitchen and poured a glass of mineral water and gave it to her but she refused to drink, placing the glass on the carpet.

He said, "Do you want a doctor?"

She shook her head and put on the sweater. Her attitude seemed to say, I owe you no explanations.

Sydney went to the window and drew the blinds. The *gardien* was sweeping up the glass, a study in slow motion. He had piled the books and the picture frame neatly to one side. The candlestick was smashed.

She said, "You hurt him."

"That's right," Sydney said. "I meant to."

"He is excitable, and he was drunk."

"He's a pig," Sydney said. "He hurt you."

"Not so much. And I was not nice to him." She picked up the glass of water and drank from it, staring at Sydney over the rim of the glass. "You are a violent man. That is your generation, violence. That is your answer to everything."

"Not usually," Sydney said. He looked at his bruised hands, which were still trembling, and put them in his pockets.

"You should not have interfered. You should be ashamed of yourself. You were like a wild man, the way you attacked him. You were not like the Sydney I have known."

Sydney considered that and did not answer. He said, "Who is he?"

She smiled her sarcastic smile. "Paul," she said. "My former boyfriend from the Kleinwalsertal."

"The sexy boyfriend?" He could hardly believe it. He remembered the sausage legs and soft belly, and the tight curls. Probably it was the curls; young women loved curls almost as much as they loved excitement. He could not imagine sexy Paul on skis, two short lengths of wurst topped with mashed potatoes, and of course the curls.

"He has been searching for me."

"And now he's found you, and you weren't nice to him. So he beat you and smashed up the apartment. He invaded us. *Me*."

"He has a terrible temper."

Sydney flexed his fingers and moved to go. "Next time, when he beats you, tell him to be quiet about it. Tell him there's a violent translator upstairs who needs silence to work."

She said, "He wanted money."

"Well, that would explain it."

"He always needs money."

"For the leather goods, I expect."

"It is from Australia, his leather."

Sydney nodded, opening the door.

"Sometimes he is a snot," Milda said. "He thinks I have money that belongs to him, but he is wrong. That money was spent a long time ago. But I said he could return when he learns to behave like a gentleman. He has been searching for me everywhere." She glanced around the room, the books on the floor and the smashed coffee table, shaking her head. "Consuela and Ingrid will return soon, so I must clean up this place. And tonight we leave for Rome."

"I'm going back to work."

"You are very strong, Sydney," Milda said. "You are stronger and more violent than you think."

"Not strong," Sydney said. "Furious." He went out the door and into the courtyard. The books and the fragments of glass, the picture frame, and the broken candlestick were in a single forlorn pile. The *gardien* was nowhere to be seen. Sydney continued up to his apartment and his balcony office, where old Hoerli had lain down to sleep and to dream. He lit a cigarette with his trembling fingers, and almost immediately ground it out. He found he could not grip his pencil, and his headache crouched now just back of his swollen eyes.

He lay on his bed in darkness. His eyes felt as big as golf balls, so large the lids seemed stretched tight over them. He lay without moving, the pain noisy behind his eyes. He felt her presence at the doorway, heard her sigh and say, "Oh, Van, is it a bad one?" He waved his hand weakly, a signal that he would not speak but, yes, it was bad. She sat on the edge of the bed a moment, then went into the bathroom for aspirin and a glass of water. He took the aspirin and washed it down, nodding thanks. She said she was so sorry, believing that the headache was the result of their quarrel. She believed that his headaches were always the result of emotional upset, and nothing he said to her could convince her otherwise. He tried to explain that they came without warning. There was no proximate cause. They were like a thief in the night or a summer storm. They were not a punishment for anything, nor a consequence of upset or unpleasantness. He had them when he was cheerful and he had them when he was worried. And when they ran their course, when they had what they wanted from him, they withdrew. This one was beginning to falter, yielding ground. Perhaps it had outrun its supply lines, like an invading army deep in hostile territory. His father had had a number of sensible theories about the rapid advance, the pause to consolidate, and the estimate of enemy morale. The pause was dangerous, for if the enemy morale was strong they would counterattack. His morale was lousy but the invading army was yielding anyway, having got what it wanted. He opened his eyes.

She said, "I got the ticket."

He nodded, smiling bleakly.

"Cheap, too. Only trouble, it's TWA. The World's Worst Airline. I tried Air Egypt, Air India, Finnair, even BA. But the best deal was TWA, alas. And it's direct to Boston."

"Good," he said.

"I go tomorrow."

"So soon?"

"They had a seat, and I took it. No sense in waiting."

"I suppose not," he said.

"I have to stay a week."

"You'd better call your father."

"I'll call him tonight," she said.

"He'll like it," Sydney said. He would, too. Well, it was done now. Perhaps it would be all right. He had been mulish, and now it was time to let go. A week was a long time, though. He couldn't remember the last time they had been apart for a week. Probably it was a good thing, because he had Junko's business, which he was forbidden to talk about. He said, "It'll be a good surprise for Carroll."

"I hope so," she said. "Thanks, Syd."

"Shall we have a glass of wine and think about being rich?" He reached for his cigarettes.

"*Syd!*" She watched him light his cigarette. "What did you do to your hand?"

"I'll tell you," he said. "But you won't believe it."

"I'll believe it," she said.

"You won't like it, then."

"Maybe you'd better not tell me." She was looking at his bruised hand, which had begun to swell.

"I beat up Milda's boyfriend."

She stood up, her face clouding, turned away now.

"He beat up Milda. Did you see the mess in the courtyard?"

"There wasn't any mess in the courtyard."

"He wanted money. He broke up the apartment and slapped

her around, so I went down to stop her from being killed, I thought. He was a sausage dressed in leather, a punk. And he was drunk, according to Milda."

"How chivalrous, Van."

"She didn't think so. She said I should be ashamed of myself for interfering."

"That's the first intelligent thing she's said since we've known her."

Sydney blew a smoke ring, staring out the window. It was dark, and he wondered where the time had gone.

"Milda seems to've entered our lives lately in ways that I don't like and can't understand. Every time I turn around, Milda's there."

"Why don't you go down to her apartment and take a look at her, Angie. She's quite a sight. Maybe she's got the blood off her face by now. Probably she has, she's always cared about her personal appearance. Take a good look at her nose while you're at it; it's about the size of Charles de Gaulle's. And I'm sure she's managed to clean up the place so you won't cut your feet on the broken glass." His voice had begun to rise, although he could see the humor in it.

Angie sat down again on the edge of the bed. She looked at his hands, first one and then the other.

"Milda called me violent. That was my answer to everything, violence. A generational problem, apparently."

"I can hardly believe this," Angie said.

"Odd, I know. Not the usual thing at Fortress America. But Paul is excitable. And he has a terrible temper. Wanted some money that Milda has or was supposed to have but doesn't have anymore. So he beat her up."

"I hate this place," she said slowly.

"Angie," he said, taken aback by her vehemence.

"I don't want to live here anymore," she said.

Sydney's headache was in full retreat now. His hands were steady. He looked at her on the edge of the bed, her head down. She looked defeated. "This is the modern world, Angie. The girls lead complicated lives with their sheikhs and flying seraglios and now Paul-from-the-Kleinwalsertal, broke and out of sorts. Excitable. Drunk."

She said, "Don't make jokes." Then, "What's the Kleinwalsertal?"

He said, "Mythical kingdom, box canyon south of Munich, north of the Vorarlberg. Rich people go there and seduce the natives."

She grinned faintly. "Was he big?"

"As a house," Sydney said.

"Muscular, too, I'll bet."

"Bigger than Schwarzenegger."

"And yet you hit him."

"He kicked me first."

"Kicked you?"

"In the thigh with his boot. There's a bruise, I'll show it to you. So I hit him in the stomach a couple of times. I hung him out to drip."

"*Dry*, Van. You hung him out to dry."

"Is that the idiom?"

"That's the idiom." She shook her head. "Your hands look terrible."

"I kept hitting his zipper."

"That's not sporting," she said. "No wonder Milda complained."

"He wore a leather jacket with a zipper. Australian leather, according to Milda. Hurts like hell."

"And what was Milda doing all this time?"

"Yelling at me," Sydney said.

"For you to stop hitting her boyfriend in the zipper?"

"Former boyfriend, Angie. Get it straight."

She laughed out loud then. "And why didn't you?"

"My vicious streak," he said. "My violence. Everyone knows that translators are violent. It's how we get our work done."

"I guess I'll have to believe it," she said, "because the alternative is too awful."

"Here's the bruise," he said, lowering his trousers.

"My God," she said. She went into the bathroom and brought back a jar of salve and began to rub it on the bruise. She worked slowly, her tongue between her teeth. Sydney cried out once and then began to laugh. He told her what Paul looked like, his sausage legs and his curls, and Milda distraught, comforting Paul as a mother might. Then she denounced Sydney as a wild man who did not know his own strength.

Angie listened to all this in silence, applying the salve. "Syd?"

"That hurts," he said.

"I think you liked it," she said.

"I think I did," he answered.

"But you're *not* violent. I've never seen you violent."

"Only one time," he said.

"Yes, there was that time when you became so angry and you spoke to me in German."

"This time was like that time," he said.

Part 4

One

FALSE SPRING arrived the next day. The wind swung south, the ash-colored clouds disappeared, and the morning sky filled with light, Renaissance blue with feathery mare's tails for painterly contrast. Everyone in the Fortress had thrown open their windows to the lush air, the courtyard filled now with music, violins, bongo drums, and Billie Holiday. Tables and chairs appeared on sidewalks in front of the cafés and bistros on rue Caulaincourt, and by midmorning they were all filled. People went to the little park to sunbathe, although the ground was cold and hard, and the trees bare and damp. Parisians sat in the sun and yawned, spending the unexpected windfall. Easy come, easy go.

They were waiting in front of the Fortress for Angie's cab. She had a heavy winter coat over her arm, and her head thrown back breathing the air of the false spring. They could hear the music inside the courtyard behind them. He said it was an unlucky day to leave and she agreed with him. What the hell, he said, put America off until the weather turns bad. This ought to last three days. We won't see the sun again until April. She gave him a sour look and went back to breathing. They stood in silence, waiting. When the cab came they embraced a long moment. They were still embracing when the driver got out of the car to put Angie's suitcase in the trunk. He held her tightly and she felt light in his arms.

All right, she said. Time to go to America.

We have a minute, he said.

She said, Take Max for a little walk today, will you?

He said he would.

It's so *warm.* Better take some T-shirts to him.

I'll see to it, Sydney said.

And take care of yourself. Say hi to Junko. Will you be here when I get back?

Yes, he said.

I have to go now, she said.

Good luck with your Homer, he said.

Take care, Sydney, she said.

I love you, Angie.

He said it with such vehemence that she looked at him queerly and smiled, blushing. She gave him a final kiss and climbed into the cab, which accelerated at once down avenue Songe and through the light into rue Caulaincourt. Sydney stood on the sidewalk and waved but Angie did not turn. She was already chatting up the driver, bending forward to tap him on the shoulder as if she were cutting in at a dance, saying something clever, laughing and turning at the last minute to wave and give him Churchill's V-sign, which he returned with counterfeit enthusiasm.

The cab shot away and was lost to view. He hated it when she went to the United States. The United States seemed to him like a dangerous and powerful relative, one that he had never actually met but one that determined his present and his future, everything from the films he watched to the value of the currency he used to the identity of the states he must despise and die fighting. Like Flaubert's authorial god in the universe, the United States was present everywhere and visible nowhere. Sydney lost touch with his wife when she went home, though that was not the word she normally used to describe Maine. Her jokes were different. She paid attention to different things, things outside his ken. Her language became coarse. When she was in the United States, Sydney feared that one day she would call and announce that she'd run off with a ski instructor or film director or crooked congressman. Why have you done this, Angie? Oh, Van, don't you understand anything? It's the pursuit of happiness, darling.

He turned and walked through the porte-cochère and into the courtyard and up the stairs to his apartment. He dreaded the telephone call to Herr Kaus but felt he had to warn the author that there would be a delay in the translation. Hoerli was home in his kitchen now, and there Hoerli would have to wait. Sydney hoped to make his excuses over the telephone, avoiding face-to-face explanations. There was a delay; the reason didn't matter. But Josef Kaus, after pausing and sighing deeply, insisted that they meet at Number Eighty-nine and talk where they would not be disturbed. Disappointment was evident in his voice, which seemed to drop two octaves.

"A delay? This can't be. How long a delay? A delay is very damaging. We agreed that the translation would be completed by April so that they could publish in November. I did not tell you this, but they have invited me to come to the United States. I am to speak at an important conference in Colorado."

His hand was hurting, holding the telephone, so he sat in the chair next to the bookcase and tucked the receiver between his shoulder and his ear.

"It isn't a long novel," Herr Kaus said. "The Americans are waiting for it and they expect it by a date certain so that they can arrange the printing, the publicity, the conference in Colorado, and so forth. You agreed to deliver by April and you have a duty and a responsibility to live up to your agreement. It isn't a long novel by any means."

"No," Sydney agreed. "It isn't."

"Well, then," Herr Kaus said, as if that settled the matter.

"Perhaps a fortnight's delay," Sydney lied. It would be three weeks' delay minimum, and the time was not in his control. "And I can make up some of the time, with luck."

"I never rely on luck," Herr Kaus said morosely.

"When I get back," Sydney added.

"Where are you going?"

"I have to go to Germany."

"Impossible," Herr Kaus said.

"Not impossible, unfortunately."

"It's monstrous."

Sydney did not reply, hoping that the old man would be satisfied with the small change he'd been offered. He turned his head. General Grant's memoirs were at eye level. It was the only book he had taken from his father's military library, and he had never read it. He remembered his father telling him that General Grant had terrible headaches, often just before an engagement. He drank to pacify the headaches. U. S. Grant was a great general but not always shrewd personally, his father had said.

"You have never failed me before."

"Don't worry," Sydney said.

After another deep sigh, Herr Kaus explained again about the conference in the mountains of Colorado. The Americans had sudden new interest in contemporary German writers, and even some from the East were expected. He said, "In any case, come at three this afternoon. We can drink German beer and you can explain in detail about your delay. I know it can be avoided."

Sydney hung up the telephone and sat quietly a moment, his legs stretched out in front of him, listening to the music in the courtyard. Madame Butterfly competed with Billie Holiday. He yawned, the morning was so warm. He looked at his watch, imagining Angie at the check-in counter, demanding, and not getting, a window seat in the smoking section. She had been so absorbed with her trip west and the sale of her Homer that she had not inquired again about Junko's venture, taking Sydney at his word that it was mostly routine but lucrative; she did not believe the sum he mentioned, but that was just as well. As to whether he would be in Paris when she returned, only Junko knew. But he was sorry that he had been so quick to say yes when she asked him.

Almost noon. He did not have a headache but that was no reason not to have a drink.

He chose a restaurant on the quieter east side of Place Clichy, an old favorite although he had not been there in months, and when he went Angie was always with him. He sat in a spray of sunshine and ordered half a dozen oysters, the small papillons with the icy metallic bite, and watched the *écailler* shuck them and place them on the tin tray with ice chips and a cut lemon. The waiter presented them with a flourish, adding coarse rye bread and butter and a tiny cup of vinaigrette. The waiter was brisk with the half-bottle of Sancerre, pouring a little into Sydney's glass and putting the bottle in a bucket. He ate the oysters quickly, taking a swallow of Sancerre with each oyster. The first six tasted so good he ordered another six and a second half-bottle of Sancerre.

The service was outstanding because the waiter enjoyed loitering in the sun near the *écailler*'s bench. When young women walked by he looked at each one with an appraiser's eye, occasionally shaking his wrist and muttering ooo-la. The false spring had brought them out, along with the blackbirds and pigeons that crowded the square, and in their short skirts and loose blouses they looked like Riviera girls swinging down to the beach for a swim.

He ate the second six oysters slowly and rationed his wine. He imagined he was getting a tan sitting in the sun. At length the owner came outside, smiling because business was *formidable, superb*. They shook hands and talked about the false spring, so unexpected. None of the forecasters had predicted it. And Madame? Madame had left for America, alas. She was probably in the air that very moment, looking down at the tedious countryside of southern England. But she was not eating oysters nor drinking Sancerre and was probably forbidden to smoke.

The Americans are exceptional in their concern for health, the owner said.

It's only a bourgeois thing, Sydney said.

When the owner went jauntily away he said something to the waiter and in due course a pony of Calvados appeared, along with espresso and a plate of chocolates. The taste of oysters was still on his tongue, one half-bottle of Sancerre upended in the bucket, the other still partly full, and the Calvados, coffee, and chocolate still to go, happy days in Place Cliché. The morning had been unquiet but now it was composed. He sat in the sun, alternating sips of coffee with sips of Calvados. He unwrapped the chocolate but did not eat any.

Sydney left a generous tip and hailed a cab, thinking that if he was going to be rich he might as well begin acting like it. He arrived at Number Eighty-nine twenty minutes early. He was ushered to the upstairs salon, where Herr Kaus was impatiently waiting. They sat in the silence of the somber room while the pilsener was drawn and served. Everything was as it had been before. Herr DaMurr was asleep in the chair near the fireplace, a large heavy-breathing Labrador at his feet. Herr DaMurr's mottled fist lay inert on the dog's broad back, a leather leash wound around his fingers.

Sydney was disoriented, feeling the effects of the wine and the Calvados. He could still taste the oysters at the back of his throat, and of course the Calvados. A bright shaft of light fell across the figured carpet, reminding him of the false spring outside. He felt out of place and directionless. It seemed a high price to pay for a quiet lunch on the sidewalk in the sunshine of Place Clichy.

At last the beer was brought and Herr Kaus tipped the glass at Sydney, nodded and muttered a greeting, took a long draft, and sat back to listen. His attitude was that of a stern and skeptical schoolmaster preparing to listen to the obviously fabricated excuse of a favorite student.

Sydney explained that he had been occupied with family affairs almost from the moment he had seen him last at Junko Poole's roulette wheel. The translation of *Die Katastrophe* was moving very slowly. Not badly, but slowly. He had not been able to give it his full attention; and of course it required nothing less. Now he was obliged to break off work entirely for at least a fortnight, owing to an unexpected emergency.

Well, he amended apologetically, not an emergency. Not exactly that. You could not accurately call it an emergency in the sense of crisis. You could call it an unexpected event. A business opportunity not entirely unrelated to the family affairs. And he needed a break, that was the truth of the matter. He was stale. He needed to put his mind at rest as Herr DaMurr had put his golden hands at rest. So the translation had to be set aside for a little while, perhaps a fortnight. Sorry, he said. Truly sorry. But the circumstances were unavoidable.

"What are these family affairs?"

Sydney shrugged and sipped his beer. And when Herr Kaus made a little impatient gesture he looked up sharply and said, "My son is ill."

Herr Kaus started. "I am very sorry, of course. I had no idea."

"Yes," Sydney said.

"I see," Herr Kaus said.

"He is in the hospital." Sydney thought a moment and added, "He has been sick for a very long time." There was silence between them, with only the breathing of the dog to interfere. Herr DaMurr was motionless in his chair; defenseless was the word Sydney would have used, had he not known Herr DaMurr. He noticed that the shaft of light had disappeared, the sun under a cloud.

Herr Kaus reached to turn on the lamp at his elbow. "It has been a bad time then, for you and your wife."

"It has been upsetting," Sydney said.

"Of course," Herr Kaus said. "How old is your son?"

"Almost fifteen," Sydney said.

Kaus said, "I did not know you had children. You and your wife were always alone when I saw you in the quarter. But of course, as you said, he has been in a hospital. Well. This is distressing."

"So as you might imagine for the past few weeks I have not been able to work as I normally do. My wife."

"Yes?"

"Left for America today." When Herr Kaus leaned forward, nodding in sympathy, his manner indicating that now he understood, Sydney said, "Not that. She will be there for one week only." He did not continue in that direction. He said instead, "And then this other matter arose."

"Your emergency," Kaus said.

"As you like," Sydney said.

"What did you do to your hands?"

Sydney looked at his hands, turning them over and making a fist. He had forgotten about them except when he was manipulating the oysters. He smiled and shook his head. "Too complicated to explain," he said.

Kaus smiled back. "Try."

"It's not important," Sydney said.

"And the other fellow?"

"He survived."

"And this is related to your emergency."

"No. It is unrelated. A small misunderstanding in my apartment building. My fault, I'm afraid."

"They are badly swollen."

Sydney did not reply. He had already said more than he intended.

"Business," Kaus said. He took a long swallow of beer. "It wouldn't be Mr. Poole's business, would it?"

Sydney shrugged.

"He worries me," Kaus said.

"Junko worries everybody," Sydney said.

"He has no sense of proportion. No sense of equilibrium. But as you told me, he goes from success to success."

Sydney smiled. You couldn't fault the old man's memory.

"I hope you are being well paid."

"Very well paid," Sydney said.

"And you need the money for the boy, your son who is in the hospital."

Sydney remembered then that Angie had asked him to take Max for a walk in the sun, and that he had said he would, and bring him T-shirts because it was so warm. He had forgotten entirely about it and now the sun had gone under a cloud, and it would be dark before long. He sighed and said, "Yes."

Kaus was silent a moment, chewing on his lower lip, looking at the ceiling and then across the room at Herr DaMurr and the dog. "My poor, poor Hoerli. I don't know what to do now. While you're gone, while the translation is inactive, he'll be like poor Felix, at rest and unable to rise. He'll be in a coma. There's a phrase for it in English."

"Suspended animation," Sydney said.

"Where is he now?"

Sydney did not know what Kaus meant; then he understood. He cited the page number and the moment in the action, Hoerli at home preparing sausages, his thoughts as always far away. He was recalling his father. Present time seemed to not exist for Josef Kaus's stubborn hero. Present time was merely a convenience, a promontory from which to scan the past, in the sense that the past cannot exist without the present. In any event, only the past had meaning.

Sydney had finished his beer and watched Kaus rise and move to the door, calling for the waiter to bring two more glasses of pils.

"Yes," Kaus said, resuming his seat. "It is the passage following the cavalry troop in the field. He is waiting for winter, my Hoerli. And what a terrible winter it will be, ships lost at sea and stock frozen in the fields. Windmills will cease to turn, trees will split. Snow and wind, storms in the North Sea and storms in the Baltic, frigid in January and February, thawing in March, then frigid again, when the book ends. But Hoerli, in the kitchen with his sausages, does not know this yet. He does not know his fate." Kaus described the weather on the Polish-German plain, then old Hoerli standing in his kitchen looking out the window at the bare trees and the threatening sky. Presently rain arrives, sharp taps on the windowpane. Kaus's voice was soft, almost dreamy, as he described daily life in Mimerheim, the life that was infinitely closer and clearer and more intimate than his own, more deeply felt and consequential. Perhaps it was the life he wanted for himself. Probably it was the life he understood best, having created old Hoerli to put inside it. Herr Kaus sipped his beer, collecting foam on his Stalin mustache. Turning to look at Sydney, he said that this life was now suspended, old Hoerli motionless in front of his kitchen window, the clouds motionless, the fire motionless under the sausages, the cat in midleap from the bed to the floor, packed suitcases in the parlor.

This is inexpressibly sad, he said. It is the grief of uncompleted action.

Sydney sipped beer and waited. Could it be said of writers that they were self-absorbed?

"Have you ever been to Colorado?" Kaus asked.

"I have never been to the United States. There have been opportunities but something always interfered. It's one of the things I regret."

"Colorado is in the West. My publisher is excited, so many Germans in one place. The conference will be at a mountaintop place. Can you imagine it? All of us Germans in the thin air of Colorado, talking about our work and of course the political events. I would hate to miss it."

"You won't," Sydney said.

"They are going to give me a prize," Herr Kaus said shyly.

"Congratulations."

"Five thousand dollars goes with the prize."

"That's wonderful, Josef."

"It's your prize, too. My books in English are partly your books. My canvas, but your paint. So I have asked them to give half of the money to you, and to invite you to Colorado to accept the prize with me. It is only just."

Sydney was touched by the old man's words and sat back, silent a moment. He shook his head, not trusting himself to speak.

"I decided this weeks ago. It has nothing to do with what you have told me today. But perhaps it will help."

Sydney said, "I'm very grateful. You don't have to do it."

"I know," Herr Kaus said. "One enjoys most doing the things that one does not have to do. So you come to Colorado with me. Your wife, too. We will have a fine time in the thin air with our

German colleagues. I will give a little speech in German and you can translate. Then you give a speech of your own. Tell them what it means to be a translator. Speak to them about fidelity."

"With pleasure," Sydney said.

"But you must do this other business first."

"Yes."

"With our friend LeMessurier Poole."

Sydney nodded.

"I understand that he has investments in the other Europe and that these require his attention."

"Yes," Sydney said.

"And you will be going with him?"

"I suppose I will be."

"To the other Europe, east."

"That's our arrangement."

"I wish you success, for your son's sake."

"My wife is upset," Sydney said.

"It is natural," Kaus said.

"What is natural?" Herr DaMurr's voice was harsh in the heaviness of the room. The Labrador was rousing itself, rising by stages, forelegs and then haunches, stretching and giving a great yawn before collapsing again at his master's feet. DaMurr kept a firm grip on the leash.

"Herr van Damm was speaking about his wife," Kaus said.

"And what upset her?"

"Their son's illness."

DaMurr made a little rippling motion with his hand, as if to say that one illness more or less in the world was unremarkable.

Sydney finished his beer and rose. It was dusk outside. He had a headache from the wine and the Calvados; it was only a small skirmish and would disappear when he got some air. He felt overheated and knew that his face was red and drawn. His eyes were tired. He was sweating in the heat of the room.

"I want to thank you again," he said.

"Stay and have another pils," Kaus said.

"I must leave now. I must visit my son."

"Of course," Kaus said. "Say a word to him for me."

"I'll do that, Josef."

"And I wish you a pleasant journey east. Where will you be going exactly?"

"Hamburg first, then to the Baltic Coast."

"That is my part of the world."

"And mine, too."

"And Hoerli's. Have a successful journey and return quickly. I will not be able to rest until my Hoerli begins to move again. The cat must complete its leap."

"You have my assurance," Sydney said.

"And remember Colorado."

"I will not forget Colorado," Sydney said.

"It's time," DaMurr said.

"Games again?" Sydney asked.

"A short game," Kaus said.

"Cards," DaMurr said. He was standing now, his egg shape in silhouette, a benign smile on his heavy face as he leaned down to pat the dog's neck and body. He made the sounds that one does when loving animals and small children. The Labrador yawned and raised its head so that DaMurr could scratch its chin. Sydney watched the sometime golden hands as they patted and scratched, roughing and then smoothing the fur. He was talking to the dog in a private language. He unsnapped the leash from the dog's collar and let it hang from his fingers, but the dog did not move. It did not know it was free to go. Sydney wondered if Herr DaMurr had ever loved a human being as he seemed to love the dog. Probably not. Probably he had had no opportunity or reason to love human beings, perhaps with the exception of his daughter.

"Poker," Kaus said.

"I will talk to you when I return," Sydney said.

"It's a gentleman's game," DaMurr said.

"Felix," Kaus said mildly.

"You couldn't afford the losses," DaMurr said to Sydney.

"Good luck with your short game," Sydney said to Kaus.

"And as you've said, you're not a gambler." DaMurr grinned, raising his eyebrows.

"Good luck in Hamburg and the East," Kaus said. "It will be very cold in the Baltic region."

"They'll eat him alive in Hamburg," DaMurr said.

"Don't worry about Hoerli," Sydney said.

"What do you know about Hamburg, anyway?" DaMurr said.

"I worry all the time," Kaus said.

"Hoerli's resourceful," Sydney said. "Hoerli and his cat know how to take care of themselves. They've been together for years, haven't they? They've had good times and bad times and know each other. Besides, he has his suitcases."

"You don't know anything about suitcases," DaMurr said.

"I hope so," Kaus said.

DaMurr laughed. "You aren't the kind of man who knows about suitcases. You haven't the background."

"Good-bye then," Sydney said. He and Kaus shook hands.

"Be careful, Sydney," Kaus said.

"A fortnight," Sydney said.

"I wish you Godspeed," Kaus said. "Hurry back."

"I will," Sydney said.

"Hoerli," Kaus said.

"Poole," DaMurr said. "That confidence man. That shyster. That clown. It is criminal to have business with such a one as LeMessurier Poole. Only a fool would engage in business with a piece of *merde*. He has the morals of the Gestapo." DaMurr turned, kneeling now beside the dog, taking its face in his cupped hands, kissing its muzzle, muttering something in its ear, causing the dog to moan softly and rub its body against the old man's spindly shins while its tail whirled like a whip.

The sun was down and a wind had come up. Sydney stood on the sidewalk in front of Number Eighty-nine getting his bearings and collecting himself. He thought about Colorado and Josef Kaus's prize, half his now. Poor Kaus, poor DaMurr even; their fates had long been cast.

He did not have the energy to go to Max.

The streetlights threw an orange glow to the end of the block where a bus waited. It was suddenly cold. False spring was at an end. Sydney raised his face to the chill breeze, believing somehow that air would relieve his Calvados headache. And it seemed to, for a moment.

Two

LEMESSURIER POOLE was balancing his accounts, always an agreeable chore. He had seven accounts, two in Paris, two in New York, and one each in London, Düsseldorf, and Zürich. Four were private, three were company accounts. He devoted one morning each week to them, verifying the arithmetic of the various banks, and then moving the funds around, depending on current rates and his own expenses, personal and business. This month he was heavy in British pounds and light in deutsche marks, but hedged in dollars and Swiss francs. He never bought gold, because he was not afraid of political instability. Indeed, political instability was his friend, always welcome.

Junko was whistling while he worked, partly because he had discovered an error in his favor at one of the New York banks; and the morning paper had brought news of a fresh crisis in London, which would put increased pressure on the pound. He was whistling, too, because that morning in the bathtub he had read that Alexander the Great had wept bitter tears when he discovered that there were no more worlds to conquer; the writer was making a clumsy analogy to the Republican Party in the United States. Alexander the Great in his tent in the desert, his face in his hands, boo-hoo. And he was dead at thirty-three! Like all generals, he suffered from tunnel vision. Like all generals, he always fought the last war. He did not understand that there were untamed worlds beyond the skirmish line. To subdue them required fresh insights. Alexander wept then and would weep today because the skirmish line was obsolete; that business was bankrupt. No one believed in it anymore. Alexander would rage, his beautiful army suddenly irrelevant; he would be as desolate as Heifetz forbidden to play his Strad. The audience had disappeared. In the industrialized world, people no longer believed in their masters. This was evident in all walks of life; politics, as a pact between leaders and led, had disappeared. In some ways people yearned to return to a medieval state of stability and fixed rules, and in other ways to democratic anarchy. No one wanted to fight a war except those with spiritual grievances, and they would be discouraged whether they be Iraqis or Lithuanians because the financial world could not afford military solutions. The market economy depended on consumers. For that reason the state of affairs in Islam would bear scrutiny. Peace had become the natural condition of Europe, but it was the natural condition nowhere else. In time, Europe would become a played-out mine, for any investor with an adventurous spirit and — grievances of his own.

Junko looked up from his accounts and laughed out loud. Through the large window in front of his desk he could see the crowns of the trees in the Champ de Mars. He watched a yellow balloon rise, floating free, and then catch on the topmost branch. It shuddered, nodding, turning this way and that like a person pestered by an insect. Junko imagined the child below, near tears, not understanding the physical principle of negative gravity. Tether the balloon or it flies away, snags or floats free; either way it is lost. This one was snagged on a thin gray limb, the yellow brilliant against the pale blue sky. The child's tears would be no less bitter than Alexander the Great's, except that the child would get over it and Alexander never did.

Junko looked at the clock and turned back to his accounts, mentally preparing fax messages directing a transfer of funds from London to Düsseldorf, and from Paris to Zürich. But his subconscious was elsewhere.

The point was this. Governments would now set about redistributing wealth. That was the meaning of the consolidation of the two Germanys, and the coups in Poland and Czechoslovakia and Hungary. It was what Thatcher was doing in Britain and what Gonzales wanted to do in Spain. Italy was hopeless but it would happen there, too. Only the government of the United States had failed to grasp the point, lost as it was in the past. The redistribution of wealth was the tremendous task of the moment, and the equally tremendous opportunity. Money never moved without a piece falling away here and there. Money was like a river, continually changing course, eddying here, slipping its banks there. It was necessary to understand the hydraulics, the current, and the location of the eddies, the depth of the stream and the shape of the bank in order to siphon off the piece here and the piece there. The smallest pebble interfered with flow. Trail your finger behind a dinghy at Sauk Center and a month later a leaf changed course at New Orleans. You looked for a sudden dribble or the dream deluge. Of course you had to concentrate, focusing your energies on the channel every hour of every day, because things were subject to change without notice. Today was not yesterday. Tomorrow would be another moment altogether, yet the stream had its own logic and at times of turbulence — it was a witching hour! In this laudable redistribution of wealth mistakes would be made; the situation was novel and the mistakes therefore natural, the consequence of the many unk-unks — unknown unknowns. So you used people. You used them without prejudice. Money was neutral but the people weren't neutral. They were all adults. In every capital in Europe hands were out, bankers' hands, bureaucrats' hands, consultants, middlemen, academics, journalists, diplomats, attorneys, ten-percenters of varying provenance. They were the ones who testified that they knew a certain part of the river, the location of a beaver dam or a tributary the size of a hairpin, and could predict with certainty when the current would shift and water therefore spill, "redirected," "replotted" you might say, or "reformed" or simply: "Redistributed."

The misanthrope's iron law: history never repeats itself except perversely. Yet the idea of the soft underbelly of Europe had a certain romantic fin-de-siècle appeal. This underbelly was fully exposed as Central Europe did its dance of welcome. They wanted it so badly, with the fervor of a middle-aged man in a sexual frenzy for the sweet thing next door, believing she would save his life. Capitalism was wanton, Darwin's bleak law according to Marx. Perhaps the other Europe had forgotten that, perhaps the propaganda had been too strident, too clumsy and old-fashioned, and people had ceased to believe. But no one could say they hadn't been warned.

Chat them up, love them a little, offer them the sweet thing, and let the sweet thing give them dat ole black magic. No one fell in love faster or more completely or blindly than a fucking poet.

When his bell sounded, Junko gave a start. His reverie ended. Marx and Darwin disappeared, the soft underbelly of Europe disappeared, the sweet thing and the ten-percenters disappeared. Only the shimmer and humidity of the great money-river itself remained, as it always did, at the threshold of Junko Poole's consciousness. He had not completed his accounting, had not sent his faxes; nor had he thought through what he would say to Sydney van Damm, who was now at the iron gate in the courtyard waiting to be buzzed up. Junko saw him on the small screen embedded in the wall, Sydney looking at his wristwatch, trying to avoid the camera's eye. Sometimes it was wise not to write dialogue in advance; each seduction had its own characteristics. Junko looked out the window at the yellow balloon still struggling in the winter breeze. And he thought, as he pushed back his chair and stepped to the front door, that a stroll in the Luxembourg Gardens might set the discussion on the right course. The thing to remember about Sydney van Damm was that he was absolutely trustworthy and often naïve.

Above Junko's desk was a framed cover of the Foundation magazine, defunct these many years, a list of contributors in blue against a red background. There were recognizable names, an ambassador, a deputy prime minister, a minister of culture; in those days they had been dissident writers. The cover was now more than thirty years old, a collector's item. It had been a while since Sydney had seen the office, and now Junko pointed out the new word processor with its laser printer, the latest model fax machine and the ancient telex, as out of place as a telegraph key. In the corner was a dated computer. Directly above it hung the Beerbohm caricature of Joseph Duveen, the great art dealer and Junko Poole's hero. Duveen: a Renaissance man of business. The markets were no different from an art appraisal and subsequent auction. They both required thorough preparation and an inside track, a network of alliances and an understanding of fashion, and knowing where the money was. And a killer instinct no less feral than a prehistoric beast, reversing the evolutionary process. All computers had codewords for access. Junko's cipher for his dated computer was "Berenson."

Sydney made appropriate noises, noticing that Junko's eyes kept straying to the cover of the Foundation magazine. Finally he reached over to straighten the frame.

Sydney was squinting, trying to read the names. He said, "Not exactly household names."

"Jesus," Junko said. "Jesus Christ, a basketful of failures, except for one or two whose reputations are inflated and who're now feeding at the state's trough. That one." He pointed at the first name. "Married well, went to live in Ischia or some god damned place. Never wrote another line, which is probably just as well. That one." He pointed to the second name. "Lost somewhere in America; no safety net was fine enough to catch him. These three." He continued down the list. "Are dead. The next one is the ambassador, you can catch him from time to time on Antenne 2, he's as *médiatique* as Madonna. The next one I knew pretty well in the old days and then she turned dike and went to live in Berlin, east sector, probably cozy with some Stasi thugess." Junko shook his head. "So it didn't turn out well for them, did it? But back then when they thought they were geniuses it was just a matter of time before everyone agreed and they'd be typing out their speeches for the ceremonies at Stockholm and be recognized by the waiters at the Flore for the rest of their sorry lives. They didn't care who knew it, either. I had to hear how great they were every time I'd collect a manuscript while shoveling some green into their sweaty palms, as if they were doing me the fucking favor instead of the other way around. So I don't care for them much, Syd. I think they're hypocrites and whiners. Poets and their hangers-on, it's a racket like any other, as I have cause to know because the German-American Foundation kept them alive until the time that it leaked out that some of them had been on Uncle Sugar's tit for years and years and that caused some embarrassment in the international salons. Some unpleasantness with their security services, too. And who do you suppose did the leaking, Syd? One guess."

Junko paused then, looking out the window at the crowns of the trees in the Champ de Mars and the Eiffel Tower beyond. He had worked himself into a state, his hands trembling slightly and his voice thickening with each fresh denunciation.

Wrote a poem myself, he said. Just once.

He insisted on telling the story, which began in his old flat in Montmartre, cold water in the tap, W.C. down the hall, Boho country. Two North Africans lived in the flat next door and fought every night until the man sliced the woman's ear off her head. It was a clean cut, blood everywhere. Junko had never seen a severed ear, nor had the intern at the American hospital. The North African woman held it in her hand during the fifty-minute ride on the Métro to Neuilly; Junko tried to stanch the flow of blood. No dice, they couldn't sew it back on. How did this happen, madame? It is a private matter, she replied. He wrote a poem about it but the poem was not a success because no reader could suspend disbelief. You must try to avoid these overdone themes, one of the poets said, ignoring Junko's deft comparison of the ear to a seashell. He had a sunflower in there, too.

"Those were the days," he said to Sydney.

He carefully stacked his accounts and laid them to one side. He switched on the telephone answering machine and checked the fax. He looked closely at Sydney, who had been listening attentively, stone silent. Was that a skeptical expression on van Damm's face?

"That's why I've got that old magazine cover on the wall, and why I like looking at it. It reminds me of my salad days in fast company in Montparnasse, the German-American Foundation, the Lord providing. It reminds me of where I am and where they are. Just keeping score, Syd."

The fax machine began to chatter and Junko looked at it, waiting for the message to clear. He ripped off the copy, read it, bunched it, and threw it in the wastebasket, smiling maliciously. One of my banks admits to an error, he said.

Sydney smiled politely.

"The hell with it. Let's take a walk, Syd. Let's go to the Luxembourg."

"First time I've heard about the ear," Sydney said.

"Well, it's true," Junko said defensively.

"And the Luxembourg's a hike."

"It'll do us good," Junko said.

They walked out of the office and into the living room, Sydney pausing to look at the Matisse and the Meissen horse and the backgammon board at which Angie had won two thousand francs. The Eiffel Tower was visible through the high windows and it was easy imagining Erich looking at it, wondering at the turn of events that had brought him to an American's apartment in Paris, drinking Champagne and eating caviar and pâté de foie gras.

Junko said, "Want a drink?"

Sydney laughed, remembering the long lunch yesterday, the beer with Josef Kaus at Number Eighty-nine, and the stiff whiskeys before and during dinner. He said, "No."

"Let's go then," Junko said, pushing buttons to activate his security alarms.

It was cold outside, the wind gusting in the Champ de Mars. They walked across the esplanade to Suffren and Sèvres, and then the jumble of streets to the Luxembourg. Almost noon, and the garden had its usual complement of elderly men playing chess with their mittens on, and elderly women taking their morning constitutionals, accompanied by small dogs on leashes. There were a few young women wheeling baby carriages. A gendarme moved with the slow step and gravity of a priest, nodding politely at the women. Junko and Sydney walked in silence until they reached the steps leading to the terrace and the great pool, Marie de Médicis' cold Florentine palace looming over it like a balustraded Alp. Stone statues of robust French queens and other notables ringed the terrace, a tableau mort. The many iron chairs were empty but arranged as though they were occupied, chairs facing each other or side by side, companionable in the cold. The chairs themselves appeared to be in conversation. A patina of ice had frozen a child's silver sloop on the surface of the pool, the sloop crippled and listing to starboard.

At the edge of the pool, so still they were not noticed at first, two lovers faced each other under the blank gaze of a queen of France. The boy and girl stood with their foreheads touching, bookbags on the ground at their feet. The girl was as tall as the boy, but slender and supple. Even at that distance Sydney could see how sexy they were, how pleased with each other in that opulent setting, on the deserted terrace under the pale blue sky.

Junko said, "How's little Max getting on?"
"All right," Sydney said. "No change."
"But he's comfortable?"
"Yes," Sydney said. "He seems to be."
"And it's a good place, isn't it?"
"I think so. There are many that are much worse. And a few that are better."
"I heard about one the other day, I meant to tell you."
Sydney nodded. He had a file full of such places.
"It's in Normandy, a village outside of Caen. It's a farm. There are animals and so forth and so on, a real working farm." Junko rubbed his hands together, blowing on them. He was watching the lovers fifty feet away. The boy had said something and the girl had raised her eyes to the sky, a brilliant smile on her face. The girl's breath came in little urgent gusts. The boy couldn't keep his eyes off her, kissing her now on her neck while she smiled at the sky. "You still see him on Sundays?"
"Most Sundays. It isn't possible to take him out to lunch anymore, so we see him for a few hours there. And Angie goes over about every day. The Sisters are wonderful with him. They knit things for him and of course they pray. They pray to St. Jude."
Junko nodded without comment.
"She wants to take him to the country."
"Yes," Junko said.
"Did she ever mention that to you?"
"I don't think so," Junko said, rocking back on his heels, coughing shortly.
"She said she did," Sydney said.
"Maybe she did," Junko said. He was watching the girl, her arms around the boy's waist, kissing him. They were turning in an adagio.
"So that's what we're going to do, with all the money I'm going to have. Who knows if it's right. I don't know. Angie says she knows. And maybe she does. She thinks about him often, more than I do because I'm occupied with my work. I think to her Max has become larger than life, which is a little bit of an irony, isn't it?"
"He was an appealing child," Junko said.
"Do you think so?"
"Yes, Syd. Of course."

"To us he was. Not to anyone else. He wasn't universal, like those two." The girl had light hair cropped short and swept back, that season's mode. She wore a shapeless yellow parka. Both she and the boy were wearing skin-tight jeans and carried identical bookbags. Watching them, Sydney remembered old Hoerli in the wheatfield, feeling no desire. These two weren't actually making love with their clothes off but they might as well have been; it was what they were thinking about, you could almost hear their thoughts, the words in a balloon over their heads like cartoon characters. They continued to turn slowly in the cold, the girl on tiptoe now, whispering into the boy's ear. Such a bella figura had sent old Hoerli spinning back in his memory to a family lunch fifty years before, the sudden moment that divided a life; but of course that was a fiction. Nothing came to Sydney but a vague regret that Angie was in America. These two were almost young enough to be their children, his and Angie's. Sydney shifted his eyes and saw the priestly gendarme sitting on a stone bench, eating a chocolate bar and staring stubbornly into the middle distance. "But it doesn't make any difference," Sydney said. "He won't live more than a couple of years. He won't see his twentieth birthday, although Angela won't accept that. She doesn't believe it. She says the doctors don't know and maybe she's right about that also. I think she can't imagine life without him. He's a kind of myth, always there even if you aren't thinking about him consciously. It's like the Revolution if you live in France, part of the emotional atmosphere of life, a kind of profound turbulence. Except Max doesn't stand for anything. He isn't a symbol of anything except a gene that went haywire. He's an accident, and entirely and completely defenseless."

Junko pitched his cigarette over the steps and onto the terrace gravel, where it bounced in a glum shower of sparks. The lovers didn't notice and kept turning to their private music. Junko sighed; dat ole black magic once again. Perhaps they were poets. The cigarette could have been a hand grenade and they still wouldn't've noticed.

"She wants to do as much for him as she can, even if he doesn't know she's doing it. Or care. If you see what I mean."

"Of course," Junko said, nodding vigorously. This had gone farther than he intended, and now he was stuck with it. He hadn't seen Max in years and what he remembered was the boy's mottled, wrinkled face, like an old man who had led a hard life. Max bore a passing resemblance to Sydney, in the shape of his face, his turned-down eyes, and his powerful body. He never would have noticed, except that Angela had mentioned it once. Sydney and Angela rarely talked about him and now Sydney wouldn't shut up. He wouldn't let it go and his monotone was unnerving.

Junko lit another cigarette, offering one to Sydney; but Sydney shook his head.

"I told her I was going to work for you. I didn't explain what it was, except that my end would be translating. I love it, you know. That's where my heart is, with Josef Kaus and his haunted Germans, his ghosts. We are not a bad people, we Germans. We are in a constant struggle, though. We struggle with ourselves and with the outside world. It seems to be a condition of our life. Eyes are always upon us, watching us as we are watching those two children. Isn't it miraculous that they do not see us and if they did see us that they would not care? Perhaps they are immortal, those two. Perhaps we have died and gone to heaven, Junko. And they are the entertainment." A shaft of pale sunlight fell across the façade of the palace. At one of the windows a uniformed guard stood staring at the sky with the sentry's usual motionless boredom. He was waiting for something unexpected to turn up, something suspicious. Sydney thought that Max often stared in that way, concentrating on a thing that only he could see and was unable to describe. Perhaps that was Max's entertainment. That was the optimist's viewpoint, anyway. He moved to a bench and sat down, beckoning to Junko Poole. "Let's go to work. What do you have?"

Junko sat beside him, digging into his jacket pocket. "This letter," he said.

"Is that all?"

"There's more back at the office. And when you finish the letter, there's a transcript of a telephone conversation."

Sydney stared at the letter. It was written in pencil on coarse paper. The writer was barely literate, the letter filled with misspelled slang. He said, "Axel is writing his girlfriend. They cannot meet on Monday as planned. The literal translation is that Axel will be unable to look at her cunt. He thinks Wednesday instead because of the oafs in charge of the shipment." Sydney handed the letter to Junko. "This Axel is not German. I would guess Czech."

"You guess right."

"You mentioned a transcript."

"In a manner of speaking." Junko dug again into his pocket and produced a tiny recorder with earphones. "Push the button marked 'Start,' Syd."

Sydney fumbled for a moment. He was wearing gloves so that Junko could not see his hands. He put the earphones on and began to listen. The quality was excellent and he let his mind wander a moment, to the uniformed guard still standing motionless at Marie de Médicis' window. He wondered if it was a grace-and-favor sort of job, the kind a politician got for his unambitious brother-in-law. The guard suddenly gave a tremendous yawn, smiling at the end of it as if he had performed a complicated task. The recording had gotten away from him and he stopped it and reversed the tape and began again. At length he stopped it and sat quietly a moment, organizing his thoughts. There was some technical material that he did not understand but Junko would. The rest of it was clear enough.

"The material is coming from Martin, in Czecho. It's manufactured at Dubnica but Martin is the assembly point. They'll be sending nine T-72 tanks and four thousand automatic weapons to the arsenal near Anklam, East Germany. They're happy to be rid of them, by the way. The Czechs don't like the arms trade anymore. It's a Warsaw Pact contract, so the material has been paid for. The shipment will include a — we'd call it a dividend. That's to be paid for separately. All clear so far?"

"Admirable, Syd. Keep going."

"The dividend includes nine dozen missiles of Soviet manufacture and another one thousand automatic weapons, mostly Kalashnikovs. With ammunition."

"One thousand?"

"One thousand."

"Nine dozen?"

"Nine dozen."

"Not five thousand?"

"No."

"Not ten dozen?"
"No."
"Crafty little devils, aren't they?"
"As you know, there are two men on this tape. I would say they are very nervous. They are nervous about the transfer, and they are nervous about the payment. They say that things are secure but they don't seem very confident about it."
Junko thought a moment. "Can you identify them in context?"
"One's a soldier, the other's a bureaucrat."
"That's right, Syd."
"Erich's voice sounds different on tape, but that's who it is."
"My faith is shaken," Junko said, and laughed.
"One last thing," Sydney said.
"Tell me, Syd."
"Erich says the buyer is a shit. He has to be watched every minute, particularly as regards payment. Nothing leaves Anklam until the bank notifies them that the funds have arrived intact, the agreed-upon amount and so forth and so on. There's some complaining about the papers you're making them sign. Then they're laughing because they don't believe you can transship. They don't think you can get the goods out of the country."
"And then what?"
"Then they're talking about women. But the laughter seems genuine."
"As if they know something I don't know?"
"Maybe," Sydney said.
Junko Poole was silent, lighting a cigarette.
"How did you get the tape?"
He made a little impatient gesture. "A wire," Junko said.
Sydney looked at him, waiting for more. When nothing more came, he said, "How are you going to do it?"
"That's not your worry, Syd."
"You've got missiles and automatic weapons in an army depot in East Germany. It's not Kleenex or citrus fruit, for Christ's sake. Where do they go? How do they get there? Who receives them?"
"Shush," Junko said. "All in good time. As I said the other day, that's not your end." Junko looked at him sideways, blowing a thin stream of smoke into the cold air. "There are some twists and turns to this deal that are not perfect. I could wish them otherwise,

but wishing isn't worth a crap. You can throw your penny down a wishing well and if you're a child you can clap your hands and believe the Jolly Green Giant'll appear toot sweet, and for that moment while you're wishing it's a tremendous feeling. Followed by letdown, I'd say, Syd." He sighed deeply, hesitating. "You have to look things straight in the face and decide how much it's worth to you. First, you have to want it, then you have to know how to do it. And it isn't as easy as it sounds with these two because they've been fucked by experts and think they know what to expect. You have to blind-side them. You have to come at them from a direction they've never seen before, and then you can make it stick. Also, it earns you respect the next time around." He rubbed his hands together. "That's fundamental."

Sydney was silent, watching the lovers. They had ceased their slow dance and were talking confidentially. The girl was speaking and the boy was listening and nodding, his feet scuffing the gravel. Whatever the girl was saying he wasn't happy to hear but he was listening hard. Sydney looked up, thinking suddenly of his manuscript unattended on his office desk so far from Junko's worldly Luxembourg. Nothing moved in the great garden except some winter birds flitting from statue to statue. He had the idea that the birds had been there for centuries. Probably the boy and girl had, too, along with the priestly gendarme and the old men playing chess with their mittens on, and his unattended manuscript, and Max; all centuries old.

"I lead a dull life," Sydney said suddenly.

"I wouldn't call it dull, exactly."

"I would. It's narrow. It's a life of routine, and not a very interesting or rewarding routine, except for the work itself. The product. My life has disappeared inside the product."

"You need to give Kaus a rest, Syd."

"Is that it?"

"When we finish up our work you ought to do something spur of the moment. Take a trip somewhere with Angie, spend some real money. You don't look well, you know. Take a trip to London, see some shows. I'll get you a visitor's card to my club. Rent a car, go to the Lake District for a few days. In the middle of winter, London's exciting. And there's the January sale at Harold's."

"Harrod's," Sydney said.

"I know that, Syd. It's a joke."

He turned to Junko, who was smoking serenely with the air of a man at ease on the grounds of a country house somewhere, perhaps waiting for the clatter of the cocktail tray. His expression was composed. Not a hair was out of place. His suit was pressed to within an inch of its life, and his shoes glowed with their usual high shine. Rising now, he leaned forward on one foot, a figure from an eighteenth-century print, Junko Poole a pillar of the Enlightenment, prosperous, Godless, and confident. Beside him, Sydney felt like a degenerate monk of the Middle Ages, knowing that the wind was blowing from the underworld and helpless before it, weary of science and skeptical of prayer, more concerned with the attitude of God than the rights of man; not caring, really, in the way that he should. Another inscrutable miracle. He led a dull life. The world went around him, willy-nilly, anyhow. He had his work and his family and there was nothing extraordinary about either. They all tried to get on, as people did, though Junko's world was more spacious, altogether more unpredictable, various, and fun, absorbed as he was in the great task of capital formation, working at it with the protean intensity of Voltaire on *Candide,* and to a roughly similar subversive end, except that Junko's scientific garden was the wide world.

Sydney said, "Missiles?"

Junko said, "Not your concern, Syd."

"Where are they going?"

Junko leaned forward on the toes of his shoes, scuffing the gravel, whistling between his teeth. "Maybe they're not going anywhere."

Sydney said nothing to that, but he was moved to smile.

"Maybe they're staying right where they are." Junko dropped his cigarette at his feet and ground it into the gravel viciously, as if it were alive and might strike. "Let's move along, Syd."

Sydney was laughing.

"It's pretty as a picture, this operation. As I said, there're some things I would wish different, I wouldn't lie to you, a twist here and a turn there. But the hell with it. Nothing's perfect."

"I'm glad to hear it," Sydney said, still laughing.

"You won't be sorry, Syd. You've never seen anything like this.

This is state of the art. And the thing is, it's just as old as the god damned hills. It's the oldest story in the world, and it's state of the art."

"State-of-the-art what?"

Junko thought a moment. "Think of us as navigating a mighty river."

Sydney nodded, knowing that he had gotten all he was going to get. He was getting used to the idea. He did not know how Junko intended to play his game, but game it surely was; not perfect, but not vicious either, neither evil nor malignant. Now he watched the lovers pick up their bookbags and begin to stroll away in the direction of the balustraded palace. They never looked back. The boy's arm was around the girl's waist, squeezing. Whatever she had been telling him, he apparently had accepted. She said something and the boy laughed and held her tight, relieving her of her books. Then they disappeared around the corner of the Médicis fountain. All this time Junko had been whistling under his breath.

Sydney said, "Nice-looking kids."

Junko wasn't listening. "I've got some stuff in my apartment, letters and tapes and a document or two. Arrived yesterday. I'll need a translation right away. If they're what I think they are, it's unbelievable. It won't take you long, maybe the rest of the afternoon, an hour or two tomorrow, depending. Then we're going to Hamburg. We're going to Hamburg on the night train to meet the advance men for lunch. There'll be some back-and-forth at lunch, and forty-eight hours later we'll go east. Claim our goods, have a final conversation."

They walked back along the jumble of streets to Sèvres and then up Suffren to the Champ de Mars. Along the way, Junko bought a newspaper and began reading it, whistling under his breath. He looked up every few moments, but depended on Sydney to keep him from bumping into things. Sydney was silent, thinking about Hamburg, believing that if things went as planned he would be free of Junko's business by the end of the week. He would be finished by the time Angie returned and they could take a trip together, not London. Not anywhere in France or Germany. Somewhere warm, perhaps North Africa, perhaps Portugal. And not a long weekend either; a week or more, lying on the sand in the sun, bella figuras to begin the day and bella figuras to end it. That left

Herr Kaus, but in any great enterprise there was neglect. For Herr Kaus, the cat would have to remain in midleap a while longer.

They approached the monument to Marshal Joffre, the hero of the Marne. The wide esplanade of the Champ de Mars swung away to the Eiffel Tower. There were a few tourists and many young mothers with small children and vendors selling hot dogs and candy. A clochard was panhandling without success.

Junko suddenly began to laugh, throwing the newspaper into the sidewalk trash can.

"Hostages," he said.

"What about hostages?"

"It's in the paper. They've released three French hostages in Beirut. Some concession we'll never hear about but they're home now and the interviews're all over the paper. God, they're whiners. It's disgusting. The food's no good. They can't get anything to read. The water's foul and there's not enough of it. They can't bathe. No shampoo and the soap's coarse. Their teeth hurt. They miss their wives and children. Boo-hoo. They're bored. They aren't allowed to talk to anyone and at night it's chilly cold. They can't keep track of time. It gives me a pain, listening to hostages bitch and moan. The French're no worse than the others. Why can't they grow up?"

Sydney was listening to Junko's tirade and watching the young mothers and their children. A little group of them was standing under one of the plane trees in front of Junko's apartment, looking skyward. A little girl was crying.

"Every time one of them gets released and they show the interviews on television, I turn the god damned set off because I can't stand the whining."

"What's going on over there?"

"I don't know," Junko said.

"Those people under the tree."

"Oh, those."

"What are they looking for?"

"That kid that's crying," Junko said.

"Yes," Sydney said.

"She lost her fucking balloon."

Three

SYDNEY went to bed at once, leaving Junko Poole alone and dispirited in his wagon-lit as the night train slipped from the vast gloom of the Gare du Nord. Junko had brought a bottle of Mumm's and a tin of caviar and a bag of toast points, believing that the journey would be festive. That was the reason for taking the train, a nineteenth-century conveyance where things, as they said in the advertisements, were possible. Sydney seemed cheerful enough, though his eyes were more turned-down than usual and his manner tense and distracted. Junko was left alone in the empty corridor holding a paper cup of Mumm's and watching the suburban stations flash by. At this hour they were deserted, woebegone in the neon glare. Junko was waiting for the dark countryside north of Senlis, terrain he knew well, northeast through St.-Quentin and the western Ardennes to Mons, and beyond Mons, Liège and Aachen. The countryside was lit by a full moon and Junko returned to his compartment, shut the door and turned out the light, and sat down on his bed with his Mumm's, watching the featureless landscape, the German invasion corridor in 1914 and again in 1940, flat fields through which flowed sluggish rivers, meandering and tangled as ganglia, all the familiar rivers, the Aisne, the Oise, the Meuse; to the east the Somme, to the west the Marne. Many of the campaigns were named for the rivers and the Marne had two, First Marne and Second Marne. There was the Meuse-Argonne salient, the Somme offensive, the Aisne front. They were not great rivers, like the Seine or the Rhine, only slowly moving streams that were not advantageous either for defense or attack. In 1940 the German advance had been so swift that all the battles were merged into one descriptive noun, *Blitzkrieg*. Junko lay back, thinking how useful the wars had been. The trench warfare of the First War made fixed lines a no-go in the second. The Second War in Europe was a war of fire and maneuver. The humiliation of the French — what was Sydney's theory? That humiliation was a luxury for the well fed and the cowardly — made it unimaginable that the French would ever fight again. They had been humiliated, and they had survived; they carried a deep psychic wound, but wounds healed and in a generation or so they could pick at the scab and perhaps then it would vanish or become merely a thin white line, like any scar from some youthful misfortune. The Germans had always been frightened of themselves and the Second War made them terrified, and although irony was never a German trait, they saw the irony of their situation now. Defeated utterly in 1945, they were now the strongest power in Europe, stronger by far than if the Third Reich had triumphed. The fascists did not have the intelligence or vision to administer a continent. Ten years after the war, Germany would have been bankrupt; and France would now be what Germany was. Of course this was logical but did not take into account mischance, perversity, and God's will. There were also the legends.

Junko Poole sipped his Mumm's and thought about the Angel's Elm, due any time now outside the window. Years ago a sentimental German army colonel had told him a wonderful story he had heard from an aged British brigadier. Junko and the German were having a drink in the bar car, the German traveling from Hamburg to Paris to attend a war game at Versailles; Junko had got on the train after mischief in Bremen. They reached an empty stretch south of Mons where the fields were as level and barren as a pool table. The colonel laughed and pointed out the window at an enormous elm whose summer crown resembled angel's wings.

A famous elm, he said.

Well known to my regiment.

And well known to the brigadier's.

One of the great myths of the First War was that angels had protected the British retreat at Mons. Inexplicable otherwise. The British should never have escaped, pursued as they were by the 24th Brandenburgers of General von Lochow's III Corps. The regiment was the finest in the German army, its service dating from the Napoleonic wars. The only criticism of this regiment was that it was too brave, officers and men. But somehow at Mons the British slipped the noose and then Falkenhayn ordered the regiment to pull up at the Marne. This blunder, plus of course the angels, allowed the British to retreat, regroup, counterattack, and sideslip west. Both armies were fearful of being outflanked. This was in 1914, early days.

Remember, Herr Poole, that the casualties had already been high. The Germans lost a million men killed, wounded, and missing, in the first five months of the war. And the French lost an equal number. The British lost somewhat less, perhaps because they believed in angels. In any case, that was soon to be set straight.

The benevolent angels at Mons preserved the British Expeditionary Force to fight at Ypres, where incidentally Falkenhayn authorized the first use of poison gas. The gas tore an enormous hole in the British lines but again the general failed to *pursue*. In battle, audacity was everything and Falkenhayn had every military attribute except the salient one. The British closed ranks and the fight went on for weeks. The angels at Mons preserved the BEF to fight at Ypres, as bloody a contest as there was in the First War, which made it as bloody a contest as there was in the history of human conflict. In the few weeks British losses amounted to 55,000 men killed, wounded, and missing. It was a slaughter.

Some angels, the colonel said with a huge laugh.

Junko had been waiting for the elm tree with the angel's crown, but it had flown by unobserved because they had arrived at Mons station, and were as suddenly beyond it. The countryside was much darker now. That afternoon the colonel had gone on and on, retailing myths about the First War. Very few attached to the second because men were too self-conscious and unwilling to *believe* — Freud's legacy, the colonel said. Of course it would happen again; not the Germans this time but the Russians, if they could sober up the infantry. Or perhaps the French, frustrated by their inability to influence events, would strike north. Or the Americans, frustrated by whatever, the Americans had an enormous capacity for frustration and paranoia, would invade once again. This time the invasion would be south-to-north rather than the other way around and Germany would be the killing field.

It is plausible, no?

No, Junko had said. It is not plausible. He had gestured out the window at the morose Flanders landscape. All this is behind us. First Marne is as quaint as Little Big Horn. It will never happen again, Ypres, Sedan, Verdun, Dunkirk. There will not be a European war in our lifetime because everyone understands that if you win you lose and if you lose you win. Except that it might, sometime, be the other way around. It was in 1870. We must look forward, to the day after tomorrow.

The colonel had laughed and said, I think you are naïve, Herr Poole. Men have always fought. It's what men do. They like to do it. It's bred in the bone.

Naïve? Junko said. *Me?* And grinning wolfishly, to the colonel's evident puzzlement, he described his vision of the future. As it happened, he agreed entirely with the colonel's shrewd reading of human nature. But the modern world was not accommodating. Alas, if they gave a war the day after tomorrow no one would R.S.V.P. Not the Russians, the Scandinavians, the Spanish, the Italians, the French, the English, or the Americans. Perhaps the Germans, but there were not enough of them to make a real war. It's obsolete. It's last year's car. So the fight must be carried on with other weapons, just as exciting, except no one dies of visible wounds. The aggression is the same but there are no concentration camps, no mass graves, no cities pounded to rubble. You read the body count each day on the Bourse.

They had argued until the train eased into the Gare du Nord, where they exchanged cards and promised to stay in touch, but didn't.

That was years ago. In many ways, Junko had been prescient. But in the heat of his discovery he had forgotten the great exception. Of course the Third World was exempt, because megalomania flourished in the humidity of the southern climates. Humidity made men dreamy. In the same way, murderous zeal flourished in conditions of spiritual excess. They were so close to God, so far from humanity. The belligerent cycle of history in the northern hemisphere would repeat itself in the southern, so there would always be war business; the colonel had only misidentified the theater.

Junko was pleasantly tipsy, enjoying the motion of the train as it hurtled toward the Rhineland, and then north through the Ruhr Valley to Schleswig-Holstein. He was sorry to have missed the angel tree at Mons, always an agreeable talisman on his frequent journeys to mighty Hamburg. He pressed his face against the cold glass, noticing that the countryside was much darker now. There were no lights anywhere, nor any sign of life, and the moon had disappeared. Junko poured the last of the Mumm's into his paper cup and stared into the blackness, beginning to smile because he thought of poor Sydney, who did not see the romance of business. He did not see the humor of a paper cup of Champagne in the middle of the night, wondering where the light had gone. He did not appreciate life's variety, living as he did inside others' texts. Perhaps it was a mistake, involving Sydney van Damm with these ambitious Germans. But it was Sydney's choice, concerned as he was about his wife and his helpless son; value given, value received. And he had only a supporting role, because he did not understand that you had to lie. You created your own story because no one would do it for you; it was part of the oxygen you breathed. You had to lie to people to make them believe. In that way you gave them the gift of faith.

He pressed his nose against the cold window, smiling broadly now. Then he noticed tiny snowflakes brushing against the glass and reflected on the short life of false spring.

Junko had rented a spacious suite in a hotel overlooking the frozen Aussenalster. The meeting was set for noon. He arranged for fresh flowers and a full bar, German beer, Russian vodka, British gin, American whiskey, and the mixers to go with them. There was ice in a glass bucket and wedges of lemons and limes in porcelain bowls. Here and there were packs of American cigarettes and a humidor of Havana cigars, and various hors d'oeuvres, appetizers to the four-course lunch, which would be served promptly at one. He had conferred with the maître d', who proposed a tub of shrimp followed by grilled sole fresh from the North Sea, a cheese board, and a baked Alaska to finish, all of it accompanied by a Sancerre blanc and a Morgon rouge from reliable Socialist

France. Of course Cognac and the usual *eaux de vie* would be served with coffee. No waiters. The party would serve itself. The maître d' found that odd, but said nothing. Herr Poole was an old and valued customer, and knew his business.

He busied himself with the refreshments, arranging the bottles as a general would arrange his troops, the hardiest front and center. Vodka was the equivalent of the 24th Brandenburgers, one hundred proof and counting. Junko was dressed in a heavy worsted suit, a brilliant white shirt, and a silk tie. He had the day before exchanged his gold Rolex for an authoritative Audemars Piguet, enough dials (as he said) to navigate an aircraft. Junko looked like any prosperous investment banker with an urbane turn of mind and an infinite line of credit, a flexible businessman who understood that the durable deal was the one in which both parties left the table slightly dissatisfied. But — a shrewd adversary would look for asymmetries, and this adversary might guess that Herr Poole was not very bright. Perhaps Herr Poole was too quick to smile, to offer his hand, to make an uninteresting joke, altogether too porous and inattentive to read the fine print. In such a circumstance, a shrewd adversary would want to close at once, perhaps while proposing a toast to mutual trust, respect, and confidence.

All this, Junko had carefully prepared. And prepared Sydney as well. The translator, as instructed, wore corduroy trousers and a black turtleneck sweater and a tweed sport jacket out at the elbows, looking rather like an overage graduate student, perhaps one with proletarian antecedents and an eye for the main chance.

Your attitude's important, Syd. Remember, these are the advance men. You're a little out of place here among the costly vintages and the American in the bespoke suit. Erich will have briefed them, so they'll know we're friends. But you're somewhat skeptical. With these two, you're friendly but not too friendly until we sit down at the table, when your sympathies become obvious. You're here to protect them against me.

I'm their pal, Sydney said.

Not their pal, Junko said. You're their counselor. That's what you become as the afternoon wears on and on, although it may end sooner than you think. You don't want to see your countrymen screwed by a slimy American from Paris, probably a Jew. You go next door now, wait till they come, then knock about five minutes later. It'll give me a chance to meet Bernhard, demonstrate that I know a few words of Kraut and not much more. When you come in, make free with the drinks yourself to show that you're one of them. I'll drink Perrier so they'll think I'm an American pansy, worried about his weight and his liver. I'd like you to talk again to Erich, chat him up a little. Find out what's on his mind. It's Bernhard who's in charge, so I'll handle him. This is just a little get-acquainted meeting. We're just verifying that we're all in the same foursome, playing the same course under the same strict rules of golf, because they're our escorts when we go east.

Sydney nodded.

My big one's the one to watch out for. Bernhard is heartless. Fifty years ago he'd've been a concentration camp commandant, proud of his efficiency. And as a matter of fact, I think that's what he was. There aren't very many of them over there, most of the fascists came to our side of the line because they hated the Reds so. And weren't we happy to have them? But of course you know that, don't you, Syd? Probably he had something they wanted or maybe he was theirs all along. Bernhard understands a little English but less than he thinks he does, which is an advantage for us. I don't worry about Erich and you shouldn't either. Erich's tired, Syd. Erich's a little sick at heart, because he's been walking the tightrope between politics and culture for so long. He bills himself as an intellekshul but he's dumber than horse cock. The point is this, Syd. We have to give them confidence and I don't think this is going to be difficult. I'm not even sure that you and I will have to stay beyond the shrimp bowl, because I have a trick up my sleeve, too.

Sydney went down the hall to his own room and lay down on the bed with a copy of *Der Spiegel*. He found it hard to concentrate despite the picture spread on East Germany's Baltic riviera; that was where they would be going. He read for a moment and then went to the window. The Aussenalster was frozen solid, the day overcast with a bitter north wind. He watched pedestrians struggle with it. Everyone was wrapped in heavy greatcoats with mufflers and fur hats. Sydney stared at a high-shouldered statue that suddenly moved and became a man, walking slowly now in the direction of the city center. Sydney shivered, feeling the cold through the windowpane. And then there were noises in the corridor,

Junko's baritone and Erich's bass, and he knew that the Germans had arrived.

When he walked into the suite, Junko was standing in front of the bar, offering his wares. Introductions were made, Bernhard nodding and Erich smiling, everyone shaking hands. Bernhard accepted a tumbler of vodka and Erich a beer. Sydney took beer. Junko poured himself a finger of bourbon and Sydney wondered what had happened to make him change his drinking plans; it was doubtless some remark Bernhard had made. Junko was brimming with confidence and bonhomie, solicitous of his guests. Bernhard was a mountain of flesh, perhaps seventy years old though he looked younger. He was drenched in cologne. He wore a double-breasted blue suit with side vents, a fashionable affair that fit poorly. Sydney knew from his slurred German dialect that he was from the south, somewhere in the vicinity of Munich. Bernhard looked the way a Socialist functionary was supposed to look: stolid, satisfied, suspicious, slow to move, slow to think, quick to anger.

They had been chatting in fractured English and German, but when Sydney arrived Bernhard switched entirely to German. Erich said very little, nursing his beer, listening. Erich had the looks and bearing of a subordinate, yet he could not suppress a small sarcastic smile from asserting itself at casual moments. Junko was telling them a preposterous story about an elm tree south of Mons. It took Sydney a moment to get it, Junko's singular slang, the German army colonel, the retreat and regroupment, the counterattack, and the bloody dénouement at Ypres.

"Some angel," Junko said, Sydney translated, and the Germans dutifully laughed.

Bernhard helped himself to more vodka.

"But we don't have to worry about that anymore."

"No?" Bernhard looked at him doubtfully.

"It's over and done with, dead and buried." Junko passed the plate of hors d'oeuvres, caviar on toast, quails' eggs, thumb-sized German sausages with mustard, Greek olives. "No winners, no losers, only survivors. It's time at last to think about a Europe free of rivalry, where everyone has a community of interest. The modern European choir: basses, tenors, sopranos, all singing the same song. The economy, for example, the mighty engine of Western civilization. And what is the bottom line of this civilization? Sell the people what they want! When the people have what they want, there's a spirit of public happiness. Nationalism's for the squirrels. It's not ownership that's important, it's production. And after production, distribution. After distribution, sales." Junko poured a thimble of bourbon into his glass and raised it in salute. "To profits!" he cried.

There was general silence after this fantastic tango.

Then Bernhard cleared his throat.

"We need money," he said in English, moving to the window, nodding at Junko to follow him.

Erich said, "Squirrels?"

"Junko is often — carried away."

Erich nodded, sighing.

Sydney said, "Hamburg is a beautiful city, is it not?"

"It is my first visit," Erich said.

Sydney was surprised and said so.

"Believe it," Erich said. "I have been out of the Democratic Republic only a few times, to Prague and to Moscow of course, and to Paris once. That was when I saw you. I have been a good Communist all my life. My father was. When I was a young man I taught at a gymnasium near Dresden. Some years ago they told me I must work for Bernhard, so I did. Bernhard knows nothing of mathematics and therefore nothing of computers. Yet he ran the depot." Erich looked at the hors d'oeuvres tray and took a sausage and a quail's egg. Sydney opened a bottle of pilsener and poured it into Erich's glass. Across the room, at the window, Junko was talking and Bernhard was listening. Erich watched them a moment, then seemed to make up his mind about something, for he shook his head and laughed sharply. "And do you have an opinion about our unification?"

Sydney shrugged and did not reply.

Erich took silence as a rebuke. He said, "We know the contempt you in the West have for us, the sort of people we have been, the sort of government we allowed. We allowed the West to buy our citizens, so many west marks for this citizen, so many for that. We never gave them our terrorists, though. We protected our terrorists the way the Soviets used to protect their Jews. A nation of fools and thugs is what we've been. We live worse even than the Turks. My brother-in-law is in the Stasi, so I knew roughly what it did and how it did it and with what authority. But I had no idea of the excesses, the killings, the torture, the espionage, the surveillance. We were a small country and had to remain vigilant. That was obvious, our enemies were numerous. No one questioned the need for a security apparatus. But."

Sydney smiled broadly.

"I know," Erich said. "It sounds familiar. It is identical with those German citizens who lived in Munich during the war. They professed to know nothing of Dachau. Dachau was a suburb a few kilometers away, perhaps some people were interned there, the usual misfits, perverts, enemies of the state." He smiled coldly. "Truly. Aren't we an amazing people."

"Amazing," Sydney said.

"Much is concealed in our Germany. Your Germany, too."

"I live in France," Sydney said.

"For a long time?"

"A very long time," Sydney said.

"Then you have been left behind, as regards the development of the two Germanys."

"Yes," Sydney said.

At the window, Bernhard was laughing at something Junko had said, splashing vodka into his glass, ice following the vodka, lemon wedge following the ice. Junko had switched to Perrier.

"I was a good Marxist," Erich said.

"Was?" Sydney asked.

"It has no utility anymore. It is a dead language. In a few years, we will be just like you."

"I hope not," Sydney said.

"Life in Paris is not pleasant?"

"Sometimes it is," Sydney admitted.

"As Sebastian said. The bottom line — wasn't that what he called it? It is an accountant's term, is it not? — is to sell the people what they want and the people want automobiles and television sets and sexy films and wine and weapons. If bullets were digestible there would be no hunger in the world." He paused and gestured around the room, taking in the bar, the round table with white linen and place settings for four, Morgon and Sancerre cooling in their separate buckets, the chairs and long davenport, the figured carpet, the hotel art on the walls, and said, "They want this."

"You're forgetting the little vacation apartment in Torremolinos," Sydney said.

"What is Torremolinos?"

"A nasty Spanish resort, popular with Germans and English."

"Nasty, is it?"

"Very," Sydney said.

"And here, I didn't even know it existed." Erich thought a moment. He had not touched his beer but held it delicately between his thumb and forefinger. "It seemed to many of us at the gymnasium that our Berlin was no more corrupt than your Berlin or Washington or Paris. It was corrupt in a different way, and the reforms were no easier for us than they are for the Americans or the French. In fact they were harder because of the party control and your economic warfare against us, and it is fair to say that in the West the people are lulled. They do not care in the way that we care. They do not want to build a society, they want to live off it. We thought that once we reformed the party then we would have decent politics and a modern society. A number of us thought that. Quite a lot, really. You must not think that all of us are bewitched by automobiles, television sets, and dirty films. The weapons are another matter. But there are not enough of us and probably we are naïve, although naïveté was never a conspicuous trait with us. I will say that perhaps we are too romantic. But the party fell in an instant. And when it broke apart we saw how corrupt it was. It was just a sick old man without energy enough to be paranoid, even. The proletariat rushed into the streets, not knowing what it would find. And it found Herr Kohl. And here we are." Erich reached down to the coffee table and picked up a pack of Marlboros, slit it open, and extracted a cigarette. He looked around for a match but Sydney offered his lighter. Erich inhaled deeply and blew a smoke ring, as he had seen Sydney do. "So I have spent my life chasing that," he said, gesturing at the smoke ring as it collapsed. "And what have you been chasing, Herr van Damm? Can it be true that you have no opinion of our unification, as certain now as if it were ordained by God?"

Sydney watched Erich's face as he spoke. There was a tic in his cheek and his eyes moved inward toward some imaginary landscape. How different they were, he and Erich. Like the two Germanys themselves they had no common memory and no agreed-upon history. Perhaps there was a common search for equilibrium, though Erich's would be the equilibrium of the collapsed smoke ring; probably he believed that politics was conscience. Sydney remembered suddenly the German legend, the itinerant dwarf who with his raised sword was the height of a normal man. He and Erich and the dwarf, too, sought a Rightful Place. In Germany there would always be dreaming. Germans were great dreamers, hence their talent for mathematics. Germans sought a unified field, some ruling principle that all Germans could live by. You could draw a common boundary and call it unification, but it wasn't unification in any sense other than economic, an arrangement supervised by Düsseldorf banks. It was only a common skin. A schizophrenic inhabits one body and looking at that body in repose you assume that inside is an integrated personality. But when the schizophrenic awakens and begins to speak and move about, you discover not one but many personalities, some in harmony and others in opposition. He said to Erich, "We Germans have not one history but many histories. The Americans solved the problem by democracy, which many of our great philosophers denounce as vulgar anarchy. Heidelberg for us, Hollywood for them. We despise the common culture of the Americans and then fear it because we see our own young drawn into its orbit. We Germans love stability and order, strict exactitude. We are nostalgic for medieval times. We are nostalgic for the Teutonic Knights, for the slayers of giants, for the heroes who lie asleep to issue forth at the hour of the nation's greatest need. We search for a Rightful Place. *We want to be Europeans.*" Erich had taken a step back and now looked at him with dismay. "But I wonder if we are not going against the tide of history," Sydney said softly. "It would not be the first time. The Soviet Union is breaking up, the Balkans will soon be breaking up, capitalism itself is disintegrating. Yet the Germans come together and no romantic soul can be less than thrilled, since it is what the people want. The people from the East want it more than life itself. They want to enter the postwar world of the Federal Republic, and who can blame them? Who can say we must not do this because of German history, the behavior of our fathers and grandfathers? The Wall is a symbol nearly as grotesque as the swastika, not only dividing Germany but dividing Europe. Unification is what the people want and that is what they will have, but applause must be withheld until the crisis that cannot be solved by a deutsche mark. This will be a crisis that will call for sacrifice and generosity, the product of a culture rather than the product of politics. Then we shall see." Sydney smiled and leaned forward. "Have you seen my mother lately?"

Erich recoiled, seeming almost to lose his balance.

"Her health," Sydney began.

"No," Erich said.

"I wonder what she thinks about it," Sydney said. "Probably she is opposed. Old people despise change."

"Not only the old people," Erich said.

"I thought you might have seen her lately. In your travels."

"No," Erich said. "Not for some months."

"Perhaps," Sydney began, but did not finish the sentence.

"I am glad to know you have thought about our country," Erich said quickly.

"I have thought about it a little," Sydney said.

Erich smiled, glancing at Bernhard and Junko Poole by the window, deep in conversation. "You are right about Hollywood," he said finally.

"One of my earliest memories," Sydney said. "A Hollywood movie. A cheap American film, my mother called it." When Erich did not reply, Sydney said, "Do you have a family?"

"Yes, a wife. Two children. We were married because it was the only way to get an apartment. It was not a romantic business but we get along. The children are at the gymnasium where I used to teach. I suppose now they will learn about Bentham and Mill and Reagan and Thatcher instead of Marx. I suppose that instead of Goethe they will read Lewis Carroll. They will learn about Lenin, I think, except Lenin will be taught as a great national hero, a kind of Napoleon with an unfortunate ideology and a secret police. The ideology will be secondary to the personality. You can forget about Karl Liebknecht and Rosa Luxemburg, though. Karl and Rosa will be described as bandits and neurotics, cosmopolitans, Jews."

"Maybe Thomas Jefferson," Sydney said.

Erich looked at him through a cloud of tobacco smoke. "Do you really think so?"

"No," Sydney said.

"I don't either."

"It's too bad you can't save something for the future generations to study, some of the artifacts of your civilization. The way archaeologists study Etruscan pots."

"Don't make jokes," Erich said. "We were stabbed in the back. Our leaders stabbed us first. And then the West. We had our chance but when there is treachery all around. When there is treachery in every corner. At every turn. When you are surrounded by treachery. When it is in the air that you breathe." He took a long swallow of beer. "What can you do?"

"Complain about treachery," Sydney said.

"More than that," Erich said.

There was a sudden blast of laughter from the window, Bernhard and Junko roaring at some story, arms around each other's shoulders.

Erich watched them a moment, his mouth a thin line of distaste, and said, "Is he as stupid as he sounds?"

"No," Sydney said.

"I didn't think so," Erich said.

"Let me tell you something," Sydney began, but Erich put up his hands in a show of surrender, shaking his head.

"We both know what's happening here," he said. "What is happening now and what is going to happen. The form of it doesn't matter. The details don't matter. Herr Poole and his associates, whoever they are, will take delivery of our goods. What happens to them later isn't our affair. How we got them isn't your affair. It's a simple business transaction of the sort that happens every day, isn't that right? We have no other way of disposing of our goods. We do not have your free market here. So we needed another party, one with experience in the commercial world. The one who was introduced to Bernhard was Herr Poole. Bernhard assigned me to work out the details with Herr Poole and that is how I came to be in Paris, eating caviar and drinking Champagne, listening to jokes."

Erich was silent a moment, and then he sighed. "I think this business arrangement will not benefit us, but who cares. We are accustomed to the stab in the back."

"If you say so," Sydney said.

"Is that his real name?"

"Sure," Sydney said.

"What does he do actually? Is he a spy?"

"He is a businessman," Sydney said.

"And you, Herr van Damm. What do you do actually?"

"I translate for him."

"This is how you are employed?"

"Occasionally. Normally I translate books. You may know of Josef Kaus."

"Yes, of course," Erich said. "His books are available here."

"I translate him into English," Sydney said.

Erich frowned. "I cannot imagine his English readership."

"American," Sydney said.

"He is our greatest writer," Erich said.

"I agree," Sydney said.

"He is a *German* and without remorse."

"Perhaps we see him differently," Sydney said.

"And he too lives in Paris."

"Around the corner from my apartment," Sydney said.

"Yet he does not write of Paris."

"No one does anymore," Sydney said. "In any case, Paris does not interest him."

Erich looked at him suddenly and said, "You should not be involved in this business."

"But I am," he said.

"I think it could end badly."

"How?"

"Bernhard is a fool," Erich said.

Sydney looked at them by the window, laughing again. "You could put a stop to it."

"Oh?" Erich smiled. He drained his beer and put the glass carefully on the side table. "I think that would not be productive." Then, "Perhaps it is good that you are involved. Good luck to us."

"May I ask you something?"

"Of course, Herr van Damm."

"Will the goods actually be there? In your depot? When we go to collect them? You have made me nervous."

"Naturally," Erich said.

"To table!" Junko cried. Bernhard poured more vodka into his glass, Erich fetched another bottle of beer, and the four sat. Junko busied himself with the wine bottles, uncorking them and sending them around the table, all the while chattering aimlessly, Sydney translating each ricochet. When the bottles were safely in their buckets, Junko looked around the table, beaming, and clapped his hands.

The bedroom door opened and the two servers appeared, pushing wheeled tables laden with food. In the sudden sharp silence each man moved, to touch the knot of his tie or to adjust a wineglass or pull his nose. The servers were about twenty, dressed in blue miniskirts and T-shirts. One was fair and the other dark. Sydney thought they were the prettiest German girls he had ever seen and, in the stale hotel atmosphere, lascivious. They radiated desire. They were barefoot, perfect small feet at the base of slender curvy legs, and waists as supple as ballet dancers'. They swayed when they walked. Adorable, they passed the tub of slippery shrimp, smiling prettily, touching each man's shoulder as they leaned forward, ladling the wet shrimp and the various tasty sauces. They spoke softly in a kind of drawl, occasionally to each other, using sexy nicknames. Their eyes glittered with worldly amusement. Their manners said that these moments were the apex of their young lives and perhaps — perhaps! — if these experienced older men would consent to lie with them after the meal, this adventure would remain with them for the remainder of their human existence, enchanted as that existence might turn out to be. These girls were so young and fresh, so untouched by life; yet they were avid. And of the four men at table, the large one promised the most. Was it not well known that young women liked large, fat men? Balding, clumsy men with heavy breasts and thick useful thighs. Ach! The afternoon of a lifetime, a thing to be pressed into the memory like the petals of a flower in a diary. No service would be too oppressive or arduous.

And as the girls served, paying particular attention to the two guests, Sydney glanced at Erich, glaring openly at a taut T-shirt no more than six inches from his nose. Hard to know what his expression signified. Sydney thought it was hatred, though it may have been desire.

"Dig in," Junko said.

What happened then? Angie asked.

Sydney listened to the transatlantic hum, Hamburg to Old Harbor.

The endgame, Sydney said. Bernhard had fallen in love completely and without reservation and couldn't keep his mind on his food. Shrimp kept falling out of his mouth. Romy or Brigitte, or whatever the blond one was called, laughed merrily, picked up the shrimp, and put it back in his mouth as if she were feeding pablum to a baby. She'd lay the damned thing on his tongue and he'd say, *Gut.* Then she'd smile, wiggle her behind, and clap her pretty hands as if he'd performed an incredible athletic feat; and all the while she'd be pouring vodka. Erich was staring at Bernhard, not, I think, believing what was in front of his eyes. Meanwhile, the dark-haired one (she had very long eyelashes and a turned-up nose, a soft voice and a modest manner and a body better than any statue in the Louvre) was making certain that Erich had his napkin arranged properly in his lap. It was then that Junko motioned for me to lean close, that he had a question or two for his friend Bernhard. He raised an eyebrow at the girls and they stepped back, their expressions alarmed, for it was evident that Junko was displeased; and if Junko was displeased, perhaps they would be sent on their way. Their alarm was nothing compared to Bernhard's, but the situation was resolved. Junko wanted to settle a discrepancy in the number of machines that were being delivered, and the money that was being paid for them. It took about a minute and a half, including translation, and Bernhard never took his eyes off the blond one, and when she winked at him I thought he would break down. Then the telephone rang and Junko answered it and spoke a few words and hung up and declared that we, he and I, had to leave at once on urgent business. Naturally Bernhard and Erich were to remain and enjoy themselves, the girls would attend to their every need and we'd be in touch.

It was a nightmare, Sydney said.

Not that it wasn't funny in its own way, he added.

Angela had been listening carefully but she was not amused. She was thinking about the girls. No doubt they had been told what to expect. No doubt they had been handsomely paid, rewarded above and beyond the usual fees. But what a chore, and the fact that they had chosen it made it no less odious. She hated that Sydney was involved.

In what way was it funny, van Damm?

But Sydney could not tell her in what way it was funny; perhaps it was funny in an untranslatable German way.

And what happens now?

We have the correct manifest and we're going east the day after tomorrow, escorted by Bernhard and Erich. Then it's over and I'm going home. I have a car, and tomorrow I'm taking a drive. I may visit my mother, Angie.

Your mother?

It's about three hours by car. The border's open.

Well, she said. Good.

What about you? he asked. How are things in Old Harbor?

Not so hot, she said. I'm not sorry I came, but it's been a trial. You were right, van Damm. Please don't say I told you so. What I have to say is, Thank God for Junko Poole, that bastard.

Four

SHE HAD NOTICED the missing shingles when she stepped from the cab, standing alone with her bag in the driveway in the snow, waiting for some sign of life within. Tommy Borowy's tiny Toyota was parked next to the garage, a light dusting of snow on its hood. Angie blew on her hands and picked up her bag, noticing that her fingers were grimy and stiff in the cold. She buried her chin in her coat collar and mounted the steps, turning to peek through the big window into the living room. Her father was asleep in his wing chair, the reading light on, his book open, the magnifying glass still in his limp hand. She recognized *The Education of Henry Adams*. Tommy Borowy was asleep in the chair in front of the television set, some sporting event in vivid color. She smiled. They looked like two ancient children having their afternoon naps, except that instead of milk and cookies each man had a highball near at hand, the whiskey tepid now. The living room was disheveled, magazines and newspapers here and there. Through the window she could hear them snoring lightly.

They were both so old, her father now eighty, Tommy over seventy. Parents were always old. She tried to remember Carroll at middle age, the age she was now, and could not. However old you were, they were always a generation ahead. And then they got very old and reminded you of ancient children. Her memories of Tommy Borowy went back as far, though somewhere she had a recollection of him on the back lawn playing croquet in white ducks and a straw hat, saddle shoes on his feet, a mint julep in his hand, dapper as Fred Astaire. That was when her mother was alive and Shake very young; the house and grounds were groomed, or as groomed as you could get in rustic Maine. There was a gardener and a housekeeper and various mechanicals to keep things running; "mechanicals," her father's word. An appliance failed and he would cry, "Get a mechanical!" They were all gone now — the roofer, the plumber, the furnace man, the electrician. Their trades did not appeal to their children, either sons or daughters; so the mechanicals closed their businesses and moved to Florida. Help had to be imported from Bar Harbor or even Bangor. The price was always high, so after a while Carroll let things go, a battered roof or a toilet that flushed incompletely or a furnace that banged. Carroll complained that they seemed to be living in a Third World country where nothing happened without a bribe, where the authorities were invisible except at tax time, and where no one was proficient, unlike the old mechanicals, who were crackerjacks. Repairs now were carelessly done by anonymous workmen. But you couldn't do without heat or plumbing or a roof over your head; so you begged people to come. And then Mrs. Steen, who had looked after both of them for years, went to live with her daughter in Springfield, Massachusetts, leaving them in the care of a sullen teenager who listened to rock music while she worked or, rather, loitered. Carroll on Mondays, Tommy on Wednesdays. Really, Angela, the child's good for nothing. I can't get her to iron my socks.

Angela tried the door and found it locked. That was new. It was only four in the afternoon, though dusk was coming on; no one ever bothered to lock up during the day. And God, it was bleak after sunny Paris. There were no leaves on the trees, and all the colors were various shades of gray, even the firs. She put down her bag and tapped lightly on the glass, twice. She was looking into the living room sideways through the glass, the only movement on the screen of the television set. Her father did not stir and Tommy looked dead. She tapped a third time and they both shuddered, first their legs and then their heads. They gathered themselves like collapsed marionettes. Carroll turned then and saw her in the window, gave a wide grin and rose, standing unsteadily, saying something to Tommy.

Welcome! Carroll cried, opening the door. Welcome home!

* * *

Tommy had bought a roast and Carroll went to the basement to fetch a bottle from his dwindling wine cellar. Dwindling, he said, but not so dwindling that I can't find a bottle from the sixties, when they still knew how to make wine. Angela prepared the roast, a seven-pound affair that would feed them for a week. Tommy and Carroll sat at the kitchen table and talked while she cooked and cleaned up. The kitchen was filthy, as it never was when Mrs. Steen was doing the chores.

Carroll uncorked a bottle of Burgundy and let it sit on the sideboard.

Angela halved onions and listened to their news.

All their close friends were dead, so the obits had to do with acquaintances or celebrities, actors they had seen in their youth, or writers or politicians. The roofer had died of cancer in Bradenton, Florida. Tommy's law partner's widow died in a nursing home in Portland, age one hundred and two. Her husband had died in 1958. You remember, Angie, old Harold Williams and Priscilla, you went out once or twice with their son, Ivan. Nice boy. One hundred and two, think of that; two of her children were dead, and one grandchild. She was one of the oldest citizens in the state of Maine, the last of six generations. Ivan moved away, I can't remember where.

Carroll looked up. That's not much older than I am.

You're still in double numbers, Tommy said.

I'm on the back nine, though. I'm damned near in the clubhouse.

Tommy said, Every year she got a birthday card from the White House. The past couple of years, anyway.

That Yalie tries to send me a birthday card, I'll stick it right back in his face.

You've got twenty years to go, Tommy said. Maybe we'll have a good one then.

Fat chance, Carroll said. The last good one was FDR.

He's doing the best he can, Tommy said.

Carroll cackled loudly. That's the trouble, he said.

Priscilla was a suffragette, Tommy said.

Dean Acheson is dead. So is Hemingway. Sidney Bechet, Emily Post. *Wiley* Post.

Nixon's still alive, though.

Nixon will never die, Carroll said. Never. He has eternal life. He's Nosferatu.

Angie was washing and slicing vegetables, listening now and then. She was thinking how large and efficient the kitchen was. The appliances seemed to her oversized. When Tommy asked her how things were in Paris, she gave him a one-sentence answer that told him nothing. But they weren't listening. They wanted to deliver their own news report, the obits first, then the weather, the economy, how they were getting on, how things were from day to day and how they felt about it. Tommy thought to ask about Van, and when she replied that he was fine, Tommy said that didn't surprise him. Germans had wonderful constitutions. All Northern Europeans did, particularly the Scandinavians. Tommy lectured for a moment on the nutritional habits of Norsemen. And natives of the state of Maine lived long though not necessarily productive lives. And things were more difficult in Maine than they were in Europe. Carroll went on to talk about the difficulties of living in America's Third World, dispirited, undernourished, and debt-burdened, where you couldn't get anything repaired or cleaned. Service wasn't available at any price, and of course things were always breaking down because they weren't manufactured properly. Oh, yes, and the newspaper went out of business, just like that, shut up shop one day. They couldn't give it away, although they tried.

The wind picked up and the old house whistled with it. The kitchen was drafty. When Angie looked outside she saw it was snowing, hard little flakes that clicked against the window like iron filings. Carroll said he was going to have a whiskey, and Angie said she would join him, a double, please. Tommy declined. Whiskey made him sleepy and then he couldn't drive properly and the storm troopers of the highway patrol had warned him once already.

The economy's going to hell, Tommy said.

Did you hear what happened to them in Massachusetts? They're broke.

Mismanagement, Tommy said.

No one was minding the store.

They wanted to run the country but they couldn't even run itty-bitty Massachusetts.

They're ding-a-lings, Tommy said.

Worse than that, Carroll said, returning with two glasses filled with whiskey. Much worse. They've turned their faces to the wall like poor Milly Theale.

I remember her, Tommy said. She was Priscilla's friend, a sister suffragette.

Jesus Christ, Tommy. For Christ's sake. Henry *James*.

Was that her husband? No, you haven't got it straight. That was the kid down at the car wash. And his name was Jimmy Henry.

Carroll turned to Angie. You see what I have to put up with?

Tommy spun his finger in a circle around his ear, and laughed.

It's probably as bad in Europe as it is here, Carroll said.

No, Angie said. She had been listening to them with growing amazement. No, it's not bad in Europe.

Thanks to our foreign aid, Tommy said.

Angie laughed, not too loudly. She said, That was the Marshall Plan, Tommy. That was forty years ago.

Tommy nodded. Now that they're back on their feet they feel they can kick us around. Poor old Uncle Sam, everybody's patsy. He began to laugh, and it was evident that he had been struck by a new thought. He said, Harold Williams was a great supporter of Senator Joe McCarthy. Harold hated the Reds. He always called McCarthy 'Tail-Gunner Joe.' That was his campaign slogan up in Wisconsin, where he was a war hero. Harold thought Senator Joe would save the Republic from Ike and Dulles, the fellow travelers. Then things went badly for Joe. Cohn got him into trouble and the Senate censured him and he sort of went to pieces, started drinking Scotch with his cornflakes. Then some smart newspaperman dug up his war record and Tail-Gunner Joe turned out to be an exaggeration. There were some financial irregularities, too, I think. The IRS got involved. Poor old Joe died and none of us could think of anything to say to Harold about it, he was so broken up. Harold revered Senator Joe. Except one night Carroll asked Harold what he thought about Senator Joe now — this was a year or two after he died — and Harold said that Joe's death proved the point. The liberal press got him, the pinko *New York Times*. The *Times* killed him, just as surely as if they'd stuck the bottle in his mouth. Of course that was before we knew anything about the Gulag.

That was the end of the story.

Angie looked at her father, who smiled.

Time to eat, Carroll said.

They sat down at seven and an hour later Tommy said he had to go, the roads would be slippery and the Nazis looking for him. They didn't get the snow-removal equipment out as early as they used to, a consequence of the budget squeeze, the shortfalls, and the cutbacks. So it was like driving in the old days, only worse because the cars were now so damned light. It didn't stop the storm troopers, though. They catch a man with a little whiskey on his breath, it's good-bye. Angie promised to come by and see him at his office before she left for France. He reminded her that he went to his office every day, mostly to read the obits. He still had more than fifty wills in his files, several of them the testaments of the grandchildren of clients long since dead. Of course his secretary had passed away, too, but occasionally someone from the courthouse came over to help him with his correspondence. And your dad's, too, of course.

He blew his nose and said it was wonderful to have her back.

Carroll and I've been counting the days.

This old house looks a lot better with you in it.

Sorry we were asleep, Tommy said.

After they had seen him to his car, and watched him laboriously back-and-forth out of the driveway, spinning his tires and racing the engine, Angie and Carroll returned to the kitchen for coffee.

I'm feeling pretty well, considering, Carroll said.

You look well, Angie said, although she thought his eyes cloudier than usual and his complexion pale. But in a Maine winter, everyone's complexion was pale.

You look tired, Carroll said.

She said, Jet lag.

He nodded, turning slightly to look out the window at the snow. The big firs were shrugging in the wind, the snow blowing every which way. The blowsy firs looked like heavy peasant women in aprons. She had grown up in snow, the way an islander grows up with the sea. The first fall often came when the leaves were still turning, well before Thanksgiving. They called it locking-in time, and it was not welcome, a signal of the length of the winter to spring's horizon. The other seasons were a parenthesis in winter. When she was a girl she looked at the first snow with a mixture of dread and delight, so many days until Christmas, so many days until Easter vacation, so many, many days until June. Winter in Maine was an eternity of ice, darkness, and bad temper, when the world seemed to stand still, without color or vivacity. Yet it was their way of life, and so they took a perverse pride in their exertions, the effort that it took not to advance but to maintain. She looked out the window at the fir, curtseying now in the wind, and wondered if it would be a three-day blow. She doubted it; it was too cold for a three-day blow. But if it was, the airport would be closed and her flight to New York delayed. She said a little silent prayer.

It's bad out there, Carroll said.

I don't think it will last, though, Angie said.

Maybe not. I wouldn't count on it.

I don't think so, Angie said firmly.

They're getting warmer, you know. It's not as bad as when you were growing up.

It's warmer in Europe, too.

Would you like a little French Cognac, Angie? I want to talk to you about something.

I would, she said. Yes, I would.

Sit still, he said. I'll get it.

She watched him smile and rub his hands with pleasure, ambling out of the kitchen in the direction of the living room, where the drinks were kept. He seemed cheerful enough and there was no trace of the stutter that had come when Shake died; and he rarely talked about Shake now. She noticed the snow collecting on the window ledges and said another prayer. Once they had been snowed in for four days, huddled around the fireplace because the power had failed. It was the year after her mother died, a February; they were burdened with memories of her, her long illness and death, all of it unaccountable, unimaginable even. They awoke to a blizzard that lasted all day long. The house was so tight that the living room was cozy, the fireplace giving both heat and light, even though the pipes in the basement froze and the snow reached almost to the eaves. They ate Campbell's soup for lunch and dinner and melted snow for drinking water. There was a cord of split wood on the porch. Carroll was happy because there was plenty of ice for his drink, icicles snapped from the eaves. He made a show of good humor, though in fact he was worried. I have to keep up my strength, he said. I'm the skipper of this ship, and the skipper needs his rum ration. He stood at the window for long minutes, sipping his drink while he watched the storm. During the day they played countless games of Monopoly. Shake quickly got the hang of the game and they let him win a few. It's important to keep up the morale of the men, Carroll said, giving her a conspiratorial wink. They were very close and companionable by the fire, listening to the storm outside. When she asked him to read them a story he consulted his bookshelves and brought down *Heart of Darkness*, reading by the light of the fire, the story taking exactly as long to read aloud as Marlow's version on the page. And when he finished, the sun was rising in Maine as it was rising in central Africa. The storm had ended, and a little later the lights went on.

He returned with a bottle of Cognac, poured two ponys, and sat down, frowning.

She said, I was remembering the time we were snowed in for four days and you read *Heart of Darkness* all one night.

I did?

She said, It was very exciting. You read it very well.

Yes, he said. That was just after your mother died. I was worried as hell. We were cut off from the outside world. We might as well have been living a hundred years ago. We might as well have been living in Afghanistan, but it was just poor cold Maine, so close to God and Canada. Shake shivering all the time, though you could hardly blame him, poor kid.

Shake was fine, she said.

That was the worst storm I ever saw up here and I've seen plenty. The house took it, though. The house stood up to it. They knew how to build things in the old days. Houses or novels. I'd forgotten about the *Heart of Darkness*. It doesn't sound like a good choice for children in the middle of a storm.

I think you read it for yourself, not for us, she said.

I suppose so, Carroll said.

Remember, they found the hunter, a couple of weeks later? He was in a tree with his rifle, frozen solid. They couldn't get him down except with a saw, and the family wouldn't allow it. They had to wait until spring. They covered him with a tarpaulin so you couldn't see him. Apparently he thought he'd be safe in the tree.

He was only a few hundred yards off Ridgfield Road but in the storm he didn't know where he was. They tried to keep the location a secret but they didn't succeed. We all knew where he was. We'd go there sometimes after school to sneak a look.

He said, I never knew that. How grisly.

God, she said. What a terrible year.

He nodded but did not reply.

Sometimes I'd pretend that she wasn't dead, only gone away, and that she'd be back and everything would be the way it always was. I can still remember some of the conversations we had. I think she hated it up here. That year, it seemed that nothing moved. Our family had no moving parts. You were remote, Shake so quiet all the time —

I'm not so well fixed, he said loudly.

— he'd go days without speaking, she concluded, her voice falling. He was glaring at her, turning his glass this way and that, the Cognac reflecting the light. In that moment, she thought he looked thirty years younger.

Angie? Listen to me. It's terrible, living in this country. You don't know what's what. You can't add things up properly. And suddenly everything changes and you don't know where you are. Living where you do, you don't know what's happened. You don't know what things cost. The cost of living is out of sight, in Maine and everywhere, hell's bells, everything from a light bulb to a bottle of whiskey. I don't know what makes money anymore. It happened when my back was turned. I've got to start thinking about the future, because I'm about busted.

Everything's less here than it is in Europe, she said. Much, much less.

I'm about busted, he said again.

She said, That's impossible.

No, it isn't. I'm like that fellow in the tree. I chose the wrong port in the storm. I got bad advice and I took it. I've never been good with investments, but there was always enough so that I didn't have to be. I could hire people to look after it, and that's what I did. And now I've got to liquidate. This house will bring something, and my library, and the Homer and the Remington. Those are my assets, plus your mother's Boston property, worth half what it was two years ago. God damn them, they should go to jail in Boston but probably won't. The fix is in, Angie, and there isn't a jail big enough to hold them all.

I didn't know she owned anything in Boston, Angie said.

Well, she did.

And it's *gone?*

It might as well be, he said. I have some securities also, not many. I don't know where it all went, I really don't.

She said, You're broke?

This is a fine house but no one wants it. No one wants to live up here, it's too far away from Mount Desert. And the house is too big. I suppose if I had a swimming pool it might be more attractive, that or a tennis court. And I'd do it, too, if I had the money, even though the roof's in bad shape. This country's hard on a house, even a house as well built as this one is. You've got to keep on top of it. You can't let it go even for a season or you wake up one morning and the thing's a wreck, even though the foundation is sound.

This is a good house, Angie said.

It's two hundred years old, Carroll said. Or the main part of it is. Plenty has been added on over the years.

Trouble is, he said, and fell suddenly silent.

What? she asked.

I've been meaning to tell you, Angie. I can't count on the pictures. The Remington is probably a fake. Your grandfather wasn't above a little sharp practice where the art market was concerned.

Mother had it appraised, she said. I remember that very well.

Yes, well, Carroll said sarcastically. Up to a point. Appraised by that friend of your mother's, the Polish screwball from Beacon Hill. It's not an appraisal that I'd walk into Sotheby's with, I can tell you that. No way. The Homer's all right, though. I'd stake my life on the Homer, which'll fetch a pretty good price. That is, if anyone's buying Homer. That's what I have anyway, plus the odds and ends that everyone accumulates. I still have some of your mother's jewelry, and that might bring something. I just found out how bad things were.

She was horrified. The jewelry was hers; it had been promised. She was listening carefully now, not knowing how much to believe, and therefore not knowing what to say or how to react. He had always complained about money, though he loved giving it away, to friends, to various cultural institutions, and the Boy Scouts — some irony there — and then later in his life to the people who made things easier, liquor stores that delivered, limousines for hire by the day. He had never earned anything himself. He had always lived on capital.

You can't sell my mother's jewelry, she said.

It's an asset, he said. I have to.

It's mine, she said.

I'm eighty years old, Angie. And I intend to live for a while.

And she promised me the Homer.

I never knew that, Carroll said.

She promised me the day she died. She said the Homer was mine. She wanted me to have it. It had been her mother's and now it was mine. I want it, Carroll.

He picked up the pony of Cognac and set it down again, turning in his chair, patting his thighs. He did not look at her.

I'm going to take it with me, she said.

It isn't here, Angie.

She didn't say anything for a moment, watching him.

He said, I don't have it.

She said, Where is it?

He said, It's in Boston. It's being sold in Boston.

I see, she said.

I have debts, he said.

You're selling my Winslow Homer to pay off your debts, she said.

He nodded sadly.

What about your library?

I'll sell it, too, one of these days. It won't fetch much except for the Conrads and the Melvilles. One or two other items, the James and the Twain. I don't have to sell them right away, though. That's the sale of last resort. I can't afford to live here anymore. I can't afford to live, period.

Carroll, she said. I can't believe this.

I made some mistakes, he said.

She said, What do you need to live on, a year?

I don't know exactly, he said. I've never figured it out. Too much. More than I take in, and that's less each year because I'm selling assets. I had some government bonds and I sold them. But most of the securities are so old, and I bought them so low, that the capital gains kills me.

You'd hate it somewhere else, she said. And where would you go?

There are some condos they built, near Bar Harbor.

She turned toward the window, searching for the firs. They were motionless now. The snow had stopped and the wind abated. She did not know what to say to him. She could not imagine him without money; and she had always counted on something for herself, beyond her annuity, smaller each year. She had definitely counted on the Homer. She and van Damm never spoke of her inheritance because they never believed it was real, or at any event reliable. And now it wasn't.

Her father smiled at her and shook his head helplessly, summoning a shadow of his ingratiating boyish charm, so formidable for so long to so many. But his daughter did not smile back.

I don't quite know how it happened, dear.

Inattention, Dad. Inattention, she said.

No, he said. It was Shake. When your brother died in the war things just seemed to go to hell for me. I lost my concentration, I didn't have any confidence in anything anymore. Oh gosh, he said suddenly. That reminds me. How's Max?

She said, What reminds you of Max?

He looked at her blankly.

You said, 'That reminds me. How's Max?'

Oh, he said. I don't know. The poor kid.

You said you didn't have any confidence anymore. Was that what reminded you of Max?

No, he said.

Max is fine, she said.

That's good, Angie.

I see him every day, she said.

Good, he said.

He's *healthy,* she said.

Why did you want the Homer, Angie?

She said, Because it's mine. Because Sydney and I are moving to the country so Max can be with us. I intended to take my Winslow Homer to New York and sell it, even though Sydney didn't want me to because it was a family treasure. But it doesn't matter now whether it's a family treasure or not. I know I won't be able to sell it in New York because you're selling it in Boston. But I'd counted on it. I want you to know that. Syd was counting on it, too.

It can't be helped, he said, rising, leaving his Cognac untouched.

That's what you have to say? It can't be helped?

There was a piece in the paper the other day, he said.

Yes?

That this is only temporary. The economy is fundamentally sound.

He went to bed and she stayed to put away the dishes and drink a last Cognac. The taste and the bouquet reminded her of Paris and Van, late nights in Fortress America. She looked again out the window to the firs, and the stone benches in front of them, the benches covered with snow. Her mother used to knit there in the summer. Sometimes Carroll would join her, reading aloud while she knitted. Their laughter would carry across the lawn, when he read her a passage from Twain or James. Once at school a classmate asked her what her father did and she was at a loss to explain. Reading was not a profession. She described him finally as a collector. He collected books to read. Her father had had a good life, and if he had been inattentive perhaps that was only the most obvious price he had paid for it.

She was trying to gather it in without prejudice but when she looked at the stone benches she remembered the spacious garden in front of them, and her heart surged. The garden was a miniature paradise, as gardens were supposed to be. Often her mother and Carroll would stroll its paths, picking flowers for the living room and the dinner table. Carroll walked with his book under his arm. The garden was an annual surprise, always overflowing. No one knew what it would look like year to year, and in that way it seemed to define or express possibility. Some years were more riotous than others, but there was always something unexpected and delightful, and the more thrilling for being extemporaneous. When her mother died, Carroll continued to tend the garden but each year it became more prepared and predictable, until finally the rows of blossoms were as strict and regular as a sonnet, the colors harmonious, the heights just so. Carroll was a great respecter of form. Then when Shake died he let it go and the garden became a thicket of dead and desiccated plants. He sat on his stone bench with a book and watched his garden decay. One April he had it plowed under and seeded so that now it was a part of the lawn. No trace of it remained. The benches stayed, but now there was no view from them except an ordinary lawn.

So she was not to have her watercolor. There would be no inheritance, large or small, and not even a memento of her mother. She wished she were with van Damm in the Fortress so that she could tell him in person. Sorry, Van. No Big Bucks, no Dilion's Millions, nul, nada, zero. He's broke. We might get some first editions out of him if we ask nicely and offer to pay. She was trying not to think about her mother's jewelry, but there it was and it would go with the rest of the assets. What had he said? "The odds and ends that everyone accumulates." Perhaps she could rescue a few of the less choice items — for sentiment, Carroll, because she was my mother and the jewelry was hers and her mother's and now, by rights, should be mine. She didn't promise them but she didn't have to; it was understood. There was a pearl necklace and a small sapphire ring and a cameo brooch and a gold pin with her initials on it. Angie had asked for them once but Carroll had temporized; they were in a bank vault, difficult to get at; let me keep them for you, or you can get them next time you come. So she had not insisted. She had let them go, as Carroll had let their money go. She had been inattentive.

Probably it was an inherited characteristic, like the Dilion Trill.

But he had no right to the picture, none at all.

Van would ask what happened. And she would explain, he spent it. And it sounds as if he made a bad investment or three, junk bonds or gold mines in Iowa. And now he has debts and has to sell my Homer to cover them. Van would listen and smile and say he never counted on it anyway, had looked on her inheritance as he would look on a lottery ticket or a turn of the wheel at Biarritz. And now everything depended on him, and Junko Poole's venture, whatever it was. She wished she had been more inquisitive, had asked questions and demanded answers. Junko's schemes were often not entirely aboveboard, though they were usually profitable. She remembered that it involved a trip to Germany, and perhaps that was where van Damm was now.

She pushed the thought away. She was having enough trouble trying to understand the one big thing without considering what came later. It was inconceivable that her father was broke. Dilions were rich. They had been rich since the middle of the last century, surviving war, panic, depression, and scandal. It was as if they had second sight; or, as a Marxist would argue, money protected itself. The Dilions had always managed to pass on a legacy, in the manner of European families, who passed on their customs, their way of looking at things, along with their valuables. Often history intervened, a revolution or other natural catastrophe, causing the inheritance to vanish for a while, though rarely entirely; and the next generation would do what it could to square the account. The next generation was obliged to do it, for that was the price they paid for the name they carried. Her family had just let it go. She did not know what she could do to square the account, and she and Van did not have an inheritor to bequeath what she had evidently been given: inattention. Perhaps it had only been bad luck, though luck seemed a soft explanation, a kind of anaesthetic like the cry of the capitalist or the gambler. She and Sydney would have no heirs, and in fact their family names would die with them, as if they were species that could not adapt to the modern environment, owing to underdeveloped lungs or brains. What they could claim was this: they were natural in their own way. They were able to console each other and that was something. A great many people had less.

She and Carroll could not console each other after her mother's death or after Shake's either. They did not have a common language of grief or solace, and she thought she would go to her grave without ever expressing the terrible desolation that she felt, to one who could feel it as she did. But Sydney felt it. Sydney had an instinct for it, as an animal had for the noises of nature. He had even understood about Max, though there had been an anxious week when she felt she would be let down by him, in her despair anticipating it almost. But he came to her aid. He had his memory of his mother in the war, a mother who would do anything — pray night and day, go hungry, lie, hate with the appetite of a Teutonic warrior, refuse to move, go through the pockets of dead men looking for chocolates and cigarettes, cheat, steal, anything to keep her son alive and herself, too, because she knew he would die without her protection; and all the time insisting that you forget about this, Siggy. Sydney's serenity rose from the conditions of his childhood at Ilsensee. Nothing that could happen in his life would be as frightful as the day his father was taken away, the day the bombs fell, and the day the American soldiers were slaughtered. All that had given him a stubborn courage, though he admitted daily fear, a fear of what the future held. And as soon as he could decently quit the Federal Republic he did, one of a dwindling number of nomadic Germans. Of course Sydney's coin had another face, melancholy and pessimistic; cold, too.

Too bad she had never said any of this to Carroll, not that he would have listened carefully. She did not know how to reconcile him with her life. She could not picture him in the modern world as it was but saw him only in Old Harbor with his library, his Scotch, the bad weather, his fake Remington, and Tommy Borowy for company. A capitalist who complained that he had been victimized by bankers was like a swimmer who despised the wetness of water. She did not know where he fit into her life, or where she fit into his.

Well, they were both alone. In that way they fit.

But he treated her like a stranger. She was a visitor to him as he was to her. They were father and daughter and that was all they were, linked by genes that supplied something called the Dilion Trill and a specific way of walking and talking. He had a certain squirely angle of vision because he had been rich for a very long time. No one could doubt, seeing them together, that they were related by blood. They might have been distant cousins or he might have been her godfather — the genes, in this instance, being Eastern Seaboard genes mixed generations back, tribal genes, as all Gypsies are said to be related — and their connection with each other a chatty card at Christmas and a United States government bond on her birthday. Her family was a house divided, it always had been. Her mother and brother both gone, she felt an orphan and knew she would have to make her own way in life.

Of course she had Sydney. Carroll had nobody.

He was a relic of the century before. That was the truth of it. He had a hopeful temperament and a trusting heart, living blamelessly, as he once said, reading his first editions, making it through from year to year. Everyone's friend, he wouldn't hurt a fly. He told her once that money bored him. It was not *interesting*. It had no moral weight. Henry James could make it interesting and he loved reading Henry James. But he was not Poynton or Ransome or even Strether, and he did not identify with them. He was interested in their adventures but the adventures were theirs, not his. Neither had he anything to do with Europeans. His own money was not interesting, it was only specie acquired and spent — as inert and cold as a stone bench in the snow. Perhaps if his son were alive, his son would have kept an eye on things, posed a rude question from time to time, and listened to the answer. Money would have been interesting to Shake.

You say there's a gold mine in Iowa?

Between Davenport and Des Moines?

And you heard about it in Bangor?

At the bar of the Ramada Inn?

From a gent with a flower in his lapel?

And a pencil-thin mustache?

And spats?

Who called himself Bunky?

And what did he call you? Squire Dilion?

She picked up her Cognac and walked out of the kitchen, turning off the light. She was laughing now, thinking about whatever investment it was that had gone bad. Probably there was more than one. Well, even his name would be gone soon. Dilion — The Lion, according to family legend, almost certainly bogus. The name and the inheritance, both gone; the house, the library, the jewelry, her Homer, all gone. And she did not know what would happen to him.

She crossed the hall and stepped into the living room. Moonlight was soft on the figured carpet and brilliant on the snow outside. Her prayers had been answered, and the storm had blown itself out. Of course now she had no place to go, except home. In the moonlight she filled her glass with Cognac and stood looking at the vacant space on the opposite wall. Her mother's photograph was in the middle distance, its frame shimmering in the glow. Angie looked past it to the place where the little Homer watercolor had hung. It was luminous in her mind. She had seen it all her life, a mariner alone in a boat, the wind rising, the mariner troubled. Probably he could not find the horizon, and therefore did not know his location. The horizon defined every life. She took a step forward, touching her mother's photograph on the table, her mother so young and pretty. The pearl necklace was barely visible at her throat and the pin with her initials partly hidden by a fold in her sweater. Angela stepped into the full moonlight in that great silent room with its weight of books, a two-hundred-year-old room in a house that would no longer belong to Dilions. She sighed deeply in the stillness, shadows seeming to crowd around her. Somewhere upstairs a floorboard creaked and she knew he was peeking into her bedroom, ready for a good-night kiss and perhaps another apology. He had mentioned Max only once, but once was enough.

Carroll would make out all right, she was certain of that; he always had before. But he seemed so depressed and discouraged now, almost frightened. He was frightened in the way that she was frightened when she thought about Max alone. If something happened to her or Sydney, what would become of Max? The thought terrified her. Carroll was not Max, but he was used to certain things and she did not know whether he would cope — not could, *would*. He had been on hard ice all his long life and was not prepared for the thaw. "I'm like that fellow in the tree," he'd said, smiling boyishly, amused at the comparison. They would love him in the condo at Bar Harbor, the ladies would find him the cutest thing; and he could tell his stories again and again to people who had never heard them. His natural charm and optimism would assert themselves.

She was not prepared either and just then did not know whether to laugh or break down, and wished Van were there to interpret for her. He would know where things were leading and how to survive. He would dissect their situation as if it were one of Josef Kaus's novels, parsing it and putting it into language she could understand. Just then she realized how much she missed him and wondered where he was and why he hadn't called. All they had was each other and the boy and the life they had made. This cold, distressed country, she did not know how to live in it anymore. It was no longer hers. She knew her childhood and that was all she knew, and her childhood was as out of reach as her mother. She looked at the photograph, and the vacant space where Winslow Homer's watercolor had hung. It was so bright outside it might have been daylight. The floorboard upstairs creaked again. She had forgotten her Cognac and picked it up now and sipped at it thoughtfully, and then took it all the way down.

She was so tired. She looked at the time; it would be about the hour she went to see Max, playing with the farm animals and talking in the language she used only with him. She wanted to be home in the Fortress, listening to Van stirring in his office, muttering, wrestling with text. She wished she had never left Paris. She wished she had not come to Maine. Her life seemed suddenly shallow and insubstantial, almost weightless. Her poor distracted father, she remembered him suddenly as he had been in the dining room of the Ritz, someone's rich American uncle, picking up the tab. She would try to be better with him because he was alone and had no one else. She rubbed her eyes, sighing, feeling water on her cheeks. And water was on her sweater. She looked at the floor, and then up at the widening stain on the ceiling. The roof was leaking.

Going East

SYDNEY had not driven in years and he had mislaid his license. Junko Poole agreed to rent the car and turn it over to Sydney in the parking lot, then discovered he had to show Sydney how to operate it, a Mercedes sedan with an automatic gear shift. The last car Sydney had driven was a deux-chevaux, about as complicated as a can opener. Sydney sat in the driver's seat while Junko pointed out the emergency brake, the lights, the windshield wipers, the gas gauge, the radio, and the various locks, plus the myriad extras. Sydney stared at the instrument panel as if he were in the cockpit of an aircraft. Junko took him through the steps of the security system. There was no way to disarm it, so Sydney had to learn how to operate it.

Christ, Sydney. It's just a *car.*

I'm out of practice, Sydney said.

Try to get back here in one piece, Syd. We have serious business tomorrow. I'm going to need your undivided attention.

Don't worry, Sydney said.

What kind of music do you want?

Mozart, Sydney said.

Junko tuned the radio and found not Mozart but Brahms. When Sydney marveled at the quality of the sound, Junko explained that there was no better place to listen to music than a German car with a Blaupunkt stereo. It's better than Carnegie Hall, he said.

Sydney nodded grimly and drove out of the parking lot, narrowly missing a motorcyclist. His car filled with Brahms's Third Symphony, he drove east, miraculously leaving Hamburg without incident. He stopped to buy bread and sausages, cheese and two bottles of beer, since the porter at the hotel had told him that restaurants in the East were filthy. Sydney thought of detouring through Ilsensee but didn't. He was worried about time. He calculated the journey to his mother's would take three hours. He showed his passport and the car's papers at the border and was waved through by a supremely bored control officer, who barely gave the documents a glance, though the license number of the car was carefully noted. And then Sydney was in East Germany.

He was stopped by the side of the road eating lunch when the Americans appeared. They pulled off the road in a gigantic Mitsubishi and approached him, the man smiling, the woman frowning and clutching their map and a German phrasebook. *Bitte? Woh ist Stralsund?* the woman said and when Sydney answered in English she laughed helplessly and shook her head, so pleased to hear an American voice. They were lost. They were unable to read the map. They didn't know where they were, the signs few and far between and confusing as well. It was hard to get your bearings. Sometimes the countryside looked like Kansas and other times like Minnesota; but really it didn't resemble anything in the United States, with the stands of birches and the slate churches and the constant wind, not the prairie wind of the Middle West but the sea wind from the frigid Baltic. And the hordes of evil-smelling Trabant automobiles polluting half of Central Europe. It was disgusting. We're a long way from home, the woman said.

It was noon. When the Mitsubishi appeared, Sydney was eating lunch in the pale sunlight, dead fields all around him and an occasional Baltic gull for company. He kept his back to the rutted highway because there was more traffic than he expected, the Trabants along with heavy-footed diesel trucks and old people on ancient bicycles. He thought it only an hour more to his mother's village and was in no hurry to leave, enjoying the sea wind and the low flat line of the horizon. He had laid his picnic on the hood of the Mercedes, listening to the ticking of the engine as it cooled. It was very quiet and he ate slowly. The food tasted good, and the beer that went with it was very good. He offered some to the Americans, who accepted with thanks. They had spent the night in Lübeck. The woman explained that her husband wanted to see the Buddenbrooks house.

They introduced themselves, Ed and Kathleen on a sentimental journey to Stralsund. They were lawyers in upstate Wisconsin. He was the counselor and she was the litigator. We do pretty well, Ed said. Can't complain. It's a mom-and-pop law office, Kathleen said.

"What do you do?" Ed said to Sydney.

"I'm a translator," Sydney said.

"Well, that must be interesting," Ed said.

"It is," Sydney said. He looked at his watch, suddenly anxious to be driving again.

"I'm a Thomas Mann freak," Ed said. "So I dragged her to Lübeck. That little square looks just about the way it did when Mann lived there. I like the way the Germans preserve things, don't you?"

When Sydney asked about their sentimental journey, Kathleen replied that her husband's people had immigrated to the United States from Stralsund in the nineteenth century. The usual story. Two brothers, broke but healthy, arrived at Ellis Island and changed their unpronounceable name to Strasland and lit out for Minnesota. One Strasland stayed and the other went to Oregon. Both brothers prospered.

"It wasn't unpronounceable," Ed said. "It was Kroger."

"Why did they change it then, Ed?" his wife asked.

"Damned if I know," Ed said.

"And when they changed it they got it wrong, not Stralsund but Strasland. So we're going there to see if there are any Krogers left and if any of them look like Ed. That thing on Ed's face is called the Strasland nose. It's unique. Only Straslands have it and Ed's willed it to the Smithsonian when he dies. It'll be hanging from the ceiling next to Lindbergh's airplane."

Ed laughed good-naturedly, turning his profile so that Sydney could see his nose, which was very long and sharp at the end, indisputably a family heirloom. "I just want to see what the place looks like," he said, "because my grandfather used to talk about it all the time, the way the Krogers were at odds with Stralsund. He had one of those love-hate things with it. Maybe there was some trouble before he left. I think there was, as a matter of fact. Some family matter. The brothers were the black sheep of the family, so they left for America, or maybe fled to America, and never went back to the old country. But my grandfather couldn't get Stralsund out of his system, and when the Reds took over after the war he said it served them right. And in the next breath he'd wonder about the Krogers left behind, how they were getting on and whether the Communists had killed them or sent them to the Gulag. Years ago they were landowners. He wrote letters but never got any satisfaction. Before he died I promised to try to find out for him. So Kathleen and I decided to visit. I don't give a damn for myself, it's ancient history. But I promised the old man. What I see of East Germany, I don't like."

"The Wall came down and we took advantage of it," Kathleen said.

"It's our first trip to Europe," Ed said. "We're a little unsettled by it."

"He is," she said. "I'm not."

"I like Wisconsin," Ed said.

"Well," Kathleen said. She brushed crumbs from her sweater and looked at her husband, who showed no signs of wanting to leave; and Sydney was obviously impatient, she could see it in his forced smile.

Ed said, "I don't know what it's going to mean when these two countries get together. I suppose it'll be a poke in the eye to everyone else, including the U.S.A. But, hell, if they work harder than anyone else. Have some pride in what they do. Why shouldn't they be king of the hill? It's the American way. When we were king of the hill we took it as an act of God, as if we were ordained, like it or lump it. This part of the country doesn't look like much, though. It's like the Rust Belt without the belt."

Sydney laughed.

"Mr. Foreign Policy Expert," Kathleen said, rolling her eyes. "Let's take our show on the road, Ed. You've been very nice to us, Sydney. We appreciate it. We were famished. Lost, too. We never expected to meet an American on this stretch of road. Where are you headed?"

"East, about an hour," Sydney said. He moved to collect the wrappings of the sausage, cheese, and bread. They had eaten everything. He handed the last of the beer to Ed Strasland, who took a sip and handed it back. He said, "I'm going to visit my mother."

"She lives here?" Ed said. "In East Germany?"

"About an hour away," Sydney said. "Close to Poland."

Kathleen looked closely at him. "Has it been a long time since you've seen her?"

"A while," Sydney said. He balled the wrappings and tossed them into the rear of the Mercedes. "It's been more than thirty years."

"My goodness," Kathleen said.

"My God," Ed said.

"So I'd better be off," Sydney said. "Good luck in Stralsund."

"Thanks for the grub," Ed said. "And the brewski."

"Thirty years," Kathleen said. "Good luck to you, Sydney."

"You were born in Germany," Ed said.

"West," Sydney said. "I was born in West Germany."

"And I thought you were an American," Ed said.

"I'm married to one. And I wish she was here but she isn't. She's in the state of Maine with her father and won't be back for a week, damn it." Sydney was surprised that he had said what he did, they were strangers after all.

"Well," Ed said uncomfortably.

"Let me show you again where you're headed," Sydney said. He spread the road map on the hood of the Mitsubishi. "You're here" — pointing at the map — "and you want to go there. You turn left at the next town. It's about ten kilometers, you can't miss it, and another fifty to Stralsund." Sydney folded the map and handed it to Kathleen, then got into his own car. He said, "You'll smell the pollution before you see the town. There's plenty of rust in Stralsund. I hope you find your Krogers."

Kathleen moved close to the car window. He was wearing his good leather boots, tan corduroy trousers, and a black leather jacket, unbelted now. He wore a heavy white turtleneck sweater under the leather jacket, presenting an altogether conventional, and slightly alarming, appearance. He looked like a policeman and not your friendly neighborhood policeman either, but someone special, someone they would call "inspector" or "superintendent" or perhaps avoid entirely, as he would be from another section, one that was not, strictly speaking, the police. "I hope you have a nice reunion with your mother," Kathleen said shyly.

"Reconciliation," Sydney said, and pulled away onto the highway.

Miles and miles of bloody East Germany, Sydney thought as he looked at the disabled landscape. He drove slowly, avoiding potholes and vigilant for road signs. The glare of the winter sun hurt his eyes. The Straslands followed him for ten kilometers and then turned, flashing their lights and honking. He wondered what Ed and Kathleen made of him, enough to make a story certainly when they were back in Wisconsin and telling friends about their trip. A German going to visit his mother whom he hadn't seen in thirty years, mad at his wife who was visiting her father in Maine, for God's sake; his name was Sydney and he looked like a rough customer, spoke absolutely fluent, accentless English, damnedest thing . . .

He wondered what they would find in Stralsund. Perhaps everyonc would have a long nose with a sharp point at the end, women as well as men; children, too, and their pets. Probably the authorities would give Ed and Kathleen keys to the city and ask them if they wanted to set up a law practice. Lawyers were the priests of the free market. That was what happened when you stopped for a private picnic, two Americans from the Midwest drive up in a Mitsubishi and ask you how to get to a city that's been forgotten since the fourteenth century and the Hanseatic League. They were gregarious Americans. You heard the family history and you knew that they were doing all right because they couldn't complain. Ed was looking up his ancestral ground because his late grandfather asked him to, perhaps stricken with nostalgia or guilt at the end of his life. The Krogers were at odds with Stralsund, so it was fair to assume that Stralsund was at odds with the Krogers. So they boarded a steamer for the U.S.A. One brother became rich in Minnesota and the other brother in Oregon. But it was Stralsund that had stayed with them. And if you were broke, it was good to be healthy.

A Trabant passed him, honking and spitting dirty exhaust.

Sydney wished he had a different car, the Mercedes was as conspicuous as a neon sign. The two men in the Trabant had ostentatiously looked the other way when they passed him, as if black Mercedes sedans were an everyday sight in the Democratic Republic. And then the driver stared into the rearview mirror, checking the license plate. The miles and miles of bloody East Germany were coming to an end now, fields giving way to clusters of houses, tract houses, small and functional, identical. All the trees had been cut down. On the front stoop of one of the houses a middle-aged man sat smoking in the cold. There was an old joke about East Germany, that smoking was the only pleasure left, the only pleasure not forbidden or circumscribed, and so expensive you could only do it on weekends. He was in the subdivision and immediately out of it, flat fields again with brick farmhouses. The gulls had disappeared. He turned on the radio and spun the dial but found only static and rock and roll. He thought he had never seen such cheerless terrain, and then he remembered Angela's descriptions of the state of Maine. Played-out whacked-out Maine, existing now on the margins of the consumer culture, fast-food stands, used car lots, discount warehouses, lobsters sold from the back of a pickup truck. Here there was nothing but flat fields and an occasional stand of birch trees or firs and now and again a store or shop set back from the road; no telling what they sold, or if they sold anything. A painter of a particular cast of mind would be attracted to it. Emil Nolde was, finding in the monochromes a riotous imaginary rainbow. Looking at this motionless land, he seemed to feel the spirits of centuries inhabiting it, or imprisoned just below its crust, a permanent underworld that had claims to occupation and sovereign power. They would be the characters of the German legends, alive and animated, changing character as the times matured, a feverish mythology without obvious origins or end. He shivered. Probably he was nervous and being sentimental, so close to his destination. He began to drive faster despite the ruts and the traffic. Then he was in a village that seemed empty of people, and he knew it was where she lived.

I hope I haven't made a mistake, he said aloud.

I should have warned her.

She won't know what to think.

He stopped and asked directions of a woman who looked at him and at his black Mercedes and refused to reply, turning abruptly and hurrying away. Unnerved, Sydney tried again with an old man in a heavy wool jacket and a black cap. The old man listened carefully and took his time before nodding and saying yes, he knew the street. There were not so many streets in the village that he did not know each one intimately. It was straight on one kilometer, and then a right turn.

"Who are you looking for?" the old man asked.

"Frau van Damm," Sydney replied.

The old man considered that a moment, nodding.

"Do you know where Frau van Damm lives?"

"I might," the old man said.

Sydney waited.

The old man went around to the front of the car, looked at the license plate, and returned. "You are from Hamburg."

"I have come from Hamburg, yes."

"Why do you want to visit Frau van Damm?"

"I am a friend," Sydney said.

"Frau van Damm knows no one in Hamburg."

"She knows me," Sydney said.

"That may be," the old man said, removing his cap. "But it won't do you any good."

Sydney said, "Thanks for your help."

"Frau van Damm is dead," the old man said.

Sydney closed his eyes and found not blackness but a vivid scratch of orange.

"She died just before Christmas."

His eyes squeezed shut, Sydney imagined the road in front of him, straight as country roads tended to be. One kilometer on, then a turn to the right.

"We had the funeral the day after Christmas."

Sydney nodded.

"It was not so large. We found someone from Swinemunde to conduct the service."

"How did she die?" Sydney managed.

"She was very old."

"I know that. How did she die?"

"Pneumonia," he said. "That is how old people die. It is how I will die, when it is time."

Sydney said, "She did not suffer?"

The old man looked at him queerly. "Of course she suffered. Do you think dying is easy? It is a struggle. She fought it."

Sydney said, "Yes."

"It is said she had a son."

"She did."

"But the son did not live in Hamburg."

"No," Sydney said.

"The son lived somewhere in the West."

"Paris," Sydney said. "I am her son."

"We wondered," the old man said.

"Yet no one thought to notify me."

"Frau van Damm kept to herself," the old man said.

"Still," Sydney said.

"She never spoke of her family."

"She never spoke of her husband who died in the war?"

"Notification is the responsibility of the authorities," the old man said.

"But they did nothing."

"There has been confusion since the events. The government does not govern."

Sydney stared straight ahead, gripping the steering wheel hard, his hands at ten and two. He was trying to bring her into his mind, a small sinewy woman, her arms brown and gnarled as roots. Erich had told him that she wore her hair in a bun wound tight as a spool of thread. Her health was good, though she walked with difficulty. She was a model citizen of the German Democratic Republic, according to Erich. And what would she have thought of 'the events'? Sydney remarked, more to himself than to the old man, "She was happy here."

"Yes, of course. This was her home after all."

"Did she have an opinion of the events?"

"She gave none," the old man said.

Sydney smiled. "Her house," he said.

"What about her house?"

"I want to go there," Sydney said.

"It is locked."

"If there is a lock, there must be a key."

"Probably that can be arranged."

"I suppose the authorities have the key."

"Her neighbor has the key."

"If you would be good enough to show me," Sydney said.

"I live nearby," the old man said. "Perhaps, if you could give me a ride as far as my own house —" Sydney opened the door and the old man climbed in, slowly because his joints were stiff. He was careful to use the seat belt. He sat ramrod straight, his black cap pulled low over his forehead. His hands began to move tentatively over the leather, almost as if he were caressing a woman. His eyes took in the instrument panel, the dials and switches, the buttons and the silent Blaupunkt. He took a deep breath, inhaling, smelling the leather, smiling with satisfaction. When Sydney had driven the one kilometer, the old man told him to stop, that Frau van Damm's house was to the right and the neighbor across the street had the key. Watch out for the dog, the old man said, a cur that should be put away. He gave the leather a last touch and opened the door and got out.

"The house has not been disturbed," the old man said.

"I'm glad to hear it."

"I am sorry about your mother."

"Thank you. Did you know her well?"

"Not so well. As I said, she kept to herself. I think she was lonely. She had not so much to live for."

Sydney nodded and put the car in gear.

"The winters here are harsh."

"Thank you for your help," Sydney said.

"And when one has no family —"

"Good luck to you," Sydney said.

"Still, she enjoyed her garden."

"Good-bye," Sydney said.

"This is a beautiful car," the old man said. "You must love it very much."

The neighbor was reluctant to give him the key, and did not invite him in; because of the dog, she said. She looked him over — leather boots, white turtleneck sweater, black leather jacket, Mercedes sedan in the street — with undisguised suspicion and said his request was irregular. She did not know him. She was not prepared for such a request, and certainly not from anyone who lived in the West. Of course it was strictly forbidden to remove anything from the house. The dog was growling but she had a firm grip on its collar. Sydney reminded the woman that Frau van Damm was his mother, and he had only just now learned of her death. No one had informed him. He was distressed naturally and wanted only to visit his mother's house for a few moments, after his long drive. The woman stood thinking a moment, then with an irritated sigh went inside and came back with a heavy key on a steel chain. Return it when you are finished, she said. The key is state property.

He walked across the street to his mother's cottage. It was very old and obviously unlived-in. The front yard and garden were dead and matted in January and the cottage seemed to sag. Across the level fields was a small flat lake, white in the pale sun, as there had been at Ilsensee. But there was no other comparison. This was terrain without color or contour. The cottage was a natural feature of the landscape, as if it were not man-made at all but grown from the soil. He could imagine his mother in this house very well, as he could imagine her forebears.

The key turned easily in the lock and the door swung wide. The sitting room was sparely furnished, a worn velour couch and two ladderback chairs and a narrow dining table set for one. There was a plate and cup and saucer and flatware either side of the plate as if the householder were expected momentarily. The china was familiar, causing Sydney to close his eyes and draw back, leaning against the wall. He thought he felt her presence in the room, an aura of disapproval mixed with curiosity; and then the thought vanished. The fireplace was cold, dust everywhere. Behind the couch was a rolltop desk with a framed photograph of a young man in an army officer's uniform. It was a straight-on shot, black and white, its lighting and composition reminding Sydney of a wedding photograph. There was a resemblance to Sydney in the turned-down eyes and the set of the shoulders. Klaus van Damm was a handsome man, finer boned and leaner than his son.

Pale sunlight spilled from the windows. A wooden crucifix hung over the fireplace, and under it a carved figure rested on the mantel. In the pale light Sydney could not make out what it was, and wondered suddenly if it was an Ilsensee dwarf. But peering closely at it, he saw it was not. It was the carved figure of an old woman leaning on a cane. If the artist had given it a name it would have been *Patience* or *Endurance*, possibly *Submission*. He did not remember it from the Ilsensee house and wondered where it had come from and who the artist was. Probably it represented his mother's view of herself, survivor of some never-ending wrong, Germany's shipwreck, all hands missing and believed lost.

The wooden crucifix was in her plain style.

His attention was focused now on the bookcase, volume after volume of military histories, memoirs, biographies. He wondered how she had got them across the border in the bad old days, probably secreted in trunks. Who would question an old woman? Propped on one shelf were the photographs of Ulysses S. Grant and Robert E. Lee. He looked at them and smiled, quintessential American faces, but all generals formed a kind of International, like soccer players and orchestra conductors. It was a fine library and there was no book in it written after 1941. On a lower shelf were other books, German books, none of them written later than the middle of the last century. The books looked as if they had not been moved from their shelves for many years. He searched the room for some evidence of her, but there was only the crucifix and the photographs and a basket of yarn, and the table setting. The rest was impersonal, as if she had led her life as a guest in someone else's house.

He could not find her, not in body and not in spirit, but it had been so long and they did not part on good terms. She would remember every word of the quarrel, as he did. And then he recalled something she said about politics. It was just after the war when the Americans were in charge. She said that politics had no essence, it was only a thing that men did to occupy themselves. A few women enjoyed it. It didn't matter what you called it, politics was their affair. There was nothing they could do to harm you if you stayed close to home, kept to yourself, did not travel, and did not demand choices. Life wasn't so difficult then. And later she explained that she went to the Democratic Republic because she could no longer tolerate Ilsensee and the economic miracle. She heard airplanes at night. She heard the bombs. The dwarf came to her in her dreams, offering its forehead and proposing fantastic adventures. And often in her dreams her husband was standing at his place at the head of the table, the meal concluded. He took a large cigar from his breast pocket and lit it, the smoke billowing as smoke from a bomb. In the parlor the radio was on, the Sunday opera, Puccini. Klaus was distracted and worried. She had cleared the dishes from the table and now they waited; in her dream they waited all afternoon, but there were no visitors.

She believed the only safe place for her was her parents' village and the house she was born in and grew up in and was loved in, and where she and her husband were married and lived for a year before he was sent to Hamburg and they bought the house at Ilsensee. She wanted only to live in past time with no distractions, among her sister Germans. No doubt she would recollect the fury of the war, that time when the earth was hot under their feet and everyone suffered. When she recollected the war, her faith would be tested because no good came of it; evil origins, evil consequences. It was not redemptive. So she would keep to herself, living quietly without remorse, and disclose nothing of her life, of her fierce heroism during the war, of her dead husband and indifferent son living in the West, the son who thought her an accomplice of the fascists. The essence of Martin Luther's teaching was faith. She knew nothing of this son, of the life he lived or the woman he married or the damaged child they bore. Perhaps in her despair and tenacity she would have taken a certain satisfaction in the boy. She would see him as the natural product of the impious and unprincipled cosmopolitan modern world; and the Russian proverb had its German variation. Perhaps it was true that she had not so much to live for, yet when her time came to die she did not surrender to it but struggled with it, taking what she could. God did not send what could not be borne. She went through death's pockets as she had gone through the pockets of the American soldiers, and perhaps this time she found something of value. He was sick that he was not with her at the end. No one should have to die alone and unattended. He did not know why he had waited for so long, and now he was too late.

He almost heard her voice in the wind whistling in the eaves. He looked at her basket of yarn, and the photographs of the American generals and of his father, dead now almost fifty years. How remote this was from his own apartment in avenue Songe, his and Angela's bedroom, the small empty bedroom, and his balcony office with *Die Katastrophe* unfinished on his desk, the cat in midleap. How remote, too, from Junko Poole and the fine hotel in Hamburg, or the rented Mercedes in the street outside. The sunlight in this room seemed to him thin and washed out, and the bare walls and wooden floor unbearable in their austerity. But this was how she lived and it suited her. The view from the parlor window was not memorable, a flat dead field with a small flat lake beyond. The water was the color of mercury, ruffled now by the wind that had come up. There were many such lakes in north Germany, small, shallow, and picturesque. There was a German legend that the lakes had been made by the hooves of a great golden stallion. The stallion had looked after the country and kept it prosperous and free. It had guarded north Germany for millennia until one winter's day it stormed away, vanished utterly, and was never seen again. Frightful calamities followed, war, plague, famine, and pogrom supervised by tyrants. The population endured, confident that one day the beast would return and claim its rightful place as guardian of the country. All the old people believed this.

Sydney did not know how long he stood with his back against the wall, not daring to move or to explore further. He was thinking of his wife and son and how much he loved them both. His sight was blurred as he stared out the window at the two black sedans stopped now in the street, the doors opening and men alighting, stamping their feet, looking at the tiny cottage and talking quietly, taking their time before two of them detached themselves and sauntered up the path to the door. They walked as slowly as priests focused on some disagreeable pastoral duty. The others leaned against the cars. Across the street Sydney could see the sullen neighbor standing in her doorway with her arms folded across her chest, the dog alert at her side.

Sydney heard two sharp raps but did not move. He said softly that they could enter, the door was not locked.

There were two of them in trenchcoats. Three others remained with the cars. A fourth was seated in the rear seat of one of the sedans, and although his face was in shadows Sydney recognized him as Erich.

The two in trenchcoats entered, leaving the door ajar. One of them went to the kitchen and looked inside, then to his mother's bedroom, stepping into it, muttering something. The other one stood stolidly in the doorway.

The one in his mother's bedroom looked at him and said, "Herr Poole?"

Sydney had been unable to enter his mother's bedroom. Now he watched the German lift a corner of the pillow and let it fall. His hands were filthy. Sydney said coldly, "Who are you? What do you want?"

The German fingered the pillowcase and said mildly, "I am a major of state security. Are you Herr Poole?"

"No," Sydney said. "I am not Herr Poole."

"I have a warrant for Herr Poole's arrest."

Sydney said nothing to that.

"The charges are serious."

Sydney shrugged.

"Your identification," the major said.

Sydney walked to the doorway of his mother's bedroom and handed him the passport. Her closet door was open, revealing black dresses and shoes neatly aligned. On one wall was a mirror in a wooden frame that he remembered from Ilsensee. The room seemed small and unwomanly with the major in it.

"Where is Herr Poole?"

"I don't know," Sydney said.

"The car outside was rented to Herr Poole."

"He rented it for me," Sydney said.

"Why would he do that?"

"As a favor," Sydney said.

The major nodded, smiling broadly. "So Herr Poole is not here."

"As you can see," Sydney said.

The one in the doorway moved then, in such a way as to alert Sydney to danger. The other Stasi had come up from the street and were gathered outside the door.

Sydney said, "Get out of the bedroom."

The major was examining Sydney's passport but did not look up, or give any sign that he had heard or was listening. He said after a moment, "Erich? Who is this one?"

"He is the translator," Erich said from the doorway.

"Name?"
"Van Damm," Erich said. "I told you about him."
"So you did," the major said. He was still turning the pages of Sydney's passport. "Of course they would need to have one, engaged in their dirty business. They would need a man fluent in the language of espionage, German and English. What sort of man would volunteer for such an assignment when the penalties are so high?"
"He is the one who thinks we are schizophrenic. He thinks we are nostalgic for the Knights. He has an American wife."
"Ah," the major said, making a noun of it, the soft sound implying that the fact of an American wife explained much. "But of course it is not the wife who will stand trial, nor go to prison when the trial is concluded."
There were four of them crowding the door now but Sydney found Erich and looked into his mournful eyes. The tic in his cheek beat a tattoo. Erich was standing easily against the doorjamb, his hands in his pockets. His eyes were watery and suddenly he sneezed. As Junko had said, Erich loved his DDR; that was his rightful place. Erich did not think it necessary to wander the earth in search of his lost half. Let the other side endure unsatisfied longing. The look Sydney got from Erich now was blank and his face still, unless you detected the very slight smile pulling at the corners of his mouth. It said that the German Democratic Republic was not finished yet. It remained a *state*. The Stasi was not finished either. There were a few cards left to play if not very much time to play them in.
"So we missed Herr Poole," the major said.
"Erich can find him for you," Sydney said.
"Erich?" The major smiled. "Erich is a fool."
There was some movement in the doorway and when Sydney looked he saw that Erich was no longer there. He saw to his surprise that dusk was falling, the pale blue Baltic light weakening. The lake was indistinct in the distance.
"You are under arrest," the major said softly.
"What is the charge?"
"We will find one," the major said. "Tell me something. You were born in Germany?"
"As you can see from my passport."

"You have a strange accent. You have the accent of a foreigner."

"Get out of my mother's bedroom," Sydney said when the major turned, grinning, looking at himself in the mirror, preening almost. Sydney moved forward, shuffling, his hands in front of him. Who were these people? He saw the hard old lady vividly now and knew that he must do this one thing to protect her memory, equivocal as that memory was. He knew he would get the major out of her bedroom if it was the last thing he did. His head was mercifully clear and free of pain, and now he felt a murderous surge of anger. He leaped forward, but when he reached the bedroom door he was suddenly down on the cold floor with a tearing spasm in his gut, knowing at once that he had been hit by the stolid one, hit very hard, much harder than was necessary and to his infinite surprise knew that he was badly hurt. His head scraped the floorboards. The stolid one hit him again. Sydney tried to say something but was unable to form the words from the shadows in his mind. So he reached out, as a cat might do, his nails scratching the cold wooden floor. He raised his hand, reaching, but that did not seem to work either and he slipped away, first deaf, then unconscious, and then past all understanding.

2

Fortress America was quiet in late afternoon. A light cover of snow, the first in two years, gave a festive appearance to the Weimar face. The snow had arrived without warning, along with an arctic wind. Many of the inhabitants were away on their winter holidays and Milda and her roommates were in Rome with their sheikhs, so there was no music in the courtyard except for the very faint sound of American jazz from number 18. All the windows were closed because of the cold, minus 9 degrees C. The ferns were moribund in their green glazed pots.

Junko Poole knocked at the van Damms' door, knocked once and again and again, and was about to turn away when he saw a note folded in the lock. *Come in*, the note said, no signature. The door was not locked and Junko walked in, calling loudly and receiving no answer. The room was cold and he turned up the thermostat. He switched on the lights in the living room and the kitchen, threw his coat and hat on a chair, and went to the liquor cabinet. He fetched a bottle of Scotch, poured two fingers into a wineglass, and went in search of ice. He found three ice trays in the freezer and set about extracting the cubes, cursing because they were nasty little French ice trays, about the dimensions of a paperback book, icecubes the size of marbles. Sydney and Angela had lived in the fucking apartment for fifteen years and had not bothered to buy an ice maker or even American ice trays and it wasn't as if they didn't take a drink now and then. It was habit and they were always hard up and who could resist a forty-franc saving, for Christ's sake. They lived like graduate students. He searched for something to eat, peanuts or olives or a wedge of Camembert, but found nothing; the fridge was bare except for a jar of cornichons, rancid from the look of them. He filled the wineglass with ice and added a thimble of water and walked into the living room. Her suitcase was on the floor, unopened. Junko stood for a moment at the bibelot table and began to rearrange the ornaments as he had seen Sydney do, scrimshaw forward and dolls back, eggs among the ivory.

He sat in Sydney's chair, but that was not comfortable for him so he went to the window and looked out into the snow, waiting for Angela.

He would have met her plane, insisted on doing it, but she didn't know when she would get a flight. Everything was booked. She was crying, almost hysterical, so Junko spoke with her father, who did not seem to know the score, demanding information in a rough voice while his daughter bawled on his shoulder. And then the next morning she called from London and said to meet her in the apartment at five that afternoon. Her father had arranged for a private plane to take her from Bar Harbor to Boston and she had talked herself onto the first available flight, London, knowing that it was simple to get from London to Paris if there was no weather delay. And of course there was a weather delay, owing to the snow in Paris and the fog at Heathrow. She was sure she could get to the Fortress by five P.M., by train and boat if necessary, but if she wasn't there, to wait for her. Angela's voice was high and thin but composed. In her fear and hysteria the day before she had asked no questions and the old man didn't know the questions to ask. But she had questions now.

What about Sydney? she asked.

He did not know what she meant and muttered something vague and reassuring.

His *body*, she said. Sydney's *body*.

Yes, he said. Of course.

I want to have a service in Paris, she said.

Good idea, he said. That's an excellent idea, Angela.

Junko, she said, her voice rising. She was almost shaking. Where is Sydney's body? Where is it *now?*

In the East, he said. But he did not know where it was specifically, which hospital or morgue.

Find out, please.

Yes, he said.

Will they return him?

I'll see to it, Junko said.

But will they return him? Will they return him to me in Paris?

Yes, Junko said. Of course.

He's all alone, she said.

Junko Poole recovered himself then and began to speak in his usual confident you-can-rest-assured-things-are-in-good-hands manner. And in the middle of his improvisation she had rung off, no good-byes, no nothing. That was unnerving. The conversation itself was unnerving. And he was not thinking clearly; it had been a miserable three days and he had lost a good close friend and came close to being lost himself, a miserable fuck-up all along the line. Now he would have to think about a eulogy if Angela carried through her threat to have a memorial service. There was a problem with the body and he did not know how to explain that to Angela, beyond the usual maledictions against the Communist bureaucrats and their cumbersome procedures, autopsies and the like. They would return Sydney but it wouldn't be any time soon. Still, you could have a service without a corpse. He would speak and Angela would, certainly, and probably Kaus. There were a number of things to be said about Sydney, his tact and loyalty and sense of duty; he was essentially harmless, a German removed from the life of his nation. He had withdrawn himself; recused, as the lawyers liked to say. Sydney was sometimes his own worst enemy and was never what you would call a player and had his naïve side, perhaps too willing to take things on faith. You couldn't help liking him. He was a good close friend and they had had many adventures, going back thirty years and more. He remembered Sydney at the Gare du Nord, gawking like a student tourist, his square head and thick body as German as Otto von Bismarck. He was just a kid, and in some ways still was. That was what happened when you lost your father at an early age; you either grew up before your time or never grew up at all. Sydney had never come to terms with the Nazis, that was his trouble. Wherever he went, Klaus van Damm was at his side, looking over his shoulder; a filthy legacy. Philip Poole was something else altogether, a bon vivant, a man who took life on his own terms, refusing to be bound by any convention. Somehow he had managed to pass that on. Probably it came through the genes; everything of value did. They had both lost their fathers when they were boys but their reactions were different, having drawn opposite lessons. Well, it was a damned shame. Sydney had been caught in a tight spot. But in the last analysis you had to look out for yourself. No one did that for you. That was Lesson One. Sydney was often careless.

Junko took a long pull on his Scotch, pressing his forehead against the cold windowpane, staring into the empty courtyard, almost dark now. No sense having the blues. What was done was done and there was no undoing it and tears were always a fucking waste of time and energy. The days were getting longer now and perhaps in a few weeks, when this was done with and forgotten, he could take a trip, the Seychelles or London. It would be good to see a show, visit the baccarat table at Les Ambassadeurs. London was always a tonic, good for what ailed you. Perhaps he could take Angela with him, his treat, give her a break from the desolate Paris winter. And where was she? Probably she had gone for a walk in the snow, it was now after five, though why you'd want to walk in the snow was a mystery and where you walked in Montmartre was a mystery also. It was a suburban district having none of the charm and élan of the real Paris, *centre ville*. On avenue Songe the petit bourgeois huddled in their tiny Renaults and cramped apartments. Narrow horizons all around. They might as well be living in Chicago. Fortress America itself was queer, with its curves and precipitous balconies and circus history, all bogus. There was nothing to hold on to, nothing solid you could count on. Sydney called it a Weimar face and he was correct but not in the way he thought he was correct. The architecture was self-indulgent to the point of anarchy or parody, which only proved that opposites attract. The tenants were déclassé, air hostesses and marginal businessmen, and of course the rapacious photographers. The fucking press, sanctimonious leeches. At least Angela would not have to endure the paparazzi. There were still a few things that money could buy, although you had to be awfully careful how you went about it. In the event, it wasn't as difficult as he thought it would be, or as expensive. In his distress he had forgotten one thing. No one gave a good god damn about Sydney van Damm, West German citizen, translator.

He could hold pretty close to the truth with Angela because Sydney had promised he had told her nothing, no details, and Sydney did not lie. Old Syd never gave the gift of faith. So: they were buying machine tools and heavy pipe and while the transaction was somewhat irregular, it was not illegal. They were buying the goods in East Germany and reselling them in East Germany to unknown parties who were acting through nominees, a practice common in the Communist world. Some commissar wanted a cut, probably. Doubtless the unknown parties were transshipping the goods elsewhere, but that was not their affair, his and Sydney's. The preliminary negotiations in Hamburg had gone very well, with the parties agreed to conclude the sale in forty-eight hours, contracts exchanged and so forth and so on, the usual bullshit and whatnot. We were to meet them in Dresden, East Germany.

And that's all there was to that, Angela.

I know it sounds like a spy story, Ange. But it's normal business, pretty much straightforward and aboveboard.

Sydney had a free day, so he decided to visit his mother. He was excited about it, he hadn't seen her in so many years. He wanted it to be a surprise. I rented a car for him because he'd mislaid his license. Typical. You know Sydney, head always in the clouds. I never should've done it because if anything had happened my neck was in the noose but what the hell, the poor guy was determined. I was worried because he'd never driven a Mercedes. He didn't know how to work the Blaupunkt. He almost hit a motorcyclist driving out of the lot. He arrived at his mother's some time around two in the afternoon and discovered that she had died, Angela, in December. No one had told him. Imagine the shock, poor Sydney.

The best we can discover is that he had a heart attack. He was in his mother's house when they found him. He'd borrowed a key from the neighbor, who reported that he was very upset and abusive, an arrogant Westerner. That wasn't the Sydney we knew, Angela. Our Sydney was never abusive. The heart attack was sudden and massive. He could not have suffered. All he wanted to do was look around his mother's house.

I suppose he wanted to see how she had lived.

I'm sick about it, Angie.

He was my oldest friend.

Close enough to the truth. Close enough to be believed. And who was to contradict him? It was too ludicrous for words. Sydney had no one to stand up for him. If he had been an American citizen, there would be an official inquiry. If he were French, the grapevine might produce a cause célèbre. Perhaps if he had lived in Germany and possessed a close circle of concerned friends, there would be suspicions and unwholesome rumors that would have to be dealt with. But he was an expatriate. He lived among foreigners. No one owed him anything. Neither of the two Germanys wanted an incident, not now with the Wall down, the Reds in retreat, and the glorious unified future so near at hand. Another destabilizing spy scandal? Now? A respected middle-aged West German translator beaten to death by Stasi goons? The respected translator involved somehow in the arms trade, and not ordinary arms but stolen Warsaw Pact property? And in the background an American with known connections to Western security services, though at the critical moment the American was nowhere to be found. No, no. This was a scandal that no one wanted or needed, there were higher matters of state at risk. So the authorities would turn their backs, misprision a patriotic duty. East Berlin had brought that Stasi unit under control damned fast, got Sydney to a military hospital, where he was DOA, ruptured spleen and other internal injuries, which caused his heart to stop. The translator had inexplicably tried to attack a Stasi major and naturally had been restrained. They said it was an accident, and maybe it was.

Of course Junko knew nothing of that until the following day, when word came from Erich. Get out of Hamburg. Get out right away, boat, car, first available aircraft. Erich explained what had happened to Sydney or what he had been told had happened. He had not been present. There were parts of it that were not clear, but it seemed to be the usual story of betrayal and stupidity. No doubt that weasel Bernhard, he should be a *Bombenbrandsschrumpfleiche*.

A word coined in Hamburg, Erich explained.

It meant "body shrunken by fire-bombing."

They're embarrassed and prepared to forget it now, Erich said, but don't wait around. Don't wait a minute. So Junko had roughly disengaged himself from Romy and departed immediately for the *Bahnhof*. He did not bother to collect his things or Sydney's. He took the express to Paris, Gare du Nord, as he always did. On the train there was never a passport check.

Snow continued to fall, blowing now. It was entirely dark in the courtyard. Junko Poole looked at his wristwatch, wishing Angela would hurry. He had unfinished business at home. But he remained by the window to watch for her, the drink tepid now in his hand. He had turned off the lights in the living room so that he could not be seen from the courtyard, though if he had been asked why he did this he would not have been able to say. Perhaps it was a cautious instinct inherited from his unconventional father. Perhaps it was only dusty habit, as it was habit not to wonder why Sydney van Damm would assault a Stasi major, nor to be curious about what Angela would do with her life now that Sydney was gone. He did remark to himself that she knew how to take care of herself, Angie had always been clever with life. She had a natural gift for survival, as women generally did. Her great fault was introspection, trying to get to the bottom of things that had no bottom. It was always a mistake to look backward and try to undo what had been done, or account for it or atone, still less to apologize or explain. You accepted the facts you were given and made a tapestry of them, made the story that you wanted to have, a bedtime story if need be or a love story, a lullabye. In any case a life was mysterious, real only to the one who was living it. It had no meaning for anyone else; for anyone else, that life could be said not to exist. It was no more real than a movie. He had mentioned once to that fool DaMurr that he had visited Dachau, and DaMurr had flown at him. You didn't visit *Dachau*, he shouted. You visited some barracks, looked at a gas chamber, stared through barbed wire. Perhaps you shook your head as you did so and said something pious, in your case a Christian prayer. But it wasn't *Dachau* you visited. You can't visit *Dachau. Dachau* no longer exists, except in a few memories.

And he had to admit, DaMurr had a point.

The time was almost six. Suddenly the white lights in the courtyard blinked on, and Junko saw Angela moving slowly through the falling snow. She had that wretched child with her. He watched them advance in the harsh light and then they began to turn in a slow circle. The child was unable to walk a straight line and he was batting his arms at the snowflakes, a midget windmill gone out of control. Angie tried to hold him close but he slid away again and again, chasing the falling snowflakes as if they were alive. She looked up suddenly at the windows of her apartment and, seeing nothing, bent her head.

It was a damned shame, Junko thought. People never learned. You could never tell them anything. The more painful things were, the better they liked it. People worried life, picked at it, quarreled with it and diminished it, not understanding that they were issued only one. You had your own life, not anyone else's. And that was the life you were responsible for and had to justify every minute of every day and understand what you were capable of, and that meant escaping the curse of memory. But it had to be done. People refused to forget. They refused to look at what was in front of their eyes and say, Forget it.

The boy and his mother advanced, struggling, leaving ragged tracks in the snow. The boy began to whirl again, his arms churning, chasing snowflakes. In the white light Angela's face was ghastly. She moved to restrain Max but in a wild motion he threw his arms around her waist and for a brief moment they were simultaneous, one body motionless in the snow.